BLUES FROM DOWN DEEP

GWYNNE FORSTER

BLUES FROM DOWN DEEP

Dafina
Books

KENSINGTON PUBLISHING CORP.
http://www.kensingtonbooks.com

DAFINA BOOKS are published by

Kensington Publishing Corp.
850 Third Avenue
New York, NY 10022

All Kensington titles, imprints and distributed lines are available at special quantity discounts for bulk purchases for sales promotion, premiums, fund-raising, educational or institutional use.

Special book excerpts or customized printings can also be created to fit specific needs. For details, write or phone the office of the Kensington Special Sales Manager: Kensington Publishing Corp., 850 Third Avenue, New York, NY 10022, Attn. Special Sales Department. Phone: 1-800-221-2647.

Dafina Books and the Dafina logo Reg. U.S. Pat. & TM Off.

Library of Congress Card Catalogue Number: 2002112550
ISBN: 1-57566-920-X

First Printing: March 2003
10 9 8 7 6 5 4 3 2 1

Printed in the United States of America

One

Regina Pearson had everything a forty-year-old woman could want. Everything, that is, except a feeling that she belonged to someone or in some place. That she was an intrinsic part of a warm, loving family. When she looked at the people and the place she'd known all of her life, she didn't think, *I'm a part of this; it's me; it's who I am.* Even the sunshine that greeted her every morning and the ever-present scent of the tropical blooms the world loved seemed to her a foreign thing, and it always had. It didn't mean to her what it meant to the people she knew best—the Native Hawaiians. Many of them worshiped the sun as a deity, just as they paid homage to Kanaloa, god of eternal hope and happiness, but Papa had admonished her that that was a form of paganism. It wasn't her place, and the people around her were not her people. But they were all she had.

She sat with her best friend, Kalani, whose ancestors had lived for centuries on the island of Oahu, in her late father's bedroom sorting out his belongings. Kalani didn't think it proper to wade through a dead person's private dreams, goals, personal successes, and failures, and told Regina as much.

"It's Papa's wish, Kalani." Just one more of the numerous cultural differences between herself and the Hawaiian people with whom she had lived all of her life. Mainlanders tended not to socialize with the Native Hawaiians, though her father had intentionally settled among them.

"What about your people? None of them came to the burial." Kalani's people didn't have funerals.

"Papa never told me anything about his family or his life," she said, "just that he came from the southern part of the United States and never wanted to see the place again. I don't even know why he left there and settled here." She hadn't even known of her father's considerable wealth; they certainly had not lived as people of means, and he never spoke to her of his finances. It surprised her that his will made her a wealthy woman.

"Didn't he leave some relatives on the mainland?" Kalani asked her. "What about your mother, if you don't mind my asking?"

"She died when I was two, and he never talked about her. If I mentioned her, he'd just look off in space and act like he didn't hear me. I guess it hurt him to talk about her. When I would ask him about our kinfolk, he'd say we didn't have any. Watching television and seeing African Americans on the screen, I used to wonder if any of them were related to me."

"Why? You can't like what you see of them on TV and read in the papers; most of the time, they seem to be doing something bad."

"I know. Or stupid, like in those sitcoms. Papa always said the media likes to show us in a bad light, and that's as far as he would go on the subject. You know, Kalani, I'll be forty April twenty-sixth, and I don't know hardly anything about myself. I wish I had some relatives, some people who look like me and who care about me. I'm tired of feeling like a freak."

Kalani tied a piece of cord around a box of clothing and marked it for the seniors center. "Regina, we don't see you that way. Besides, there are African Americans living in Honolulu, and a lot of them visit here."

"Right. One in every two hundred thousand, and they don't go to my school, my community center, the local library, and the other places I go."

"It's too bad you didn't insist on some answers from your dad. What are you going to do now?"

"I'll get to that when I finish with . . . Look at this, will you?"

Kalani rushed to her. "What? What's that?"

"It's an envelope from somebody named Maude Witherspoon, addressed to my mother, and it's dated the year before I was born. I can't make out the month and day. New Bern, North Carolina? Never heard of the place."

"What does it say?"

She pushed back the envelope flap. "Nothing. There's no letter inside." Although she fixed a smile on her face, she couldn't hide from her friend the sudden depression that spread over her.

Sensing Regina's dampened mood, Kalani tried to cheer her. "Regina, why don't you come to my family's party next week? It's our family reunion, and you'll meet people from the states, Canada, Sweden, Japan, and a lot of other places as well as Hawaii. We always have a luau, a Japanese tea ceremony, and a Texas barbecue. You'll enjoy it, and maybe it will pull you out of the dumps."

How was the company of a hundred strangers supposed to make her feel better? The local customs dictated that she accept, so she thanked her friend and prepared herself for another experience of isolation in the midst of a crowd.

They lugged a dozen boxes to Kalani's old station wagon and left them at the seniors center. "You should have buried your father's precious things along with him," Kalani said, "but you didn't, so you should burn them."

"I have to do exactly what he asked me to do," Regina said, aware that she was contravening a sacred custom of Kalani's people. "My father didn't believe in wasting anything. He wanted poor people to have whatever I can't use."

They said good-bye, and Regina headed for her own apartment on Huauni Place, taking the long route along Diamond Head Road in the direction of Diamond Head, the 761-foot peak that dominated the Oahu Island skyline before the advent of skyscraper hotels, and which loomed above an extinct volcanic crater that was the site of an ancient Hawaiian burial ground. Diamond Head was the one thing, other than the Pacific Ocean, that she liked about Honolulu. She could count on it; after thousands of years in that spot, it never changed, and when she looked out of her kitchen window, she knew it would stand there, gazing at the Pacific's enormous waves and swirling foam.

"Mustn't get sentimental about the Pacific," she told herself, remembering that it took her mother.

Several days later, primed for a Hawaiian family reunion, she reached number 22 Kahoaa Street in heightened spirits, although she did not relish the company of so many people who were likely to wonder about her presence among them. She couldn't know that this April day would mark a turning point in her life—that the warmth, love, and friendliness with which Kalani's scores of relatives greeted her would motivate her to find her own family.

"Sorry to hear about Miles." She swung around, knowing who she would see. "He had a rough time of it," Ken Pahoa, her Native Hawaiian former lover, said of her father, "so we shouldn't begrudge him his rest. What are your plans?"

"I haven't made any yet."

"I suppose now you're sorry you walked out on me. If you want to come back, we'll have to have some ground rules. For one, you'll accept that I'm head of the house, and do as I say."

She laughed aloud. Not in amusement, but as a cleansing emotion that seemed to scrape itself from the bowels of her being. He grabbed her shoulders, but still she laughed.

"You're hysterical," he growled. "Cut it out. I don't see anything funny."

She brought herself under control. "I do. I left you because I couldn't tolerate living with you any longer. What do you think changed in a month's time? And I was laughing at myself for having been such a nitwit. Trust me, not having a man in my life is a blessed state compared to what it was with you the past months." Oh, how sweet it was to know she'd shaken his self-assurance, that she'd punched a hole in his ego. "I need you the way a car needs a flat tire."

His mouth twisted in anger, but she didn't care. He hadn't believed her when she told him he was out of her life for good.

"I hope you and Ken aren't planning to get back together," Kalani said later as they leaned against a banyon tree, inhaling the scent of freshly mowed grass and sipping cold coconut milk.

"Not a chance. That's all behind me now. I've had my fill of men— two of them as lovers—and my papa was no prize."

Kalani didn't question her about that; asking personal questions wasn't the way of her people. Instead, her raised eyebrow showed her bafflement.

"You don't know how fortunate you are. A hundred and thirty- some relatives all around you, embracing, swapping jokes, telling tales about each other, and reminiscing about those who are absent. I've never had any of that. You know your background, your culture and where you fit in"—she waved her right hand—"among these people. You know who you are, but I can only guess at who I am."

"Please don't be sad. With my family here, we're supposed to be merrymaking."

Regina looked toward the vast Pacific. "I'm not one bit sad. I real- ize I've been making up my mind to leave Honolulu. Tomorrow, I'm going to begin searching for Maude Witherspoon. I want to know what it's like to be a member of a family. If she knew my mother, she may know my mother's relatives."

"But Regina, you said the envelope was postmarked more than forty years ago."

"When my mother got that letter, she was twenty-one years old, so some of her relatives are still living. I'm going to find them. I have to. You don't know what it's like to be alone. There are people around me, yes, but they don't know who I am, and they don't show me who they are. If you look at it closely, you'll see that around here, I'm really a nobody."

From that day, Regina's search occupied her mind every minute of her waking hours, interfering with concentration on her work as a publicist and event planner for Hawaii's Mt. Royal Hotels. Hours of searching on the Internet yielded no clues as to the whereabouts of Maude Witherspoon.

One afternoon, not long after Regina's father died, Kalani stared at the Pacific from a window in Regina's office at Oahu Royal Hotel and spoke with her back to Regina—a signal that her words would not bring pleasure. "She may not be living. Maybe you just have to accept that you're not going to find her. Anything can happen to a person in forty years."

"I can't give up. She's the only thread I have. I wrote the chamber of commerce but haven't gotten an answer. I may have to hire a lawyer or somebody in New Bern to look for her if I don't find her in one of those nineteen-ninety census tract volumes I ordered through the university."

"Did you try the phone company?"

Regina looked to the ceiling, as she had so often seen her father do when nonplussed. "First thing. 'Please speak the address clearly' was the reply I got from that digital operator. I hate those recordings. I don't have an address, but tell that to the recorded voice."

She despaired of waiting for the census tract records, sent to New Bern for some newspapers, and began searching them for a legal representative. Weeks passed, but she made no progress. Mountains that she couldn't climb, rivers she couldn't cross—insurmountable objects impeding her flight from danger—plagued her in her dreams, and she awakened night after night panting and soaked with perspiration.

When a reply arrived from the chamber of commerce, she ripped open the letter in frenzied anticipation, only to yield to exasperation when she saw that it contained only a brochure.

But Regina refused to give up. Perusing the brochure, she found a telephone number, dialed it, and stated her problem.

"Lots of Witherspoons around here," the woman in New Bern said. "One of them used to be a blues singer. She's famous, but I can't think of her name right now. Wait a minute. Maybe one of the colored women in here knows her."

Regina's breath hung in her throat as she waited for what seemed like hours but couldn't have been more than two minutes.

"You're looking for Maude van der Kaa," the woman said, and gave Regina the address. "I wish you luck."

She hung up, reached for the receiver to dial the New Bern telephone operator, and immediately withdrew her hand. She couldn't risk causing the woman to have a heart attack, and a phone call might net her a snap-judgment rejection. She wrote and rewrote a letter explaining who she was and inquiring about the woman's relationship to her mother. Finally, certain that she would probably never hear from Maude van der Kaa, she mailed it and returned to the unpleasant task of sorting out her parents' effects. Her father hadn't disposed of her mother's personal things but had locked them in a steamer trunk and stored it in a crib beside the house.

It was a Saturday morning in late May when her gaze landed on a packet of papers enclosed in a plastic envelope and tied with brown string. She knew at once that the papers contained something of value to her, and struggled with trembling fingers to untie the tightly knotted cord. Finally, she saw her mother's handwriting in love letters to her father, and then a certificate of marriage naming Miles Pearson and Louise Witherspoon as the celebrants. She nearly choked on her breath as the realization hit her that the Witherspoons of New Bern were her mother's relatives. She hadn't known her mother's maiden name, because she had learned as a small child that any questions to her father about her mother caused him to withdraw from her. As the years passed, she stopped asking questions.

Tears pooled in her lap as she stared at the treasure in her hands. She accepted them as tears of joy for having discovered something important about herself, and of sadness because she knew no one who would understand what she felt. Still, she had a sense of relief that she no longer depended on an answer from Maude van der Kaa as the means of finding her family.

She ordered copies of more recent issues of New Bern's daily and weekly newspapers and searched them for job possibilities, reasoning that nothing prevented her going there for a visit and staying if she found a job. A little over a week later, she received a letter from Maude, but her anxiety as to its contents was so acute that hours passed before she willed herself to open it.

> *I'm your Aunt Maude,* she read, *your mother's younger sister. We gave up hope long ago of ever hearing from her or anything about her. None of us knew where she and Miles went. I'm sorry to know they're both gone. I want you to come visit me right away and stay a while.*

She phoned Kalani to share her joy and excitement, then began looking in earnest for work in or near New Bern. In *The Sun Journal's* classified advertisements, she found a job possibility, a chance to manage a hotel that was near completion. With trepidation she applied for the job and waited. She had given up hope when, in late July, the hotel owner called, interviewed her by telephone, and promised to get back to her. Three days later, the manager of the Hotel Hawaii told her that the owner of the Craven Hotel in New Bern had asked him to interview her.

"You'll get the job," he said after talking with her.

On that August evening, one day before her scheduled flight to New Bern, she walked at sunset along Waikiki Beach for a last look at her beloved Pacific Ocean. As she strolled, she let her love of the ocean, the sand, palm trees, and warm gentle breeze lift her out of herself and erase from her thoughts any disquiet about what she might face the next day and the next. She sat in the sand with her back resting against a palm tree, removed her sandals, and dug her toes into the warm white grains that, eons earlier, had been fertile soil. Oahu had never given her a reason to love it, and she didn't, but as the big red disc slipped into the ocean, she lamented its descent and the forty years of her life that seemed to vanish along with it.

"You can always come back here," Kalani said as they waited in

Honolulu International Airport for Regina's American Airlines flight to the Raleigh-Durham airport. From there she would take a local flight to New Bern.

Hawaiians reserved gestures of affection for intimate family members, but as the reality of what she was doing took possession of her thoughts, and the pangs of severing ties with her dearest friend became almost unbearable, Regina hugged Kalani. "I admit I'm scared leaving the only home, friends, people, and way of life I know, but I have to do this." *Trading all I have to search for a family, a bunch of strangers to whom I mean nothing, in hopes of finding that sense of belonging that I've never known. I wonder if I'm out of my mind.*

Kalani tried to smile. "Go with the gods."

Without looking back, Regina stepped through the gate and headed for her future. She took her seat in business class, closed her eyes, and made herself a promise. From now on, she would be assertive, stand up for herself, demand her rights, and be independent. She wanted a family, but if she didn't find one, she'd be the best hotelier in North Carolina and get on with her life.

Scared? Yes, she was scared. Not because it was her first flight or because she had never before left the island of her birth. Her fear stemmed from the growing awareness that achieving what she so badly coveted didn't rest with her alone. Even if she found scores of kinfolk, she couldn't make them like her or even want to be in her company. And as badly as she wanted a big loving family, there was one price she would not pay. Never again would she beg for love and affection, and if she spent every day of the rest of her life alone, she'd gladly do it rather than tolerate disrespect, unfaithfulness, and psychological abuse from a man. Any man.

She would never forget the day she rushed home to tell her father that she had been elected class valedictorian. She had worked so hard, getting straight A's all through school, to achieve that honor. At last, she had accomplished what would surely make him proud.

"Look, Papa. Here's the principal's list of class honors, and I'm the valedictorian." In her ebullience and without thinking, she threw her arms around his neck. "Oh, Papa, I'm so happy. I'm speaking at commencement."

He shifted from her embrace, looked up briefly from his paper, said, "Good. good," then continued reading.

She hadn't meant to hug him, and she backed away, petrified, be-cause he hated being touched. "I uh . . . I'll need a cap and gown, Papa."

He used his finger for a marker and, with what appeared to be re-luctance, dragged his gaze from his precious paper. "Of course. Just let me know how much money you need."

"Yes, sir. I . . . uh . . . Papa, will you go with me to the party for par-ents of graduating honor students? Will you, please, Papa?"

He didn't look up. "I don't think that's necessary. But if you want to go, ask one of your little friends." Always the same. Generous with money and stingy with himself.

He might as well have dropped a wrecking ball on her head, for she felt as if her whole insides had been smashed. But it was in her heart that she felt the pain. "I'll never ask him to go anywhere with me again," she vowed as she fled the room, fully aware that he didn't know she'd left. She hadn't bothered to cry; she was seventeen years old, and she had already cried enough for a lifetime because her father didn't love her.

Six months later, then a freshman at the University of Hawaii, she fell for Helmut Neukirk, a graduate student with a ready smile, who seemed unable to keep his hands off her. Older than she by eleven years, he quickly embroiled her in a sexual affair that she mistook for love. Hoping for the love she'd missed all her life, she moved in with him. But she soon learned that he was undemonstrative and unfeeling, that he touched her only when he wanted sex.

She gazed at the clouds through the window of the Boeing 747 that was roaring with her to the unknown, and tried to clean all thoughts of Helmut from her mind. But the picture of herself in the orange-and-yellow dinner dress she bought for the office Christmas party would not leave her. She would never forget it.

"Do you like it?" she'd asked Helmut, swirling before him, model-ing the dress.

He'd barely glanced her way as he chewed Pringles potato chips and watched the Cowboys lose to the Saints. "What do you want from me? It's garish. You look like one of the Natives in that thing." She had stopped dancing. Suddenly, she was seventeen again, begging her fa-ther to go with her to her high school's party for parents of graduating honor students.

She had needed more than he gave, but thinking his behavior and attitude normal, she didn't try to extricate herself from the affair.

One day after Regina saw an old movie, *Gaslight*, about a psychologically abused woman, one of her colleagues at work asked her, "What does your father say about you and Helmut?"

"Why, nothing. Why?"

"I'm surprised. Helmut is self-serving, mean, arrogant, and overbearing. How can you love him?"

Stunned, she replied. "What do you mean?"

"I mean no man at all is better than that one," her colleague, a Seattle-born Caucasian girl, said. "You can do better, and you should."

What yardstick did she have for judging a man? After fretting over it for months and accepting that Helmut was the source of her unhappiness, she had severed ties with him. But she could hardly bear the loneliness and eventually formed a liaison with Ken Pahoa, a Native Hawaiian, who offered love, affection, and understanding. She would learn that, in matters of love and affection, Ken was even more of a charlatan than Helmut.

The smell of barbecued beef and heavily roasted coffee brought her back to the present. *What's done is done, and I'm not going to let it weigh me down.*

Eleven hours later, the tiny US Airways Express plane to which she had transferred at Raleigh-Durham rolled to a stop in Craven County Regional Airport, which served New Bern and nearby towns. With a thirst for the unknown and brimming with excitement, she walked down the steps and went to the cart for her hand luggage.

"Here you are, Miss." The voice belonged to a stocky black man who seemed to look right through her.

She thanked him, and when he didn't respond, she picked up her bag and started toward the building. Half a dozen African-American men performed various tasks around the plane and the entrance to the airport building, but none paid her any attention. Strangers had always taken a second look at her, and forgetting that she was no longer an anomaly, she found it disconcerting to be ignored. A stranger in another strange land.

In the waiting room, Regina looked for a red dress—Maude wrote that she would be wearing red—but at least half a dozen African-American women wore that color. Her heartbeat accelerated when a tall, very attractive dark woman of indeterminable age, who wore a red dress and long gold earrings, walked toward her.

"Are you Louise's daughter?" the woman asked with something akin to a smile hovering around her eyes.

Regina nodded, and the woman opened her arms. "I'm your aunt Maude. We hadn't heard a single solitary thing from Louise since Miles took her from here. You can't imagine how glad I am to see you." She picked up Regina's bag. "We've got a lot of catching up to do."

On the drive from the airport, Regina learned that Maude didn't make small talk. She paid no attention to the speed limit, either, and by the time they reached Maude's red-brick bungalow, Regina surmised that she had personally slammed on the brakes a dozen times.

"You must be tired," Maude said, "so I'll show you your room."

"I'm not tired." She didn't know what she had expected, but she had a feeling of contentment as she walked through the attractive, modern home. "Aunt Maude." She repeated it, liking the sound and its meaning for her. "Aunt Maude, I've got so many questions that I hardly know where to start. I don't know a thing about myself. Tell me something. *Anything.*"

"You might as well relax. It'll take forever to cover forty years of total silence. I want a beer. What would you like?"

The words *a glass of cold coconut milk* were at the tip of her tongue when she checked herself. "Something . . . uh . . . cold."

Maude braced her hips with knotted fists. "I don't believe in fencing. Say what you mean, honey."

"I'd rather not have beer, but I'd like something cold."

Minutes later, she sipped iced tea and stared in wonder as her aunt enjoyed a glass of Heineken beer and a Havana cigar. She hadn't thought the ban against the importation of Havana cigars had been lifted, but as she would have done in Hawaii, she refrained from pressing the question. Working as a hotel event planner, she had imagined she'd seen about everything, but a woman puffing a cigar was something new. She asked her aunt whether cigar-smoking was common among African-American women.

"Not that I know of. I've never cared what other people do, Regina. I do as I please." For a few quiet moments, she savored her beer. "The nights are getting cool. I hope you brought some real shoes, 'cause your feet'll freeze in those sandals."

"I knew I'd have to buy some things, and I'd appreciate any tips."

"Sure. Plenty good stores around here."

Regina leaned back and relaxed in the rocker—an apple-green

color she disliked. "Aunt Maude." *How beautiful that sounded!* "Aunt Maude, I hope I've got scores of relatives, and I want you to introduce me to every one of them and help me get them all together."

Maude's stare nearly disconcerted her. "I sure hope you're kidding. I don't think I could stand being in the same house with them."

Regina felt her lower lip sag. "Why? It's my dream to have a family, to be around my kinfolk, people who look like me and care about me."

"For goodness' sake, don't get carried away. Sometime you're better off without a bunch of relatives hanging around." She jumped up from the low rattan chair. "I'd better call Pop and tell him you're here."

Regina sat forward. Tense. "Your father? My grandfather?"

Maude sauntered over to the wall phone beside the door leading to the hall. "One and the same. Abner Witherspoon." She dialed his number.

"Pop, this is Maude. Louise's daughter is here with me." She leaned against the wall, listening. "No point in that, Pop. Let's let bygones be bygones. She didn't know anything about us until after Miles passed and she went through his things. *Now, Pop.* All right. All right, I'll tell her."

"What's the matter? You look as if . . . What is it?"

"He's a stubborn man, and after forty years, he's still mad with Louise and Miles for getting married. He was against it. Intractable."

The bottom dropped out of her belly, and goose bumps covered her arms. It hadn't occurred to her that her own blood kin wouldn't want her.

With effort, she camouflaged the fear that snaked through her; nothing would stand in her way. She had it—the family she longed for—within her grasp, and she refused to be defeated. Then she asked Maude, "Is it here, as among Native Hawaiians, that the family usually does whatever the elder says?"

Maude took a slug of beer and puffed her cigar. "No, indeedy. If that were the case, your mother never would have gone off with Miles Pearson. Pop was mad enough to raise a gun to her. He just stood on the front porch and watched her go, and as far as I know, he hasn't mentioned her name in over forty years."

Regina told herself not to let it upset her, leaned back in the rocker, and spoke calmly as if the experience of having her grandfather reject her was an everyday occurrence.

"Do you think he'll change if I go talk with him?"

Maude cut the cigar with a pocketknife, relit it, and puffed some more. "Child, Pop's ninety-one. I left here thirty-seven years ago and hit just about every country in the Western Hemisphere. When I came back last year, Pop was still having half a grapefruit, wheat toast, two soft-boiled eggs, a slice of cheddar cheese, and one cup of coffee for breakfast. Pop is like the tree planted by the river of water, as the song goes. He's not about to be moved."

Regina leaned forward, fighting off consternation as her heartbeat accelerated to a gallop. "Maybe we'd better start at the beginning. Why didn't Grandfather want Papa to marry my mother?"

"He never would tell."

Maude's right foot swung like a pendulum from her crossed leg. "I'll tell you one thing. Your daddy's people, the Pearsons, look down on all us dark-skinned folks, and the Witherspoons think all light-skinned folks descended from black women who slept around with white slave owners. The circumstances of that don't bother them one bit. They don't care that most of the poor women were forced, ravished. When I got to Europe, I wanted to spread my wings and fly under my own power. Free of all this stupidity. In the twenty-some years I stayed over there, I didn't encounter any of this foolishness about race and skin color. You want family? I wish you luck."

The phone rang repeatedly, and she watched in amazement as Maude took her time getting to it. *If she doesn't hurry, she'll miss the call,* Regina thought, and could feel her face heat when Maude, seeming to have read her mind, raised an eyebrow in her direction. "The caller wants to talk with *me,* not the other way around," she said, "so why should I break my neck getting to the phone?"

"Maude speaking. How y'all doing this afternoon?" She listened for a few seconds. "Don't even think it. I'm through with that. Listen, come over and meet my niece from Honolulu. None of that, Harold. Besides, she's your first cousin, and she wants to meet her relatives. Day after tomorrow is fine. Supper." She hung up.

"Who's Harold?"

"Harold Pearson. His daddy and yours were brothers. You'd better get some rest." She walked over to Regina. "You here for good?"

"Yes. Honolulu is behind me. I want a life with my own people."

She thought Maude looked skeptical, but she wasn't sure. The woman's face was anything but open. "Don't expect too much,

Regina. I got relatives right here in New Bern that I haven't laid eyes on in the almost two years I've been back here. Don't prime yourself for heartache."

"If you love people, Aunt Maude, they love you back. In a year, you and I will laugh about this conversation." She forced a smile. "And Grandfather will get over his grudge."

"I take it you've got the help of the angel Gabriel. We'll eat supper around seven-thirty." She went into the house and closed the door.

Regina sat there for a few minutes, digesting Maude's words and behavior. As for her brave words, she knew she would like her aunt, but wasn't sure she hadn't set her goal for a large, loving family too high.

She tossed in the bed for a few hours, excited, anxious to begin her new life. Her talk with Maude was the first intimate conversation she'd ever had with a black woman. She'd read about the sisterhood, and television had taught her that African-American men called each other "brother." She could hardly wait to become a part of the African-American community and of the Witherspoon and Pearson families.

Propelled by her eagerness, she got up, dressed, and went out to the garden, where she found Maude gathering bell peppers. "How do I get to the Craven Hotel?" she asked Maude.

"Why? It's not open yet."

Regina explained about her job there as hotel manager and earned her aunt's obvious admiration.

"Well I'll be doggoned. You sure are resourceful," Maude said. She straightened up and braced the back of her right hand against her hip. "Darned if history isn't trying to repeat itself. As far back as the twenties, first my granddaddy Witherspoon and then Pop owned and managed the only hotel in this town where our people could stay. It's in your blood; you'll do all right." She cut some chrysanthemums and laid them on top of the peppers. "Pop ran that hotel till he was eighty-three. Wait'll I tell him about this." Her eyes sparkled with deviltry. "Boy, I bet that'll shake him up."

Maude didn't blame Regina for wanting what most people took for granted, but neither did she welcome a renewal of the dislikes, grudges, and especially the nasty whispers that Regina would stir up with her plans to bring the Witherspoons and Pearsons together. Not even all the Witherspoons could bear one another's company, and putting the two families together could be like pitching a Molotov cocktail into a blazing furnace. She had battled the Witherspoon family herself from the time she was seventeen, and she got along with them now because she no longer cared what they thought of her.

Maybe she shouldn't worry Pop with information about Regina, but Abner Witherspoon needed to learn the art of forgiveness. She dialed his number. "Pop, you wouldn't believe this. Regina, that's Louise's daughter, is going to manage the Craven Hotel, and she had no idea that around here the Witherspoon name is synonymous with hotels. Looks like she's a chip off the old block."

"Humph. When you seen Robert? You brother acts like he doesn't have a father. Hasn't been around here in over a month."

Maybe you really couldn't teach an old dog new tricks. Knowing that his strict rules about good manners would prevent his hanging up on her, she made a stab at creating a little remorse in her father. "Pop, suppose you get to heaven and the Lord won't let you come in because Granddaddy set old man Beidermeyer's silo on fire and destroyed a year's wheat crop?" His silence emboldened her, and she went on, "If you blame Regina for what her parents did . . ." She let him finish it. Stubborn though he was, she knew he had a conscience.

"Well, Pop?"

"I had three boys and two girls. My boys never talked back to me. You watch your mouth. You hear?"

In for a penny, in for a pound. "Pop, you know I don't say everything I think. If I did, none of y'all would be speaking to me. Regina's staying here with me at least for the time being. So remember that if you come over for supper before Wednesday night prayer meeting, you'll have to eat at the table with her."

In her mind's eye, she could see him purse his lips and let a frown darken his countenance when he said, "She can take a walk for an hour. A little exercise won't hurt her, and I'm not giving up my Wednesday night chili and cracklin' bread."

"Pop, I can't ask Regina to leave home because her grandfather doesn't want to meet the grandchild he's never seen."

"Case is closed. I'll be there Wednesday for my supper as usual."

He won that round because he knew she wouldn't deprive him of his favorite meal, and she had a feeling she'd been too hasty in encouraging Regina to come to New Bern.

* * *

The following morning, anxious for a look at the town she hoped would be her home, Regina rose with the sun, dressed quickly, and stepped outside, but she hadn't expected the frosty air and discovered that she didn't tolerate it well. Nonetheless, she stood on Maude's front steps, captivated by the quiet, idyllic setting: houses of red or white brick, set well back from the broad street, among groves of pine, cottonwood, and white birch trees interspersed with the crape myrtle and magnolia trees that would bloom in spring. Yes, she would miss the Pacific Ocean, but she could be at home in New Bern. Her roots were there, and an inner sense told her she would find in that town of 30,000 people what she lacked and wanted most.

Around ten o'clock, armed with instructions from Maude, she struck out for Vanguard Department Store. "Do you have any more of these in size three-X," she asked a clerk as she held up a package of hosiery.

"Just what you see over there."

Taken aback by the clerk's nonchalance, she said, "I didn't see any more. Perhaps you have some in your storage room."

The woman stopped chewing her gum. "I *said*, just what you see over there."

Astounded by the clerk's attitude and disinterest in her patronage, Regina walked around until she saw an employee who wore a large pin on which was written, *Service is our business; we aim to please.* She approached the woman, who favored her with a luminous smile, and related her problem.

"Could you help me, please?"

"Just what's over there in aisle three."

"But I looked, and this is all I could find."

The smile disappeared. "Lady, if you didn't see it, it's not there."

So much for the sisterhood. Sisters, indeed! She finished her shopping and went home, considerably less ebullient that when she left.

"It's nothing to be concerned about, honey. That's just the way they act," Maude said when Regina mentioned it. "Service is out of fashion these days, so unless you go to a high-price shop, you gonna have to put up with ornery salespeople."

"But they were African-American women, and I thought they'd be helpful."

Maude's hands went to her hips. "You got some sentimental notions about black people, and you might as well get rid of that right now. We're just like everybody else—nice when it's convenient."

She didn't like thinking herself naive, but in regard to black Americans, the term seemed to fit. "Where should I look for a place to stay?" she asked Maude.

"Plenty of room right here in this big house, so take your time. And don't forget your cousin Harold will be here for supper."

"What's he like?"

Maude removed her glasses and gazed toward the ceiling. "Harold? He defies description. No way you can stick Harold in a pigeonhole. You have to know Harold."

Harold arrived promptly at seven. Maude ate at seven-thirty, a habit cultivated while in Europe, and made an exception only for her father, who ate supper with her every Wednesday. Regina hadn't prepared herself for Harold's expansive welcome and embrace, nor for his seeming diffidence. She noticed that he walked with a slight limp, and wondered if that accounted for his self-consciousness.

"Harold plays the saxophone."

"Yeah," he said, and she thought he stared at her as would one greatly perplexed. He shook his head and grinned, though his expression remained troubled. "I'm trying to get Maude to do a program with me. Regina, this woman is considered one of the great blues singers of our time."

Regina swung around and faced Maude. "You didn't mention that to me. I didn't know you were famous."

"She acts modest," Harold said, "but that's wasted on me. If you got it, flaunt it. You good at something, admit it. Humility is tiresome. Truth is, most people don't have anything to be humble about. What about it, Maude? Six-week run, three nights a week. That's all I'm asking."

"I invited you to meet your cousin and to eat supper with us. That's all. The blues are in the past."

Harold raised both eyebrows. "Don't kid yourself, Maude. It's in your blood the way music is in mine. I'll bet you go to sleep nights hearing that applause. The first year back here, you were building your house and furnishing it, and the past six months, you've been enjoying it. You're due for a good case of boredom. Then you'll sing."

"Must be nice to know it all," Maude said. "Come on. Let's eat."

They sat down to supper, and she noticed that Harold hesitated and Maude began eating. She was about to emulate Maude when Harold rapped his glass with a fork. "Okay, you two infidels, I'm used to blessing my food before I eat."

She watched him say grace and wanted to ask him to write it down for her but didn't. The less her relatives knew of her ignorance about their lives, customs, and beliefs, the better. She'd speak to Maude about it.

"Not much to do around here, Regina," Harold said later, savoring apple pie à la mode as if it were as precious as gold bouillon. "Want to go with me to the Zanzibar some time? You do like jazz, don't you?"

He said it as if it were a given, causing her to wonder how far out of step she was. "I . . . uh . . . I'm not sure I understand it."

Harold positioned his fork properly on the side of his plate, folded his hands in his lap, and stared hard at her. "What do you mean? You don't bother about *understanding* it; jazz is something you feel all the way to the pit of your gut. It's like great sex. Opens you up, makes you vulnerable, and rocks you till you feel like you're flying. Awesome."

Her eyes widened, and she felt her lower lip drop as she gaped at him. Native Hawaiians didn't talk about sex, and especially not in mixed company. Maude snickered, adding to her discomfort.

"I'll have to inform myself," she said. "I take it you're an expert when it comes to jazz." She figured that would get him off the subject of sex.

"I hold my own, Cousin. I can hang out with the best of them." He served himself another slice of pie. "I see I'm gonna have to educate you. You ever heard of the blues before tonight?"

"Don't patronize me, Harold. When do we go to the Zanzibar?"

He looked directly at her then, a worried look clouding his dark eyes. "I hope Maude warned you that neither the Witherspoons nor my folks approve of me. It hurts, but I can't change to suit them." He gave her his phone number. "Talk it over with Maude and let me know whether you want us to be friends."

Regina looked from Maude to Harold, but nothing in their faces hinted at the reasons for his odd remark. She was getting used to Maude's complex personality and her penchant for plain speaking, but Harold appeared to relish playing catch with a person's mind. She wondered if every relative she met would be a jigsaw puzzle.

"Regina wants to get to know her kinfolk. She feels she needs them around her, though I can't imagine why."

"Me, neither," Harold said, standing to leave. "If you've got one little thorn in your otherwise starry crown, they'll find it, stick it in you, and make you bleed. And guess where every single one of 'em will be at eleven o'clock Sunday mornings. You got it. Biggest bunch of hypocrites that ever breathed."

Regina angled her head to the side and took a good look at Harold. If there was anything wrong with him, it wasn't obvious. "Let me know when you want us to go to the Zanzibar. And thanks for coming. I've a feeling we'll be good friends."

He kissed her cheek. "Maybe what this gang needs is new blood, somebody who doesn't buy into their prejudices and pretenses. I'll call you next week."

After Harold left, Regina asked Maude, "Why do I get the impression that a friendship with Harold could amount to a big risk?"

Maude lifted her left shoulder in a careless shrug. "Not with me, it wouldn't, but you'd tick off the Pearsons and the rest of the Witherspoons. If you're trying to pull your families around you, hanging out with *two* social misfits won't cut it."

A slow flush of dread seeped through her. "Who're you talking about?"

Maude stacked the dessert plates and displayed an air of nonchalance. "I'm talking 'bout your cousin Harold and your aunt Maude. If our folks were passing out grades, I'd get a D and Harold would get an F. And if I was grading most of *them*, they'd get a double F."

Regina stared at Maude's retreating back and prayed that she hadn't jumped into a hornets' nest.

Two

Regina dressed in a rust-colored linen suit, silk beige shirt, and black accessories and went into the living room, where Maude sat on a stool playing a guitar. "How far from here are they building the Craven Hotel?"

Maude's face bore the expression of someone impressed, and favorably so. "Well, well. I got a hunch you're going to bring some class to this hick town. Craven's about a mile. Walking distance. Why?"

"I'm supposed to start work today."

Maude rubbed out her cigar. "Do you realize that's a thirty-story hotel and that it's got a huge conference center? You're taking on plenty with a hotel that big."

"I'm trained for it; I've had experience working in hotels, and I'm not afraid of the challenge."

Maude lay the instrument aside and dropped her hands into the lap of the caftan she wore. "No, I guess you're not. It's in your blood. Like I said, Pop ran the only good hotel in this region that catered to blacks, just as his papa did before him. You'll do fine. You really are here for good, then?"

With her shoulders laid back and her chin just a little higher, Regina looked her aunt in the eye. "I haven't changed my mind, Aunt Maude. I want a life here with my own people."

"Well, you're my niece, my sister's child. I'm here for you as long as you act like folks, but don't expect that from all the rest of them."

She stood, lithe, sensuous, and attractive for her sixty years. "Much as I enjoyed the adulation and company of my European friends, I got lonely for these back-biting kinfolk of mine; I was never sure whether it was me or my singing that turned on my husbands and lovers." She exhaled a long sigh. "Eerie as the devil. I used to wonder about that at the doggonedest times." She laughed, evidently nursing a treasured memory.

"I always knew I needed more, Aunt Maude. Maybe if Papa and I had been closer, I wouldn't have had this gut-wrenching need for my own people. If you'll make a list of my mother's and father's relatives and some way of contacting them, I'll do the rest. See you later."

Craven Hotel stood among its neighboring structures as a Parthenon among huts, soaring thirty stories. New Bern had not previously boasted a building or monument of its ilk, and some said that it transformed the town of 30,000 people into a modern city. Others said it made the rest of the town inconsequential. Regina gazed at the bronzed pillars, door handles, and moldings and the sedate brownstone-faced facade that promised inner luxury; straightened her shoulders; and quickened her steps. She would be mistress of New Bern's architectural gem.

"Good morning. I'm Regina Pearson," she said and extended her right hand to the receptionist, who sat in front of a door marked *James Carlson, Proprietor.* With an air of deference, the woman reciprocated. "Good morning, Miss Pearson. We've been expecting you, ma'am. Mr. Carlson is waiting for you."

The door opened, and Justin Duval arose from his seat beside James Carlson's desk, with his gaze glued in that direction and his bearing appropriate to his status as colonel, United States Army, retired. Ever since he'd been advised that a Hawaiian woman would manage the Craven, he'd been tempted to revoke his contract to design the hotel's furnishings. All the Hawaiian hotels he'd been in were decorated in what he liked to call "early ugly." He hoped she didn't subscribe to that style of decorating.

The woman, tall, elegant, and right to his taste, stepped into the room, and barbells began a war in his belly. She took a few steps and stopped, her gaze darting from Carlson to him, where it lingered. She didn't smile, but the expression in her eyes set him afire. Cool. And interested. He swore under his breath.

Carlson, who had seemed stunned, must have recovered his aplomb, for with his face wreathed in smiles, he walked to her with his hand extended. "I'm James Carlson. We're glad you're here. This is Colonel Duval. He's designing our furnishings." Her eyebrows shot up, and Carlson hastened to explain, "Justin has retired from the Army. He's an expert designer of furniture and interiors. One of the best."

"How do you do, Mr. Carlson?" She turned to him but didn't offer to shake hands, and that suited him. "I'm glad to meet you, Colonel." Her voice, low and sultry, did nothing to arrest the weights that battled in his gut.

He didn't say he was glad to meet her, because he wasn't. "I've been looking forward to meeting you." That much was true. "Switching from a tropical to a temperate climate won't tax you too much, I hope."

Daggers seemed to shoot from her eyes as she seated herself in a chair opposite him, serving notice that Ms. Pearson understood his comment and that she welcomed a good fight. He wondered at the quick animosity. Unless she had a short fuse, she would have thought all he did was show concern.

"Won't tax me at all," she said, and turned fully to face James Carlson, in effect dismissing *him*. She didn't look his way while Carlson explained to her that all furnishings were being designed especially for the hotel, which would open in six months.

"Is Colonel Duval designing all of it?" she asked in a tone that suggested she thought it ridiculous.

Justin leaned back in the chair, folded his arms, and smiled. The lady had inscribed his name on her blacklist, and he couldn't have been more pleased. "Right down to the last ashtray," he said in answer to the question she put to Carlson. "It's my job to coordinate every thread, shard, and splinter, and I intend to do precisely that."

Her long leg swung carelessly and rhythmically from her knee, and he quickly diverted his gaze. "I certainly hope you have good taste, Colonel."

"No one has ever questioned it," he shot back. "In any case, taste is subjective; there is no universal law as to what is elegant and what isn't."

Carlson cleared his throat—rather loudly, Justin thought, and told himself not to show his hand. "You'll want to look over the floor plans and review Justin's drawings and sketches, Regina—I hope you don't mind if we use first names—and let's meet again next Monday after you've had time to digest all this." He handed her a folder and stood. "Let's go around the corner to Drake's and get something to eat."

Justin observed that she put the sketches in her briefcase with great care so as not to crease them. That earned her high marks, but he'd rather she had given him a reason to distrust her professionalism. Working in a combative relationship with a woman who attracted him and who was smooth, elegant, and, he hoped, competent wasn't something he relished. Not that he'd let his feelings get in the way of his work. The interior of that hotel was his business, and if she didn't like his taste, he couldn't care less.

At lunch, Regina ordered fried catfish, collards, candied sweet potatoes, and corn muffins. "If you eat all that for lunch, what will you eat for dinner?" Justin asked her.

She seemed surprised that he would ask her a personal question. "I could eat this at every meal." Her gaze rested on Carlson. "Are we going to serve soul food at the hotel?"

He shrugged. "I hadn't thought about it."

"In that case, I'd better have a chat with the chef." She stopped eating and rested her fork. "This hotel does not discriminate." Even if she had meant it as a question, it emerged as a statement.

Carlson's eyes darkened to a fern green, and his fingers plowed through his wavy blond hair. "It has never occurred to me. And when you begin hiring staff, remember that we are an equal-opportunity employer."

"We damned sight better be," she said, shocking him with the vehemence of her tone.

As they left the restaurant, Carlson handed her his business card. "Call me if you have any questions." Then he paused as if he had second thoughts. "Actually, you should call Justin, since the two of you will be working together and those are his drawings."

Her demeanor said she didn't like that. Neither did he, but he didn't think it prudent to say so. However, she had no qualms about expressing her views.

"Who am I satisfying here? If you expect me to please you, then it's you I'll call."

Carlson stopped walking and detained her with a finger at her elbow. "Let's get this straight. I'm not going to waste my time refereeing, and I don't intend to deal with plans and sketches that I barely understand. The two of you have to work it out; I'm leaving for Dallas tomorrow. Justin, I'm sure you can walk her through those plans if she needs it."

"In that case, I'll see how much progress I make by Monday." He nearly laughed. Regina Pearson either didn't understand that Carlson didn't like her suggestion, or she understood and was letting him know she'd do it her way. He suspected the latter. Some woman!

Regina did indeed understand. She had also targeted Justin Duval as the enemy, a threat professionally and personally. She didn't relish working with him, but James Carlson didn't give her a choice.

Her longing for her father's affection had once ruled her life, and she had transferred that legacy—a lack of self-worth—to her lovers. But no more! Life was more peaceful without them, and she was putting Justin Duval on the back burners of her mind and keeping him there.

"How'd it go?" Maude asked her as she entered the house.

"All right, but I won't know what I'm dealing with till I study these plans. By the way, you wouldn't know a Colonel Justin Duval, would you?" She said it with an air of disinterest, as if the man and the question were of little import. But Maude made it clear that she wasn't taken in by Regina's casual manner.

"An army colonel? I doubt he's from around here. Never heard of him." She lowered her voice. "Hmm. What's he like, honey?"

Her blood quickened and seemed to flow faster at Maude's suggestive tone, reminding her of the man's rough masculinity and frank sexuality. "He uh . . . I'm not sure I liked him. I have to work with him, because—"

Maude cut her off with what was half a laugh and half a giggle. "No explanation needed. Your high color says it all. Take my advice: if you work with the man, don't sleep with him. When a man is on top, whether you're in the office or in the bed, he's dealing the cards, and you have to play the hand he gives you. Be smart."

She took that like a punch in the belly and stared at her aunt, who sat before a mirror, brushing her long tresses with an almost aggravating patience. "Any more morsels of wisdom?" Regina asked her, not bothering to conceal the sarcasm. She knew she had to get used to having her privacy invaded. It hit her then that, because her father hadn't indoctrinated her with his own culture, she had adopted the habits and customs of the Native Hawaiians. And she'd have to get rid of them.

"No point in getting testy," Maude said. "I already told you, I don't care for pretense and sham. The man threw you for a loop. Just proves you're human. I hope he's not your boss."

She explained the relationship. "James Carlson is my boss," she said of the blond, green-eyed man who owned the hotel, "and I got the impression he thinks Colonel Duval is hot stuff."

Laughter spilled out of Maude as she sprayed lavender oil in her hair. "Maybe he is. I could use some hot stuff myself." When Regina's eyebrows shot up, she jested, "I shocked you, did I? Well, I may be sixty, but I definitely am not dead. By the way, your cousin Harold called, and I'm not ashamed to tell you I encouraged him to take you out Wednesday evening."

"Why Wednesday?"

"Pop has chili con carne and cracklin' bread for supper over here every Wednesday, but he doesn't want to see you and insists he's not giving up his chili."

She wasn't prepared for that. "Oh, yeah? It would serve him right if I met him at the door." That piece of information cut, and deeply, but she'd had forty years' experience with shrugging off the pain of her father's rejection. She hadn't stood up to her father, but . . . "Tell Abner Witherspoon that his granddaughter hopes he enjoys his dinner, because she certainly intends to enjoy hers." Big words, considering the tears that dripped down her insides.

Maude regarded her niece with admiration. The course Regina had set for herself didn't suit a wimp, and nobody could accuse Regina of being that. But she would need more than average stamina and perseverance to mold her relatives into a family that she could love or, indeed, that she would want to love. She angled her head to one side, her signature three-inch earrings grazing her left shoulder.

"That's exactly the way to treat Pop. He'll walk right over you if you plead or beg. Tell you the truth, a little arrogance is good for him because he sure can dish it out."

"If he doesn't want to see me, I don't want to see him," she lied, and prepared to spend Wednesday evening at the Zanzibar with Harold.

* * *

"Come on in, Pop," Maude said, opening the door in answer to his knock. His banging, actually. She'd often wondered why he refused to acknowledge that doorbells had been invented. "One of these times, you're going to bruise your knuckles."

He stood with both feet firmly on the door sill. "You here by yourself?" His voice, deep and strong for his great age, possessed an authority that she had always admired even if she couldn't stand the harsh pronouncements for which he sometimes used it.

"Would I have the nerve to disobey you?" she asked him with tongue in cheek.

"You don't need nerve for that. It's natural for you. Well, now, this place sure smells good. Did you put a little garlic in it?"

"Yes, sir, just like I always do."

He didn't pause until he reached the dining room and took his usual seat at the table. She put the food on the table, joined him, and waited while he said grace.

He savored a spoonful of chili. "If you'd made this for your husbands, you wouldn't have had so many of 'em. A woman ought to cook for her man."

"I cooked, Pop." She didn't want him to get on his favorite topic, which always began with "In my day . . ." "The trouble was, I made lousy choices."

"What about the last one, that fellah with the three last names? From what you said, he didn't sound so bad, except that he was white. Don't they have any black men in Europe?"

She couldn't helping laughing at that. Black men all over Europe getting a taste of heaven. "They've all got white women, Pop. Besides, I married two of our men here. You know that. Lawrence pushed me down the stairs. Julius was a good man, but he soon figured out that I wasn't right for him. It's funny when I think about it. He looked at me one morning with a sad expression on his face and said he was sorry, but he realized he'd married the wrong woman. And he was right. After that, I think I was entitled to cast my glance elsewhere." She served him more chili, sat back, and watched him enjoy it. "Anyhow, Pop, I was in Europe more than thirty-five years, and I took what was available to me."

"Humph. I don't like it. Never did. Why'd you leave this van der Kaa fellow? I got half a dozen letters from him asking how you are and why you don't write. Tired of speaking Dutch all the time is no ground for leaving your husband. That's the reason he said you gave him."

She took a deep breath and shot for the bull's-eye. "You think my leaving Johann is worse than your refusing even to lay your eyes on your own granddaughter? She told me to tell you she hoped you enjoyed your dinner, because she was certainly going to enjoy hers."

"Wh . . . what?" he sputtered. With his head angled slightly and his lips pursed, he nodded. "Sassy, is she?"

That chili con carne must have opened him up, and she intended to take advantage of it. If the way to a man's heart was through his belly, she'd soon verify it. "Smart, too. She's got a five-year contract to manage the Craven Hotel."

"She *what*? What did you say?"

She repeated it. "You'd love her, Pop. You always said you had a bunch of offspring and descendants but you didn't have a family. She took that job because she was lonely for a family, and she's determined to get this bunch together and squeeze some love out of 'em. I tell her she's hoping to get blood out of a bunch of turnips, but she doesn't believe me."

She knew she had his attention when he stopped eating his precious chili con carne and stared at her. But stubborn as he was, he wouldn't readily admit that she had impressed him.

"I hope you made some apple turnovers. The perfect finish for a meal like this one."

He'd think about what she said, because his eyes held a faraway look, a strange kind of sadness. "I'll be right back," she said, leaving him to his demons. She returned quickly, served the turnovers, and then placed a bag beside his plate. "I put some of these in this bag for you, Pop."

At the door later, he said, "She's really going to manage that huge hotel?"

"Yes, sir."

His head moved from side to side. "No telling what I'll hear next."

She kissed him good night and stood on the porch until he was out of sight. He wouldn't admit that she'd touched him. Not yet. But she knew how badly he'd wanted his sons to take over his hotel, to follow in his footsteps. He'd come around. Maybe not soon, but he would.

That night, Harold kept his promised date with Regina. "You need a car in this town," he told her as he drove them to the jazz club. "And for goodness' sake, don't get a Cadillac. So many of our folks driving them that the white people started buying Lincoln Town Cars."

"In that case, I'll buy a Town Car. Oops. Just kidding," she said when he aimed a hard stare at her.

She liked Harold because she felt at ease with him. His unaffected, down-to-earth manner reminded her of Kalani and some of her other Hawaiian friends. "I wish I'd had you for a brother."

"Don't get carried away, cuz. I come with built-in baggage. And siblings can be problems. My sister, Jewel, might as well be a foreigner for all I see of her, and believe me, I don't get any pains about it. If I'm in her company for three minutes, I get a friggin' headache. Here we are."

They sat at a small table near the band, a six-piece combo that featured a saxophone, and she tried to decipher the comments—cracks, actually—that the musicians aimed at Harold, who took it good-naturedly.

"Good evening, Ms. Pearson."

Her head jerked up at the sound of that voice. "Well, hello," she said to Justin Duval, and introduced him to Harold.

"I'd hoped you'd be in the band tonight."

"I might sit in for a couple of pieces if Regina doesn't mind sitting here alone."

"I'm surprised you like jazz, Ms. Pearson."

Before she could answer, Harold sucked in his breath and said, "If she doesn't like it, she'll soon learn to. Where else can you go in this town? Church and the library, and both are closed at night. Say, man, why don't you sit down?"

Her expression must not have been comforting, for Justin hesitated. "May I?"

She let a smile suffice for a yes, and he took a seat on the other side of Harold. She liked that until he turned his chair to face her. Doggoned if she'd let him see her squirm, but his penetrating gaze nearly lifted her out of her seat.

Almost immediately, the band leader went to the microphone. "We're *on* tonight, folks. Harold Pearson is in the house. Give it up for Harold, everybody. Let him know you want to hear a few choruses of ' 'Round Midnight.' "

As the patrons clapped, stomped, and cheered, Harold jumped up on the bandstand, grabbed a sideman's cornet and began playing. She tried to concentrate on her cousin's genius but couldn't shake her awareness of Justin Duval.

As soon as Harold returned to the table, Justin stood and nodded to Harold. "Great job, man." With his gaze on her, he said, "Nice being with you, Ms. Pearson. See you Monday."

"He comes in here a lot lately. What's between you and him?"

"Nothing, Harold. He's the interior designer for the Craven Hotel, and I'm its manager."

Harold's eyebrows shot up. "Well, hell. Congratulations. Abner Witherspoon must be walking on air."

She told him about Abner's attitude toward her. "Humph. That old coot! He'd snub the angel Gabriel if he got a chance. The whole town knows Abner's a hard man."

She didn't want to focus on her grandfather, a man who cared more for chili con carne than for the granddaughter he'd never seen. "I loved your playing. I could listen to you all night."

"Thanks. We can . . . hang out some time." She wondered at his hesitation.

"How's it going, man?" a stranger asked just before they stepped out of the club.

"Cool." Harold didn't glance in the man's direction. Not her idea of brotherhood.

She was getting the feeling that the media had fed her a lot of untruths and half-truths about African Americans. She hated that she had been so gullible in accepting their messages without question.

Harold interrupted her thoughts. "Cephus, my half-brother, wants to meet you. We have the same father."

Forging ties with her relatives wasn't half as difficult as Maude seemed to imagine. "Fantastic. Oh, that's wonderful. When can I meet him?" she asked, rubbing her hands in delight.

"Hold it," he said, easing the car to the curb in front of Maude's red-brick bungalow. "Cephus and I are as different as a flute and a saxophone. Both are wind instruments, but the similarity stops there."

"What's that supposed to mean?"

She knew before he answered that he intended to dampen her enthusiasm. "Cephus is an out-sized ass. Period."

"He can't be that bad," she said when she could stop laughing.

"People who know Cephus don't believe he's for real."

"I don't care. I want to meet him."

"Suit yourself, Cousin. I'll tell him I know a person in this world who wants to be in his company."

"Oh, Harold. How could you?"

"Easily. I like my poison in minuscule amounts, and brother Cephus is six feet six and weighs two hundred and fifty pounds. Next Wednesday?"

She closed the gaping hole that was her mouth. "Uh . . . yes. I hope you'll play more next time."

"Okay. I'll bring my sax."

What's wrong with Cephus?" she asked Maude the next morning.

Maude stood at the stove, frying breakfast sausage. "What's *right* with him? Hmmm. I do love the smell of this sage sausage."

First Harold and then Maude whetted her curiosity about Cephus Pearson. She got Maude's list and put a check mark beside his name.

Monday morning arrived, and Justin made his way to the Craven Hotel for his meeting with James and Regina. In his briefcase were samples of the fabric he'd designed and ordered. Picking his way carefully among the stacks of tile and boxes of fixtures destined for the top ten floors of the Craven, he focused on his mission. He hadn't let James Carlson know how much that job meant to his success as an interior designer and sculptor of fine furniture—hobbies he adopted as he made his way up the ranks from army private to colonel.

He could thank the army for that and much more. Having enlisted at age seventeen, the day after graduating from high school, by the time he was twenty-one he had a bachelor's degree in engineering and a solid grounding in the hobby that would sustain him after he put in his twenty years. He retired three months after his thirty-seventh birthday. After polishing his skills at furniture making and interior design for a year at Parsons School of Design, in New York, he showed James Carlson his work and got the Craven Hotel contract. If he let his mind dwell on how much depended on that job, he'd be a basket case.

The first hurdle awaited him in Carlson's office. Opposition from Regina over the fabrics and carpets he'd designed was a given, but she'd be mad as the devil when she learned that he had already ordered patterns for the lobby and the first through the twentieth floors.

She didn't look at the materials but fixed a steely gaze on him. "Why was I wasting my time poring over your designs this past week if you've already placed your orders? Well, you can just cancel them."

He cautioned himself not to overreach, mentally counted to ten, and then repeated it. With his temper reasonably controlled, he bared his teeth in what he hoped would pass for a smile.

"I didn't think the distinction between your jurisdiction and mine was debatable." He spread the samples on James's desk. "These are for the third through the twentieth floor. I'm planning six themes for this section of the hotel." He ignored her gasp. "Every three floors will have a different theme and color scheme."

She let her eyes express the ferocity of her anger and spoke in a low, carefully controlled voice. "I'm the one responsible for making this a profitable venture, and it's going to make a profit. Do you understand? I am not used to failure."

This was a woman who didn't play feminine games in matters of business, who based her appeal on facts, and she got to him more solidly than if she had attempted to rope him with womanly wiles.

"Are you saying you have more at stake here than I do?" he asked her, injecting as much gentleness into his tone as he could muster. "It's my job to make this an elegant showplace, where people will willingly pay the high prices you're going to demand."

James cleared his throat, seemingly undisturbed by their combat, though he had to see the fury in both of them. "You two settle that . . . uh . . . later. The top ten floors will house club rooms, corporate suites, business facilities, and private conference rooms. For the club rooms and suites, the interiors will have to match the tenant."

James stood, stretched, and let his gaze linger on Regina. "I heard you're from a family of hotel managers. That so?"

Justin watched as she leaned back, crossed her knee, and swung one of her fabulous legs. "So it seems, but you probably know as much about that as I do."

James stuffed some papers into his briefcase and zipped it up. "Interesting. Your name plates will be on your office doors by tomorrow, and you can settle in."

"Which one of them is mine?" Regina asked.

James's green eyes flashed a twinkle. "Doesn't matter. They're identical. Side by side and the view's the same. See you tomorrow."

The door closed, and immediately Justin felt the air crackle with electricity, bouncing between them like lightning streaking through the sky in an electrical storm. They had to work together, and James had just punctuated that fact, though he couldn't imagine how they would manage it. Now that they were alone, she wouldn't look at him, and he couldn't think of a word to say.

After what seemed like forever, Regina's voice sliced through the silence. "This job is terribly important to me. I didn't uproot myself because I needed a job. I had one. A good one. What I needed was a family and people like me. I discovered that my relatives are here, and I got this job and moved to New Bern so I could have what others take for granted: a loving family."

She had knocked the wind out of him, and he seated himself with a lot less grace than he would have wished. He'd been prepared to fight her at every turn and on every issue, but she discarded her armor and let him see her as a human being without defenses. She hadn't done it in order to gain points, either; he knew an act when he saw one, and she wasn't acting.

"Didn't you have any family in Honolulu?"

"My father, but he died a few months back. Even before he passed . . . I mean . . . for as long as I can remember, I have longed . . ."

Suddenly, her eyes widened and her demeanor changed. He knew she'd surprised herself, and she confirmed it when she said, "I don't know what got into me."

He did his best to hide his stunned reaction to that revelation. "Don't apologize. I guess we all have moments when the tongue speaks for the soul rather than the mind." She didn't respond, and he searched for a way of drawing her out, of making her talk. "How is this job connected with your getting a family?"

She threw out her hands in a gesture of resignation. "I've been here over two weeks, and they know I'm here, but they haven't come to me in droves. So much for Southern hospitality. If I'm successful, they're more likely to accept me as one of them."

He had some strong thoughts about that. "You could say that having achieved the rank of colonel by the age of thirty-five was commendable, and at thirty-eight, I'm reasonably successful, but if that cuts any ice with the Duvals and Spriggs of Baton Rouge, Louisiana, nobody told *me*. I loved them most when I was in Australia, which was about as far away from them as I could get."

What kind of person would make such a statement, she wondered, staring at him in awe. "You can't be serious." It was rhetorical, reflexive. She didn't doubt that he meant every word.

His shrug, careless though he obviously intended it, didn't match his grim expression. "Family can be a yoke around your neck, which is why I avoid mine. Look, Regina. We have to work together, so let's agree on a modus operandi. We both need to succeed here. I won't hinder you, and you won't hamper me. Right?"

She uncrossed her legs, braced her hands on the arms of the chair, and stood, her movements drawn out, almost in slow motion. She didn't lack self-assurance, so as she stood before him motionless, he wondered what her problem could be. Protocol, maybe. He didn't know whether Hawaiian men and women shook hands with each other, so he took a couple of steps toward her and extended his hand.

She met him then, holding out her hand, her face breaking into a slow but brilliant smile. "All right. Shake." Their hands locked.

"I guess you'd better let me have my hand," she whispered, evidently refusing to ease the moment by laughing or making a joke. "James could at least have put us at opposite ends of the building." He understood her and wished he didn't.

"How much difference do you think *that* would make? You don't need skates to get from one end of this hall to the other in a minute's time—that is, if you're in a hurry. See you." He grabbed his samples, crammed them into his brief case, and left.

"Now that we've acknowledged it, we can stay the hell out of each other's way," he said to himself on his way out of the building, surprising himself at his own bitterness. Neither she nor anyone else was going to stop him from making that hotel a showplace.

Regina hoped that Justin *would* deliver a splendid, elegant hotel, but a place where people lived—even for a short time—needed a woman's touch. Asking a man to choose furnishings for bedrooms and bathrooms didn't make sense to her. She started down the hall to inspect the offices James had assigned them. *I've got to stop thinking with a Hawaiian mind,* she cautioned herself. *Half of the decorators in this country must be men, and he's not merely decorating; he's designing everything.* The office doors were locked, so she went home to begin work on staffing the hotel.

"If it's equal opportunity hiring," Maude said, "you have to put ads in the *Sun Journal.* I can't imagine many white people read *The Craven Challenger.*"

Regina threw up her hands. "All right. All right. I keep forgetting that over here, people think about race before anything else. It's one piece of my culture that I hope I don't absorb."

"You trying to tell me nobody in Hawaii discriminated against the Native Hawaiians, or you just didn't notice it 'cause you weren't one of 'em?"

"I didn't get my face washed with it at least twice a day."

"No point in getting bent out of shape, honey. It's something you're going to deal with on a daily basis in that job. And the more I think of it, the more certain I am that you may be the best person for it. Our folks gonna expect special treatment, but you'll be fair-minded."

"What folks are you talking about?"

Maude leaned back in the apple green porch rocker. "After a while," she said, "the whole town, starting with the Pearsons and the Witherspoons."

"Well, put the word out. Only those qualified need apply." She meant it, but if she enforced that rule, what would happen to her dream? If only she could affect a relationship with her grandfather. He would know how to handle it.

At work in her room, she began a list of the types of employees she would need, but soon threw up her hands. Six months in which to get all of that in place. She needed a walk along a beach. Any beach. She had always done her best thinking with her toes in the sand of Waikiki Beach.

She went back to the glass-enclosed porch, where Maude sat rocking. "How far am I from the water, Aunt Maude?"

"About ten blocks. Why?"

She supposed her eyes widened and her face lit up. "Is that all? Which way is it?"

"You can't go in the water now. It's too cool."

"I just want to walk along the beach."

Maude stopped rocking. "What beach? Honey, that river's got banks. If you want sand, you got to go all the way to the sound, and it's too rough for that today."

She dropped herself into the apple green swing. "I keep forgetting that you don't have warm weather here the year around."

Maude walked over to the swing, sat down, and took Regina's hand. "You made a huge jump from there to here. I know. It was the same when I left the States and went to Europe. I had to get used to a whole new way of life, and that changed from one country to the next. You moved from one state to another, but you went from one way of life to a very different one. Be patient with yourself."

"I guess I'm trying to do too many things at once. Maybe I'll walk up to Drake's, get some lunch, pick up some newspapers, come back, and write the ad." She thought for a minute. Well, it wouldn't hurt to ask. "Aunt Maude, you don't think my grandfather would let me talk this over with him, do you?"

She shrugged. "Child, only the Lord knows what's in Pop's head. You can ask. He always says 'Nothing beats a trial but a failure.' "

"I'll . . . uh . . . I'll think about it. If he won't talk to me, I'll wish I hadn't bothered." She batted back the moisture that accumulated in her eyes. "You can't know how awful I feel. He's my grandfather, and if this was a normal situation, he'd love me."

"He would. The more I get to know you, the more certain I am that of all Pop's children and grandchildren, you'd be his favorite."

"Don't tell me that, Aunt Maude. I could easily get a false sense of security about all of you. I don't want any superficial relationships; that's all I've had in my whole life—except perhaps for the two years I had my mother, though that's beyond my memory." She looked at her watch. Unlike Honolulu, where you could get a meal from early morning until midnight, restaurants in New Bern served three meals a day during specific hours. She took out her writing pad and made a note in large letters: *The Craven will serve food in one or the other of its restaurants from six in the morning until midnight.*

"I'd better go; Drake's stops serving lunch at two o'clock."

She was about to enter the restaurant, and as she reached for the door, a man pushed it open and held it. "You wouldn't be Regina Pearson, would you?"

She stopped, frozen in her tracks, and stared at the man. A big man who'd wrapped himself in an air of importance. "Yes. I'm Regina Pearson." She waited for him to identify himself, and for a minute she thought he wasn't going to bother.

Seemingly crestfallen, though she couldn't imagine why, he said in a voice that boomed, "I'm Cephus Pearson, assistant to the governor."

Her first thought was of Harold's description of Cephus, but she quickly shoved it to the back of her mind to avoid laughing. "I'm so glad to meet you. When can we get together for a visit?"

He pushed back the left cuff of his white shirt, displaying what was certainly a gold watch. "We don't have time right now, because I'm in an awful hurry. Another day."

It had been her impression that *he* wanted to meet her. "Are you off today? Or don't you work in Raleigh?"

"Well, of course I work in the state capital with the governor, but I'm here on an . . . uh . . . errand for him. I'll be in touch." He dashed across the street and into a place that bore a sign reading, *Mr. John's Hair Creations.* She couldn't be sure, but he hadn't had enough hair to allow anything creative, no matter how imaginative Mr. John was. Seconds later, he emerged with a beautifully coiffed blonde, looked from left to right, and ushered her to a black limousine parked nearby. Regina couldn't read the license plate.

After a so-so lunch, she walked down to the Neuse River, not far from the Craven Hotel. Several old men fished on a pier that jutted way out into the river, and a radio blasted the rusty voice of a gut-bucket blues singer playing a twelve-string guitar.

What kind of blues did her Aunt Maude sing? And why couldn't she sing at the opening of the Craven? She leaned against the mooring post to which boats were tied, and surveyed her surroundings. From the upper floors of the Craven, patrons would be able to see the Outer Banks, which separated the Pimlico Sound from the Atlantic Ocean. She put her brief case on the pier, beside her feet, and began to make notes. Maybe she needed the water for inspiration. She wrote rapidly, unaware of the passing time.

"Tide's coming in, ma'am," one of the men said. "Hadn't you better go? I've known the Neuse to cover these boards."

She thanked him, and as she walked back to the shore with him, an idea formed. "Do you happen to know Abner Witherspoon?"

"Sure do. Who is it in New Bern that don't know old Abner?"

She felt a rush of blood as excitement coursed through her. "Does he ever fish out here?"

"Right often," the man said, "but you got to come out early. Abner fishes starting around six in the summer and seven-thirty or eight along now. But if you want to see him, why don't you just go to his house?"

She felt like kissing the old man. "Thanks, and you have a wonderful day."

She didn't intend to give up on Abner Witherspoon, because she didn't believe a grandfather existed anywhere who wouldn't welcome and embrace a loving granddaughter.

Over on Kalb Drive, Abner sat on his back porch, battling with himself over that same question. Maude piqued his interest about the girl, and what was more, she'd done it with her usual feigned innocence, hoping to inveigle him into breaking down and meeting the girl. Everybody knew how badly he'd wanted one of his sons to take over his hotel. Seventy-two years of Witherspoon labor and sweat—his and that of his father—and yet his children willingly saw him sell it for peanuts in his eighty-fourth year when he could no longer run it.

And now his granddaughter would manage the finest, most modern hotel in the region. Pride suffused him, and he didn't try to stave it off. But he couldn't release his bitterness toward her parents, either. Not the daughter who disobeyed him, or Miles Pearson, who hadn't even let him know when his oldest child, the one who was his very heart, died. He still didn't know what could have taken the life of a healthy twenty-two-year-old woman. The sun hung low in the autumn sky, and he went inside, turned on the light, and opened the Bible to the Seventy-first Psalm. *In thee, O Lord, do I put my trust: Let me never be put to confusion.*

He read until Robert—to his knowledge the only survivor of his three sons, since nobody knew Travis's whereabouts—opened the door and walked in. He didn't lock his house; locks didn't thwart a determined thief.

"How are you, Pop? I hear Louise's daughter is in town, living at Maude's house. Where'd she come from?"

"So *that's* why you're here. Well, you know where she is. Ask her. I don't know a thing about her."

"The way I heard it, she's got some weird ideas about getting the family together. Who's she kidding?"

Abner motioned for Robert to sit down. "Don't knock it. The bunch of you never did act like a family. Maybe it's 'cause you grew up without your mother. You don't even get together for Thanksgiving and Christmas like other families. If she manages to bang it into your heads that people who have the same father and mother usually care about each other, it'll be more than I ever could do. When I had brothers, we were close, and we loved each other. If she brings you into line, she'll do you all a favor."

"But we don't know anything about her, Pop."

He thought for a moment about those words he'd just read. If his own heart wasn't pure . . . "You didn't. Now you do. The next time you come, you bring those young'uns to see me. You hear? And pay your niece a visit if you want to know what she's like."

Robert rubbed the stubble on his chin. "*Me* go see her! I'm told she's been here about three weeks, Pop, but you don't know a thing about her. You seen her?"

"What you signifying? I don't answer to nobody but the Lord."

"I was just wondering, sir. It's definitely not like you to reverse yourself after forty years."

"Humph," Abner snorted. "I don't ask you to walk my walk. When I wanted you to take over the hotel, you had to be a peanut farmer. You take care of your responsibilities, son, and leave mine to me."

"Yes, sir. And I'll try to bring the kids over next weekend." The last thing he was expecting was Robert's kiss on his cheek. Guilt made a man do unusual things. Robert left, and he tuned the television to CNN, but the wretchedness of the world wouldn't engage his thoughts. He kept wondering what and who Regina Pearson looked like, and if people could inherit a liking for a specific kind of work. Imagine! Manager of the Craven Hotel.

Three

Several days after that, Justin knelt on the porch of the condo he'd sublet for eighteen months, comparing the desk he'd just received from Lymann Manufacturers with the model he gave them and sniffing the wood to make certain they had used the odorless wax he specified. He considered it fortunate that the Craven was in a region known for the manufacture of fine furniture, and while his designs were being replicated in the factory, he could check on them. He looked down at the hole in his jeans that exposed his right knee, and laughed. If the men who'd been under his command saw him, they wouldn't believe their eyes. "Old Shitshape," they called him behind his back—an adulteration of the term *shipshape*, which he used frequently—referring to his impeccable carriage and attire and voicing their resentment that he demanded the same of them. He took out his cellular phone and called the foreman at Lymann.

"This desk is perfect. Go ahead with the order. How soon can I see some of the chairs and sofas I ordered for the lobby and cocktail lounge?"

"Two or three days. I'll call you. Glad you like the desk."

He hung up, and immediately, the phone rang. He rushed inside and lifted the receiver. "Duval." It had taken him months to stop answering as Colonel Duval. He held the phone away from his ears. Would it never end?

"Justin, you ought to come back here and help us deal with Oleana. She just had a sold-out concert, and we hear she must've made a few hundred thousand dollars. Does she share any of it with your mama? Not a penny, and after all Simone did for her . . ." On and on it went. He stopped listening, closed his eyes, and tuned out his aunt's voice. His mother did not need the money; she had money of her own. But his aunt Jo used every occasion to foment dissent within the family. He had long been sick of the in-fighting that she caused.

"Is Mama broke?" he asked, knowing that the question would have the same effect on his aunt as torching a stick of dynamite. Without waiting to reflect, she exploded at him with admonishments that he should stop ignoring his family, come back home, and give them moral support. She did the same when he was in the army, and no amount of explanation that he couldn't walk away from his post and move to Baton Rouge ever satisfied her. He covered the earpiece with his hand, waited a reasonable amount of time, and then listened again.

"Well," he heard her say, "are you coming?"

"I'll try to get down there Christmastime . . . if I can. That isn't definite, so don't spread it around. Thanks for calling." He hung up, exhausted from what his aunt's tirade represented to him: the continuous calamities that enveloped the members of his family. His sister, Oleana, knew that their mother was financially independent, but his aunt was as stingy as an empty udder was with milk, and couldn't imagine that anybody wouldn't need money. No matter how you shaped it, he was happiest when he was no place near Baton Rouge.

The autumn chill seeped through him, and he got a few pieces of fatwood, lit a fire in the brick oven he built in the corner of the garden, and dumped a bag of charcoal on it. After a few minutes, he slipped on his government-issue khaki sweater and hunkered before the flames. The scent of roasting pecans soon teased his nostrils, reminding him of nights as a child when the family sat around the fire roasting nuts, potatoes, and slices of pork belly. Restless. Nothing he could put his finger on, just a niggling little ache.

He could go to the Zanzibar, but it was closed on Mondays. He cocked his ears at the sound of a whippoorwill, probably its last call of the season, and laughed at himself. Since moving to New Bern to work on the Craven, he'd done nothing but that. Hadn't made one friend that he could call for dinner, fishing, or a movie. Still mired in his army ways; he'd wanted to stand out, and that meant walking alone. Right then, being alone wasn't pleasant. What the hell!

He bounded into the house and telephoned Regina. He wasn't after a date, only company.

"Witherspoon residence. Maude speaking. How y'all doing this evening?"

Hmmm. A new slant on phone manners. "Good evening, Maude," he said before reminding himself to be informal. "This is Justin Duval. Is Regina there?"

"Uh . . . just a second. She was here a minute ago." Covering her flank in case Regina didn't want to talk, was she? He waited.

"This is Regina. How are you, Justin? I'm surprised to hear from you." He wasn't used to women as candid as she and who didn't mind shooting from the hip.

"I'm as surprised as you are, Regina, if you don't mind my calling you that. I was sitting out there by the fire in my garden, and this sweater just didn't cut it, so I phoned you."

After a brief hesitation, she said, "I gather you don't want to talk about what we're doing at the Craven. What happened?"

"Damned if I know precisely, but I just had a conversation with one of my relatives, and she can provoke all kinds of moods in me."

"Why is that? Doesn't she approve of you?" He imagined that she was sitting down, swinging one of her fabulous legs. Indeed, he was so sure of it that he was tempted to ask her to confirm it.

"As far as I know, most of them do. If they don't, I certainly wouldn't spend any time worrying about it."

"Justin, did you eat yet?"

His lower lip dropped. The woman fired off one bomb after another. Nobody he knew was that forthright. He told the truth. "Not since lunch. Why?"

That laughter again. Bubbly. Tinkling. As if she were ringing a temple bell. "Want us to eat dinner together? We could meet at Drake's."

He leaned against the wall, feeling the need for support. "I . . . I'd love it. How much time do you need?"

"Forty minutes?"

He agreed, hung up, and dropped himself into the nearest chair. She didn't want a personal relationship with him, and she'd taken pains to let him know it. For that matter, he didn't want one with her, but he wouldn't lay money that it would never happen. According to his watch, she'd be there in thirty-eight minutes. He pulled the sweater over his head and headed for the shower.

* * *

Justin was sitting at a table near the back when she walked in, and he stood at once. "Thanks for the company," he said, holding the chair for her. "We have such a peculiar relationship that I didn't dare ask you to have dinner with me."

Nearly speechless with surprise in view of the barely veiled hostility evident at some time during each of their previous meetings, she arched an eyebrow. "I don't bite, Justin, and I've never known anybody who found it necessary to tiptoe around me."

"Come on, now, Regina, you can pitch barbs with the best of them. But since we have to work together, I'd like to ease the tension, if possible. Tell me about yourself."

She scanned the menu and then looked straight at him. "What did you have in mind?"

He didn't bat a single eyelash. "Age, marital status, and whether you plan to move permanently to New Bern." Then, as if deciding to get as much information as possible once she began talking, he added, "for starters."

This man was crafty, and she'd best watch herself. She didn't speak again until after they placed their orders."I'm planning to live on the mainland, and I hope to settle here in New Bern with my family. How old are you, and are you married or single?"

He leaned back in his chair and strummed his long brown fingers on the white linen tablecloth, rhythmically, as if playing a game. "I'm thirty-eight. I've been divorced for five years, and I was separated for three years prior to that. Now you can tell me about you."

"I've had a couple of serious liaisons, no marriages. And I'm forty. So mind how you treat your elder. Among Native Hawaiians, age carries some enormous advantages, so in the future, I'll expect proper deference."

His gaze bore into her. "I've been deferring to you ever since I met you. Imagine what I'd have said to James if he'd ordered me to cancel those fabrics in the tone of voice that you used."

She remembered doing that when she thought he was trying to usurp her authority as hotel manager. She still wasn't sure he wouldn't try it. "If you think I should apologize for that, I do. Hawaiians have a saying: 'If you know a tree has to be removed, don't let it stand another minute.' That and 'Weeds are easiest to pull when they are little.' You'll forgive me if I get these cultures mixed up."

A smile didn't quite make it to his eyes. "Of course, and you won't hold it against me if my association with the Cajun culture causes me to slip up where women's equality is concerned. Huh?"

Her eyes narrowed in a squint. "Are you confirming that the equality of women is a problem with you?"

His fingers resumed their strumming, so slowly that she wouldn't have been surprised if he'd counted to ten. Aloud. "What I'm confirming is the need for both of us to resist doing and saying things that might anger or hurt the other."

She tried not to hear the gentleness that lay beneath his words, but she admitted to herself that she wanted a good relationship with him. "You're right, and I'd rather it were that way. I'm not used to having poor relations with colleagues."

"Neither am I. Friends?"

She held out her hand and hoped she wasn't bartering with the devil. "Say, so do you ever go fishing?" she asked him, formulating a plan to "accidentally" meet her grandfather.

His eyes widened. "Who, me? Next to horseback riding, swimming, surfing, and fishing are what I like best."

"Want to go fishing early one Saturday morning?"

"Well . . . sure. Fishing, eh? Sure. I'd love it."

They ate in companionable silence, and for the first time, she felt completely at ease with him. Not even her growing attraction to him distressed her as it had previously.

When they reached Maude's house, he put the car in park, cut the motor, and turned fully to face her. "I enjoyed the company and the dinner." Then he got out of the car, walked around, and would have opened the door if she hadn't already gotten out. "Why didn't I know you were going to do that? I'll walk you to the door. Thanks for rescuing me," he added with a slight bow. "See you at work tomorrow."

She smiled because she felt good. He would probably never be a close friend, but at least he wasn't an adversary. She corrected that. *Right then*, he wasn't. "I enjoyed it," she told him, and it was true.

With a wink, he walked away, and she went inside, closed the door, and followed the voices till she reached the den.

Regina walked into the house and heard Maude and Harold engaged in a spirited conversation. From what Maude had told her, some kind of calamity always surrounded Harold, so she wondered about his obviously unscheduled visit.

"You gotta come out of those mothballs and get back to work, Maude. What do you do all day? You got your house fixed up. Now what?"

"Say what you want, Harold, I'm not busting my butt trying to please these folks here in New Bern. Half of 'em think automobiles and airplanes have been here since the beginning of time, and maybe even more of them think a woman entertainer doesn't deserve respect. This town is backward. Besides, Pop would keel over."

Harold released a long breath. "If he heard you sing, he sure would, and he'd probably spend the rest of his life berating himself for not supporting you."

"That's water under the bridge." She cut the tip of her cigar and relit it. "I wish I got along with my kinfolk as well as I do with you."

"Honey, don't compare yourself to me. At least you and your folks are on speaking terms. My sister Jewel's got her nose so far up in the air she can't even see where to walk, and you know Cephus is not of this world. I'll be glad to have you as my honorary cuz."

Regina hung her jacket in the hall closet and walked into the cozy room just off the hallway. "Hi, Harold. Hi, Aunt Maude."

"How's the colonel?" they asked in unison.

"We had a nice dinner at Drake's, and he's gone home. That's it, and that's all you can expect." She looked at Harold. "I met Cephus."

"So I heard. I hope he was on his best behavior."

She explained the circumstances of her meeting with Harold's half-brother. "He was on an errand for the governor. Who was that good-looking blonde? About five feet four, slim—"

Harold pulled a large volume of air through his front teeth and interrupted her. "Errand, my foot. I'll bet he went with the governor's wife to the hairdresser. She was born in New Bern and still comes here for most of her services. Cephus might have let you believe he's deputy governor, but he's the gov's friggin' bodyguard, for Pete's sake."

She digested that, wondering at the collection of characters with whom she shared genes, and what she'd stumble onto next.

Why had Harold begun to stare at her as if he hadn't ever seen her? Both he and Maude had hinted that Harold was a misfit, and she hoped he didn't have some kind of psychological dysfunction that was about to get out of hand. However, she needn't have worried.

Harold turned to Maude. "Has she met Juliet?"

Maude closed her eyes, hummed, and puffed on her cigar. "Not as far as I know." She knew it wouldn't be long before Harold or some of the other Pearsons brought up the matter of Juliet, although there was little chance that Regina wouldn't eventually meet her.

"Who's Juliet?"

"One of your Witherspoon cousins," Harold said.

"First I heard of her. What's she like? I mean, how old is she and what does she do?"

"Juliet's kicking forty," Harold said, "and she writes for *The New Bern Chronicle*. She'll be all over you when you start hiring people for the Craven."

"Juliet Smith's not a day over thirty-five. My brother left here in 'seventy-two or 'seventy-three when she was about three, maybe four years old. Her husband's a conductor on Amtrak's Boston-to-Jacksonville, Florida, run," Maude explained to Regina. "So Juliet has plenty of time to write for the *Chronicle* and that magazine she works on, too."

"That gal's such a downer, I suspect Herbert took that job just to get away from her," Harold said.

Maude rubbed out the cigar. "Harold, if there's one thing I know, it's that Herbert Smith is crazy about his Juliet. So you stop that story right there. She's not so bad."

Regina had already decided that Maude was honest to a fault, rarely wasting words, and certainly not on gossip, so she tried to put their disagreement into perspective. Maybe Harold loved to chat about people and tended to be critical, but that wouldn't explain why he'd stared at her as if she were an oddity, or why Maude was at pains to discredit everything Harold said. An uneasy feeling snaked through her.

The feeling persisted after Harold left them. She suspected that she had to face an unpleasantness involving Juliet, and she didn't believe in sweeping problems under the rug. "Solve it," her father had preached, "or accept it as your life and forget about it."

"Aunt Maude, I want to meet Juliet."

Maude turned to face her, the ever-present long, gold earrings bouncing against her shoulders in a seductive dance. "If that's what you want, I'll see to it." She got up, yawning as she stood. "Good night. See you in the morning."

Appalled at the speed with which her aunt terminated the conversation, circumventing any discussion of Juliet, Regina went to her room and checked the list of relatives Maude had made out for her. Juliet Witherspoon Smith's name was the last on the list of twenty-seven.

As if he couldn't wait to get it over with, Justin had suggested they fish the following Saturday morning. The idea of fishing off the Neuse River pier at six o'clock on a Saturday morning in mid-September did not enthrall Justin. The greatest advantage to being out of the army was the opportunity to sleep late at least twice a week, and he had discovered since his retirement that he cherished sleeping until nine on those Saturday and Sunday mornings when he was at home. He also didn't like sitting out of doors in forty-five-degree temperature. But he had promised her the previous week, so he'd do it—this once.

"You sure picked a nice, warm morning," he said, tightening the scarf around his neck as they walked out on the pier. "Do you know how to bait a hook?"

"I was hoping you'd show me."

Don't glare at her, man. Be calm and act as if it were a common thing for a sophisticated woman to invite you to fish with her when she's never had a rod in her hands. He baited her hook with a lure—he didn't touch worms—did the same for himself, and settled down on the pier. Cold soon began to seep through him, and he knew the expedition would be a short one, at least for him.

"You have to concentrate on what you're doing, Regina. Don't you see your little red-and-white bobber bobbing up and down?"

"Humph?"

"Wait a minute. What's bothering you?"

"Who, me?"

"Yes, you. That was probably a fish testing at the lure, and you let him get away."

"I'm sorry, Justin. I thought maybe my grandfather would be fishing out here this morning, and I'm disappointed not to see him."

"Why didn't you call him and ask whether he'd . . . ? Say, what *is* this? Don't you talk with him?"

She shook her head, reeled in the bait, and cast it out again. She didn't fool him. She was upset, and trying not to betray her feelings. He put his rod aside, walked over, hunkered beside her, and asked her grandfather's name. Between sneezes, she told him.

"I don't know him. Look. It's cold out here, and you're getting a cold. Let's go somewhere and get some breakfast. I could drink a gallon of hot coffee."

"I sneeze sometimes when I'm frustrated."

He raised an eyebrow at that. "I know you don't like talking about yourself, but why do you let it bother you if he doesn't want to talk with you?" he asked her after they seated themselves in the White Castle restaurant.

"He's my grandfather, my mother's father. I haven't done anything to deserve this, and I'm not going to hold still for it. He's nursing a forty-one-year grudge against my parents."

What could he say to that? From where he stood, family and yoke were one and the same. Yet, though it made him uncomfortable, he felt for her, and would have given a lot to tell the old man a few things.

"If you know where he lives, go see him. I don't believe he'd slam the door in your face, and I doubt he could resist you; fathers and grandfathers love their daughters and granddaughters, and he's probably not different from others."

He savored the coffee, and from the expression on her face, he must have appeared rhapsodic. "You don't know how I needed this. I hadn't even had water when I picked you up, and I'm a breakfast man."

"Well, you look happy now. I wish I hadn't suggested this, but some men I saw on the pier one day last week told me that Grandfather fished out there mornings around six, so—"

"He may. If I were you, I wouldn't rush it. Wait until you get the hotel operating, or better still, since he used to own one, call him and ask his advice. Do you think he could resist that?"

"I thought of that, but . . . well, I'm sure I'll have problems that he can help me with. He's ninety-one, and change won't be easy for him."

"He's not too old to love his granddaughter."

They finished breakfast, and he drove her back to Maude's house. "Are you planning on finding a place of your own?"

"I want a house, but I intend to wait till I know more about New Bern. I've always lived where I can see the ocean from my windows, so I want to be able to see the sound."

"You could see it from the high floors of the Craven, but not anywhere else in town, I don't think."

"The river, then. Thanks for this morning, and call me when you get into another blue funk."

"Who said I had a . . . ?" He had to laugh at himself. He no longer had to maintain an image as an all-knowing, fearless, and perfectly capable colonel, and he couldn't get used to it. "How about tonight? I feel one of those . . . uh . . . blue things coming on right now."

Her laughter was an aphrodisiac, wrapping around him like warm sunshine. "I'm not going to make you a habit, Justin, so let up on the charm."

He stared at her. "Damned if you don't say whatever comes into your head."

"Don't you believe it. You'd be surprised at what's up here." She pointed to her forehead. "See you Monday." Seconds later, the front door closed.

What a mercurial woman! She could mess up a man's head if he was foolish enough to let her.

The following Monday morning, Regina inspected her new office, furnished with contemporary walnut desk, conference table, chairs with leather cushions, and built-in walnut shelving. A sofa covered in heather blue velvet and two heather blue leather visitor's chairs also rested on the royal Bokara carpet. She walked around, examining the place, getting the feel of it. Looking up, she saw heather blue velvet valances atop the windows. She wouldn't have liked it better if she had decorated it herself. The man had taste, and she hoped that taste extended to the remainder of the hotel. Yes, he knew his business, and before her eyes, all around her, was evidence of his expertise as a furniture designer. She let out a long breath, half in relief and half in trepidation; a man with that much skill had to be cocky and a problem to work with.

The phone rang, and she looked around for it. A mobile phone. What hadn't he thought of? She lifted the receiver. "Regina Pearson speaking."

"Do you like it? Your office, I mean. Mine's just like yours, except that the upholstery's an avocado green and the carpet's brown, same pattern. If you'd rather have this one, I don't mind. Most people either like green or blue. What do you think?"

A frown creased her forehead, and she stared at the receiver. She couldn't believe he wanted her approval of his work. "This is perfect, Justin. I wouldn't give it up no matter what yours looks like. I feel good in here. Very classy. No flies on you, mister. I'd love to see James's office."

"Exactly like ours, except that his upholstery is beige, and his carpet is identical to mine. I'm glad you're pleased."

They hung up, and she began the task of listing her staff needs. Questions about Juliet Smith plagued her, but nevertheless, she managed to work. Maude hadn't mentioned the woman again, and Regina had a hunch that she wouldn't.

At home that evening, she asked Maude, "Did you happen to look up this woman named Juliet?"

"Yeah, I did, but she's in Jacksonville, Florida, and won't be back for some months. Herbert, her husband, works on Amtrak's Silver Meteor Boston-to-Jacksonville run, so down there, she can see him every third day. Don't worry. You'll meet her."

Six weeks later, with her managers in place, Regina sat with her secretary, front-office manager, and bookings clerk, drafting letters to African-American sororities, fraternities, and national professional organizations—social workers, lawyers, physicians, dentists, and others.

"These people aren't going to hold a convention in this town, Regina," Marlene, the bookings clerk, said. "If we ever had a black national convention here, I don't remember it."

"First time for everything, and I don't like negative vibes around me. If you don't have faith in what you're doing, I need somebody else."

"You think white groups will book here if you have all these other people?"

Regina leaned back in her chair and scrutinized her bookings clerk. "Are you suggesting that *you* would rather not be a guest here along with conventions of African Americans, Marlene?"

Marlene reddened and shifted her gaze. "Well, no, but some might."

"Then they can stay at another hotel." She made a mental note to shift Marlene from bookings to responsibility for ordering housekeeping supplies.

The phone lights blinked, and her secretary answered. "Mr. Duval."

"Hello, Justin."

"I'm working on the executive floors. So far, you've given me specifications for three corporate clients. Could you check this one out?"

"I'm in a conference right now. Can you give me half an hour?"

"Well, I'd have to hold my hands for half an hour."

"Hard as you work, you probably need half an hour's respite. Be there in half an hour."

Forty-five minutes later, while she was engrossed in discussions with her staff, the door flung open, and Regina bolted upright, her mouth agape. "What—"

"How long is half an hour in Honolulu? I've been warming my chair for the last forty-five minutes while you sit in here like some kind of imperious magistrate, feeling your oats and wasting my time."

She'd gotten so deeply involved in what she was doing that she hadn't paid attention to the time, and she was sorry, but he wasn't going to berate her in the presence of her staff and do it with impunity. So much for their good working relationship.

She asked the women to excuse her. "We'll get back to this shortly."

"Close the door," she said to Justin when they were alone. She had cut Ken Pahoa out of her life for his arrogance and disrespect, and no other man would ever be able to boast of having put her down and gotten away with it.

He stood in the open doorway, erect, his head slightly tilted and his nostrils flaring. "You don't ever order me to do anything. Do you understand that?"

"And you don't burst into my office and disrespect me, either. If you want to talk, come in and close the door."

He stood there for a long while, his breathing notably harsh, his stance uncompromising, and his anger rising rather than abating. It occurred to her that they might not be able to continue working together. She didn't care; nothing in her contract said she had to deal with a furniture designer. She leaned back in her chair and waited. Standing there, he made an impressive sight, but he would never know it from her.

His voice, cold and impersonal, could have been directed to a company of discredited soldiers. "You've planned your opening activities and mailed invitations to half the country, but unless you cooperate with me, this hotel won't open February the fourteenth. Period. Is that clear? I'll be in my office."

He left and didn't close the door. She hadn't paid attention to the time—a throwback to her other life among people who rarely stressed themselves about time or anything else—and the problem was her fault. However, that didn't mean he should give rein to his temper and act out of turn. If he expected her to genuflect to him, he'd better rethink it. *So what do we do about this?*

She phoned James, explained that the breach was her fault, and asked him to mediate their dispute, so that they could air their grievances and get back to working together.

"All right," James said, "I'll be around there in a minute. You say it's your fault; are you willing for us to meet in Justin's office?"

"Either there or in yours, because you won't convince him to come in here."

"I'll be there in five minutes, and please remember to check your watch, Regina."

Since her door remained ajar, she heard James knock on Justin's office door, waited five minutes, and went to Justin's office.

"I want an understanding," Justin said, "that I don't need Regina's approval for anything."

"You don't," James agreed, "but I've yet to meet a person who's one hundred percent right every time. After these few months, I'm more certain than ever that I hired the right interior furnishings designer and the right manager for the hotel. Regina told me this . . . er, problem was her fault and that she's sorry, so bend a little, Justin. See you next Monday at managers' meeting." He headed for the door, opened it, and turned around. Slowly and deliberately.

"The two of you are going to cross swords until you deal with the real problem. And that has nothing to do with violating each other's jurisdictions."

"Spell it out, man," Justin said in a tone not suited to addressing one's boss.

A grin formed around the corners of James's mouth. "If I thought you meant that, I would. Take care of business, man. You know what I'm saying?" He pulled the door open, walked out, and closed it.

Justin tapped his pen repeatedly on his desk. He could imagine grabbing her shoulders and shaking her. She wasn't only indifferent to wasting other people's time, she was irreverent and high-handed to boot. Gazing at him, she didn't show an ounce of humility.

"Why are you staring at me?"

"I wasn't . . ." She stood there rubbing her arms up and down, not caressing herself, just rubbing. Creating the kind of friction a man liked to build inside a woman. He bounded out of his desk chair, strode to the window, and settled his gaze on the cooling waters of the Neuse River.

"Get off your high horse, Justin. We have to work together," she said, misunderstanding his move. "I'm not one of your troops, and I said I was sorry."

He whirled around. "Woman, would you please . . ." The words hung unuttered in his throat. The sight of her standing there, vulnerable as he'd never known her, seemingly defenseless, uncorked him. She sucked in her breath, her eyes darkened, and her breathing quickened.

"What are you?" he blurted out, partly as a defense mechanism, "somebody who changes faces like a chameleon switching skin?"

She started for the door. "How can you say such an ugly thing? You're not what I thought you were," she said in a voice that wavered—and not with anger. The door closed behind her, and he slumped into the chair. She would never know how close he'd come to . . . He rubbed his hand over his forehead with punishing force. He'd wanted that woman worse than . . . To hell with her. He slammed a compass across the room, went to his drawing board, and got to work.

If she had been within the sphere of his vision then, he would have seen that Regina's strength matched his own, for at that moment, she stood at her desk, grateful that her self-control had not deserted her. She had never thought of what she would do if he ever touched her the way a man touches a woman he wants. She thought of it then; if it ever happened, she would be at war with herself, and she wasn't sure she would win.

The fingernails of her right hand scraped across her chin as they always did when she was perplexed or uncertain. If she worked herself to death doing it, the Craven Hotel was going to be the pride of New Bern, always fully booked and glittering with special events and programs that would make it the most prestigious and renowned establishment in Eastern North Carolina. That meant she had to keep Justin Duval at a distance and out of her hair. With its inherent pitfalls, the job required her full concentration, and she refused to allow passion for a man—any man—to doom her to failure and ruin her chances of having the family she craved.

She punched her intercom and told her secretary that she was ready to resume the meeting, but without Marlene. "I putting Marc Harris in charge of bookings. Ask him to join us."

She phoned Marlene. "Would you be satisfied with responsibility for ordering household supplies?"

"Yes. As long as I have a job, I'm all right."

That done, she set her thoughts to the business of getting corporate clients.

The light blinked on her phone. "Yes, Justin."

"You never did see what I'm proposing for that airline company."

"I'm sorry, I've just called my folks to continue that meeting you . . ." She caught herself. No point in starting trouble.

"This will take five minutes, Regina."

"All right. Meet you on twenty-four."

"Right now?"

"Right now."

She stepped off the elevator; saw the hall carpet on which tiny Raphael angels were replicated in antique gold, brown, and beige; and wondered what he'd think of next. The color scheme continued in the entrance to the suite, which bore a mural of Raphael angels consorting in the heavens. She liked the hand-polished pecan-wood furniture that stood out against the dark-rust upholstery. He had taste, all right, and hadn't overlooked a single essential accoutrement.

"You like it?"

"It's wonderful. Just the thing for an airline company. Are you planning a different theme for every suite?"

"For the most part. But I'll duplicate the designs wherever I can."

She looked at him but only briefly, although long enough to see that he had divested himself of the authoritative personality that made him seem so formidable. He was doing his part to maintain good working relations, and she'd do the same.

"This is first class, Justin. I can't wait till you finish."

"Thanks. I'm glad you're pleased."

She went back to her office, grateful that they had bridged what had seemed an insurmountable chasm. Now if she could get the rest of her life on track that easily.

Four

After venturing to the Neuse River pier on two consecutive Saturday mornings, weathering the cold in attire suited for skiing, without finding her grandfather there, Regina had to accept that he had given up fishing for the winter. She discovered that the library opened late on Wednesday nights, and used it to allow Abner Witherspoon to avoid her company. She hadn't given up on seeing him and demanding that he recognize her, but she was learning the efficacy of patience. Taking her cue from Maude, she didn't mention either her grandfather or Juliet Smith, but bided her time.

She didn't have as long to wait as she'd feared. Opportunity knocked when her personnel manager faced her with the question whether the Craven would be a union shop. She didn't expect that James would have the answer, and if he did, it was her job to solve the problem. When neither the library nor her employee manual yielded the answer, she sat nonplussed in her office until it occurred to her that it was a matter she could legitimately put to her grandfather. She located his telephone number in the telephone book.

"Abner Witherspoon speaking."

At the sound of his voice, her heart seemed to sink into her belly, and for the first time in her life, her tongue seemed tied.

"Who's this?" Though craggy and seemingly worn, the voice still carried a warm resonance and masterful sound. "I said who *is* this?"

"Uh . . . I'm having a problem with union shop. Can you please tell me how to . . . to deal with it?" That didn't sound professional, but she couldn't help it; her emotions had her twisted into a knot.

"Of course I can tell you. Who'm I talking to?"

If he hung up, she didn't know what she'd do. She had to tell him. "I'm Regina Pearson, sir."

"Regi . . ." He sputtered.

She had the presence of mind to plead with him. Quickly. "Please help me, sir. I don't know how to handle this."

She waited for what seemed like hours, though hardly a minute passed. Finally, he said, "You scared to identify yourself?"

She told the truth. "Yes, I was. I was afraid you would hang up."

"I've got manners, young lady, and I demand it of everybody else. What's wrong?"

More comfortable now, she resumed her normal manner of speech."The head of the local said I have to have a union shop, and—"

"You don't have to do no such thing. You put up a proper ballot box and let your employees vote on whether they want a union shop. Have an officer and somebody from both political parties there while you're counting, and abide by the results."

"That's all?"

"It's enough, isn't it? Don't do that till you hire somewhere nigh three-quarters of your people."

"Thank you, sir. I couldn't find anything on that in my manual."

"Course not. Manuals are for the people who write 'em."

"Do you . . . mind if I call you again, Grandfather? If I need you, I mean."

After a deafening silence, he said, "You can suit yourself."

Heartened, though she didn't know whether he meant her to be, she had to stifle a laugh—laughter of pure joy—lest he misunderstand. "Thank you, Grandfather. I'll do that. Good-bye."

"Same here." He hung up.

She'd made a dent, though not a big one. He hadn't said good-bye, nor had he invited her to visit or even to phone him. "Suit yourself," he'd said, but he hadn't slammed the door, so to speak, in her face, and she sensed that he wouldn't.

The phone line blinked, and though she wasn't ready to release those precious minutes, she answered. "Regina Pearson."

"Regina, we're going to have to put a timer on your mind. Didn't you remember that you, James, and I are meeting for lunch right about now? We're down in the lobby."

She wasn't about to confess that in her euphoria about speaking with her grandfather for the first time and finding him at least civil to her, everything else had vacated her mind. "On my way this minute."

"What's the story on the union?" James asked her as they left the restaurant about an hour later.

She repeated the advice her grandfather gave her and added, "It's a great opportunity for us to get some good publicity, what with two leading politicians observing us as we pay homage to democracy. In fact, we could get newspaper coverage and—"

Justin interrupted the thoughts that flew from her in the form of spontaneous words. "Now, that's creative. Got any ideas about what we could do with the space on top of the hotel? We could have a sun deck, but it's so windy."

"Then why not enclose it with some kind of glass?" she said, her voice brimming with excitement.

To her surprise, Justin snapped his fingers in agreement, obviously excited. "That would be the perfect place for the community swimming pool. Free to all patrons. Not every guest will visit the spa in order to swim. Too expensive. What do you say we put a year-round pool and sun deck up there?"

James removed a small notebook from his vest pocket. "I'll speak with the architect tomorrow to see if it's possible." A grin crawled over his face. "Didn't I tell you two that if you got it together, you'd be a perfect team?"

Justin ran his fingers over his hair and regarded her with skepticism. "You talking about her and *me?*"

"You got it, man. Regina, let me know when you schedule the labor vote. I don't care how it comes out, just that we do it right."

"Sure thing," she said, not quite in agreement with him. "But first, I'll give them a talk about our labor policy."

"That's a piece of genius, solving the labor issue with a vote," Justin said as the two of them walked together from the elevator to their offices. "How'd you come up with it? I couldn't imagine how you'd work around it."

She wanted to avoid personal discussions with him, but saw no alternative to telling him the truth. "I was as frustrated as I've ever been, and when I remembered that at least one person's word on that would be gospel, I called my grandfather."

"You *did?*" They reached his door first, but he accompanied her the next few steps to her office. "That's the first time you spoke with him? How'd he react?"

"Well, reluctant, but he's obviously honorable, and I suspect it pleased him that I brought him my problem. It was clear that he knows I'm the Craven's manager, though he didn't say a word about it. We didn't mend any fences, but when I asked if I could call him again, he said, 'Suit yourself,' and I intend to do exactly that."

He rubbed the back of his neck with his left hand. "Well, I'll be damned. You keep at it. He's got to be proud of you. Next time you talk with him, find out what he thinks of using one of the rooms for a small chapel—nondenominational, of course. James thinks it's a great idea, but I think it stinks, and I told him so. I've already discovered that this is a very religious town."

"Why don't you like the idea?"

"Because Catholics want to see a cross and a statue of the Virgin. Protestants like the cross, but most don't want the statue, and what about Jews, Moslems, Hindus, and . . . ? There must be a dozen religious groups in Craven county alone."

Her eyes narrowed to a squint. Why couldn't he see how unreasonable that was? "If people want to have a service, let them bring their own stuff and remove it when they leave."

"James might like that, but I don't. Tom, Dick, and Harry shouldn't be handling religious articles. But who am I to talk? I haven't been inside a church since I got married."

He didn't need to know her history with the church. "Why don't we settle for a meditation room?"

He gazed down at her, his eyes bright with an intensity with which she had no familiarity, not with respect to *any* man. "James may be right. You have a habit of pleasing me without trying." He swung around, strode into his office, and closed the door.

Regina told herself that dwelling on that cryptic comment wasn't in her best interest. She left work early, hoping to prevail upon her Aunt Maude to go with her to look at a house. Maude opened the door before Regina could use her key.

"I thought I'd warn you. Your cousin Odette is here, and she takes some getting used to, so psych yourself up. She never stays long."

Her eyebrows eased up. "Oh? Witherspoon or Pearson?"

"Witherspoon, honey. My late brother Andrew's daughter. Don't worry; she's harmless even if you get the impression she's not."

"What y'all whispering about out here?"

Regina whirled around to see a tall, dark woman who bore a resemblance to her aunt Maude. Her knuckles rested on her hips in a stance that suggested she may be aggravated. Maude ignored the question, walked past her niece to the back porch, and sat down. Odette followed her.

"With your high color, you don't look like no Witherspoon to me," Odette said when Regina joined them. "I heard so much talk about you, managing the Craven and all, that I had to come over here and see you for myself."

Taken about, Regina opted for humor. "I'm glad to meet you, Odette. I hope I pass muster."

Odette leaned back and crossed her ankles. "Muster? Don't be throwing them big words at me. All the college I had was in evening school. What they pay you for running that big hotel?"

True, the people she'd met in New Bern tended to get a lot more personal than the Native Hawaiians, but this cousin bordered on rudeness. She cautioned herself not to react.

"I haven't gotten paid yet." She tried to change the topic. "Thanks for coming by to see me. Aunt Maude listed you as one of the relatives I should look up."

Odette stood, reached for her coat on the rack beside the door, and stared at Regina. "You're not gonna get me to believe Aunt Maude told you to look for me. I haven't seen her but twice in the almost two years she been back here." She scrutinized Regina. "Girl, you definitely don't look like no Witherspoon to me. You too high-yallow, and besides—"

"Odette, for the Lord's sake, do you always have to say whatever pops up in your head?" Maude asked, her impatience seeming to border on anger.

"I ain't lied, and you know it." Odette continued to stare at Regina. "You met your cousin Juliet? No, I guess you haven't. Somebody told me she's down in Florida keeping tabs on Herbert." She buttoned her coat and pulled on her gloves, pressing each finger. "Gimme little something before I go, Cousin."

A frown creased Regina's forehead, and she could feel her eyes narrow into a squint. "Like what?" she asked Odette.

"Like nothing," Maude said. "Odette begs everybody stupid enough to stop and talk with her. Don't give her a thing."

Regina reached in her pocketbook and got a bill. "What's so special about my cousin Juliet?"

Odette snatched the dollar bill, her white teeth glistening in a broad grin. "When you meet her, won't nobody have to tell you. Y'all take care, now."

"Don't pay any attention to Odette," Maude said, and changed the subject. "Harold is after me to do a few gigs with his band. Music won't make you rich in this part of the country, and I'd like to do what I can to help him. He travels in the spring and from Thanksgiving through New Year's, but I get the impression he doesn't take the band on those tours. I don't know. Harold has always been so secretive. Still . . ."

Maude's words triggered an idea. Why hadn't she thought of it before? "Why not? You don't have to revive your career just because you sing with Harold a couple of times a month, and you'd probably enjoy it. Sing something for me."

To her surprise, Maude leaned back in the rocker, closed her eyes, and began to sing "Keeps On Raining" in a voice low and melodious. By the time she finished, Regina was standing and staring at her. She'd heard that voice over the radio in Honolulu and often wondered about the identity of the singer.

"Aunt Maude, Good Lord! You're . . . I recognize that voice. You can't sit around here and not use it. My goodness!" That settled it. Maude Witherspoon would headline her first musical event. In her enthusiasm, she forgot to tell Maude that she'd spoken with her grandfather and neglected to query her as to why first Harold and then Odette wanted to know if she'd met Juliet.

"This house is expensive," Maude said to Regina later that afternoon as they examined a two-story white-brick town house. "Don't you have to give the builder cash for these condos? The monthly maintenance is high, too."

"I can afford it. Papa left me in good shape. He exported pineapples and exotic fruits to Europe, Canada, and mainland United States, and he certainly wasn't a spendthrift. Last August, when I sold his house, it was about the same inside and out as when my mother lived. He didn't place much value on material things."

Maude sat against the railing of the sun deck and crossed her legs. Well-tapered legs must be a Witherspoon trait, Regina thought, remembering that as Odette's best attribute—as far as she could determine.

"If your relatives hear you make a statement like that," Maude said, "before you know it half of 'em will want to move in with you. I love this house. Good neighborhood and close to the water; I'd buy it if I were you."

Regina took a small tablet from her purse and made some notes. "I'm glad you like it, because I've fallen in love with it. It's walking distance from you and Pop and just a few blocks from the Craven. I won't need a car."

Maude tightened her beaver coat—dyed green because she disliked brown—and walked out into the garden area. "Nobody who wants to be independent in this town can make it without a car. Nobody but Pop, that is. You need a car. Odette goes around crying poor mouth, but she still drives a Mercury Sable."

Maude's thoughts lingered on Odette and the problem that had plagued her since she met Regina in the airport: Juliet. But never one to let her tongue do her thinking—as she often phrased it—she kept her mouth shut about it. She also didn't question Regina about her plans for Wednesday nights between the hours of six and eight; Pop could ignore his granddaughter without her help.

That evening, Abner arrived at six o'clock, half an hour early. "I never could figure out what makes this the best chili con carne I ever ate anywhere," Abner said, savoring his favorite dish. "You ought to package it and freeze it. You'd make millions."

She doubted he had ever paid anyone a higher compliment, and told him so. "Well, you can cook," he said. "You always could. I got two letters from Johann last week. Seems like a real nice fellow. Last letter, he hinted about wanting to come visit me. Does he work?"

What was he telling her? "He owns a recording company and a TV station. He's not looking for money, because he's rolling in it."

He helped himself to more chili, rested his left elbow on the table, and pointed his finger at her. "For the life of me, I can't figure out why you left him. You're not telling all. I'm going to write and let him visit me if he wants to. I had two daughters, and neither one of you gave me a decent son-in-law. I want to see what this one's like."

She knew there was no use trying to change his mind, and didn't try. "All right with me, Pop, as long as he knows it's you he's visiting and not me."

She flinched beneath his piercing gaze. "Does he speak English?" She nodded. "Well, I thought you said you left because you got tired of speaking Dutch. Over here, you can speak English."

She wasn't going back to the Netherlands no matter what Pop said or Johann did. If her former husband—present husband, really, since they hadn't divorced—figured he could get her in bed and change her mind, he was right, which was why she planned to stay out of a bed if

Johann was in it. Johann van der Kaa in bed was a sexual tornado. Oh, no!

"Pop, that's a closed chapter."

"Humph. Where's your niece tonight?"

Her niece! Sly as a fox, he was, but he wasn't going to get away with it. "Odette was over here this afternoon, Pop."

He paused in the act of savoring the brown Betty and looked at her. "I am not talking about Odette, miss, and you know it. Mind your manners."

She wasn't ready to yield. "I can't read your mind, Pop. I didn't figure you were asking about Regina. Were you?"

He shook his fork at her. "You're almost two-thirds of a hundred, and you're still as contrary as you were when you were twelve."

She reached over and patted his arm. "I won't be sixty-one till February seventeenth. Two-thirds of a hundred is sixty-seven." She beamed a brilliant smile at him. "You know, Pop, since I was knee-high to nothing, everybody said I was just like you, and I was always so proud of that. But I'm not as stubborn as you are. If you want to ask me about Regina, why don't you?"

He took a bite of the brown Betty and let her wait for his answer while he chewed and swallowed it. "She called me today."

Maude's fork clattered against her plate. "She did? Did you talk with her?"

"She needed some advice, and she had sense enough to know I could help her. She'll do well. She will."

Next, somebody was going to tell her she'd won a million dollars. "What did she want, Pop?"

"Old Strayhorn's trying to force a union shop on her. Nothing wrong with it if that's what the workers want. I told her what was what, and she'll do it, too. That's a big job she's got there."

She didn't miss the pride with which he said it. "I'm glad she called you, Pop. If anybody knows the hotel business, you sure do."

"Well, I better be going. The chili was first-class tonight, and your cracklin' bread tastes just like your mama's used to."

"Really?" She hugged him. "Thanks, Pop. I'll drive you to prayer meeting."

"Naah. The walk's good for me, and it's only a few blocks."

She stood at the door, watching until he was out of sight, as she always did. He was softening toward Regina as she'd known he would, though he wasn't there yet.

She didn't want him to encourage her husband's visit. It had taken her a good long year to get up the courage to leave him and Amsterdam. Wherever she lived in Europe, and no matter how long she stayed there, she remained a stranger. She'd gotten tired of being different, of never knowing whether their friends liked her, admired her for her singing, or were patronizing her with their smiles and backslapping. And she'd gotten sick of parties; whenever she and Johann went to the homes of their friends, the hostess would ask her to sing. Finally fed up, she stopped obliging them. It was a reason why she welcomed Regina so quickly and so wholeheartedly. She'd walked in those shoes, and she knew how they could pinch.

If Johann came to New Bern, she didn't know how she'd resist him. She hadn't made love in the almost two years since she left him, and hadn't had any use for celibacy since she was seventeen and Lawrence Hicks—eventually her first husband—introduced her to orgasms. Maybe if she got a job, Johann would understand her refusal to leave New Bern, and he could see that Pop was old and needed his only daughter. She crossed her fingers and looked toward heaven.

As Maude would eventually learn, Abner was busy mending fences with his granddaughter, though in a very left-handed kind of way. He didn't call her, or say any unnecessary words when she called him. On the other hand, Regina understood that her grandfather needed excuses to bridge the chasm he had dug, and she fed them to him.

Abner didn't mince words. "Why on earth do you need a church in a hotel? If there's anything people in this town—black and white— have too many of, it's churches. Every time some joker goes broke, he gets holy and starts a church. His congregation makes him rich, and the IRS smiles and tells him he doesn't have to pay a cent in taxes."

He certainly doesn't hesitate to speak his mind. "James Carlson, the owner, thought it would be good to have one, but Justin ridiculed the idea," she told her grandfather.

"Humph. Smart man, Justin. Who is he?"

"He's uh, he designed all the furniture and furnishings and did the interior decorating."

"Hmmm," he said after a couple of minutes. "Well, you don't need it. People who get married in a hotel aren't interested in a church anyway; those who are will find a real one."

She asked if he'd come to the opening on February 14. "Nope. I don't go to outings anymore. I need my sleep."

"All right, then. Thanks for helping me, Grandfather. I'll tell James it's not a good idea."

"Humph." She wished she could see him and know how he looked when he said that. "Humph. It's a rotten idea. And I . . . uh . . . You can call me Grandfather if you want, but the rest of 'em call me Pop."

She thanked him. "Maybe you can come to the hotel one morning and look around. Bye, Pop." She terminated the conversation, not wanting to give him a chance to say no to that as well. He was a tough one, but she had reason to hope now that he'd come around.

By mid-January, the Craven was almost ready for guests, and Regina called a press conference as part of a publicity campaign. She dressed smartly that morning in a brick-red designer suit and black accessories. She hated high heels but figured the suit called for them. With her hair in a French knot, and diamond studs in her ears, she grabbed her briefcase, got into her new Buick Century, and headed for the Craven.

Justin had implemented his plan to have three different floor designs for the third through twentieth floors, and it gave the hotel a richness that she hadn't imagined. She invited the media for a guided tour, prefacing her talk with information on the roles of her grandfather and great-grandfather as the only hoteliers in the region catering to African Americans. But when she reached the seventh floor, and the reporters got an understanding of the designer's scheme, their attention shifted to Justin and remained on him. She wouldn't have minded if he had once attempted to bring her into the discussions, but he didn't. He was man of the hour, and he spoke to the reporters—admirers all—with such authority that they seemed to swallow his words as if they were choice morsels of the finest Swiss chocolate.

Regina fumed, hating the smell of newness that reeked from every artifact, and hating Justin. When had New Bern ever had a female manager of a major institution, and a black one at that? By the time they reached the sixteenth floor, she could taste the bitterness in her mouth.

I ought to let Justin host the luncheon. Whirling around, she started for the elevator and stopped dead in her tracks.

"Who . . . ?" Her heart seemed to plummet to the bottom of her belly, and perspiration dampened her palms. "Who *are* you?" She stared at the woman who leaned against the wall as if waiting for the elevator. Horrified, she said, "Oh, my Lord. Don't tell me! You're Juliet Witherspoon Smith."

The woman straightened up and stood head to head with Regina. Her face contorted into a scowl. "And you're Regina Pearson. I heard so much about you that I high-assed it back here from Florida to make sure Cephus wasn't lying. Just stay out of my way." With those words, Juliet stepped into the elevator.

Regina stood there, dumbfounded, as the door closed. She slumped against the wall, and a dozen horrors flitted through her mind, the worst being the near certainty that she had jumped into a tangled nest of individuals bound by genes but apathetic to one another and indifferent to her. Recalling how she burned her bridges when she left Honolulu, cold tremors skittered up and down her arms.

Justin walked with James, the reporters, and cameramen to the dining room, so furious that he could feel his anger slugging his senses. Where the hell was she, and how could she disappear as she had? Didn't she know that the media would berate her or, at best, indulge in unflattering speculation?

"Where do you think she went?" he whispered to James Carlson.

James's shrug further aggravated him. Didn't the man care what happened to his manager? "She's probably somewhere near your office, waiting to annihilate you when you show up," James said, working hard at not erupting in laughter.

Justin stopped walking. "What the hell are you talking about?" He'd donned his army-officer personality with his threatening stance and authoritative voice, but he couldn't care less. He didn't take mocking from any man.

"Cool it, man. You stole her show, and don't think she'll let you do that with impunity. She's not the type."

He stared at his boss. "You're out of your mind. All I did was answer the reporters' questions. I *am* the designer, for heaven's sake."

"This is true, my friend. But it's her hotel, and I'd rather meet a wildcat right now than run into Regina Pearson. A woman scorned is a furious creature."

"Are you saying I scorned her?"

James laid his head to the side as if contemplating the question.

"Maybe not exactly, but who else can she take it out on? Huh? Suppose you'd worked as hard as you did and the press ignored you when I tried to show your work? Justin, that woman is mad enough to chew nails."

However, when they reached the dining room, Regina stood at the door with a smile frozen on her face and greeted each one of her guests with a handshake. He couldn't help being amused at the skill with which she avoided looking at him and her boss and so managed not to shake their hands. After the luncheon, he wanted to congratulate her on the elegant meal but couldn't find her.

"She left for the day, Mr. Duval," Regina's secretary told him when he phoned her from the lobby. "She'll be in Monday."

"She sure knows how to throw a luncheon," James said. "You couldn't beat it for elegance."

"No, you couldn't," Justin agreed. "I wonder where she went."

"Let it lie, man. She's somewhere cooling off, and I suggest you do the same. Then find her and fix it up. You'll both feel better."

He ignored James's remark; his mind dwelt on Regina and whether he might have hurt her either by deed or omission. She could make him mad enough to explode, but he wouldn't hurt her if his life were at stake. He stopped walking. She couldn't mean *that* much to him.

Justin thought Regina was distressed because the news conference hadn't gone as she had wished, but what he didn't know was that she'd gotten a double whammy. She didn't go home but drove straight to her Aunt Maude's house. Maude answered the door.

"Come on in, child. I got a look at Justin Duval this morning at the press conference, and let me tell you he's quintessential male. If I ever saw a stud in my life—"

"Aunt Maude, the man's a recently retired army colonel used to throwing his weight around; what do you expect him to look like?"

"Well, 'scuse me. Who put rocks in *your* bed?"

Regina flopped down into an overstuffed living room chair. "Aunt Maude, I ran into Juliet Smith, and nobody had to tell me who she was or why everybody's been asking if I'd met her. Except for skin color, we look like identical twins. And not just in the face, we're the same height and size and we have the same figure. We could impersonate each other. This doesn't make sense."

"There're a couple of unmistakable, telltale differences, Regina.

Juliet's voice is high-pitched and yours is low and sultry. She also has an unpleasant disposition. But you're right; she's a dead ringer for you."

"I felt like somebody had kicked me in the stomach. And you're right about her nasty disposition. She told me to stay out of her way. I'm beginning to think I shouldn't have left Honolulu." She looked into a mirror and patted her recently permed hair. "I didn't straighten my hair for this. If I'd left it kinky, there'd be less similarity."

"Don't sweat about it, Regina. All you have to do is walk into a room, and nobody who knows Juliet would mistake you for her."

Regina stood to leave. "I thought she was in Florida with her husband."

Maude shrugged, but Regina could see that her aunt feigned the nonchalance. "She was, but maybe she came back for your press conference. She's feature editor for *The New Bern Chronicle,* you know."

Just what she needed: bad press in the only black newspaper in New Bern. "Well, swat my cat," she said under her breath, reverting to an expression she commonly used in Honolulu. "So she can write a negative review, huh?"

"Don't let that bother you. All of our folks who can afford to patronize the Craven also read the *Sun Journal,* and the ones who don't will scrape up their little change and go just because the place is new. Besides, word of mouth beats newspapers for spreading the word."

Still unraveled by her encounter with Juliet, she left Maude's, drove down to the pier, and parked. Water had always soothed her, and she walked along the riverbank hoping to find the peace and calm that the Pacific Ocean always gave her. As she walked, her eyes accustomed themselves to the changing light. Dusk settled around her, and she took comfort in the shadowy eeriness of her surroundings. Comfort in the aloneness in which she so frequently dwelled before coming to New Bern.

"Regina!" She whirled around, hearing her name but seeing no one. It was as if the sound had flown to her on the rising wind.

"Regina!" She heard it again, stopped, and cocked her ears in the direction from which the sound came. "Regina!" It was closer now. She recognized the voice and was torn between waiting and running. She did neither but walked on without her usual gait.

"It's freezing out here," he rasped when he caught up with her, seemingly out of breath. "I've been looking for you, and when I saw your car as it passed my place, I knew you were headed here."

She stopped walking. "Justin, it's best you leave me alone right now. Save whatever you have to say for later. I'm dealing with things that don't involve you, so please. I . . . I need to think."

He hesitated, spread his hands, and appeared helpless, a demeanor that she would have thought foreign to him. "Regina, can't I . . . What can I do to help you? I can't leave you here like this."

Without considering her action, she reached out and rested her hand on his upper arm. "Thanks, but go on back home. You can't help right now."

His hand covered hers. "I . . . Regina, I don't want to leave you like this; your shoulders were hunched over, and you were walking as if you could hardly put one foot before the other."

She patted his arm "Go on. If . . . Call me later on. I'll be fine."

"Well . . . if you insist." She stood there as he walked back toward Craven Street, bent against the cold, his hands stuffed into his pants pockets. Only then did she realize that he'd come out of his house without a topcoat or storm jacket. He hadn't wanted to leave her—that was clear—but she wasn't ready to share with him or anyone else the horrors that had settled in her mind.

Maude, too, fretted about the coming calamity that Regina would have to face. For the remainder of the afternoon, she could think of little else. Around four-thirty, when winter darkness was settling in, she lifted the receiver to answer the phone, only to have her father's words send ripples of apprehension shooting through her like a shower of bullets.

"What did you say, Pop? What're you trying to do to me? He's never written me one word since I left there, and now you're telling me—"

"How could he write you when he didn't know where you were? He writes me 'cause he found my address in papers you left there. And why should he write when you let him know you didn't want him?"

"I never told him any such thing, Pop."

"You left him, didn't you? Actions speak louder than words. Anyhow, he's coming day after tomorrow. I got plenty room here, and I could use a little company."

"Bu . . . but, Pop," she stammered. "You don't understand."

"I understand more'n you think. Besides, he's not your problem.

I'll hire a car and go to the Craven Regional Airport to meet him my-self. I just thought you oughta know." He hung up, and she sat there for the next twenty minutes staring at the phone.

Neither Johann nor Pop nor anybody else was going to deprive her of her hew life and her freedom to do as she pleased. Nobody. She got a beer and one of her choice cigars, put on an old record of herself singing "St. Louis Blues," sat down in her favorite rocker, and rocked herself. She had just about achieved the peace she sought, when Harold called her.

"I hear that was one whale of a reception Regina pulled off today. Cephus said the gov's press secretary wants the capital moved to New Bern so he can hang out in that bar."

She didn't answer him, because she knew he hadn't phoned her to say that, and she wasn't in the mood to be toyed with. Evidently sens-ing that or something similar, he finally came out with it.

"Cephus said Juliet's hot under the collar about Regina. Seems they ran into each other at the press conference. Maybe now Juliet will get her butt off her shoulders. You think it's possible they're twins?"

Maude stopped puffing on her cigar. "Harold, Juliet was born to Heddy Witherspoon right here in Craven Hospital a good eight years after Miles and Louise left New Bern. Regina was born in Honolulu to Louise Witherspoon Pearson."

Harold's whistle burned her ears. "Man, oh, man, somebody's been foolin' around. You just wait till one of 'em starts looking for an-swers. I hope I'm in New York or maybe London when that stuff hits the fan."

"Looks like good old Cephus has been totin' tales. Why's he in touch with Juliet? Are they buddies?"

"No, but they're cut from the same cloth. I'll be by in a couple of days with some music. I have a song you won't be able to resist."

With Johann hard on her heels, she might need Harold. "What's the name of it?"

" 'Monday Morning Blues.' It's for your voice and a tenor sax echo. You'll love it."

"Well, come over tomorrow around two or three."

It didn't much suit her, but the following day, she might have Johann on her hands. If Pop thought her husband would be content to stay with him and not make opportunities for himself with her, Pop was older than she thought. Besides, her memories of what it was like to lie beneath her husband were already doing Johann's work for him.

She expelled a choice expletive as her nipples tightened with thoughts of Johann, and, disgusted, she turned off the music, which was another reminder of her life with him. She laughed aloud; it also reminded her of her marriages to Julius and to Henri, a Frenchman, the most fey of her four husbands or any of her European lovers. It was her music, her singing that brought the men into her life, and sheer willpower and a resolve to be her own woman, her independent self, that had separated her from each of them. Except for Johann, she recalled. She left him because she'd just wanted to be where she could be black and speak her native tongue and not give a damn for what people thought of her or for anybody else's cultural peculiarities. And dammit, she was staying home in New Bern.

If Maude was aiming to anchor herself more solidly in New Bern, Regina was at that moment wondering why she'd ever left Honolulu. She didn't like cold weather, hated not looking out of her window and seeing the Pacific Ocean, and, worst of all, she hadn't found the family that she desperately longed for. Kin she had, but they were merely two bunches of individuals whose affections for each other had all the robustness of watered-down wine. With the wind blistering her face, she trudged back to her car and drove home. A hour later, she sat on the floor before the open fire in her den, savoring the aroma of roasting sweet potatoes, baby zucchinis, and country sausage that she planned for her dinner. She had changed into black cotton-quill pants, a red crewneck sweater with loose side slits, and a pair of black sneakers and would normally have been looking forward to working for a few hours, had not her mind shouted questions she couldn't answer. And with both parents gone, she had no one to ask.

Her body lurched forward at the sound of the chimes from her front door. No one had visited her except Maude, and she couldn't imagine who would come to her house at night without calling first. She went to the door expecting to see Maude or Harold, but her gaze landed on Justin instead.

"Oh! This is certainly a surprise," she said, unable to think of a more intelligent comment.

"Surprised me, too. Are you going to ask me in?"

"Of course." She stood back to let him pass. "I'm in here."

"You're cooking? Sorry. It didn't occur to me that I might interfere with your dinner. I didn't call, because you would have told me not to come, and I wasn't prepared to hear that."

"It's, uh . . . not a problem. 'Scuse me a minute."

She walked down the hall to the kitchen and leaned against the counter. As raw and mixed up as she was, it would have been better for her if he hadn't come. She needed him. Badly. But she hadn't forgiven him for stealing her show, though that now seemed inconsequential and petty in light of her other concerns. She braced both hands on the counter and took long, deep breaths to stave off the tears.

"Regina!" He turned her into his arms, and immediately she knew a peacefulness, an unfamiliar comfort as he held her to him, stroking and soothing her. "You're hurting. I know it. I'm not asking you to tell me what's bothering you, only let me be here with you."

She didn't fight him or herself but settled into his arms, taking what he offered and what she so badly needed: the caring and affection of another human being, a giving that asked nothing of her. With his fingers in her hair, he nestled her head in the curve of his neck, and she felt his lips brush her forehead.

"Regina. Regina. You're beginning to get inside of me."

At that moment, she wanted to be in him forever and to hold him in the heat of her body, but she made herself move away. God forbid she should take him to her bed and make the same error she made first with Helmut and then with Ken—the mistake of believing she wasn't a whole person without a man's affection. That was her father's most telling and most debilitating legacy to her, and it thrilled her to realize that she had divested herself of it. She took Justin's hand and walked back to her den.

"I'm glad you came. At least I know I'm not mad with you." She looked at the food roasting beside the fire, as must have been the way of cooks from time immemorial, and squeezed his hand. "Want to eat supper with me?"

His eyes twinkled with mischief. "That's better than . . . uh . . . Thanks, I'd love it."

If he could be reckless, so could she. "As you *almost* said, it beats nothing."

"Hey. You're calling the shots here. We can change that right now."

She could feel the grin changing the contours of her face. "Sorry.

The scent of this sausage is making my mouth water. Besides, I'm hungry."

He pinched her nose. "I'm hungry, too, but honey, that food can wait."

She closed her left eye in a slow wink. Play with her, would he? "Mind if I take a rain check on that?"

His eyes widened and his lower lip dropped. "Hey, wait a minute. You can't tease about *that.*"

She fixed her gaze on him in pretended arrogance. "Oh. You mean you were serious?"

"You were being fresh with me when you asked for a rain check, but don't think for a second that we aren't going to use it."

She didn't answer, because she made it a point not to lie unnecessarily. "I'd better give you some supper."

His finger trailed down the side of her face. "Right. I hope that sausage tastes as good as it smells, because I need a diversion."

She didn't answer but headed to the kitchen for plates and cutlery. *Diversion?* Food was no substitute for what she wanted. Tonight he was tender and soft, had let her know that he cared for her. He was still her adversary at the Craven Hotel. Maybe James was right: if they solved it in bed, they'd stop fighting at work. Maybe.

Five

The following Monday morning, a gray day late in January, Justin got an inkling of Regina's problem, or at least a part of it. He walked into his office earlier than usual—around a quarter of eight—and ran to lift the receiver before the phone stopped ringing.

"Duval. What may I do for you?" He had hoped to hear Regina's voice, but instead, a high-pitched, tinny sound reached his ears.

"Mr. Duval, I'm Juliet Smith, feature editor of *The New Bern Chronicle*. I want to run a story on you and what you've done with the Craven Hotel. I attended the tour, and I have to say, I was awed. When could I see you?"

He rubbed the back of his neck, contemplating her words. She hadn't said she attended the press conference, but the tour. Interesting. And wouldn't a features editor send a staff reporter?

"Well . . . that's kind of you, ma'am." He waited for her next move and got a surprise, one that he didn't welcome.

"I'd prefer to do the interview in your home. My readers like to know how celebrities live."

Celebrity? First he'd heard of his new status. So she was buttering him up. That always made him wary. "If you don't mind, I'll do the interview here; I don't mix my personal life with my professional activities. Could we say this afternoon at three?" The sooner he finished with that interview, the better.

"If you insist on the office, I'll be there at three. I'm looking forward to this."

He wouldn't lie and say the same. After hanging up, he lifted the receiver to call Regina and reconsidered it. Not a good move before he managed to do any work.

* * *

Promptly at three o'clock, he heard her knock so softly as to be barely audible. "Come in." He stood as the door opened, and nearly lost his balance when Juliet Smith walked in. At first, he thought it might be a joke, but her hands were as dark as her face. He stared and didn't try to cover it up; she was either an aberration or a trick.

She spoke first, smiling as she did so and giving him proof that Regina wasn't having fun at his expense. "I see I've shocked you, Mr. Duval, and something tells me I'd better get used to it. How do you do?" She walked toward him, and the closer she got, the more appalled he became.

He forgot to greet her. "Would you mind explaining this?" He gestured toward a chair, and she seated herself, though without Regina's grace.

"I'd be glad to, if somebody would let me in on it." She leaned back in the chair, and he watched, fascinated, as her gaze grew warmer.

He had never cared for cryptic remarks; when he asked a question he wanted the answer. "How are you related to Regina Pearson?"

"Cousins, or so I'm told. I saw her for the first time when you walked off with her press conference."

She had just simplified his approach to her; he was going to dislike her, and it would be a short interview. "I didn't walk off with it, as you put it; I answered the reporters' questions. What do you want to know?"

After forty minutes, he ended the interview, certain that he had denied her the personal information she tried to dig out of him, and certain that she regarded Regina as an adversary, and that she'd made more than one pass at him.

"If I need anything further, I'll call you."

Any excuse would do, eh? He wasn't having it. "I'm sure you can manage with what you have."

Momentarily, she wilted, but with the jutting of her chin, she let him know she wasn't easily cowed. Her lips flattened. "If I don't have all I need, I'll call you. Thanks for the interview."

He walked with her to the door and was grateful that she left without saying another word. Still, his instincts told him he hadn't seen the last of her. And that was too bad; he didn't remember having such a negative reaction to a woman. How could two people look . . . ? He snapped his fingers. Maybe that explained Regina's despondency. He dialed her number.

"This is Justin. I have to ask you something." He waited for that to sink in, so as to avoid shocking her. "When did you first meet Juliet Smith?"

Her gasp told him he'd touched a nerve. "You know about her? She's my cousin. I came face to face with her the day of my press conference. Scared the bejeebers out of me until I realized who she was. Two of my other cousins had asked me if I'd met her."

So that was it. "I gave her an interview a few minutes ago. Did she stop at your office?"

Her pause was long and her voice cooler. "That's the last thing she'd do."

Sounded like some of his kinfolk. "Are you still hoping to meet all of your relatives and pull them into a family?" If so, she couldn't count on Juliet Smith. He was certain of that.

"I don't intend to give up," she said in a bulldoglike tone of voice. "These people are my blood kin, and they're supposed to be my family. I've seen how wonderful families can be, and I want mine. You ought to have closer ties with yours. The people who matter most in your life are family and close friends. Don't forget that, Justin."

He was going to make her mad, but he believed in telling the truth as he saw it. "You're grabbing straws. It would be a hell of a lot easier to start your own family. Ever think of *that?*"

"Children need a father. Mine was a failure as a parent—I mean, he didn't know the meaning of the word *affection*—though I have to admit he gave me a sense of security." She spoke in low, measured tones, letting him know that she bristled at his words.

Even as he leaned back in his chair and let the warmth of her mellow voice enthrall him, it didn't occur to him to back down. A man stood his ground.

"Most guys want to raise their children as best they can. If you've had evidence to the contrary, do something about your taste in men."

"Hey! Wait a second!" He imagined she was standing then. "You brought this up. I'm not trying to start a family, and my taste in men is not your business."

He didn't know what got into him, but it was as if something was at his back, pushing him to torment her, and he couldn't stop. "Well, if you're not trying, maybe you should be."

"Who asked you to . . . ? Justin Duval, I'm hanging up on the count of four. One . . ."

He interrupted her. "Let the baggage go, Regina. Forget about past relationships and forgive your father for being what he was. You can't open yourself to change, to the good things in your life now, if you don't get rid of all that bottled-up hurt and resentment."

"Anything else?" Her words and voice told him her anger had lost its potency.

"I wish you wouldn't resent what I said. And please don't put my words under a microscope. I may raise hell with you about work sometimes, but I wouldn't harm a hair on your head."

He hadn't planned to say that. "Want to kiss and make up?" he teased in an attempt at levity.

"What I want from you right now is . . . is . . ."

He leaned forward in anticipation. "What? Tell me what."

"Nothing. Every—" She hung up.

Now, where did that leave *him?*

That evening, Maude peeped out of the living room window, half hoping to see her father come up the walk with Johann and half praying it wouldn't happen. So she was partly relieved and partly saddened when Regina's car stopped in front of her house. She'd begun to care for her niece—more, in fact, than for any of her relatives except Pop—and she welcomed the prospect of company.

"How's it going?"

Regina shivered and tugged at her scarf. "Freezing. I hope you built a fire in the fireplace."

"Right, and I'm roasting chestnuts and sweet potatoes. Come on in. You open three weeks from tomorrow; are you nervous?"

"Excited is the word. And when you and Harold agreed to perform the first few weeks, I went from excited to giddy. I put you and Harold in the Starlight Lounge. Justin outdid himself with that room: stars twinkling overhead, moonlight, shadowy coves seating two or four instead of the typical booths, and candlelighted tables for groups of six or more. It's wonderful."

"Sounds great." She hated not to show enthusiasm for what Regina had worked so hard to accomplish, but she couldn't work up an interest.

Regina paused in the act of pulling off her coat. "Is something wrong? You don't seem like yourself."

She walked into the den and sat down. "Johann is here in New Bern, staying with Pop. Pop invited him. Pop picked him up at the airport, and Pop is busy running my life. I don't suppose he remembers why I left here almost forty years ago." She got a cup of tea for Regina and a beer and cigar for herself. "Pop is a busybody."

"What are you telling me? Didn't he ask how you felt about Johann coming here?"

Maude cut the cigar and lit it. "Did *you?* He *told* me. My husband is visiting my father, and the two of them will be as chummy as macaroni is with cheese. When Pop gets ready, he'll bring Johann over here, and he won't ask my permission."

"I take it you don't want to see Johann."

"I didn't say that. But when I get onstage, I do my own singing. You know what I'm saying?"

"I sure do. By the way, Juliet came to the hotel this afternoon to interview Justin, but she didn't stop by my office, which, incidentally, adjoins Justin's office."

"Humph. Doesn't surprise me one bit. Get ready for some of her meanness. She's bound to jostle you. With you here, her Majesty is no longer queen, and she won't take it lightly."

"There's no reason why we shouldn't get along, Aunt Maude. I'd like her for a friend."

Maude sucked air through her front teeth. "Don't be naive. She's been the best-dressed, the one tossing out favors with that job of hers, the one whose picture is in the paper five times a week. With you here—and as manager of the Craven, yet—she gets a backseat, and she knows it. Don't chase her. Let her come to you."

"But we're cousins. It makes no sense to me."

Maude shrugged first her left and then her right shoulder. "Since you won't let me teach you, you can learn the hard way."

"Another thing. I can't figure out how she's such a dead ringer for me."

Maude pushed her glass aside and leaned toward Regina. This was one topic on which there should be no misunderstandings. "When it comes to genes, nobody knows why people look like they do. My mother's hair was as kinky as any pickaninny's who ever lived. And look at mine—almost straight. Some Native American blood back there somewhere. No point in trying to trace genes. 'Scuse me." She went to answer the phone.

"Hello. How y'all going this evening? Maude speaking."

"No, Pop. I want you to please stop interfering with Johann and me. You're driving me crazy."

"You're crazy, all right, and I didn't have a thing to do with it. You marry a lot of riffraff, and finally you get me a fine son-in-law and you walk off and leave him because you're tired of speaking Dutch. Dumbest thing I ever heard. I called to let you know I'll be over Wednesday night for my chili as usual." He said good-bye and hung up.

She related the conversation to Regina. "I wonder if he's bringing Johann with him. I wouldn't put it past him to do that without so much as giving me a hint in advance."

"Why don't you invite Johann to come with him?"

She wondered at times what the Native Hawaiian culture was like. "Child, that's no way to handle men. If I did that, Johann would still be here when Pop got back home. He's not a man you can push around."

"And you think he's coming all the way from Amsterdam to spend two or three weeks with Pop, go back home, and not see you? Get real."

"No, I don't think that, and I'll cross that bridge when I get to it. I want to be left to make my own mistakes. I was always pretty good at it, so I don't need Pop to help me."

Regina drank the rest of her tea and stood to leave. "Why did you agree to do the show at the Craven? I had given up hope."

"Harold got me to thinking about how good it is to hear that applause and people yelling your name. And I figured if Johann came, he'd realize that I had obligations here and couldn't go back to Europe with him."

Regina sat down. "I see. So you still love him."

She rested her left elbow on the end table beside her chair and supported her chin and cheek with her left hand. "Yeah. And Johann knows it. I'll always love him, but I won't let that rule me. I've been away from him for more than eighteen months, and I haven't shed a tear. But that's not because I haven't hurt so badly I wanted to scream and bang my head against the wall. My back's made of steel, child, and no man is going to tell me who I am. Johann knows that, too."

Minutes after Regina left, the phone rang, and following her instincts, she answered in a high, happy voice. "Hello. How y'all doing this evening? Maude speaking." She held her breath and waited.

"Hello, Maude. Why didn't you meet me at the airport?"

Same Johann. Always first things first. "I didn't know when you were arriving, though I can't say I'd have gone if I did know."

He ignored that, and she knew it was deliberate. Johann rarely did anything without first thinking about it. "Your dad's a great guy. I wish I'd had him for a father."

"I give him to you gladly. Then he can butt in your business and not mine."

"Thanks. In this case, his meddling was a good and useful thing. How are you, Kitten? I've missed you."

Kitten! He always called her that when he was loving her. The heat began a slow spiraling to her vagina, and she was back in Amsterdam, wrestling with him in their king-size bed, waiting for the second when he'd shove into her and begin driving her out of her mind. Damn him. He knew how to get to her.

"Cut it out, Johann. I'm not going there."

"Not going where?"

She had used an American slang that he didn't understand. Well, she could say it in plain English. "Johann, I am asexual these days, meaning not into sex, so don't waste your time. You got it?"

His laughter boomed through the wire. "That's the damnedest crap I ever heard. I've got jet lag, Kitten, so I'm going to bed. See you soon."

Long after hearing his beloved voice for the first time in nearly two years, she sat before the fire, gazing into the dying flames. Finally, she got up, ate a few potato chips, and got ready for bed. Supper didn't interest her. *I don't care what he says, what he does, or how he does it; I am not going to live in Europe. I love him, but I can live without him.* She got in bed, turned out the light, and for the first time in her memory, tears soaked her pillow.

"You should have invited Johann to eat some of this chili," Abner said that Wednesday evening. He'd come alone because Johann refused to go with him without an invitation. "You got this good-looking fellow young enough to be your own son, and you got the nerve to leave him over there in Europe with all those women."

She put her fork down and took a few deep breaths. He was about to go off on his tangent, and she didn't want to hear it. "Pop, Johann is fifty. I'm sixty, and I didn't reach puberty till I was thirteen, so he's not young enough to be my son. Now, could we please talk about something else?"

"After I finish. He's a good man, and you're hurting him, girl. He said you love him, but I don't know what passes for love over there. It's not love in my book. Your mother and I didn't spend a single night away from each other from the day we married till the night she passed. If I had to stay overnight in the hotel, she joined me. You're gonna regret this."

"I'm not going to live in Europe, Pop."

"You shoulda thought of that before you married him."

"Are you going to the opening of the Craven?"

"I don't go to public social affairs, and you know it. A gang of people guzzling liquor and bumping into each other. And don't try to get me off the subject of Johann. Go ahead and ignore him. He won't be lonesome; all he has to do is walk into one of those stores on Craven Street or Queen Street, and he can have his pick of women."

"I know Johann is good-looking, but that doesn't cut ice with me. He's not going to stay here, and I'm not going to live there. Period."

"Hump." He served himself another bowl of chili con carne and a slice of cracklin' bread. "Did your niece say they dropped the idea of a church in that hotel?"

"Regina said they settled on a non-sectarian meditation room. It has seating, a five-feet-high pillar, and a light that shines on the pillar."

"Good. She did just what I told her. She's a smart girl."

"You amaze me, Pop. Don't you want to meet her?"

"There you go, minding my business again. You need to be worrying about your husband, not me. You getting better and better at this chili, and if you're smart, you'll get somebody to can it."

"I'd better tell you. I'm singing with Harold Pearson at the Craven opening night. You never heard me sing, Pop. I wish you'd come."

He exhaled the long breath of a tired man. "I'm too old to change, Maude. You go on and help your niece, but I never thought decent women entertained folks. Johann said you're a great singer. He talks about you like you're pure gold." His left hand passed over his cheek, rough with evening stubble. "I can't help feeling for the man. Well, I don't want to be late for prayer meeting." He patted the bag she handed him. "You're a good daughter. Too bad you don't have any sense about men."

February fourteenth arrived at last. At eight o'clock that morning, Regina reclined in the overstuffed chair beside the window in her office, looking out at the cold gray day, satisfied that she had everything in order. Guests occupied three-quarters of the rooms, and corporate clients had leased eight of the ten corporate suites. Further, she had turned away as many ticket seekers for Maude's debut in the Starlight Lounge as she sold. The telephone interrupted her respite.

"Regina Pearson speaking."

"I'm calling to see if you got everything in order and you don't need to ask me about anything."

She nearly dropped the phone. He'd never called her. "Pop. Pop, thank you for calling. This is the best gift I could get. Thank you."

"Humph. You got the guest rooms pretty much full?"

"Yes, sir, I sent out hundreds of letters to clubs and fraternity groups, and I gave two nights free stay to the head of each group if ten or more members registered, just like you said. It worked. Pop, I'm about three-fourths full."

"Good. Good. What about those executive suites or whatever you're calling 'em?"

"Only three of them haven't been leased."

"Good. I 'spect you're plenty tired."

"I am, Pop, but I'm happy. I really am."

"You should be. You worked hard. Too bad you weren't here when I was trying to save the Witherspoon Hotel. When I finally gave it up, I was way too old for that kind of work and worry. You got honest people on the cash registers?"

"With this modern technology, we'll catch the cheats before half a day is gone."

"Nothing's that foolproof, so you watch out. Johann's got breakfast ready, so I'd better go." He hung up.

She stared at the telephone for a good minute after he hung up. *Well, what do you know? He actually called me.* It was only a matter of time. No amount of Maude's and Harold's pessimism would convince her that she wouldn't succeed in her efforts to get the Witherspoons and Pearsons to rally around her as loving families.

Justin stood on the mezzanine, at the top of the broad staircase, looking down at the crowd milling around the lobby. Evening gowns, tuxedos, miniskirts, African caftans and head wraps. Even an occasional pair of jeans adorned a body beneath his gaze. The wealthy and the powerful didn't seem to mind rubbing shoulders with those whose outfits obviously came from Walmart's or Hattie's Used But

Good. Like the parting of the Red Sea, a path opened for the governor and his entourage. The Craven Hotel was a hit, and its manager should be happy.

He took out his cell phone and dialed her cellular number. "Regina Pearson speaking. If you're not at the Craven, you should be on your way."

"Now, if that isn't a slick commercial! Where are you? You ought to be standing here looking at this fantastic crowd."

"I'm in my little apartment. The place is . . . Is it full?"

"You're not scared, are you? Want me to come get you?" He figured that would shake her up if she was nervous.

"Generous as ever, I see. Thanks. I'll be down in a few minutes. Where're you?" He told her. "Wait there."

Minutes later, an arm slinked through his and he spun around. The woman before him bore only modest resemblance to the one who wore business suits, collared shirts, and her hair in a French knot. He could barely take his gaze from the deep décolletage that punctuated the sleeveless red-silk evening gown. Every curve showing. And seeing her in makeup gave him an inkling as to why women wore it. He wanted to run his fingers through the black tresses that brushed her shoulders.

He had to say something without showing his hand. A good, sharp whistle was out of order. "Nothing swells a man's chest like the company of a good-looking sistah."

"No flies on you, brother. Whoever invented tuxedos knew you'd come along."

Whether or not she realized it, she was getting to him in the place where it mattered. And if he said what he felt like saying right then, he'd lose a lot of points with her, so he pressed a finger to her elbow and made himself smile.

"We'd better go down to the auditorium; the governor arrived a few minutes ago, and James is already there. This is your night." He kissed her quickly on the cheek. Let her think what she would. "Come on."

When they entered the auditorium, he saw Juliet Smith watching them, a scowl on her face, as she whispered to a man beside her. Seconds later the man's camera flashed several times. He'd give anything to know whether she was recording news or gossip.

* * *

With the auditorium packed, Regina joined James, the governor, and Justin on the rostrum. She introduced them and suffered through the governor's speech according himself full credit for the building of the hotel. After swallowing that with difficulty, she invited the patrons to enjoy the evening's festivities.

"Harold Pearson and the great Maude Witherspoon will be in the Starlight Lounge at nine and again at eleven," she announced with pride.

To her satisfaction, a roar and thunderous applause followed. "But if you don't have tickets, you'll have to come back Thursday night. They'll be in the Starlight Thursday, Friday, and Saturday for the next six weeks. While I'm up here, I want to thank my grandfather, Abner Witherspoon, for helping me get this hotel running. Many of you will recall that until he retired, Pop owned and managed the Witherspoon Hotel. Thank you, Pop." She waved to the audience. "Have a good time and come back soon."

"You were listening to Regina Pearson, manager of the brand-new Craven Hotel, which opened tonight and put New Bern square in the center of the map. This is Orvell Nichols, Radio Station WNXT 89.3 on your FM dial, New Bern."

Alone in his living room, Abner Witherspoon allowed himself a splash of Courvoisier VSOP cognac, and a single tear rolled down his leathery cheek.

It surprised Regina to see Odette there; after all, tickets to the opening night festivities cost fifty dollars. "I see you got everybody in town here tonight, but don't expect people to run out here every night to see Harold and Aunt Maude. Harold's a disgrace, and Aunt Maude's not far from it. Somebody said she's married to that white man who's staying with Pop. Can you beat that? She never told me a thing about a white husband. When the news gets out, people gonna stay away from her show in droves." She looked toward the sky. "She's my aunt, but I don't approve of her, and especially not with her hanging out with Harold and his jazz crowd. Jazz people wear the right shoe and drugs wear the left one. They're inseparable."

Regina had been raised to tell the truth as she knew it, and that meant speaking her mind. However, in New Bern, she didn't have to demonstrate the self-control that the Native Hawaiians demanded, and she'd discovered that she had a temper.

"Where's your proof, Odette? I never say anything about people that I won't say to their face, and I suggest you adopt that habit and quit backstabbing." She left the woman gaping and headed for the Starlight Lounge. So much for getting that one to join a loving family.

She sat with Justin at a bistro table on the right side of the room immediately facing the stage and waited for the lights to go up and the moment when the patrons would see the effect of Justin's spectacular stage design.

"Who's that blond guy on the end, sitting alone?" Justin asked her.

As her gaze captured the man, Regina saw Juliet walk up to his table and speak to him. She wondered whether her cousin was after news or merely satisfying her curiosity about the man, when it became evident that she had asked if she could join him. The man glanced up and Regina watched, fascinated, while he said a few words and turned his back on the features editor of *The New Bern Chronicle*.

Being in the same room with Juliet Smith, even with the width of that expansive room between them, gave her a sense of unease. She didn't look at her bare arms for fear that she would see goose pimples. By some miracle, she managed not to pound the table in frustration as she looked at the woman and tried to deal with the eeriness of watching herself act like a stranger. Who *was* she and who was Juliet? After forty years, she was questioning her identity.

"Who *is* he?" she heard Justin ask again, his tone more urgent this time.

She shook herself out of her reverie and apologized for her inattentiveness. "He must be Aunt Maude's husband."

Justin's eyebrows shot up. "He *what?* You mean you don't know for sure?"

She explained as well as whispers in a noisy lounge would permit. "I hope Aunt Maude doesn't get a shock when she walks out."

He wrote something on a napkin and gave it to the waiter. "Take that to Ms. Witherspoon, and hurry."

Maude adjusted the straps of her floor-length gold lamé sheath, secured her French knot with the eighteen-karat gold comb that Johann gave her for her fiftieth birthday, clipped the shoulder-length gold bangles to her ears, dabbed Givenchy's Le De perfume behind her ears and in her cleavage, and turned toward the door to meet her audience.

"This is from Mr. Duval," the waiter said when she opened the door and saw him standing there ready to knock.

After thanking him, she unfolded the napkin and read, *Didn't want you to get a surprise, but I suspect the blond man, front row and right, might be your husband. Duval.*

She closed the door, rested her back against it, and took half a dozen deep breaths. She had half expected, half hoped, and half feared that he'd come, but if she'd been thinking straight, she would have bet on it. She glanced toward the floor-length mirror at the old Maude— tall and svelte with everything a woman needed right where it was supposed to be.

"I've still got it."

She read the note again. *The devil.* He could at least have called and told her he was coming, but he hadn't said one word to her since the day he arrived. Some of Pop's advice. She'd bet on that, too.

With the first notes of Harold's alto saxophone wailing the lover's lament "When a Woman Loves a Man," Maude stepped through the curtain to thunderous applause as the audience stood to welcome her. Pop had declined her invitation, but she knew he'd be listening to radio station WNXT-FM's broadcast. Pushing back tears of joy and the excitement of riding the crest once more, she didn't look in Johann's direction but stepped up to the mike. "She'll say he's not much, just another man . . ." she began in the deep, velvet mezzo that made her name a household word throughout Europe. Lord, but it felt good to receive the adoration of her own people!

She waited out the applause, bowed, and nodded her thanks to Justin Duval. For the first four songs, she managed not to look in Johann's direction, but the moment came when Harold stepped up to the microphone beside her and began the first notes of "Mood Indigo." She was singing that song when she looked down at an audience in Rotterdam and saw Johann for the first time. He loved all of her songs, but that was his favorite.

"You ain't been blue," she sang, and of their own accord, her eyes took her to him, and his expression said he'd known they would. Lord, he looked so good. Her heart willed her to smile at him, and she knew he still had her number. Thanks to inbred professionalism, she could give the song all she had, but she could stop telling herself she wasn't going to bed with him; he was in her, and she wasn't a whole woman without him.

She gave the audience three encores, mainly to postpone the moment when she would have to face Johann. Somehow, his libido was always rearing to be recognized whenever he heard her sing, whether at a concert or at home. He said her velvet voice triggered memories of what it was like to be locked inside her.

Regina stepped up on the stage, thanked her, and announced that the band would play three dance numbers before its intermission. *Maude hadn't seen Johann in nearly two years, and she definitely was not going to dance with him in a public place.* Or so she thought. The band whipped into Duke Ellington's "Satin Doll," another of Johann's favorites, and he stepped up on the stage, took her hand, and led her down to the dance floor.

"Hello, Kitten," he said. "You're more beautiful than ever, and you sang my song the way you did the first time I saw you." He began a slow two-step that she knew was an excuse to get both his arms around her.

"Johann, we're in a public place."

"Unfortunately. Since you're playing hard to get, I'm not pulling punches tonight. You'll be lucky if I don't put you on the floor right here in front of everybody."

Giggles didn't become a woman her age, but she got an attack of them and could hardly stop. When she regained her composure, she said, "I'd hate to see the brothers pick the flesh off your bones."

His teeth flashed, though she knew he wasn't amused. "After I get what I need, let them try it." He held her tighter, and she resisted looking around to see how the gossips of New Bern were responding to the stranger's unacceptable behavior with a woman of one of the town's leading families.

His hand stroked her bare back. "Johann, that's a no-no. I'll be the subject of every loose-tongued person in New Bern."

His gaze bore into her. "Walking out on your husband is a no-no, too."

"I . . . uh . . . I'd better go get ready for my next set."

"Right."

To her amazement, he released her at once and walked back toward his table. But as she stepped into her dressing room, his hand clutched the door, and she knew she was about to begin paying the piper. He walked in behind her, slammed the door shut, and bolted it.

If he had said just one word, maybe she would have been able to prepare herself, but all he did was let out a harsh groan, wrap one arm around her shoulders and the other around her buttocks, lift her to fit him, and possess her. Heat, like showers of hot cinders, subdued her. Within seconds, he was rock-hard, and though she didn't want to leave him, nevertheless, she attempted to move away. She was a woman again, hot and eager for anything he offered. Her nipples hardened. Damn them; they were Johann's best allies—always had been, and he knew it. He felt the change in her, removed his hand from her shoulders, and plunged it into the neckline of her dress. Her breath shortened to rapid pants as he made her wait for what he knew she longed for and loved.

"Honey, kiss me. You know what I want."

"What do you want?" He spoke in the low, guttural tone that signified his heightened sexual need. "Tell me, or I won't do it. Tell me, Kitten."

She knew that as angry as he was at her, if she didn't say it, he wouldn't oblige. She also knew that if he got his mouth on her, he'd have a full arousal, but she didn't care. "I want my nipple in your mouth."

His lips, warm and moist, were firm on her. He nipped her with his teeth, the way she liked it, and pulled her into his mouth. In a panic for fulfillment, she pressed her body against him.

"Ten minutes, Ms. Witherspoon," the waiter yelled, and tapped on her door.

Johann stepped away from her. "That's all that saved you, Kitten. In the next second, you would have done anything I asked you to do. Nothing has changed with you and me. Let me know when you're willing to acknowledge that. You're my wife, and I love you. If you think it's business as usual, Kitten, think again.

"You were great out there, and you look as good as you did the first time I saw you. I'm proud of you, but I'm also tired of this foolishness. If I'd known where you went, I'd have been here as soon as you got off the plane. When I finally found Pop's address in your box of fan mail, I was on my way out of my mind." He patted her hips. "Fix your lipstick, babe. I'm going back out there."

She manage to repair her makeup, vocalize a few bars, and drink a cup of coffee. After staring at herself for a few minutes and wondering how she could glow as she did just because she'd been back in Johann's arms, she shook her head in puzzlement and made her way to the stage and the stormy ovation of her audience. If she had to choose between that and Johann, it was no contest, but between Amsterdam and her life in New Bern . . . That wasn't a contest, either. She stepped to the mike, bent her right knee slightly, and let Duke Ellington's "I Got It Bad and That Ain't Good" pour out of her.

She'd had years of singing when she was sick, lonely, tired, even hungry, and triumphing nevertheless. And she did so then, when her heart hurt and the smile on her face felt as if her skin had cracked in a dozen places. But she sang. She smiled and sang. And at the end of the set, when the last words of "Every Day I Have the Blues" left her lips, she gave the audience her best smile, waved, and bowed as they stomped, clapped, and whistled.

Finally, she escaped to her dressing room, but if she expected Johann to continue what he started during the intermission, she couldn't have been more wrong. When she realized that he wouldn't come, the triumph of the moment faded, and a depression, a weight, settled in her chest. She put on her coat, turned out the light, and left the room.

"You outdid Lady Day herself," Harold gushed when he met her leaving her dressing room. "You and I could make a mint in no time, and the band is perfect for your voice and style."

"Thanks. I didn't see any flies on you tonight, either."

"Hey, come on . . . You should be dancing. What's the . . . Oh. Oh. The white guy, huh? I hope you don't mind my saying it, but he's got your number. Is he German?"

She shook her head. "Dutch, and I didn't know he'd be here tonight."

"You gonna tell me who he is, or will I have to believe the gossips?"

"Get it from the gossips, and tomorrow night I'll tell you how far off they are."

"From where I sat on the bandstand, that guy was exercising his rights. He also kissed off your niece Juliet, and let me tell you that did my soul good."

She told him good night and went to face the worst part of entertaining—mingling with the audience. Regina and Justin met her as she entered the Lounge.

"Aunt Maude, you were wonderful. I was spellbound. This is Colonel Justin Duval."

Now, here was a man who could mesmerize a woman just by showing up. "I gathered as much, Colonel Duval. Congratulations on the wonderful job you did with this hotel." She slapped her forehead with the palm of her right hand. "Oh, yes, and thank you for warning me about Johann. If I had been in the middle of a phrase when I saw him, I am sure I would have blown my line."

"Glad I could help. I enjoyed your singing. You have a great voice and stage presence. Would the two of you like to join Regina and me for a nightcap?"

He didn't need to know how dearly she'd paid for that public persona. "I'd love a beer, but I don't even know where Johann went. He left without saying anything."

Justin stuck his right hand in the pocket of his pants and gazed hard at her. "You're telling me that after that performance he put down on the dance floor, he walked off and left you?"

A smile played around her lips as she remembered. "You believe me, that's not all he put down."

"Right," Regina said. "I noticed he disappeared during the intermission. Way to go, Aunt Maude!"

She lowered her lashes and looked at her niece from the corner of her eyes. "Maybe that's the way for you to go, but I need something . . . uh, stronger."

When Justin threw back his head and laughed aloud, she knew he understood her, and imagined what had transpired between her and Johann. "You think you two will work it out?" he asked.

She let the quick movement of her left shoulder express her uncertainty. "He stated his . . . uh, case, and when I get ready, I'll state mine. Meanwhile, I'm not worried, and I'm sure he isn't, either." She looked at Regina. "Y'all got any rules against my cigar?"

Regina turned to Justin. "Would you mind if we went upstairs?" He indicated that he didn't. "I have a little pied-à-terre upstairs, Aunt Maude. We could go up there and order whatever we want."

"Right," Justin said, "and if Johann is waiting outside, he'll get the disappointment he deserves."

Maude placed a hand on Justin's arm. "Don't blame Johann. I'm the culprit. If he has ever wronged me, I don't know it. Left to him, I would never be out of his sight. He thinks he's teaching me a lesson, perhaps, but I learned it months ago. The question is what I'll do about it."

Six

"What do you make of that?" Justin asked Regina after Maude declined his invitation and went home.

As usual, she appeared to deliberate; he was learning that Regina rarely gave him an off-the-cuff response. "I think he's showing Aunt Maude that as much as he loves her, he's not going to crawl. And I suspect that during the intermission, he was also showing her that he meant to get her back and knows how to do it." She sipped the cold Pouilly Fuissé white wine. "I'd bet on it, in fact."

Justin motioned for the bartender and ordered a shot of bourbon and a glass of branch water. "My kind of man. I hope he doesn't think it's going to be a breeze. From where I sit, she's a tough one."

"She is, but she loves him."

He splashed the bourbon against the back of his throat and followed it with a swallow of water. That was not the explanation he would expect from Regina Pearson, a modern woman in command of her life. "Are you saying because she loves him, she'll capitulate, that he's got it made? Is that what you think?"

"I'm saying a man doesn't need much more ammunition than that."

With his fingers spread wide and his palms flat, he tapped the bistro table with rhythmic beats. Nobody had to tell him he was getting close to her personal perspective—conscious or not—on the dance of the sexes, and the one of them that she thought orchestrated it.

"So if you love a man, you don't hold back. Is that what you're telling me?" He watched carefully, knew the second she pulled away from him, and knew he'd hit a nerve.

"We were discussing Aunt Maude and her husband. Remember? This is not about me, and I want you to understand that."

With his fingers still spread, he raised his hands, palms out. "All right. No offense meant. It's late, a quarter to twelve, but how about a little supper? I don't have far to drive, but I need something to soak up this tablespoon of bourbon. Join me?"

Now what? He hadn't wanted to upset her, but her hesitancy suggested precisely that. *I've really done it. She doesn't want to eat with me.* He didn't know whether to apologize or pretend he hadn't made her uncomfortable. He opted for the apology. "I think I overstepped a line. If I did, I hope you will forgive me, but understanding you is so difficult."

"Why would you bother?"

He supposed the frown on his face showed his puzzlement. For a full minute, he struggled with his annoyance but couldn't manage to squelch his temper altogether. "Why? Because around eight o'clock this evening, you walked into that auditorium in the presence of a couple a hundred people with your hand wrapped tightly in mine and your shoulder brushing my shoulder, and because you've encouraged a relationship with me, deliberately or not, and you know it. That and some more reasons I can enumerate if you still haven't figured it out."

"And that's a contract to explore the inside of my arteries?"

He reached in his pocket for his billfold, ready to pay for their drinks and leave the hotel, but an inner voice prompted him to control his irritation and keep his seat.

"If I thought you wanted to make me miserable, I'd probably be getting into my car about now. You resist real intimacy, yet you claim you want that with your relatives. We don't love people with whom we aren't intimate, Regina, because we can't love people we don't know. I suspect this is a legacy of your Hawaiian background." He hesitated, but he'd started, so he might as well tell all of the truth. "And of your father, too. You say he wasn't affectionate, but it's more than that. I'd bet a bundle you never knew anything personal about him. Tell me I'm wrong."

"Could you pick another subject? Otherwise, let's call it a night."

Her lower lip trembled. He didn't want to hurt her, but he'd begun to relate to her at a deeper level.

He leaned toward her and softened his voice. "Did your father ever tell you when, where, and how he met your mother? When he fell in love with her? What she meant to him? Did he?"

Her head moved from side to side, and though she seemed moved to speak, no words came. He thought he saw pain flicker in her eyes, although she didn't give in to it. He motioned for the bartender, put a twenty-dollar bill on the table, and walked around to where she sat.

With his right hand extended to her, he said, "I'll kick myself when we get outside."

She stood, faced him, and stared into his eyes, but she didn't touch his hand. "You don't have to say everything you think, and this isn't the army, where you can say whatever you like to your troops with impunity."

"That shot was below the belt, and you know it."

"Was it? What gives you the right to dig into my life, to open wounds and unearth problems that you can't solve? Why do you think you have to know everything?"

She gave him the uneasy feeling that he'd seriously damaged their relationship. If he'd asked her the size of her bank account or how many lovers she'd had, he'd be guilty of trying to invade her privacy, but he hadn't asked her about herself, only her father.

"I don't think that, and I wasn't asking out of curiosity, but because I have this . . . this need to understand you. But if you can't handle that . . ." He let the thought hang. "Are you going home or staying here tonight?"

"Home, and I can make it there on my own. I drove."

"Then I'll tail you. You don't mind that, do you?"

"Thanks, but that won't be necessary. Good night."

He stood by the table as she walked off, her stride purposeful, but the rhythmic lilt of her normal gait missing.

The most important day in their careers was a professional triumph for them both, but personally, it ended with a resounding thud. From the outset, he'd thought it unwise to become intimately involved with her, but either nature or his testosterone—he didn't know which—relieved him of the decision. He didn't let his libido lead him by the nose, so come Monday morning, he'd be all business.

Regina dragged herself out of the tangled sheets and blankets that might well have been the scene of a wrestling match. Justin's questions about her father rang in her ears as they had all night. Questions that she had never faced, that she had refused to deal with because it meant addressing issues that she knew would pain her. Yet, the day would come when she couldn't avoid it. She had dismissed Justin out of hand because he'd nailed a truth that she was too honest to deny. If she had answered, she would have said no to each of his questions. And she would have to deal with that also, because Justin Duval was more to her than a wind blowing through her life.

As she sat on the side of the bed musing over that, Juliet Smith's face loomed in her mind's eye—an unsolved enigma that she would also have to face. The night before, at the Craven's opening, people stared at her. She had attributed it to their curiosity about the African-American woman who came to town as manager of the city's most illustrious enterprise, its showcase, and to the fact that the smoothest brother in town was holding her hand. Now, she doubted that. The townspeople knew Juliet, who kept herself in the limelight with her columns and with her face on the features page of New Bern's only African-American daily newspaper. Even a child would wonder at their striking resemblance.

Well, she'd had a great opening, and if she stayed on top of her job, the Craven would be the region's showplace. But nothing else in her life was in order. Only two of her dozens of relatives—Odette and Cephus—had attended her opening. Her Aunt Maude and Harold were on the payroll, and she wasn't sure Cephus would have been there if he hadn't been required to accompany the governor. Even so, he didn't say one word to her.

"I can't solve anything sitting here," she said to the air around her, put on a robe and went downstairs to the kitchen. She made a pot of strong coffee, poured a cup for herself and phoned Maude.

"You and Harold made my opening real special. Money won't pay for what you contributed."

Maude's laugh, full and vibrant, sounded as if she were in the next room. "Yes, it will, too. How y'all doing this morning?"

"Not bad. Sorry I didn't get to meet Johann." She wanted to ask if he contacted Maude after she left the hotel, but couldn't make herself do it.

"You will one of these days. That man tunes up his own motor. I can't think of anything he wouldn't do for me—anything honest, that is—except crawl. Johann doesn't even know where his knees are." A laugh burst from her. "I half expected him to be waiting outside, but he made his statement during the intermission, and I guess he left it to me to make the next move."

"Will you?" This male/female, cat/mouse stuff was new to her.

She grew to maturity thinking if you wanted a man, you let him know it.

Maude laughed again, but this time the laughter carried a tremor. "Child, I don't know where my knees are, either. I didn't leave Amsterdam and a fantastic singing career all over Europe in order to drag my tail back there the first time Johann whistled. Uh-uh. Not me."

"I guess not, since you didn't even tell him where you were going. He's a handsome man. Self-possessed, too."

"Yeah. A six-foot-four, blond, green-eyed Adonis. Cool as a weeping willow tree in June, and hot as the red coals in Pop's fireplace. He's some man, and women love him. You seen the morning paper?"

"No. I'm still in my pajamas. What's in it?"

"Your Cousin Juliet, front-page center, with her hand on my husband's shoulder. If that wench knows what's good for her, she'll sniff around some other man."

Regina's lower lip dropped. "Oops! That doesn't sound as if you don't care what Johann does."

"What gave you the idea that I don't care? You bet I do. But that doesn't mean I plan to live in Europe again. I hated the segregation and discrimination here, the lousy schools and secondhand books for black kids, and I left it all, telling myself that when I shook the North Carolina dust off my feet, the place had seen the last of me. But you can't get home out of your blood. You take it with you everywhere you go.

"Oh, the people over there couldn't have been nicer or more welcoming. Half the time, they made me feel like royalty. But not a one of them ever heard of Langston Hughes, Paul Lawrence Dunbar, or Countee Cullen. They don't know a thing about Orval Faubus and George Corlley Wallace, either, or Shirley Chisolm, Barbara Jordan, and Maxine Waters. They don't know and understand my roots, so they don't know how hard it was for me to get to where they found me. They didn't know *home*, so they couldn't know me."

She pondered her aunt's words, trying to see in them an explanation for her own jumbled feelings. "I thought it was just the language you got tired of."

"Uh-uh. The Dutch language was a symbol, and I always knew that. I felt the same way about French when I was married to Henri Duprés and living in Paris, though I felt more at home in Amsterdam."

"Do you think our family will accept me. There're thirty-seven people on this list you gave me, but except for Odette and Cephus—if you can count him—they didn't show up last night."

"You send them invitations?"

"Yes, and tickets to your show."

"I already told you they look down on entertainers. And jazz? They'd put that in the category with prostitution if they could spell the word. They think Harold and I are the dregs of the cup."

"I was really disappointed that Pop didn't come, but at least he called me yesterday morning to see if he could help me with anything."

She imagined that Maude's shock accounted for the silence. "He *what?* Pop called you?"

"Yes. He's been wonderful answering my questions about the hotel and making suggestions."

"And I bet you've found plenty of things to ask him about and problems you couldn't solve. Well, don't worry. He told me he heard the program, from the governor's speech to the last note on Harold's tenor sax."

"Really? What did he say about your singing?"

"Said he'd heard worse, but he also said you put the name Witherspoon back where it belongs." Maude's pauses made her nervous because you could always expect some drama at the end of one.

"Regina, what are you going to do about Juliet? When I picked up the paper from in front of my door this morning, I thought I was looking at you."

"What *can* I do, Aunt Maude? If she was the least civil, maybe I could talk with her."

"What good will that do? Looks come from genes, and they don't talk. You going to work today?"

"I'm off on weekends, but since this is the first one, I'll pop in. If my assistant manager needs to reach me, he knows my cell phone number."

She dressed, donned boots and a shearling coat, and headed for the river. The wind, more fierce that she would have thought, whistled around her, and bits of rubbish twirled at her feet and in her pathway. She hated the cold, but needing the soothing effect of the water, she trudged on to the river. She'd only begun to stroll along the riverbank, her body bent forward to combat the wind, when specks of dampness like bits of ice flew into her face. Unable to look directly into the wind, she stopped, turned around, and for the first time saw real snow. With her arms spread wide, she walked to meet it.

As she fought the elements, Justin filled her thoughts. She had to do something about him. He'd hardly begun work on the hotel's top three floors, which meant he'd have an office next to hers for the better part of another year. And she would have to deal with him both professionally and . . . It wasn't his looks, though Lord knows, with those long, silky lashes over a pair of dark, dreamy eyes, the little patch of gray that gave him the look of a distinguished man, and that scar above his upper lip that made him look so dangerous, she had responded to him in a basic way the minute she saw him. No. It was his unwavering masculine presence.

Fortunately, he didn't know how susceptible she was to him. She quickened her steps as the snow—grainier and thicker than only minutes earlier—stung her face.

The experience of trudging along in snow for the first time caused her to wonder about other ways in which she might be different from her relatives and from other mainlanders. She'd seen the African-American children playing hopscotch and jumping rope along Opal Terrace, an experience of youth that was foreign to her. *I won't accept it. None of this makes me that different from my blood kin.*

For the first time, anger surged within her at her father for not having taught her what it was to be black in America. She knew that forty years earlier, existence with dignity had challenged every African American. Her relatives, the people of New Bern, and the rest of the South fought it; rose above it by their own means; and continued to do so to that day. That alone set them apart from her. She bought a newspaper and tramped on home.

"Hey, Cuz," Harold said when she answered the phone shortly after getting home. "I need to go over the program with you and Maude. Where can we meet this morning?"

She thought for a few seconds. "I guess we'd better go over to Aunt Maude's house." She wouldn't expect her aunt to come to her.

"Works for me. I'll pick you up. How's half an hour?"

"Super."

She phoned Larry, the Craven's assistant manager. "If you don't need me for anything now, I'll be in around three."

"No problems here, Regina."

Harold drove them to Maude's house as if the snow-slicked streets weren't a hazard. "You and my aunt need driving lessons," she told him.

"Nobody on the street but us, so why should I creep along at thirty miles an hour?"

"So I'll be alive when we get to Aunt Maude's place."

A thought occurred to her. As a native and life-long resident, Harold might be just the person to show her the real New Bern.

"My pleasure, Cuz," he said when she asked him. "I know every dive and every place of grace in this man's town. By the way, Cephus said Juliet took a shine to Duval, but from where I sat last night, it won't do her a bit of good."

"I thought she was married."

He skidded around a curve, and she grabbed the dash board for support. "She is. Herbert loves her, and that guy don't take no tea for the fever. He works his butt off and he's a good guy, but I'd hate to be in her shoes if he caught her acting out of turn."

"I'd be surprised if Justin were stupid enough to involve himself with another man's wife. Anyhow, it means nothing to me." She told herself that if Justin wanted Juliet or any other woman, he was welcome to her.

Harold brought the car to a stop in front of Maude's bungalow. "Lying's never a good idea, Cuz, especially when you're talking to me. You and the colonel have the hots for each other, and I'll bet your cousin Juliet knows it." Her gasp didn't faze him. "I tell it like it is, Cuz."

The three of them settled on the structure and timing of the shows, but Maude lacked her usual zest. "I want to do some gut-bucket blues starting next week," she said.

"Better leave that for the last two weeks," Harold said. "The staid characters in this town can't take your 'bottle up and go' blues. This ain't New York."

Maude heaved a long sigh. "If I was in Europe, I could sing anything I wanted to."

"Yeah," Harold said, "but we're in the boondocks. Is Johann coming back tonight?"

"I don't know. He hasn't spoken to me since intermission last night."

"Really?" Regina asked. "Last night, when you were dancing, it seemed he couldn't get enough of you."

Maude's laugh carried a tinge of sadness. "You don't know what that man's going to do until he does it. After you get his confidence, he's open and giving, but till then, he pours your wine from a long-neck bottle. That's what he's doing for me right now. It doesn't bother me, because I can wait him out, and he knows it."

Harold released a sharp whistle. "Y'all must be one helluva pair. Let's go, Cuz," he said to Regina. "I'll drive you to the hotel. Maybe you'd better plan on staying there tonight." He went to the window and pulled back the drapery. "This stuff is getting thick."

Regina ran to get a look. "Just look at that, will you? I never dreamed snow was like this. The flakes are so light, but they can pile up, can't they?"

"This is nothing compared to what it could be. If I were you, I'd go on home. I'm not even sure I want to drive in this mess."

Her mind told her to go to the hotel, and she told Harold as much. "Let me know by five o'clock whether you want to cancel tonight's show, Aunt Maude."

"We'd better get cracking, Cuz. This stuff won't let up anytime soon."

She didn't mind canceling the show, but she'd have to plan some kind of entertainment for her guests. "Put some movies on in the auditorium," Harold said. "Don't you have any video tapes?"

"Great idea. I'll show *Casablanca* and *Bridges of Madison County*."

She thanked Harold, whom she was beginning to regard more as a brother than a cousin. "As of now, the show is canceled. You can have an extra weekend if you want it."

"Works for me. I don't know how Maude will feel about it—she seemed kinda down. I'll call her."

Maude was more than down; being with Johann for twenty minutes the previous night had unsettled her, and she suspected that was his design. But knowing her husband's sexual appetite, she couldn't figure out why he stayed away from her, unless . . . It wouldn't surprise her if he was taking Pop's advice to ignore her. Abner Witherspoon's crash course in how to bring an African-American woman to heel.

She dialed her father's number. "How you doing, Pop? You need anything? If you do, I'll run out and get it for you before the weather gets too bad."

"Weather's already too bad. But don't let it bother you none. My

son-in-law got everything in order. I don't have to worry about a single thing. He's a right fine cook, too, and that's a good thing since your
expertise in the kitchen doesn't go beyond chili con carne, cracklin'
bread, and those apple things. Nobody can beat you cooking that,
though."

"Pop, you'd be surprised at what I can cook. If you were willing to
eat anything over here other than chili con carne, I'd cook it. Well, I
just thought I'd make sure you're all right." She paused in the hope
that he'd ask if she wanted to speak with Johann, but he didn't take
the bait. "You take care."

"I always take care; otherwise, how would I get to be as old as I
am? You take care and cut out your beer and cigars. I asked Johann if
those Dutch women spent their time smoking cigars and drinking
beer, and he said he thought that was what American women did. Is
your niece over there?"

"Regina was here, but she went to the hotel, and I haven't seen
Odette today." Her niece. Who was he trying to fool?

"You're too smart for your own good."

"You got no business meddling in my affairs with my husband,"
she said aloud after hanging up. "If you brought him here to torture
me, you're doing a great job of it."

She paced from one end of the hall to the other. She was not going
back to Europe with Johann, not even if he stripped and did the wind
at the intersection of Packard and Crane Streets. The thought cheered
her, but not enough to temper her annoyance with her father.

Pop knew he'd gotten the better of Maude, and the thought ele-
vated his spirits. "She's too clever for her own good," he told Johann.
"She called here hoping I'd ask her if she wanted to speak with you, or
that I'd tell her you wanted to talk with her." He leaned back in the
overstuffed rocker, gazing in the fire and enjoying the scent of roasting
nuts. "Maude is talented at getting what she wants, but by golly, I am,
too."

"She's talented, all right," Johann said, "and as contrary as those
tides coming in from the North Sea. I never know what to expect."

Abner stirred the coals and replaced the poker. "Just like her mother.
Never a dull moment with her in the forty-two years of our marriage.
Good years" He rocked slowly as if the passing of time was of no
moment.

"Maude's a good woman. You oughta taste that chili she makes. If it was human it would walk. I keep telling her that if she found someone to can it, she'd be rich in six months."

Johann leaned forward. Alert. Expectant. "You think it's that good?"

"I know it is."

"Hmmm. I'd like to taste it."

Abner rocked and hummed. He'd just found a way to get them together. If he had known Johann had the perseverance to stay away from his wife voluntarily when he was itching to be with her, he might not have suggested that he hold out until Maude made the first move. Johann had an iron will, and if Maude didn't watch him, she'd be like a crustacean trying to get out of a fisherman's net. He closed his eyes and let the scent of roasting pecans tantalize his olfactory senses. Let Maude and Johann get into the canning business, and Amsterdam wouldn't see either of them again except for visits. He hummed and rocked. Life was good.

She wasn't home or at the hotel, so where was she? Sensations like crawling ants shot through his nerves. Could she have driven in that snow when she'd probably never *seen* fresh snow until that morning? He paced around his den, punishing his left palm with his right fist, berating himself for having upset her the night before. Relief sliced through him when the phone rang, and he dashed to answered it.

"Duval."

"This is your aunt Jo." He had a twinge of disappointment when he heard her voice. "I hear it's snowing up there. Why don't you move back home. It's seventy degrees down here."

"What's happening, Aunt Jo?" He knew she hadn't called to discuss the weather, and braced himself for a harangue against her latest target.

"Well, your mama gave me a few pennies from your daddy's January royalty checks, and I sure do thank her." He waited, because she didn't call to tell him that, either.

"Oh, yes. And Lee Ann's gone and done it. Run off with Rose Marie Jordan's husband."

Now she was getting to her reason for calling. The woman was addicted to carrying tales. "Is that gossip or a fact?"

"Well, they're both gone, and nobody knows where."

He hated gossip and especially when it was unfounded. Peck

Jordan wouldn't look twice at his cousin Lee Ann; his taste didn't run to dark-skinned women. "I don't want to upset you, Aunt Jo, but Lee Ann is forty-five years old, and if she finally found a man to take her to bed, for heaven's sake don't begrudge her a little pleasure." He ignored her sputters. "And maybe Peck discovered you can't judge what's inside by the color of a woman's skin."

"Shame on you, Justin Duval," she shrieked. "I don't want my daughter consorting with married men."

He enjoyed needling the aunt who complained about everybody and everything. With the most somber of voices, he said, "I'd think you'd be more worried about the possibility of her dying a virgin. I doubt she's with Peck, but let's hope she's with a man." He didn't bother to say Lee Ann was probably hiding from her overbearing, autocratic mother. "How's everybody else?"

"Fine, I guess. You ought to come back home. Your mama needs you."

"I was there six weeks ago."

Her sigh was that of one greatly wearied, but he wasn't impressed. "That's true. My mind plays tricks with me sometimes. Your uncle Heston sends love."

He hung up thinking that if it weren't for his family, from whom he had joined the army to escape, he wouldn't be independent at the age of thirty-nine. For that, he ought to thank them. Regina tried to impress upon him the importance of embracing his family, foibles and all, claiming that she would give anything to be pestered by people who loved her. The problem was his inability to tolerate their gossiping and petty bickering. How his mother, the most private person he knew, stood it continually amazed him. He phoned Regina at the hotel again.

"Regina Pearson."

"This is Justin. Thank God, you're there. I tried to reach you earlier, but you must have been between home and the hotel. I was worried that you might have driven your car; driving in this weather is difficult enough for those of us who are used to it."

"I was at Aunt Maude's house. Thanks for thinking of my well-being."

"You mean that?"

Her voice carried a mild rebuke. "Of course I mean it. Harold dropped me at the hotel, so I guess I'm here until the weather lets me leave."

He gave her his cellular phone number. "If you want to leave there,

no matter what the weather is like, call me. I'll see that you get home."
And he would. He could get a four-wheel-drive Jeep from the post
anytime he asked. He took a T-bone steak out of his freezer, put it in
the microwave oven to defrost, and looked forward to one of his favorite meals. If anybody had told him that knowing she wasn't angry
with him could give him such a feeling of relief, he'd have told them to
go dunk their heads in a tub of water. He even felt charitable toward
his Aunt Jo and the cast of characters who made up his family.

With the weekend off, thanks to the heavy snowfall, Maude worked
on her interpretation of the song Harold wrote for her. She loved it but
couldn't rid herself of the feeling that she was singing her own life's
song. She'd walked away from three husbands and never considered
looking back, but Johann was not easily dismissed. She'd loved all of
her husbands and her other men, too, at least at first, but once she con-
signed them to her past, they ceased to exist. She couldn't wrap
Johann in a neat package and store him in a corner of her mind that refused admittance to her memory, but damned if she would dance to
his tune. If he came to New Bern to get her, his behavior didn't show it.

By Wednesday, she felt she was ready to debut the song the coming
Friday night, but Harold wanted to change the chorus, so she put the
music aside. She prepared the chili con carne and, after equivocating
for an hour, settled on apple cake for desert. She'd fallen in love with it
while singing in Budapest, and had cajoled a chef into giving her the
recipe. She hadn't made it for Pop, but didn't doubt that he'd love it, a
layer of cake sliced, filled with cooked, spicy apples, and topped with
whipped cream.

"I must be losing my mind," she said to herself when she recalled
that her apple cake was Johann's favorite desert. She set the table and
puttered around the house while she waited for Pop. Promptly at six-
thirty, the doorbell rang. She opened the door and gasped. Johann
loomed behind her father, a ghostly shadow.

"Why didn't I know you'd surprise me?" she said, looking at Pop,
though she didn't doubt Johann knew her words were meant for him.
"Come on in. How y'all doing this evening?"

"Did you make the chili?" Pop asked, heading straight for the dining room.

"I've heard about this chili, and I hope you made enough, because
I didn't eat much lunch." Johann stopped right in front of her, half a

breath away, blocking her movements. "You're as beautiful as ever, Kitten, and just as much hellion."

She tried backing up but found herself in a worse position, with her back against the wall. "What have I done to make you say I'm a hellion?"

He winked in that way he had that suggested things she wouldn't have let cross her mind in her mother's presence. That wink always shifted her cerebral center from her brain to her feminine tunnel.

"You want me to think it's business as usual, that my being here doesn't bother you?"

She gazed up at him, using a few antics of her own that guaranteed he'd sweat right along with her. "You think it bothers me? You couldn't have forgotten that much about me in such a short time. Man, I'm my own woman; you know that."

"With Pop sitting ten feet from here, you don't want a demonstration of what I remember. Now, do you?" He pointed to the dining room. "He's what's saving you."

She folded her arms beneath her bosom and raised an eyebrow. "That busybody in there? It would teach him not to meddle in my life. Don't think he'll let you stand here indefinitely. When Pop smells chili, he wants to eat."

"You two set your clocks later. I'm ready to eat," Abner called to them.

She couldn't help laughing. "Told you so. Go talk to Pop while I put the chili on the table." She laid another place setting, swearing under her breath as she did so. Pop could at least have warned her. She would have put on her burnt-orange velvet caftan, and she definitely wouldn't have made that apple cake. When she sat down, Pop clasped her right hand and Johann's left one and offered a grace that, to her mind, was more like an evangelist's prayer.

"Lord, you do what you're supposed to do here," he finished. From beneath her lashes, she observed Johann's satisfied look and didn't doubt his pleasure at the course the evening had taken so far.

Pop didn't taste the chili until Johann sampled it. "What did I tell you?"

"You're right, and how!" Johann said, smacking his lips. "I'd stay in New Bern just to eat this." When her fork clattered on her plate, Johann let her have his special wink. "Just checking the atmosphere, Kitten. You ought to can this stuff and sell it."

She hoped her pleasure at his comment didn't show, but it was strong praise coming from Johann, who would dine like a gourmet at every meal if he could find the food. "Pop's always saying that."

"If you want to do it, let me know. We'd make a bundle on this in no time. You could even get somebody to write a tune and sing your own commercial." The casual, breezy way in which he said it didn't fool her; Johann didn't joke about business. "How about it, Kitten?"

"You're moving too fast." She looked at her father, whose face bore the peaceful, saintly expression seen on the religious icons of Russia and Eastern Europe. "You primed him for this, Pop."

Abner helped himself to another bowl of chili con carne. "I told him it was good and brought him along so he could judge for himself. He's a man of the world, so he ought to know when something tastes good and when it don't."

"How many different ways can you make this, Kitten?"

Until he got to New Bern, he had only called her Kitten when he was making love to her. Now, it fell out of his mouth with every sentence—like she wasn't supposed to know he intended to keep her mind on what he did to her in bed.

"I've got four standards, but Pop likes it best this way, with garlic."

"Good with cheddar cheese, too."

Looking at him, she wondered if her father had always been so sly in getting what he wanted. She cleared the table and brought the apple cake, thankful for her blackness that hid the rush of blood to her face.

Johann's face bloomed with his pleasure. "Are you sure you didn't tell her you were bringing me, Pop?"

"I didn't tell her a thing. If I had, I'd have missed my chili. You ought to know how wayward she is."

Johann's expression blessed her with his message of things to come. "Then you figured it was time I showed up."

"You can make this for me again," Pop said after his second helping. "Well, I'd better be getting on to prayer meeting. Don't want to be late. It was first-class tonight, Maude."

Her heart started a slow tumble toward the pit of her belly. Now what? Johann didn't look her way, and Pop started for the door as if everything were as usual and he weren't busy mucking up her life.

"I'll drive you," she said hurriedly.

"No, I'll drive him. I rented that Cadillac just so Pop can go in style wherever he likes."

She breathed, and her heartbeat returned to normal. But it worried her that Johann would lose such an opportunity. It wasn't like him.

She walked with them to her front door, where Abner announced, "Deacon Russell always brings me home, since he lives next door to me."

"I'll be back here in twenty minutes," Johann told her in a voice that said no nonsense.

"Not tonight," she said, and leaned against the doorjamb to steady herself.

The old Johann returned then, and he let her know it didn't matter that her father stood inches away. "Unless you can show me a divorce decree, you are my wife, and I brought a notarized copy of our marriage certificate to prove it." He pulled the paper from his pocket and showed it to her father. "It's valid in every country on this earth. If you don't want a commotion in this town tonight, open this door when I get back here. Come on, Pop. I don't want you to be late."

She spent much of the twenty minutes standing where he left her—in shock. She had miscalculated because she forgot Johann's propensity to let an adversary get comfortable, thinking he had things his way, and then go in for the kill. As a prominent businessman in two very competitive fields, he never showed his hand, and he stayed on top of the heap.

She straightened the dining room, put the remaining dishes in the dishwasher, and went upstairs. With considerable willpower, she resisted the urge to put on makeup, brush her hair, and change her clothes, though she brushed her teeth.

He's not going to overwhelm me tonight. I've got just as much control over him as he has over me, and I'm not going to let myself forget that. As she stared into the bathroom mirror, a pain settled in the region of her heart. Maybe they weren't on equal footing; he was the last man she'd made love with, but with his appetite, she doubted he had abstained for nearly two years. The sound of the doorbell ended her musings. She whispered, "Lord, it's up to you" and headed down the stairs.

"My mistake," he said without preliminaries after stepping inside, "was in not coming straight here from Craven County Regional Airport, and yours was in not meeting the plane." He took her hand, walked into the living room, offered her a seat on her sofa, and when she took it, seated himself in front of her in an overstuffed chair.

Mark that one down for Johann, she told herself.

"Do you want a divorce, Maude?"

She heard herself say no and marveled that the word flew out of her mouth so fast. "If I wanted one, I'd have it."

"Don't you think I'm entitled to a normal life? Do you think I ought to settle for a woman here or there, catch as catch can, sex without love or affection? Is that what you think?" No smile creased his face, his wonderful eyes didn't twinkle, and he presented her with a harsh facial expression.

So he'd come with an attitude! "I didn't consider all the ramifications. It built up to the point where I couldn't stand it." His eyes widened, and a rush of blood tinted his fair skin. She waved her right hand from side to side. "Not you. It wasn't you but the circumstances. The climate. The language. People who smiled at me no matter what I said or did. The whole scene." She waved her hand as if to implicate the entire world. "And no collard greens." She leaned back against the sofa and folded her hands in her lap. "I guess I never realized it before, but that was it: *no collard greens.*"

He sat forward, his knees wide apart, and stared at her. "No collard greens? What's that? Don't tell me you left me for something to eat. I could have imported anything you wanted, and I would have. All you had to do was mention it."

"They just symbolize what I missed. I couldn't be me. Nobody in your country ever lets out a real good belly laugh, and I couldn't talk with anybody about the poetry, novels, and tales I grew up with. I missed my *self*, my roots. I hate a lot of things about this place, but I'm home here. I can't explain it better."

"I'd say you've done a good job. You seemed happy for eight long years—without your *self*. Why couldn't you tell me that instead of just walking out and letting me worry about where you were and why you'd gone?"

If she told him the truth, she'd heap more ammunition on the weapons he already had, but she wasn't going to fabricate a tale to suit the occasion. She straightened her shoulders and laid her head to one side. "If I had told you I was leaving, I'd still be there, because you would have turned on the charm, the sex, the—"

"Hold it. Yes, I've done that to you a few times, but never when the issue was a critical one. I'm not doing it now, am I?"

"For the time being, you're not."

"And I don't plan to. But I also don't intend to live like a bachelor."

"What *do* you plan?" She held her breath, knowing that he would follow through on whatever he said.

"Whether I remain here or return to Amsterdam, you'll be with me." He stood. "You're married to me. You are my woman, and I'm your man. If you don't start acting like it, I'll prove it to you."

What could she say when she knew he spoke the truth? "I do not plan ever to live in Amsterdam again, and I want you to remember that."

"Will you let me out, please?" She stared at him, disbelieving his words. "Right. We'll get together again soon, but tonight isn't the time for what I need." His hand brushed her cheek, and the door closed behind him.

Trudging upstairs, flustered and battling anger at him and at herself, *old and foolish* hardly described her opinion of herself. For all her vows to keep Johann at bay and to avoid the sexual quagmire into which she'd been so sure he was eager to entrap her, he hadn't allowed her to play the role of disinterested woman. If he wanted to take her to bed, he'd made that about as apparent as a micron. She had forgotten his self-control and the ease with which his mind governed the rest of him. She had talent of that order herself, but less than he, and in any case, she saw nothing to gain by playing one-upmanship.

At age fifty, he was ten years her junior, a fact to which she hadn't previously given much thought, because the possibility of his leaving her hadn't crossed her mind. When it came to leaving, that was *her* thing. Lawrence Hicks shoved her down a flight of stairs—he swore he didn't, but that wasn't the hand of a ghost at her back—and she got up and kept walking, never once looking back. She hadn't seen him since. When Julius Nickerson came to his senses and realized he'd married the wrong woman, she told him she couldn't agree more, and gave him his walking papers. Henri Duprés's passion for garlic finally sickened her, and she discovered sweeter kisses elsewhere.

Johann van der Kaa was neither expendable nor forgettable, and that truth settled on her more forcibly with each passing day. She loved him, and she needed him, and she was no longer going to lie to herself. Maybe she was no longer a match for him.

Seven

Sunday morning, the day after the first snowfall she'd ever seen, Regina sprang out of bed at the sound of the ringing phone, already attuned to the possibility that her staff at the Craven might need her.

"Hello," she said, in her eagerness neglecting to identify herself as she usually did.

"Hey, Cuz. The rain washed away most of the snow last night, and the sky's clear as crystal. Whatta you say we have breakfast together and I show you the town?"

"All right. Can I have an hour?"

"You got it. Be there in fifty-nine minutes."

After a breakfast of fried apples, waffles, bacon, country sausage, and coffee, she patted her stomach in contentment and smiled at Harold. "No wonder so many of the sistahs down here are pleasingly plump. It's hard to pass up this good Southern cooking." She heard herself say "sistahs" and prided herself on becoming more like her own people.

Harold frowned and shook his finger at her. "You'd better pass up these Southern calories unless you want to change your dress size, not to speak of your styles."

"Hawaiian men say they like a lot of flesh on a woman."

He rolled his eyes toward the ceiling. "Pu-lease. They like what they got."

"What's your preference? I mean, do you go for tall, short, slim, fat, or some combination?"

He swallowed the last drop of coffee and stood. "I don't have one. A woman is a woman. The only people I want around me are those with brains. Ready?" With his mercurial and sometimes streetwise personality, not much that Harold said surprised her.

"The town began around the edge of the Neuse River and grew westward," he said as he began the tour. "Some of the best-preserved remnants of slavery—physical ones, I mean—are in that area. As the South went, North Carolina was comparatively liberal.

"And don't it give me a pain in the butt to admit that," he added in barely audible tones. "Even so, they did their share of lynching. Damn 'em."

He parked in front of 501 New Street. "This is the Stanley-Bishop house that *the folks* are so proud of. From eighteen-fifteen to eighteen thirty-one, Stanly Carruthers, one of New Bern's most prominent free blacks, owned it."

"Did he have slaves?"

Harold drove on. "Beats me. A lot of blacks did, though. Doing the white man's thing didn't start this morning, Cuz. Right here," he said when they reached 519 Johnson Street, "is the home of George H. White. He was an African-American lawyer and served in the United States Congress from eighteen ninety-seven to nineteen-oh-one. By then, the Reconstruction period was long forgotten, and civil liberty for us didn't rear its puny little head again until after Rosa Parks's feet got tired and made their famous statement."

"I know about that, but I never related to it; I couldn't. Off there in Hawaii, it seemed like a television series, not a reality in the lives of human beings. Now, being here in this environment, so close to where it all happened, gives me a weird feeling. It's as if I have to catch up with what I missed. But what sane person would want to experience *that?*"

"Sanity is a relative thing. Is a man more sane if he's hungry and gets himself jailed in order to eat three meals a day than if he's homeless and sleeps out in the cold rather than check into a warm, roach-and-flea-infested shelter?"

One minute Harold spoke as a man of the streets, and the next, as a philosopher exposing the strength of his mind. Her opinion of him changed with more regularity than she was comfortable with. Yet, she had the sense that he wouldn't let her down, no matter what.

"It amazes me that you didn't study for an advanced degree. Why did you stop with a bachelor's?"

"Money, Cuz. It—or lack of it—can call a halt to just about anything. This place is full of history, because New Bern was North Carolina's colonial capital. That's Tryon Palace, home of the last man to govern the colony before independence. It's two hundred and thirty years old."

By contrast, Honolulu seemed new. She loved the tree-lined streets, seeing many of them for the first time, and imagined their beauty in spring and summer, and the formal gardens surrounding some of the old Georgian mansions. She was wondering what it would have been like to grow up in New Bern, when Harold cleared his throat as if to get her attention.

"There're some old slave quarters not far from here."

"That's the last thing I want to see."

"All right. Don't take my head off."

From a distance, she saw the large red, white, and blue banner that hung in front of a building on Middle Street. "What's that over there?" She pointed to the banner.

"That? Next to Tryon Palace, that's the pride of New Bern. It's hanging over the exact spot where old Caleb Bradham first mixed up Brad's Drink, which you and everybody else know as Pepsi Cola. That was back in eighteen ninety-eight. I sure wish one of my ancestors had come up with something like that. Then I could live as I please."

"What would you do?"

He stopped the car in front of the Craven Hotel, cut the motor, and looked at her, his eyes filled with a haunted expression. "I love jazz, Regina, and I make a decent living at it. But my first loves are Mozart, Haydn, and Schubert, and I can't support myself playing the music I love on occasional dates with the Fayetteville Symphony.

"I'm a damned good classical cornetist, but conductors take one look at the color of this face and say, 'Sorry, but we don't have jazz in our repertoire.'"

"You mean to tell me—"

He interrupted her. "Right. And just thinking about it makes me ill. I definitely don't want to discuss it. One of these days it'll be 'bye-bye, baby,' and I'll head for Europe."

His right hand rested on the steering wheel, and she covered it with her left one. "I'm so sorry, Harold."

He waved his right hand as if to gainsay the importance of the matter, a gesture that his words belied. "I've composed music for wind instruments, good music that's collecting dust on my piano. I have a degree in music, but for what? I could play jazz on that sax when I was eleven years old."

He turned and faced her fully. "Keep this to yourself. I mean, don't breathe it in your prayers."

"Nobody else . . . ? I mean, people here don't know this?"

"Nobody, and I don't want them to know. My family thinks all kinds of things about me." He hit the steering wheel with his fist. "Let them!"

She nodded, appreciating the fact that he confided to her something so dear to him, and which he hadn't told to any other person in his family. "I'm sorry you've had such a bad deal, but I'm happy you confided in me. I'll never tell."

A half smile hovered over his face. "I know you won't. You're probably more important to me than I can ever be to you."

She detected a tenderness about him, but she was sure he didn't want that side of him exposed. "Harold Pearson, you're the best friend I have—you and my aunt Maude. I've been wanting to ask you about that slight limp, but Hawaiians don't ask personal questions, so—"

"A fracture just below my left knee. When it healed, the leg was about a third of an inch shorter than the other one. Most of the time, I don't remember it."

"You're right. It's barely ever noticeable." She reached out with her arms wide and hugged him."Thanks for telling me that. Now I have some family—you and Aunt Maude. Pop, too, but he hasn't acknowledged it."

He rested his arms and face on the steering wheel for a minute, then faced her. "I told you already that I come with baggage—a lot of it—and I know it's more than you can handle. But I'm here if you need me." He turned the key in the ignition. "Okay. Scat. I gotta go."

"Uh . . . Harold."

"Yeah?"

"I have to do something about Juliet. She's waging an undeclared war, and I can't just sit back and take it."

"I know," he said. "I saw her account of the Craven's opening. Seven full pages in the features section plus her personal column, and she managed not to mention your existence. You'd have thought Colonel Duval built that place with his bare hands. Solo."

"I was stunned," she confessed, but neglected to add that the slight hurt her.

He dismissed it with a shrug. "Juliet's a bitch. You've threatened her Majesty's throne, and she's after your head."

"I gather she and Cephus are good friends. Is that why he ignores me?"

"No. Cephus ignores you because you don't genuflect every time he shows up, and he can't handle that. He's got a mountain-size ego."

"But surely she doesn't toady to him."

"You got a lot to learn. She'll suck up to anybody who can further her cause."

"As arrogant as she seems?"

"Look, Cuz. Juliet and Cephus are just alike. Both of 'em smash their brains every damned time they sit down. And Juliet can be vicious, sparing nobody. She's hardly on speaking terms with any of her own folks, and she latches on to Cephus because he gets tickets for her to all the gov's affairs. Poor fool; he thinks she admires him."

That didn't make sense to her. "I'd think the governor's office would send invitations to the paper."

"Don't be naive, Cuz. The only time politicians pay any attention to a two-bit small-town black paper is when they need votes. Juliet's looking out for Juliet."

"What a load of garbage!"

"Don't let it bother you. Herbert's in town, so she'll be a good little girl for the next two weeks till he goes out again."

"Goes out where?" She was learning more about family, New Bern, Southern history, and local politics than she would have believed possible in the space of one morning.

"He works on the Silver Meteor, Amtrak's Boston-to-Jacksonville, Florida, run. Six weeks on the road and two weeks home. Look. I gotta split. See you tonight."

She ducked into the hotel and headed for her office. Every conversation she had with Harold left her with more questions than answers, and this time, he crammed her head full of suspicions as well as legitimate questions. If she were a quitter, she'd get the first plane to Honolulu.

Justin hadn't thought Regina would be in her office that Sunday morning—the first day of March and the coldest of the year. He'd walked to work in order to get exercise and, within a block of his house, regretted the idea. He heard her office door close and wondered why she'd braved the weather. He sympathized with her anxiety about the top three floors, the big moneymakers for the hotel, but he was still dissatisfied with his work on the executive penthouses and couldn't let her advertise the space. He answered the phone knowing it was she and that she'd seen the light in his office.

"Duval. Good morning."

"Hello, Justin. I need the income from that space. Can't you at least show me what you've done that you dislike?"

"I've told you and told you that I won't show my work until I am proud of it. Fill up the guest rooms."

He could imagine her calming herself. Not that he cared if he made her mad; she needed to explode occasionally. All that self-control would give a person high blood pressure. If silent suffering was typical of Native Hawaiians with whom she grew up, hypertension had to be rampant.

"I'm doing that to the best of my ability," she said, and in his mind's eye, he saw her balled fist and clenched teeth.

"You've been open three weeks, and you've averaged a sixty-to-seventy-percent capacity. What's the big deal? Some hotels never do that well."

"They're not the Craven!"

"Oops. Sorry if I hit a nerve."

"If you and I can't solve this, I'll speak with James."

"Go ahead and do that."

"You're very confident."

He wasn't, but she didn't need to know it. "That's the name of the game. If I don't believe in myself, there's no reason why you, James, or anyone else should. Do what you have to do. I'd better get back to work."

Listening to the silence, her failure to close the conversation and hang up, he pushed back the feeling for her that was always there, unwilling to give in to it. He was successful and independent *because* he had never allowed personal feelings to interfere with his profession. As an army officer, he had resisted enough temptation to merit a medal, and he wasn't about to fall on his face because he wanted the woman next door.

"You still there?" he asked her, somehow hoping she'd left the phone off the hook.

"Yeah. See you."

She hung up, leaving him to wonder why she'd taken so long to do it. He tossed the sketch of an armchair into the wastebasket and began working on another one. If he could finish that job to his satisfaction, he could call his shots. Regina Pearson's requirements were not the same as his, and he didn't plan to commit professional suicide so that she could set a record in hotel management.

Regina didn't want to set a record. She wanted to meet her goal, to keep her promise to herself that by the end of her five-year contract to manage the Craven, the hotel would be operating in the black. Receipts for the three weeks exceeded her expectations, but Maude and Harold wouldn't stay indefinitely, and she hadn't found a performer of Maude's stature to replace them. At least not at the prices she had budgeted. Nobody had to tell her that when Justin finished those suites, they'd be perfect. But it was he who needed perfection; what she needed was full occupancy.

Restless and suddenly out of sorts, she couldn't stand the bleakness she saw beyond the big window. She needed the Hawaiian sunshine, flowers, some color in her life. She needed . . . *No, I don't. I am not going to talk myself into believing that I need Justin Duval. I need him to stop dragging his feet and finish those executive suites.* Pain shot up her arm when she banged her fist on the desk. Annoyed at her foolishness, she packed her briefcase and went home.

With a fire sparkling in her fireplace, she sat on the sofa facing it, propped her feet up on the coffee table, and phoned her grandfather. He'd called her only once, on the morning of the hotel's opening, but he made it plain that he delighted in her calls to him.

"Well," he said when she stated her complaint against Justin, "I 'spect you know there's such a thing as penny-wise and pound-foolish. You're prepared to take less than the man can do so you can rent out those fancy suites and get a bigger gross right now. Don't you know that in the long run, you'll lose? The better the job he does, the easier they'll be to lease and the more you can charge for 'em every month."

She knew that, and it shamed her to have to hear it from him. "I know, Pop, but he's been working on those sketches ever since I came to New Bern."

"Let him do *his* job. *Yours* is to find other ways to boost occupancy. Get those fancy college groups and professional organizations to hold their conventions there. Hook up with an airline, offer weekend specials, discounts for bridal parties—things like that. I got a ton of suggestions for getting people to stay at a hotel. It oughta be easy, considering all I heard about that place. Got some good brochures?"

She told him she did have. "You mean they came to the opening, love the place, and still need an enticement to come back?"

"Sure, they do. You think other hotels aren't trying to get their business?"

"Thanks, Pop. I'll get on the sororities first."

"You call me and let me know if I can help. You hear?"

She promised she would and added, "I'd feel a lot better if you'd come see where I work." And she'd feel better still if he'd ask her to visit him. But she understood that he'd make that move when it suited him and not before.

"An old dog won't do new tricks, child. But you call me."

She appreciated his advice, especially since running that hotel had elements she'd never imagined. However, none of it surprised him. "I will, Pop. You know that."

After hanging up, she fell asleep on the sofa and awakened later with a feeling that she was drifting, that she still didn't belong anywhere, to anyone or with anyone. And as she dressed for Maude and Harold's performance that evening at the Craven, she made up her mind to get what she'd come to New Bern to find. She'd tried it on their terms; they hadn't come to her. She'd go to them. And she'd start with Juliet Smith.

At the intermission of Maude's first performance that evening, Regina went to her aunt's dressing room as a courtesy call, to ask if Maude needed anything, whether the lighting and public address system suited her.

"If I'd had these working conditions in every place I sang in Europe, I might have been tempted to stay over there and keep singing. Honey, this is practically paradise."

"You're due to stay through this month. What will you do after your run here?"

"I don't know. Harold would like me to tour with him, but I don't want to leave my house; I don't know how long Johann plans to stay, and . . ." She spread her hands. "Right now, the plans I can make are limited to singing here, supermarket shopping, and going to the hairdresser. Pop had better be glad he's my father; if he was anybody else, I'd . . ." She threw up her hands. "He's mucked up everything. Do you know I haven't seen Johann van der Kaa but once since opening night?"

"Aunt Maude, have you forgotten that if it hadn't been for Pop, Johann wouldn't be here? Besides, I thought you didn't want to see him."

She pulled air through her front teeth. "Of course I want to see him, and what's more, he knows it. But I can hold out as long as he can." She put a hand on each knee and leaned forward. "That man must be on saltpeter. With that appetite of his, he ain't fooling me. And Pop's not helping the situation. He's keeping my husband's mind off me. Told me this morning that he took Johann sightseeing and to the antique show last week, and they're going to Washington Thursday morning. They would go Wednesday, but Pop would miss his Wednesday chili con carne."

"Threaten not to cook the chili next Wednesday."

She laughed when Maude's eyes nearly doubled their size. "Do you want Pop to have a heart attack? I wouldn't even think of such a thing."

"Ten minutes, Ms. Witherspoon."

"And that's another thing. Wouldn't I look stupid with a name like van der Kaa? Johann wanted me to change my last name, but I told him that name didn't go with being black. He acted like he didn't know what I was talking about."

"Maybe he didn't. Until I came here, I certainly wouldn't have understood that as well as I do now. You've only got six minutes. See you later."

Sadness enveloped her as Maude's velvet mezzo delivered a gut-rending version of "Every Day I Have the Blues" to the strains of Harold's haunting saxophone. She and every person in the Starlight Lounge understood that Maude was singing her own blues, pouring out her own pain. But at the song's end, Maude smiled, bowed, and strolled off the stage with her head high and shoulders back. Regina let her gaze scan the room, hoping to see Johann, but to no avail, and she wondered whether he'd come to New Bern for Maude or for the pleasure of leaving her as she'd left him.

Regina would have been surprised to learn the course that Johann's actions were about to assume, and she wouldn't have guessed

Justin's involvement. Abner Witherspoon's great age did not hinder achievement of his goals. He wanted Maude to stay in New Bern, and he wanted his son-in-law there with her. To him, Johann was a godsend, bringing new meaning and pleasure to his life, a blessing he hadn't anticipated when he invited the Dutchman for a visit. He had in Johann a chess partner, someone as immersed in politics as he, a sharp-witted friend who relieved him of his daily burdens, and a great cook. And Johann didn't watch him with a finger hovering over 911 on the telephone key pad as his children did. He hadn't enjoyed daily living so much since he retired.

Since his marriage to Lois sixty-five years earlier, his breakfast consisted of half a grapefruit, wheat toast, two soft-boiled eggs, a slice of cheddar cheese, and one cup of coffee. Johann had changed that to grapefruit, a strip of crisp bacon, Belgian waffles with strawberries and whipped cream, and coffee. After tasting the chicory-free coffee Johann made, he enjoyed a second cup. "No more calories and no more cholesterol," Johann explained, "and a damned sight tastier."

"Were you interested in canning Maude's chili?" Abner asked Johann, who was treating his father-in-law to his first trip to Washington, D.C.

"Yes. It's good food, and it will sell in the Netherlands as well as the States." He guided the Cadillac to the right lane for the exit from Route 1 to the Fourteenth Street Bridge that would carry them into Washington.

Abner rubbed his hands together, barely able to contain his glee. "How're you going to manage to do that over there in Holland?"

He saw Johann cut a glance at him as he turned onto the bridge. "You Americans have to start calling the Netherlands by its correct name. Holland is a region of the Netherlands. It's like referring to the United States as New England."

"All right. What about you and the chili?"

"Pop, with two thriving businesses, a record company, and a TV/radio chain, I'm independent. I can put that canning factory wherever I like. My moves will depend on my wife and how things square with us."

That didn't satisfy him. "I sure hope you don't feel the same way about English as she feels about Dutch."

With Pennsylvania Avenue closed to traffic, Johann turned into Constitution Avenue and headed for the Willard Hotel. "If you weren't such an angry Democrat, we'd have stayed at the Watergate. Republicans didn't taint the place, Pop."

"I know that, but I'm not staying there. And you didn't answer my question."

"No, I don't guess I did. If I were in the habit of letting people outfox me, I'd still be passing out trays on KLM Royal Dutch Airlines."

"Humph. She doesn't show any sign of softening. Gal's been stubborn since the day she was born. Don't you fool around and blow the whole thing, now. She said she's got a contract for six weeks at the Craven, but if she gets used to working, maybe she'll go to New York or someplace like that."

"She likes being back on the stage; I could see that, but I'm still important to her. She cares as much for me as she ever did, and that's saying a lot."

"Then why'd you leave her the night you had her chili con carne? You were home before I got there from prayer meeting."

"Pop, you're muddying the water, but I'll say this much: Maude is willing to settle for the present, for half a loaf; but not me—I want the whole nine yards or nothing."

"And what if she doesn't figure that out?"

"Why would I leave that point to chance? She knows it. And stop worrying; when I get thoroughly sick of Maude's foolishness, I'll end it. I didn't come here for an indefinite vacation. I came here for my wife."

"She swears she's not going back to Europe," Abner said doggedly. "So unless you like speaking English, that doesn't look promising."

Johann's laugh had a deep, gritty quality that he'd had a hard time getting used to, and he got a good dose of it then. "You're a hard man to get around, Pop, but you may have met your match. We can always speak French.

"I want to talk with someone about designing a logo and ad campaign for that chili. That would be the most costly part of getting started. When I find out how much that will cost, I'll see about the price of processing and canning."

"Ask that fellah who did the work on the Craven. Maybe he knows somebody."

"Good idea. I'll look him up as soon as we get back."

"I can get his number for you. I can even get the appointment if you want." He got a great feeling out of knowing that if she could, Regina would do that for him—that and anything else he asked.

The next evening, after using up more energy than he'd spent in the past ten years—visiting Howard University, the White House, the Lincoln Memorial, and the Washington National Cathedral—it surprised him that he could stand up straight. Johann had arranged for a limousine to take them around, but that didn't explain why he felt more like seventy than ninety-one. Maybe a man needed good company in order to enjoy life.

He went to his room to read. Although he enjoyed every minute he spent in Johann's company, he intended to make it easy for his son-in-law to stay with him. A man needed privacy and freedom to do as he pleased, so he made it a point to leave Johann to his own devices. Maude married a strong man who knew his worth and what he wanted, and Pop meant to see them back together before he died.

"Come on in," he said when Johann knocked on his door. "I've been reading this brochure about the Grand Canyon. Says here it's two hundred and seventeen miles long. Can't beat what I saw today, though. Never thought I'd enjoy anything as much as I have this trip to Washington. Imagine! Old Abner Witherspoon walking around in the White House. You've done a lot for me, son."

"We've done a lot for each other. I came in to ask what you want for dinner. We can go out or eat here. If you're tired, we can eat in your room. By the way, since you're interested in the Grand Canyon, let's go there. I'd like to see it, too."

"Wouldn't I have to fly? I never did like flying; it hurts people's ears."

"Not anymore, Pop. Pressure is different in the jet planes. Let's go."

"I'll think about it. I sure did like that beef stew you cooked the other night. Let's see if they've got some and we can eat it up here."

"Beef stew? You call my *boeuf bourguignon* beef stew?"

"I called it that 'cause that's what it was. Maude called you yet?"

"No. And she needs a little shock, which is why I can't wait for Wednesday night."

Justin liked to begin Monday mornings with a satisfying three or four hours of work; interruptions annoyed him. Well, just that one phone call.

"You want to see me?" He asked Abner Witherspoon after finding

Regina's note under his door. He wondered why she chose that method of communication, but having learned that Regina was not predictable, he decided not to make an issue of it. If she didn't want to talk with him, so be it.

"I sure do. I want to have a talk with you and my son-in-law. He's a businessman from the . . . the Netherlands. You know, Holland. Can you come over here right away?"

"Would a couple of hours suit you?"

Abner assured him that the timing was good, and two hours later he strode past two sleeping cottonwood trees and up the steps of Abner Witherspoon's white-shuttered red Cape Cod house. When the tall, erect, and obviously proud man answered the door, he realized he'd expected to see a gaunt shadow of a man. The strong handshake also surprised him.

"Don't look so shocked," Abner said, "not every nonagenarian's got one foot in the grave and the other one on a banana peel. Thank you for coming."

He'll take some getting used to. Hmmm. Don't see any of Regina in him. "I'm glad to meet you, sir. Regina speaks so highly of you."

"Humph. She oughta. I'm her grandfather. Come on in here and meet my son-in-law."

Justin accepted the introduction, took the seat Abner offered, and worked hard at not seeming overly eager to learn what Abner was treating as top secret. He listened, stunned, as Abner described Maude's chili con carne. Had he interrupted his work to listen to somebody extol a bowl of chili?

"My son-in-law here's going to can it for us, and we need a logo for the cans, stationery, the whole works." He threw up his hands, then looked at Johann. "How come you're not saying anything?"

"If I thought I could improve on what you're saying, I would."

Thinking fast, Justin decided to bargain. If there was anything he loved, it was a bowl of great chili con carne. "Look, I can sketch a logo in a couple of minutes, but if I'm going to draw one that represents your chili, I think I'd better taste it first."

Johann's jubilant guffaw settled in the region of Justin's brain that adored the farcical and the absurd, and he saw in the man a kinsman to be valued.

"What's so funny?" Abner demanded. "Maude won't mind. She loves to show off her chili."

Johann, who had been sitting on a pouf with his back resting against the wall and with his right foot tucked beneath his hip, seemed unable to shake the mirth.

"At least warn her so she'll cook enough," Johann said. "Maude does not like surprises, not even when they involve gifts of precious jewelry."

Abner sucked his teeth. "Any woman who doesn't like that kind of surprise doesn't deserve one." He looked at Justin. "Am I right?"

Not one to rock the boat unnecessarily, Justin said, "You got it, sir. Absolutely."

Abner's demeanor changed, and he suddenly peered at Justin, judging him carefully. He nearly fell off the chair when Abner cocked his head to the side and asked him, "There wouldn't be anything between you and my granddaughter, would there?"

Justin restored his composure as quickly as possible, by chance glancing at Johann, who, with a wide grin floating over his face, held up both hands, palms out, and said, "Don't look at me. I already got the third degree."

Feigning astonishment, he hoped his face bore the expression of one very much confused. "Whatever gave you that idea?" he asked, and surmised that he would have gotten away with it if Johann's laughing fit hadn't returned.

"Because I been on this earth nearly a hundred years. Not much and practically nobody surprises me. You're not wearing a ring and you are definitely an eligible man. If my granddaughter's got anywhere near twenty-twenty vision, her eye's on you."

"Maybe that's why she's mad at me right now."

"She's not mad. I told her to do her job and let you do yours." He gestured toward Johann."Never could figure out why you young people act like you're gonna live forever. Like you got eternity to get your life together. You can build sixty hotels, go home by yourselves, and have nothing."

"Thanks for speaking on my behalf," Justin said, and meant it. "Now, when do I get to sample this chili?"

"Wednesday night," Johann said. "I'll call Maude. If it's not all right, I'll let you know."

At the door as he prepared to leave, Justin shook hands with Abner. "I can't leave without mentioning this. Get to know Regina. She's longing for a loving relationship with her family, and especially with you. Well, Thanks. I hope to see you Wednesday evening."

Abner's gaze locked on Justin. "I see. So there *is* something between you. You haven't been treating her like she's got nothing but a
big hole between her two ears, have you? Is that why she got mad at
you? That one is smart." Justin leaned against the doorjamb and
waited for the old man's thoughts. "In my day," Abner went on,
"women weren't expected to do no more'n look nice, keep house, have
children, and look after 'em. But these women today do that and a
man's job, too. Ain't nothin' wrong with it; I just don't see how they do
it." He extended his hand to Justin. "Well, I'll call my daughter and tell
her you're coming with us Wednesday."

Justin was in his office at the hotel before he realized that he had
accepted Abner Witherspoon's observation about Regina and himself.
As colonel, he would have been too alert to let that pass. The quick upward movement of his right shoulder expressed his conviction that it
was too late to correct that impression and too late to tame his feelings.
And maybe he didn't want to.

A little later, he passed Regina in the corridor and winked at her,
prepared to pause and initiate a conversation, but she winked back
and kept walking. She'd done that absentmindedly, he knew, and
wondered whether her preoccupation signified continued annoyance
with him. However, he needn't have.

At that moment, Regina struggled with what was becoming for her
almost an obsession with her cousin Juliet's likeness to her. Each time
she looked at herself in the mirror, she imagined how she would look
if she were darker, like Juliet. Maude had gainsaid their likeness as genetic coincidence, Odette considered it fuel for petty gossip, and Juliet
hated her because of it. What others *thought* mattered far less than the
reason why she was the spitting image of a cousin.

She couldn't concentrate on her work, so she telephoned Harold,
who was often at home during the day since he worked nights.

After half a dozen rings, she was replacing the receiver when she
heard his "Yeah?"

"This is Regina. Sorry, I didn't think you'd be asleep in the afternoon. I'll call back."

"What is it?"

He sounded somewhat curt, so she teased, "Got company? When
are you going to let me meet her?"

"What's up?"

"I wanted some advice, but since you're preoccupied, I guess I called at the wrong time. See you this evening."

"Where's your head? Today's Monday. Call you later." He hung up and left her gaping at the phone.

She told herself he was half asleep, and dialed the telephone operator for Juliet's phone number. What would she say to her cousin that would bring a civilized response? Surely the woman realized it was to their advantage to learn why, except for skin color, they appeared to be identical twins.

Fear and weakness gripped her as she dialed the number, and she had to struggle against her inclination to hang up. Maybe she should have talked with Pop, but she doubted he could be of help.

"Hello." The man's voice projected impatience.

"Hello. May I please speak with Juliet Smith?"

"She's not here." Whoever he was, he wasn't friendly.

"Do you know what time she'll be home?"

"I don't have the slightest idea."

Maybe she had the wrong number. "Who is this?"

"Who do you think it is? Michael Jordan? What man would you expect to answer this phone, and who are you?"

Her immediate reaction was to hang up, but doing that might not bode well for Juliet if she had a suspicious husband. "I'm Regina Pearson, Juliet's cousin."

"She doesn't have any kinfolk named Pearson. You gotta be mistaken." He hung up.

So Juliet hadn't told him about her cousin and how much she looked like her. She learned something else, too: Juliet and Herbert Smith weren't getting along. The phone rang, and she didn't think she had ever been happier at an interruption.

"This is Maude. How y'all doing this afternoon? I was just about to smother some pork chops, and I know how you love collards. Why don't you eat with me tonight."

"Aunt Maude, I'd love it." She looked at her watch. Four-fifteen. "I'm leaving here shortly. Can I bring you anything?"

"Nothing. Come on, now."

She wasted no time telling Maude about her encounter with Herbert Smith. "Don't they get along?"

"Child, I have no idea what that could be about. Herbert Smith loves himself some Juliet. The whole town knows that. He worships the ground that girl walks on. If they're not getting along, you can bet it's something she did."

"But where is she if he doesn't know? Harold told me yesterday that Juliet's husband was home for two weeks."

Maude closed her eyes and turned her head to the side, as if to say, "It doesn't matter." "Whatever it is, they'll make up, because Herbert'll do whatever it takes to keep that girl. What's going on between you and Justin Duval?"

"I don't know. Why?"

"Pop just called to say he's bringing him over here for some of my chili con carne Wednesday night. I didn't know they knew each other."

Regina almost bolted from her chair. "I wonder what Justin is up to."

Maude nearly doubled over with laughter. "Justin? You mean what is Pop up to? I'll bet you anything Johann will be with them. Let's give 'em a little surprise: you come, too."

Always eager to enjoy a good joke, she supposed her face glistened with the joy she felt anticipating the prank. Pop would . . . She couldn't. Pop might not like her being there.

She recovered quickly. "That really would be fun, but I think I'll pass."

"Oh, come on, now. I'd get a bang out of that. Why not . . . ? Sometimes I feel like disconnecting that thing," she said and headed for the telephone.

"Maude speaking. How y'all doing this evening?"

"Hello, Kitten. Pop's bringing Justin Duval and me with him for chili Wednesday."

Her hands shook, but she managed to steady her voice. He would love to know he'd knocked her off balance, but he wouldn't learn it from her. "What? Fine with me, but I'd a thought you could find some time to come over here when Pop's not guarding your tail."

Laughter rolled out of him, exciting her and making her want to enjoy the moment with him. "If anybody's guarding anybody's tail, it's me guarding Pop's. You ready to give in?"

She said nothing for a few minutes. "Johann, honey, you got a short memory. I never chased a man in my life, so if you're waiting for me to do your work for you, you might as well go back to Amsterdam. It'll never happen. You're too old to be taking advice from Pop on how to play ball with your wife. Pop got married sixty-six years ago, and I suspect he's rusty on the subject of how a man gets a woman. Even so, I imagine things were different then."

"You think I'm trying to get you? I'm not. I want to make you think about what's going on here, and if you don't get it straight soon, I know exactly how to put an end to this. Furthermore, you are well aware that all I have to do is take you to bed and get inside of you. You'll promise me anything I want. Anything. I'd rather not do it that way, but what the hell! See you Wednesday."

Shaken, she walked back to the living room, biting a fresh cigar instead of cutting the end. She dropped herself into the overstuffed chair before the fireplace. "That was Johann. He'll be over here Wednesday evening with Justin and Judas. Regina, I'm fooling myself thinking I can hold out longer than Johann. If he walked in here tonight, in five minutes I'd be a goner."

Her lower lip dropped. "Justin and *who?*"

"My Judas father. You know I love Pop, but he can't see anybody's point of view but his own."

Compared with her problem, that was a trip to the moon. "I hurt for you. I don't want to sound callous, but if I had your problem, I'd be flying straight to it as fast as I could. You love him and you're itching to go to bed with him. For heaven's sake, enjoy it."

"And I'll wind up in Amsterdam."

"Play your cards right, and maybe you can have Johann and New Bern, too. Maybe he wants you bad enough to stay here. You know more about men than I do, but even I know that man didn't come to New Bern to see Pop."

"I know that, and I know he wants me as badly as I want him, but if I'd thought I could control him, I wouldn't have left the way I did." She looked at the beer in her glass: flat and uninviting. "He's good to me, Regina. And he makes me feel warm and . . . Almost two years had passed, but the minute I looked down and saw him in the audience, I felt like a woman again."

As if the condition of the beer didn't matter, she lifted the glass and drank it all down. "I'll try and meet him halfway, but that's as far as I'm going."

"I wouldn't bet a dime on that."

"I met your grandfather yesterday," Justin told Regina, glad for that excuse to knock on her office door. "Mind if I come in?"

"Of course not." She didn't take her hand off the pen with which she'd been writing.

"I liked him."

She put the pen aside and leaned back in the chair. "He didn't tell me why he wanted your phone number, but if Aunt Maude's assessment of him is correct, he probably meant to meddle."

"Not at all. He was talking business. He's obviously developed a great fondness for Johann. If that's what Maude means by meddling, she ought to relax. It's my impression that her husband is his own man."

"She said the same." Regina's lips curved in a half smile, and her whole face suddenly brightened with what might have been an inner vision. Her cryptic words confirmed it. "The man has nothing to worry about; whatever Johann wants, Johann will get."

His left eyebrow shot up. "I haven't seen much of Maude, but I'd bet my right arm that when you get down to the nitty-gritty, that sister's made of steel. You don't climb that high, sit on top for years, and voluntarily walk away from it all unless you've got tough guts. And she has. He may get what he wants, but she won't give it to him just because he asks."

He wouldn't say she'd withdrawn, but her sudden pensiveness stood between them like clouds between the earth and the sun. He couldn't figure out what caused the change in her—not that she'd been oozing warmth, but at least she'd been receptive.

"I'm going to Baton Rouge this weekend. How about dinner Thursday night?" Her lips parted in a gut reaction, and he saw the word *no* forming, but she bit it back.

"Maybe we shouldn't socialize, Justin. This seesaw business between us doesn't sit well with me. I don't understand what goes on with you and me. I like relationships I can depend on, not one that heaves me to the sky one day and drops me in a ditch the next."

He walked closer to her desk, not wanting her to mistake his words or their meaning. "We haven't tried to develop a relationship. We've been reacting to the chemistry between us, and I suppose, considering we have to work together, that's natural. But you're scared of your feelings for me, and I've tried to control what I feel for you. Let's have dinner, act natural, and see what happens."

He could hardly contain his amusement when her eyes glittered with anticipation of what they'd be like if they let it all hang out, so to speak. "You're joking," she said.

He braced both hands on her desk and leaned forward. "Oh, no, I'm not. But I'll put the brakes on anytime you say. What about it?"

Looking wary, as if she had to choose between a road she'd traveled and one she'd never walked, she nodded her head. "Okay. Thursday."

He straightened up and gazed down at her. "I'll come for you at your home. Seven?" She nodded. "Don't look so overjoyed, Regina. You're not going to your execution."

"Figuratively speaking, maybe," she mumbled under her breath.

$\mathcal{E}ight$

Maude knew Johann would expect to see her in a flowing caftan, so she put on a red jumpsuit that had wide, pleated legs, fitted bodice, and plunging neckline. It zipped in the back. He couldn't say she dressed to please him, because he didn't like women in pants, but he couldn't deny the allure of her softly feminine outfit, either. Except for the long sleeves, he'd think it a come-on. After softening the lights in the living and dining rooms, she splashed some Dior perfume behind her ears and at her throat and looked around for something else to do. She hated waiting.

Very soon, the doorbell rang. "There's not a thing at stake," she told herself, "so be calm." She opened the door and looked into her husband's eyes.

"Hello, Kitten." He didn't wait for an invitation to enter but strode past her, and in spite of herself, her gaze followed him.

"Come on in, Justin," she heard her father say. "In my day, you could expect a warm greeting when you went to somebody's house. Maude's usually hospitable, but I guess she's not herself tonight."

She spun around, ready to do battle with her attacker, and had to laugh about it. It was just Pop being Pop. She greeted him and Justin and walked with them into her living room.

"Would have been real nice if Regina could have joined us," Maude said, getting even with her father.

"We can sit in here after we eat," Pop said, leading the way to the dining room and serving notice that he didn't plan to discuss Regina. "Let's get to the chili while it's hot."

She'd waste her breath if she told him warming up chili wouldn't hurt it, not even if you did that a dozen times. "Would you care for a drink?" she asked Justin, knowing that Johann would wash his chili down with Heineken beer.

"What are you having?" Justin asked.

"She'll guzzle that Heineken beer," Pop said. He looked at Johann. "Is that the national drink in Hol—I mean, the Netherlands?"

"Just about it, but Maude was drinking beer when I met her."

"Wine gives me a headache, so I drink beer," Maude said.

"Maybe that's because wine reminds you of that Frenchman . . . What was his name?" Abner said in his usually irreverent way.

Justin found the banter between Maude and her father entertaining. Solid mutual affection between father and daughter. He envied them. Pretending to side with Maude, he said, "Then I guess I'll guzzle some, too. A Heineken, if you have one."

"Humph" was Abner's response to Justin's needling. After saying the grace, he waited, seemingly on edge, until Justin tasted the chili. "Well?"

Justin ate a few more spoonfuls. "I envision an angel playing a harp a few inches above my head while I savor this heavenly stuff. Maybe a whole choir of angels."

Abner folded his hands in his lap and looked at Johann. "What did I tell you? Nothing like it." He resumed his enjoyment of the food, his face bearing the look of a cat who'd just produced a litter of kittens.

"I was convinced last time," Johann said. "Do you have a recipe for this, Kitten?"

"I can make it blindfolded."

"Okay, but do you have a recipe?"

"You don't think I'm going to . . . Wait a minute. What's this all about?"

"We're going to can it," Pop said, "and Justin here is going to design the cans."

"With singing angels?" She threw up her hands.

"Don't knock it, Maude," Justin said. "This stuff is heavenly, and I'll be the first person to fill my pantry with it."

They discussed the pros and cons of packaging and selling the chili, until Pop reminded them that he had to go to prayer meeting. "We're going to make you a rich woman," he told Maude.

Both men left with him, and after she cleared away all remnants of the dinner, she sat before the fire, enjoying a cigar and wondering why she'd gone to the trouble to look nice. As far as she could make out, Johann hadn't noticed her.

After taking Pop to church, Justin and Johann relaxed in the Craven Hotel's Starlight Lounge. It was an off night for Maude and Harold, and they found the quiet room perfect for relaxation and conversation.

"Are you really planning to can that chili?"

Johann rested his left ankle on his right knee. "Absolutely. Do you think it's good, or were you being a gentleman about it?"

"I can't think of many kinds of food that I like better than chili con carne, and I must have eaten a couple a hundred pounds of it since I left Baton Rouge. That's the best I've tasted. Where will you set up the factory?"

A quick movement of his shoulder indicated his uncertainty. "Depends on how things go with Maude and me."

"Well, I wish you the best of luck."

"I'm going to need it."

The following morning, Regina purchased *The New Bern Chronicle* in the hotel's lobby as she arrived for work. She threw her briefcase on her desk along with the paper and was about to remove her coat when her gaze landed on the likeness of herself in the lower left-hand corner of the front page.

"I don't remember posing for a photographer," she mused as she walked to her coat closet. "Wait a minute, here," she said aloud. "That's Juliet's photo. Doggone it, I'm sick of this." Her first thought was the immediate satisfaction she'd get from a confrontation with her cousin, though common sense told her the futility of that move.

She dropped into her chair. Somebody knew the answer, and she'd find that person no matter what it cost her. After an hour during which she accomplished nothing, she checked the list of relatives Maude gave her, but didn't see a possible clue . . . except . . . What had she been thinking? She ran to the closet for her coat, got her purse, and turned on her answering machine. *I'm sick of this foolishness. I should have done this long ago.*

Fifteen minutes later, she parked in front of the white-shuttered,

red Cape Cod house that she had occasionally passed but never entered. *He's a tough old bird,* she told herself, needing assurance that her unexpected presence wouldn't upset him. Johann answered the door. What a letdown!

"I don't think we've met," she said, "I'm your wife's niece." If she had expected warmth with that disclosure, she couldn't have erred more in her thinking. He was at once unfriendly and seemed prepared to close the door.

"What do you want?"

Taken aback, she banished her smile and glared at him. "I want to see my grandfather. Would you please let me pass?"

When his glower soften to a perplexed gaze, she remembered having seen Juliet make a play for him on Maude's opening night, and her shoulders sagged. Juliet again.

"I'm Regina Pearson, manager of the Craven Hotel. I assume you thought I was my cousin, Juliet Smith."

He stepped back. "I apologize, Miss Pearson. That's just what I thought. I've only seen such a resemblance in identical twins, but now that I observe you more closely, I can see the personality difference, not to mention the voice. Come on in. Pop's watching Judge Mathis."

She hadn't counted on a witness to her first meeting with her grandfather, and she didn't want to ask Johann to give them privacy.

"Who is it, Johann?" Abner called.

She followed the sound of the voice and headed for the den. "It's Regina, Pop. Regina. I . . . Something's bothering me. I just had to talk with you."

She stood in the doorway of the room in which he relaxed in a Mies van der Rohe Barcelona chair, facing the television but staring in her direction.

"Regina?"

She tried to control the tears that welled up in her. "Yes, Pop. I'm Regina." His silence did nothing to reassure her that she'd done the right thing by coming to see him against his wishes, and, as if her feet were planted in hardened concrete, she stood in the doorway, unable to move. Minutes passed. Then she watched the incredible picture unfolding before her. As the weathered face curved itself into a slow smile, he swung his feet to the side of the low-slung chair, grasped the back of it for support, raised himself to his full height of around six feet, and opened his arms.

"I'm a foolish old man. Come here, child." She ran to him with arms outstretched and, with her head resting firmly against his shoulder, sobbed, her chest heavy and her breathing jagged.

"Maybe I shouldn't have come, but I had to, Pop."

His frail hands soothed her back. "I'm the one who's wrong. Been wrong for years, but you can't make the north wind blow anywhere but south. No more tears, now. Come sit over here and tell me what's the matter."

It wasn't so easy. She looked at him, wanting a mental imprint of his face, his physique, and his personality. Her surprise at what he was like must have shown on her face.

"Humph. You're another one of those who thought I'd be a five-feet-tall dried vanilla bean, huh? Old is a state of the mind, child. Don't you forget that."

"Thought you'd like some tea, Pop," Johann said, and placed a tray containing a tea service and ginger snaps on the table beside the Barcelona chair.

"Thanks, Johann." He looked at Regina and gestured toward Johann. "This is my son-in-law. He's visiting me from Hol—the Netherlands. Johann, my granddaughter here is the manager of the Craven. She's taking up the hotel business that I left five or six years ago, and I'm right proud of her."

"I've been there several times. It's an elegant place." He inched toward the door. "I'll leave you two alone. If you need anything, Pop, just yell."

"That man's a prize," Abner said. "You'd think anybody as smart as my daughter Maude would be able to see that. She married four men, and Johann's the only one worth the paper the marriage certificate was printed on." He crossed his knee and patted his thigh. "He'll get her, though. Sure as my name is Abner Witherspoon." He poured a cup of tea and passed it to her. "I love ginger snaps."

She thought her heart would fly out of her chest. "Me, too, but I never ate them till I came here. My secretary's addicted to them, and I started eating them because they're always on her desk." She pulled her chair around so that she almost faced him, and his pleasure at her move showed in his face.

He finished the tea and placed his cup on the tray. "Now, tell me why you left work the first thing this morning and came to see me. Does it have anything to do with Duval?"

Her eyebrows shot up, and she imagined she gaped at Abner. "No, sir. Not a thing. It . . . it's . . ." She placed her cup on the tray. "It's Juliet Smith."

"If I hadn't heard your voice before I saw you, I might have been fooled for a minute."

She leaned toward him. "Pop, I can't stand not knowing what this is all about."

His pained expression suggested that she didn't want to know his thoughts, but it was his reluctance to speak that lowered her hopes. His hand rose as if in gesture, but he let it fall back onto his thigh. "It's best to let sleeping dogs lie. Once you start probing into things like this, you get a mess of confusion. Who knows who was married to who a couple of generations back? Start digging and you're subject to raise more questions than you will ever solve."

She reached out and touched his arm, frail but warm and steady. "But what about me, Pop? I'm becoming obsessed with this. All I did this morning was push papers around on my desk. I thought I'd go out of my mind. That's why I came to you."

He took a deep breath and expelled it slowly. "So you saw the paper this morning. I can't blame you. It's unsettling for me, too, but we can't change it. Do the two of you talk?"

She told him how she met Juliet, and added, "She despises me. Told me to stay out of her way."

"I wondered why she wrote pages and pages about the hotel and didn't mention you, a Witherspoon and the first woman, black or white, anywhere in this state to have such responsibility."

"Are you saying I have to live with this?"

"No matter how it happened that you're dead ringers for each other, you can't do anything about it. Nobody in his right mind would mistake you for Juliet. She's got an unfortunate personality and a voice like a crow. At least she did have; I haven't seen her in a couple of years."

She threw up her hands. "I don't see how I can ignore this. It's . . ." Though he shook his head, from the sadness in his eyes, she knew he sympathized and cared. For the moment mollified, she smiled. "I'll come to see you all the time, if you'll let me."

He nodded his head, as if she'd merely confirmed what he already knew. "When your mother walked out of here and didn't look back, she took my heart with her—just killed something in me. She was my firstborn, and only the Lord knows how I loved her. Your grand-

mother and I used to sit and look at her in her crib singing and slap-
ping her little hands. She made up for all the things we needed and
didn't have."

His old eyes blinked rapidly several times. "No point in going
back there. Maybe I was wrong, but she was, too. She never wrote, and
neither did your father. I didn't hear a thing till Maude got a letter
from you. Forty-two years or so later, it still hurt."

"I'm terrible sorry, Pop."

He seemed to shake himself, shedding the hurt and pain. "You
come see me as often as you can, you hear? And if I can help you any
way a'tall, you call me."

"I will, Pop." She stood to leave, and he got up. "Maybe you'll
come have dinner with me at my house some time. My roast duck will
make you dance the boogaloo."

Laughter rumbled in his throat. "If it's that good, be sure you cook
some for that fellah, Duval. He's a good man."

Her eyes widened. "Uh . . . well, I don't know whether he likes
duck." She'd like to know what he had wormed out of Justin, and how
he got the idea that she and Justin were more than coworkers.

He walked with her to the door. "If you cook it, he'll eat it. A
woman ought to cook for her man. The belly never forgets where it
gets a good meal."

She hugged him. "I'll see you soon." If she didn't get out of there,
she would sob all over him. Joy suffused her. She didn't get the answer
to Juliet's likeness, but she had her grandfather.

She opened the door for Justin at seven that evening, lighthearted,
her spirits buoyed, and her face glowing. "Hi."

"Hi. All this for me?"

"All of what?"

"This . . . I can't quite describe it. Are you glad to see me? Is that it?"

She grabbed his hand and practically pulled him inside. "You
won't believe what I did." Barely able to contain herself after waiting
all afternoon to tell someone how happy she was, she clasped her
hands against her breast and then opened her arms wide. It didn't surprise her that he walked into her open arms and hugged her; she had
learned that he always seized the moment. And she reciprocated,
laughing as she hugged him. He released her and stepped back, rubbing the back of his neck, his forehead creased.

"Maybe I should have asked you what you did that makes you
bubble like this. I have a feeling it's not one bit related to me."

"You're right. I went to see Pop. I just showed up there and knocked on the door. Justin, he was so nice and . . . I feel so good. He opened his arms and hugged me. Sorry about rattling on like this, but you can't imagine how I feel."

"Yes, I can. I remember telling you that given the chance, any grandfather would love his granddaughter. I bet you were surprised when you saw him."

"I sure was. He neither looks nor acts his age, and he's tall."

"Shocked me, too. I liked him. Was Johann there?"

"Yes, but he didn't sit with us." She explained what happened when she arrived. "That's the reason I went to see Pop. My resemblance to Juliet is becoming unbearable."

"I suppose you saw *The New Bern Chronicle* this morning. That set me back a bit, too. What did he have to say about it?"

"He told me to let sleeping dogs lie. Maybe he knows something about it. As I recall, he didn't seem shocked when he first saw me. Where're we going?"

"I made reservations at the Drake, but we can go over to Havelock and have some lobster and crab cakes at Gable Gardens."

"How far is it to Havelock?"

"Not far." He pushed back his coat sleeve and looked at his watch. "Ready to go?"

She relaxed in the leather bucket seat of the gray Oldsmobile and closed her eyes. Her life was not in order, she still didn't have the big, loving family she craved, and she didn't know for certain who she was—thanks to the intrusion of Juliet into her life—but she had a feeling of contentment, a sense that she had found her niche.

"It's funny," she said, voicing her thoughts without preliminaries. "It's as if my whole life changed today. I don't remember my mother. A pat on the back was the extent of my father's ability to express affection. If he ever held me in his arms, if I ever cried on his shoulder, I don't remember it. Being that way with Pop this morning . . ." She turned fully to face him. "It's like I'm somebody special now."

"I'm happy for you and for him, too. I suspect he wanted to see you but didn't know how to reverse his position."

"Get closer to your folks, Justin. Maybe you won't ever like all of them, but try. If I hadn't persisted, Pop would still be nursing his forty-year grudge and taking it out on me."

"Did it occur to you that you may not get that huge, loving family you're after?"

"They'll come around. All of them."

"For your sake, I hope so. The thought of being with thirty or forty of my relatives makes army boot camp seem like paradise. And I'm going to Baton Rouge this weekend."

"You told me. Any special reason?"

"I want my mother to know she can depend on me, that I'll take care of her, that I'm there for her if she needs me. So I go to see her regularly. The problem is, she surrounds herself with her sisters, nieces, nephews, brothers-in-law, and assorted friends. I'll meet half of Baton Rouge before I get back here."

"But to be around that many people who care about you—"

As he eased the car into a parking spot beside Gable Gardens, he interrupted her. "They'll be arguing, bickering, accusing each other, and gossiping. And why? Money. Fourth cousins think they're entitled to royalties from my father's estate. Put six of that bunch in a room, and the din will crack your eardrums. No thank you."

He put the car in park. "Sit there. This is a social evening. Remember?"

She did remember, and she'd been pushing it to the back of her mind. He was about to start them on an intimate relationship, and she admitted to needing a more normal life. One that involved more than working ten hours a day and thinking about the job for another four hours until she fell asleep. She sat there, not so much because he requested it, but because her mind was on the likely consequences of a deeper relationship with him. He opened the door and extended his hand.

"Thanks." She took the hand that reached out to her, looked into his face, and wondered if there really was such a thing as fate. She'd had little experience with this Justin without the authority he wore like a uniform—this man who seemed eager to please, whose face shone with warmth. Maybe her world would finally right itself.

"Would you like anything else?" the waitress asked them. Justin looked at Regina, and she indicated she'd had her fill.

"That will be all. The lobster was really good," Justin told the waitress, "and don't forget the crab cakes."

"I was surprised when you didn't order your usual, miss, but you made a good choice this time. The swordfish is good, but the lobster and crab cakes are our specialty," the waitress said. "Y'all come back anytime."

When the color left Regina's face, he knew what to expect next, so he stood and reached for her hand. "Don't think about it. The joke's on the waitress. Come on."

For a few minutes, the woman's words seemed to shrivel her, and he tightened his grip on her hand. The wind's velocity had increased while they ate dinner, and bits of debris swirled around their feet as they walked to the car. Like the debris that had once cluttered his life. He'd swept his personal universe clean five years earlier, and he meant to keep it that way. Tidy and well organized. Regina was a question mark, and he wanted to know whether he could expect a personal relationship with her. He had hoped to come to an understanding with her during the evening, but first her euphoria about her grandfather prevented his introducing it, and then the waitress's unexpected monkey wrench saddened her. He'd have to wait for another opportunity.

She began to laugh, and he feared her exasperation at the waitress's remark had changed to hysteria. She tugged at his arm until he stopped walking.

"I know it isn't easy to put up with the constant reminder that you have a double, but try not to let it get to you."

"Swordfish, for goodness' sake! I hate swordfish. Maybe she and I don't have anything in common but looks."

"Nothing that I can see." He had to get her mind off the subject of Juliet Smith. "Want to go to the Zanzibar? Pearson might not be there tonight, but the house band's pretty good." Later, they sat at a corner table that offered a full view of the band. He ordered bourbon and branch water and she asked for a glass of Chardonnay.

"I asked you once before to tell me about yourself, and you told me about your life in Hawaii. What about here in New Bern? What do you want? What do you need? What hurts you?" Maybe he was rushing her, but who could blame him? For nearly five months, they'd had a peculiarly undefined relationship that didn't suit either him or, probably, her, and she was either unwilling or unable to come to terms with it.

"I'm not certain of the answers to your question. In Hawaii, I knew what I wanted, because I understood what was available to me. Here . . . Justin, all I know about African-American male/female relations is what I've seen on television and in the movies, and I do not want that for myself. I know TV and the movies exaggerate life, but even the direction is wrong for me."

Absentmindedly he stirred the bourbon, reflecting on what she'd said. "I can't help you too much with that, because I've hardly ever watched those situation comedies, though I'm told they're ridiculous." He leaned forward and held her hand. "Let me show you."

She kept her gaze on their table. "Native Hawaiian women are frank and honest about men and sex. If they like a man and want him, they let him know it, but women here play games with men. Look at Aunt Maude. She wants Johann so badly she's getting the shakes, but when she's with him, according to her, she's cool. She's my aunt, but that's stupid."

"Men play games, too."

At last, she raised her eyes to meet his glance. "For years, I just wanted a family, people I knew would love me. I still want and need it, but I'm learning that family isn't a guaranteed source of love."

"No, it definitely is not." He drank the remainder of the bourbon and toyed with the potato chips that remained in the tiny bowl in front of him. "What do you see for us? In the future, I mean."

"I've never shared such strong chemistry with a man. I know we want each other, but there has to be something else, and I'm not sure we have it."

"Want to give it a shot? See if we have anything else going for us? As a man, I'm not willing to pass on an attraction as strong as this one. I want to know what else there is."

"All right. But I warn you: back in the office, I might forget this conversation."

"That's the least of my worries." Still unsatisfied, he leaned back and closed his eyes for a second. "Do you own anything that you saved from childhood?"

"My mother's picture. I also have her letters to my father, but I only found those after he died. And I have my mother's diary, but I can't open it, because the key's missing."

"Would you read her diary?"

She lifted her shoulders in a quick shrug. "I'll never know; without the key, what's to tempt me? Oh, yes. I have a book of poems that belonged to her."

"Do you like poetry?" he asked her, fishing for something that they might have in common.

"Oh, yes. I read poetry regularly. Nikki Giovanni, Paul Lawrence Dunbar, Elizabeth Barrett Browning, Poe, Shakespeare, Donne: all the great ones. I know many of their works by heart."

He leaned closer. *"Jenny kissed me when we met . . ."*

"Jumping from the chair she sat in . . ."

A smile floated over his face. *"How do I love thee?"*

She grinned. *"Let me count the ways."*

Her grin dissolved into a frown. "When I met you, I thought you were arrogant, authoritative, too macho to recite poetry with a woman."

He laughed a short, self-deprecating laugh. "That so? Are you in for a surprise! And I thought you were a woman who would step over everybody and anything in order to make her mark, though you soon disabused me of that. I also thought you were damned good-looking. But recite poetry? I would never have believed it."

"It's getting late, Justin."

"I know, but I don't care if you don't."

"I don't give a hoot."

The saxophone did their talking for them; they merely listened, and when the Zanzibar closed at one o'clock in the morning, Justin tipped the band leader and the bartender, took Regina's hand, and left. When he parked in front of her house, he gave her a gentle shake.

"Wake up, sleepyhead." He didn't want the temptation of carrying her into her house, so he gave her a good, solid shake.

"I wasn't asleep."

"Sure, you were." He went around and opened her door. "Are you awake now?" Assured that she was, he walked with her to her front door.

Maybe she didn't understand black male/female relations—though if they differed from relations between men and women of any other ethnic group in the country, he hadn't heard of it—but when they entered her house, he still had to get his cue from her.

She didn't keep him waiting. "I won't ask you to stay, because I don't think we've gotten that far, but I'd like a kiss."

There was something to be said for candor in a woman, but it spilled out of her like shock therapy. "All right," he said, barely able to contain the mirth, "but don't lay it on thick. Remember I'm not staying here tonight."

Her lips were soft and warm against his, and he could feel her hesitate, then ignore her good judgment and part her lips. She took him in, giving without reservation.

Finally, she returned him to himself. He observed her intently for a moment, summoned his willpower, and left. She didn't unleash her passion, and he discovered that the tender, sweet woman she showed him that night was much to his liking. And very dangerous. His mind's eye strolled over her, cataloguing her feminine assets, giving him reasons why he should have stayed. His mind told him that he was a fool to walk out of there. And I'd have been a fool to stay, he answered. Once they were back at the Craven, all that sweetness could evaporate like steam in a hot furnace. He wasn't getting cold feet. But that kiss she gave him had the power to make a man run, either to her or away from her, but it guaranteed he wouldn't stand still.

Regina was in no less a quandary than Justin. However, she didn't analyze her feelings but was more concerned about his, and worried as to whether he thought she behaved differently from other African-American women in the same circumstances. The next evening, she phoned Maude.

"Aunt Maude, do black men expect their women to level with them?" Before coming to New Bern, the question wouldn't have occurred to her. African Americans boasted about telling it like it was, but Native Hawaiians lived it every day.

"I don't know for sure, child, but I expect if you told it to them just like it is, most of 'em would keel over with a heart attack. What kind of honesty you talking about, anyway?"

"I went out with Justin last—"

"Wait a minute. Somebody's at the door."

With the receiver down, bits of the conversation drifted to her, and she hung up.

"Hello, Kitten."

"*Johann!* You could at least have called and let me know you were coming over." He brushed past her, shifting her emotions from excitement to annoyance. "In fact, you should have asked whether I'd be busy tonight."

His left eyebrow shot up with such speed that she took a step backward, for she remembered the folly of testing Johann's limits. "Is it customary in this country for a man to make an appointment to see his wife, the woman to whom he is legally married? Is it?"

"Well, no. But—"

"But nothing. You knew I was going to get tired of this. We did it your way, and now we're going to do it my way. I hate to leave Pop, because he's having the time of his life with me waiting on him hand

and foot, but you either act as if you're my wife or go out tomorrow morning and file for a divorce."

Maybe if she could force a smile, he'd soften up, but she was too scared to smile. If he walked out of there the way he came in, he wouldn't be back, and if he got what he came for, she'd be in a fix. Not knowing what else to do, she went on the attack.

"You're being unreasonable. You've written some kind of scenario in your mind, and I'm supposed to dance to that rhythm. You know I don't do that. I'm my own person."

He folded his arms across his chest and relaxed his stance. "Go on and stall, baby. I've got all night. What will it be? You and me together, or you here and me there?"

"Nothing's that simple. You can't either-or somebody's life." She was grabbing at straws, but he had the advantage, and she suspected he knew it. "I wasn't happy in Amsterdam."

He moved closer, as if to make certain that she not only heard his words but experienced the emotion that accompanied them. "I am not talking about Amsterdam, so please don't mention it again. You act as if the world consists of nothing but Amsterdam and Jurassic Park." As he gazed down at her, she saw no warmth in his green eyes, only steely determination.

Her mind conjured up the canals that crisscrossed Amsterdam, the bridges spanning them, and the expensive houseboats docked along their edges. And she remembered the chill of the North Sea in summer as well as winter, and the weeks without sunshine. He moved closer, effectively pinning her to the wall, but he didn't put his hands on her.

"You stop crowding me. You hear?"

The smile on his face was devoid of warmth, put there merely to knock her off balance. "You don't like being close to me? What happened, Kitten? You used to delight in getting me as hard as possible and inside of you with breakneck speed. Out of practice?" His fingers skimmed her shoulders, and his lips burned her neck.

"Move. I'm not going to let you seduce me."

"In that case, you don't have anything to worry about," he murmured as his mouth moved down to her cleavage. He looked up at her with a grin on his face. "Nothing's changed, Kitten. Pretend all you want to. And stop wasting time. When you opened that door and saw me, you knew that tonight you'd go to sleep with me inside of you."

"I didn't know . . . Johann, take your hands off . . . Oh, my Lord."

He ignored her protest, and why shouldn't he? To her own ears its

feebleness was laughable. He made short work of it and within minutes had her clamoring for him.

In her bedroom, he threw back the covers on her queen-size bed,
stripped her, and placed her between the sheets. Her mind had turned
off and she lay there, looking up at him, ashamed of herself for her
weakness, her lack of resolve.

"The world's not coming to an end, Kitten; for us, it might be starting to turn for good."

"I know. It's just that—"

"I love you, and I've had a hell of a hard time without you." He
began to peel off his clothes. "You're not leaving me again, if I have to
hook a chain to you." His flattened lips emphasized his harsh facial
expression.

"You've got me here. Why are you making me wait?"

"How does it feel to be on fire, to want like hell to—"

She grabbed at the sheet. "I'm getting up from here. I'm . . ."

With one knee on the bed, he pushed her back down and, with his
mouth as his weapon, started his demon assault on her body, from her
hard nipples to her seething vagina. And he lingered there, controlling
her, reminding her of who he was. Lingered until he forced her surrender.

Hours later, exhausted and locked firmly to him, she wanted to
talk but didn't know where to begin. He rolled over until she was on
top of him.

"I want it this way, too, Kitten."

"Some other time. I'm pooped."

Laughter rumbled in his throat. "It's good when we're together,
isn't it? Don't be so stubborn. Admit it."

"It's good. It's always been good, and I . . . Well, I missed you. But
Johann, much as I loathed being away from you, I was content here
with my folks. I hated being different and not knowing what people
really thought of me. The awful climate didn't help. I can't live there,
and I won't."

A grin split his face, and she realized that nothing she said would
interfere with the happiness he felt right then. And why not? Hadn't
she abandoned herself to him more wantonly than their first time,
when, in too much of a hurry to walk to his bed, he had claimed her
body on his dining room table?

"I thought it was not having any collards, and I was planning to
get some seeds here and plant some. Pop said they love cool weather
and don't need sunshine."

"What? My father needs a lesson in minding his own business."

"It's his nature. He meddles in my business, too. Thinks it's his right. There's hardly anything about me that he doesn't know. Asked me how much I was worth, and I did my best to give him an accurate figure."

She didn't believe it. *"In US dollars?"*

"Of course not. Dutch guilders, for heaven's sake."

The wicked Johann that she loved. Peals of laughter escaped her. *I'm happy*, she said to herself. *When I can laugh like this, I'm happy.* "You devil. Pop's not crazy."

"Yeah. He let me know it, too. Still pooped? I'm going to refresh your memory about a lot of things you've forgotten." As he had predicted, she awoke the next morning flat on her back, with Johann van der Kaa buried within her.

"Now what?" she asked him after he showered and dressed.

"I have to fix Pop's breakfast. See you tonight at the Craven."

She didn't hit him with the urn that rested on the floor at her feet, because she couldn't lift it. "You just dug a hole for yourself," she told him.

He shook his head. "You're interested in what happens now, but I'm after higher stakes. I'm playing for keeps, and I know you well enough to realize that this one evening with you didn't change your mind about our future. It just reminded you how much you like what I do to you. If I got a plane tomorrow, it wouldn't occur to you to go with me."

She tightened the robe around her and adjusted the belt. "So this is a game."

"You know better than that. It's our lives that I'm trying to recover, and I don't intend to fail."

She didn't wonder at his self-confidence; after what she'd done the previous night and again that morning, he'd be justified in preening like a peacock. The ball was in his court because he'd put it there, and she had no option but to see what he'd do next. She hoped Regina would make the effort to understand Justin as she did Johann; if she didn't know the man, she would be in bed sobbing. But she knew him, had given him what he wanted and needed, and had no doubt that he'd be back.

Regina and Justin had no such confidence in their knowledge of each other. Even then, Justin sat on an American Airlines flight to Baton Rouge, musing about his lack of understanding of Regina and fearing that their relationship would die for want of nourishment. For although he doubted he would admit it to her, something about her warmth and fire made his daily grind more tolerable, and he'd give a lot to be alone with her for the next few days rather than in Baton Rouge with his relatives.

At the airport, he took possession of the car he'd rented, and headed for what some people would call home, but it had never been that to him. After losing his father to a hunting accident when he was five, his childhood somehow disappeared. As he grew older, he saw in his mother an inability to stand up to her parasitic relatives and disabuse them of the notion that they had an entitlement to equal shares of her husband's and his father's estate. His mother's career as a lawyer netted her a good income, which she handled judiciously, and her family decided she didn't need the money from her husband's life's earnings. Over the next two days, he would hear their reasoning, pleading, and begging for the nth time, and he would hear the same when next he visited his mother.

The closer he got to Seventy-eighth Avenue, the heavier the feel of his chest. He aligned the car with the curb in front of the green-shuttered yellow house, a four-sided structure with an open court in the center. In his estimation, its swimming pool was the only good thing about the place.

Simone Duval stood at the front door, her face bright with a smile and her arms open. Every time he came home, she greeted him that way, and he couldn't figure out why, as soon as he left Baton Rouge, he didn't remember how warm and loving his mother was. He wrapped his arms around the tiny woman who gave him life, lifted her, and hugged her.

"It's so good you're home."

"Why? Some problems?" There were always problems with that bunch.

Her shrug indicated acceptance of whatever it was. "Your aunt Jo thinks Oleana should give up entitlement to what she gets from her father's estate, and Oleana stopped speaking to her."

"Good for her. Aunt Jo has nothing to do with my sister, and I'll . . . Mama, why can't this family get along like people in other families? I get tired of this bickering."

"Oh, son, it seems that way because you're not here, and you don't know all the fun we have, the way we support each other and love each other. You're only aware of the negatives."

He had a hard time believing that. "Really! I'd appreciate it if Aunt Jo would find a way to show her love for me that didn't involve phoning me to complain about you and my sister. I don't need that kind of love."

"Don't let Jo get next to you. She's lonely."

"I can see why. Who'd want a steady diet of her negative attitude? How's Uncle Jack?"

"Great. He caught a twenty-four-pound striped bass, and it made all the papers. Can't get within two feet of him, he's swollen up so big."

"Ah, Mom. You shouldn't speak that way about your older brother. If I caught a bass that big, I'd swell up, too." She walked with him to the big country-style kitchen. "Sit down, why don't you, and I'll get you something to eat. Those airlines don't serve enough to fill up a flea."

"If they served more, I wouldn't eat it."

She put a shrimp salad, pumpernickel bread, and coffee in front of him and sat down. "Have you found a nice girl? I want to see some grandchildren before I die, and Oleana isn't even thinking about getting married."

He tasted the shrimp salad and let a smile float over his face. "This alone is worth coming home for. It's second only to your chili con carne."

"Bring a girl to see me, and I'll teach her how to make that and the chili, too. Don't they have nice girls up there?"

How much should he tell her? He didn't want to raise her hopes. "I met someone, but the relationship doesn't move. We're combatants at work; then we smooth it out, and . . ." He threw up his hands. "I don't know. Maybe nothing will come of it."

"Maybe not. Still, next time you come, bring her to see me, and I'll let you know whether anything will come of it."

By the end of the weekend, he'd spoken with over one third of his nearly one hundred relatives and managed to ask several of the married couples why they stayed together if they didn't like each other. None of them understood the question, and he stopped trying to understand *them.*

"You can't say you didn't enjoy the barbecue," Simone said to him Sunday afternoon as he was about to leave. "And you and Jack caught a lot of fish. I know you missed seeing Oleana, but you didn't seem to mind spending a few minutes with your aunt Jo. Did you? They're wonderful people, Justin. I don't know if I'd ever want to be away from them."

"Then why do they always act out when I'm here? Aunt Lucienne upset Aunt Jo by telling her she has Alzheimer's, and Aunt Jo told Uncle Jack he fishes all the time because he's lazy and likes sitting down doing nothing. And she had the crust to tell me I'm just like him.

"When I could get away from *her,* I stopped by Cousin Rex's house. He was working on his daily newspaper column, and his kids were in the next room throwing everything they saw at each other. I walked in there and said, 'Stop it!' You could have heard a pin fall. Rex is so used to it, he didn't hear a thing. Sorry, Mama. It's not for me."

"What you just told me doesn't have a thing to do with love, and if you ever get any children, you'll believe me. No matter how it looks to you, son, we love each other. When one of us needs something, everybody is there to help."

She wanted him to love his family, and he wished he could. "Mama, I had a wonderful time. Don't worry; I'll come see you no matter how badly they behave."

She kissed his cheek. "Have it your way."

He hugged her. "I'll call you when I get home."

"What's her name? Bring her to see me."

"Who? Oh, you mean Regina? I might, if she's willing and if she can get away for an entire weekend." Then maybe she'd get off his case about closer ties with his family.

"What does she do?"

"She manages the newest and most elegant hotel in Eastern North Carolina. And she's good at what she does. Very good." The amount of pride he felt as he spoke amazed him.

"I see. So she manages the hotel that you furnished. And you're at each other's throats. Right?"

He looked down at her and at the grin on her face. "What's so great about that?" he asked her.

"If she's half as hotheaded as you are, it ought to get pretty explosive. You bring her to see me."

"I'll give it due consideration. That's all I can promise. I like her a lot, and that in itself is a problem."

Nine

Regina stared at herself in the mirror, a recent habit that served only to make her unhappy. She'd give anything if she could comb her hair and rouge her lips without looking into a mirror; having a double wouldn't aggravate her so much if she knew why—or such were her thoughts that morning. She finished dressing and, feeling the need for a good scream, was in the act of telephoning Juliet when she remembered Herbert Smith's reaction to her previous call. She didn't want to risk speaking with him again, so she slammed down the receiver, got her briefcase, and headed to work. As she drove along the wide street, observed the early morning sprinters and their self-satisfied expressions, she wondered, not for the first time, why Juliet didn't approach her for an understanding of their improbable likeness. Didn't she care? *Or did she know the answer?*

No light shone beneath Justin's office door, and her thoughts shifted to his weekend and how he had fared with his relatives. She busied herself signing contracts with a fraternity organization and a lawyers' group, obligating them to hold their conventions at the Craven for the next three years. She'd have her first experience with a big convention in early April, but the lawyers and fraternity brothers would be the first African Americans to hold conventions in New Bern.

"That's the way to do it," Abner had said when she told him how proud she was of that coup. "Next, you have to obligate 'em to come back again and again." The fraternity guaranteed two thousand guests, but even as she signed the contract, joy eluded her, for Juliet's face stared at her from the page.

Wanting advice on what she might do about Juliet, she telephoned Harold, and his failure to answer piqued her further. She needed resolution, any kind, so she phoned Cephus at the governor's mansion. After what seemed an eternity, he answered.

"Pearson speaking."

What could she say to him that wouldn't seem trite? "Cephus, this is Regina Pearson. Have you got a minute?"

"Uh . . . Sure. What brought this on?"

She related her conversation with Herbert Smith. "Where could Juliet be?"

"Oh, I wouldn't worry." His tone carried an air of superiority that nettled her. "She's probably on assignment somewhere. She's a reporter, you know."

From the recesses of her mind emerged Harold's description of Cephus as "an outsized ass." What right did he have to patronize her? "I know Juliet's an editor for the local paper, Cephus. But if she's on assignment, wouldn't her husband know that?"

The sound of him sucking his teeth was so loud that she didn't doubt he intended for her to hear it. "Herbert is lucky her last name is Smith. Like I said, don't sweat it."

Alarmed at his lackadaisical attitude, she asked him, "Don't you care that her husband doesn't know where she is? Something could have happened to her. From what Harold said, I thought the two of you were close friends."

He obviously disliked the question. "Why would Harold know who my friends are? I certainly don't hang out with *him*. Juliet uses me, and I use Juliet. Neither one of us is stupid enough to believe there's anything more to it than that. Close friends, we definitely are not."

For a long minute, she heard only silence, so she thanked him and ended the conversation. "I'm sorry I disturbed you, Cephus, but if you hear from her, give me a call at my office."

"No problem. Sooner or later, they all come to me for help."

Outsized ego, too. If Cephus thought of her as his cousin, he was careful not to communicate that to her, Regina mused. "Harold's description of you fits like a glove," she said aloud after hanging up. Nobody had to tell her that Cephus Pearson would never occupy a warm spot in her heart. She remembered that Juliet was not related by blood to Harold and Cephus, and rationalized that as a source of the man's indifference. On the other hand, she could find no explanation for Maude's apparent unconcern about Juliet's whereabouts.

"Maybe she's somewhere floating down to earth," Maude said when Regina visited her that evening. "Gravity's pretty persistent, so I expect she'll eventually land. I'm not worrying my head over Juliet Smith's weird behavior. I long ago stopped stressing out over other people's craziness. I care, but I don't let it kill me."

"Me neither," said Odette, who had stopped by to see Maude after leaving work. "Juliet's the last person I'm gonna get myself worked up over. You take it from me, girl. Juliet doesn't care about a soul but herself."

She resisted reminding Maude that Juliet was her niece, and in view of their attitude toward Juliet, she didn't dare contemplate the reaction of her relatives if she was missing.

"She ain't cutting out on Herbert, is she?" Odette asked neither of them in particular. "She never wastes her precious time speaking to anybody she considers beneath her, and from what I can tell, not many people are on her level. So if she's fooling around, the man's gotta be mighty high up."

Maude pulled on her cigar until she got a good puff, then rubbed its tip in the ashtray. "You're guessing, Odette. Don't start that tale. Nobody ever heard of Juliet doing anything like that, so don't lie on her just because you don't like her."

Odette threw up her hands. "She practically stepped on me at the Craven's opening, and that wench didn't say one word."

Maude rolled her eyes to the ceiling. "Probably scared you were about to ask her to 'give you a little something.' If she'd stopped for a second, you'd have had your hand out, and don't say you wouldn't have."

Regina had to laugh at Odette's shrug, slow and eloquent. "No, indeed, I wouldn't. She poorer'n I am."

Maude eyed Odette from beneath lowered lashes. "So is practically everybody else in New Bern, except maybe the owners of Pepsi Cola. You make sixty or seventy thousand a year and you get that much begging, plus you don't pay tax on what you get panhandling."

"Now, Maude, you ought to be ashamed of yourself. I don't do nearly that well."

Regina could feel her eyes stretching. "You mean . . . ?" she sputtered. "And I gave you five dollars. I want my money back."

Odette showed her flawless white teeth between curved lips, and a deep dimple dotted her left cheek as she laid her head to the side and looked at Regina. "Did I look like I was suffering? That was your ego working, honey. I stick my hand out, and that's all people see. A man put a ten-dollar bill in my hand once, and I had on a new fur coat. Of course, it *was* kind of cold that day."

"But what about the indignity of begging?" Regina asked her.

"What indignity? When I get in my Mercury Sable, drive to my white brick town house, relax in the Jacuzzi in my bathroom or the sauna in my basement, girl, indignity don't exist. In the summer, I sit out on my sun deck, smell the magnolia blossoms, and look at the crape myrtle in my garden. If that ain't dignity, there ain't none. You go ahead and worry about indignity." She treated them to a hearty laugh.

"People just look at your hand. They scared to look in your face for fear they might see a little misery, scared they might feel something. All these years I been putting my hand out, not a single person who gave me money ever said a word to me. Not even 'dog.' " She leaned back in the chair and closed her eyes. "Except you, Regina."

"How can you beg when you don't need it?" Regina asked her.

Odette allowed herself a shrug. "I provide a service. A lot of people are bent over with guilt about something. They see a beggar and put out fifty cents or a dollar and feel righteous for a couple of days. I help 'em get rid of their guilt."

Regina asked Odette what kind of work she did. "I'm a paralegal, the only one in town, and I charge these lawyers according to their ability to pay. 'Course what I just told you ain't none of their business."

Maude went into the kitchen and returned with a bottle of Heineken and two cups of tea. "You're improving, Regina," she said. "When you first came here, you wouldn't have asked Odette what kind of work she did."

"She got rid of that wilting-violet stuff, too," Odette said in a tone of approval. "I was noticing that crust beginning to form around the edges. Found yourself a man yet?"

Regina bristled at the question. "I haven't been looking for one."

"That fellah who had you locked to him at the Craven's opening wasn't fooling. If he's any good in the sack, I'd latch on to that one. Is he?"

Regina uncrossed her legs and was in the act of standing, ready to leave, when Maude began laughing as if she bordered on hysteria.

"I don't see a thing funny," Odette said. "If a woman doesn't make that a primary consideration when she's choosing a man, she's out of her mind."

"I have to go," Regina said. "I have an appointment with a client."

Odette ignored her. "I don't want a man who embarrasses me. He has to be clean and neat and able to talk about something other than *Superman* and *The Survivors.* Soon as I get that settled, he's got to know his way around a woman's body. Inside and out. And I ain't giving no lessons in sex. If he needs instructions, he can damned well go to somebody else's school."

"Amen," Maude said, "and I don't want no guy with a little old diploma; he's gotta have a doctorate in the philosophy of what makes a woman fly."

"You tell it, girl," Odette said. She realized Regina wasn't entering into the conversation. "What's the problem, girl?" she asked Regina.

Regina thought for a moment. "Where I grew up, people don't talk about sex, so I'm just not used to it. They have no hang-ups about it, as people do here, but they don't discuss it. To them, it's one of life's needs, like eating and breathing."

Maude rubbed her forehead as if bemused, but it was soon clear that she wasn't. "We know it's one of life's essentials, Regina, but let me tell you: if you're in bed with a man and you can't discuss what's going on between you, you got a problem. And you should be able to discuss most anything with your aunt and your first cousin, too. You're in Black America now. We talk about everything."

Her feet seemed to weight her down, dragging as she left Maude's and walked to her car. She'd been a misfit for as long as she'd known herself. No matter how much the Native Hawaiians tried to make her feel that she was one of them, accepted and loved, she always saw herself as an alien among them. And at times, two or three words from her blood kin gave her the same feeling that she didn't belong. She told herself to loosen up, that finding common ground with her people would take time. It was the only solace she could grasp.

The next evening, Lucien Hayes, CEO of Hayes Medical and Optical Instruments, stood as she approached him in the Starlight Lounge, where he had suggested they meet. She hadn't previously been introduced to him, although she had corresponded with him by mail and telephone.

"I want to see the suite before I make an offer," he said, settling down to business at once in a show of professionalism that she appreciated. "For the kind of money you're asking, I have to be cautious."

If only Justin had started furnishing it! "It isn't furnished, so you won't be able to discern its potential."

He leaned toward her in an aggressive stance. "I don't want it furnished. I want it done to my specifications."

Now what? Justin was closemouthed about that suite, and she had no idea how the place looked. She tapped her fist gently on the arm of her chair. "All right. Would you like an appointment with the man who designs the hotel's furnishings and interiors?"

Hayes shook his head and flattened his lips, his jaw working in a show of vexation. "If he's here, yes. But I decide tonight or never."

With no choice but to phone Justin and pray that he was still in his office, she took out her cellular phone and dialed his number.

"Duval. How may I help you?"

"Hello, Justin. It's my good luck that you're in your office this evening." Her words and tone carried a formality to indicate that she wasn't alone.

"What's up?"

She told him what Lucien Hayes wanted. "He's interested in the twenty-ninth floor."

"He'll see walls, parquet floors, and some sketches. That's all."

She had to go with that. If Hayes didn't like what he saw, she'd lose the sale; if she didn't show it to him, she'd lose. "Can you meet us up there in, say, four or five minutes?"

The short silence suggested that he hesitated. "Sure. You all right?"

"Yes. Thanks. See you in a minute."

She introduced them. "Colonel Duval designs all of the Craven's furniture and interiors."

The man looked Justin up and down. "How'd you get to be a colonel?" Wasn't it just like those Southerners to ask an African-American man a personal question!

"Long story," Justin said. As they toured the suite, he showed the sketches for each room and outlined his plans for wall and floor coverings. Then he stuck his hands in his pockets, slouched against the wall, and looked at Hayes.

"How does that square with what you had in mind?"

Hayes contemplated the question, rubbing the fingers of his left hand over his left eyebrow as he did so. "Man, you're way ahead of me. Go on and do your thing." He turned to Regina. "When can I get a contract?"

"We can stop by my office on the second floor, and I'll have it ready in minutes." She walked over to Justin. "How much time do you need?"

"I'd say mid-October occupancy. Give me a call when you finish that."

Half an hour later, swelling with joy and pride at having sold her biggest and most expensive suite, she telephoned Justin.

"I don't know how to thank you for—"

He interrupted. "Then don't. It's my job."

"Look, I'm sorry I've been giving you such a hard time about those three suites. From now on, I'm going to do as Pop said and mind my own business."

"Really? I don't think I'll be able to stand it. Did you eat?"

"Not yet."

"Can I feed you?"

"Your place or mine?" That sounded suggestive, but what the heck! She felt expansive.

His laughter held a wolfish insinuation. "Uh . . . I was thinking of Drake's, but if that's the way you want to go, baby, I'm right with you." His laugh, seductive and challenging, startled her.

"Are we talking about the same thing?" she asked.

"You bet we are. And get rid of your notions about who Justin Duval is."

Before she could think of an answer, she heard the dial tone. A little afraid and thoroughly excited, she couldn't move from her chair. He tapped and opened the door almost simultaneously, and she figured her eyes doubled in size when she saw the rough and determined expression on his face. In seconds he pulled her out of the chair and into his arms. When she opened her mouth to protest, his tongue found its home there. She wanted more and didn't bother to hide her reaction to him as he introduced her to gentle, tender loving.

"Do you want to go home with me?" he asked, still holding her close and rubbing her back.

She wished he hadn't asked her. If he had simply taken her hand and said, "Let's go," she would have gone with him. She didn't know how to explain it, even to herself. It seemed too premeditated, not natural. She told him the truth.

"Yes, I want to, but when the time is right, you won't have to ask me."

He gazed down at her, and she realized he understood what she hadn't managed to say. "Next time, I'll make certain that the setting is right. That's what you need, isn't it?"

She nodded. "I think these things should be the natural evolution of emotions, feelings. Am I making myself clear?"

"You bet. Let's eat in the dining room downstairs. It's getting too late to go to Drake's." He closed her office door and stood looking down at her. "I realize I'm just beginning to understand you. When we get things here under control, let's take some time for ourselves. How about it?"

She regarded him closely, wanting to make certain she got his message. Warmth sparkled in his eyes, but he didn't smile. She took his free hand and started for the stairs that would take them to the lobby.

"I'd like that," she said. "I'd like it a lot."

Regina talked about herself without disclosing herself, but Justin wanted and needed more. He might be foolish, and chances were, he'd be sorry, but he needed the whole woman. And he longed to be himself with her, not the colonel whom nothing fazed, cool and indifferent. That was the shell given him by the United States Army, and he'd worn it so long that a part of it fitted him, but he wanted her to see the man inside it, to accept and enjoy that man.

They took a table for two away from the bandstand, and he breathed deeply in relief when he saw that the band was on a thirty-minute break. He didn't want the distraction of music, not even good music.

"What brought on this somber expression?" he asked Regina. "I can't keep up with these mood changes." In less than five minutes, she'd folded up.

"You're one to talk. When did you get back to New Bern?"

He was not in the mood for banalities and said as much. Maybe he was fed up with the superficiality of his relations with his family, or perhaps tired of the emptiness, the wasteland that was his life. He was reaching out to her, knew it, and knew he'd have to take the consequences.

"Open up, Regina. For God's sake, let me in. It isn't when I got back here, but what happened to me while I was there, en route, and on my way back that matters. Regina, I am up to here"—he sliced the air over his head—"with problems, good and bad habits, attitudes, and . . . hell, I'm a man who needs to be accepted and understood for what he is.

"For practically all of the last twenty or so years, I've had nothing but window dressing, meekness, and obeisance from grown men forced to acquiesce to authority. Yes, sir, Colonel Duval. No, sir, Colonel Duval. Whatever you say, Colonel Duval. I want some honesty. Some in-your-face truth. If you don't like what I say or do, tell me; dammit, care about me. Ask me if I ache, if I ever stole anything. Hell, ask me when I last slept with a woman, but don't ask me when I got back here."

He'd seen her wide-eyed before, but not along with a sagging lower lip and suspended breathing. He'd shocked her—maybe that was his purpose—but until she reacted to the pain that had just poured out of him, he wouldn't say one word. He waved the waiter away.

"Do you . . . feel this way all the time?" He watched, horrified, as tears pooled in her eyes. "I didn't realize that you hurt so badly. You look to me like a man who has the world by the throat. Every act, word, and gesture controlled." Her voice lowered to a whisper. "If we were somewhere else, I'd . . . I'd hold you."

"Being a man doesn't mean I'm all-powerful or that I don't bleed." He caught himself when he heard his words chiding her as he'd once chastened his ex-wife. He hoped his resentment toward Miriam hadn't influenced his outlook or his relationship with Regina. If he allowed that to happen, he would victimize himself.

She wiped tears with the back of her hand. "I'm so used to keeping my emotions in check that I . . . I don't know how to express what I feel right now."

He leaned toward her. Waiting. Hoping. She reached for his hand, held it, and at last asked him, "What happened to you this past weekend?"

The long, deep breath he took was commensurate with the relief he felt. "Same old, same old, but this time I cared. Your longing for the love of your family must have rubbed off on me. This time, I wanted more from them, from all of my relatives, but I didn't know how to lead them to offer more. "He shook his head. "Maybe I've been apart from them so long that we have nothing in common."

As if traumatized by his words, she stared at him for a long minute; then he could see her relax, could tell that she'd given in to whatever emotion or thought she'd wanted to resist.

"I've been so wrapped up in my own concerns that I haven't noticed your reaching out to me. You want us to be friends as well as . . .
as—"

He finished it for her. "As lovers. Yes. Plain old sex alone no longer
works for me. Hell, maybe I'm in a midlife crisis. I'm almost forty, and
the silver eagle on my army uniform is all I've got to show for it."

Her face bore the look of one suddenly aware, awakening, as it
were, from an intellectual slumber. "I've always felt something lacking
between us. Something important." She appeared to consider her
words. "Except that time when you came to my house and showed me
such tenderness."

As if a peaceful feeling stole over her, she smiled. "I had a similar
feeling when Pop put his arms around me that day I barged in on him."

It came back to him then—the sense of drifting from the time of his
father's death. He idolized his father, but his memory of him had
dimmed until he could no longer remember his father's face, not even
with the aid of the many photographs his mother kept.

He brought his thoughts to the present. "Growing up without a
mother and with an undemonstrative father, you didn't learn how to
share yourself."

"No, I suppose not. If I had, maybe being Juliet Smith's double
wouldn't upset me the way it does." She released his hand and spread
both of hers in a gesture of helplessness. "Justin, nobody seems to
know where she is."

"Isn't she married. Did you ask her husband?"

He listened to her story of Juliet and the reaction of her husband,
her relatives, and alleged friends to the question of Juliet's whereabouts and wondered whether Regina saw a lesson in their attitudes.

"If she and her husband had a spat, his reaction is understandable,
but the others . . . they don't make sense. Did you speak to your grandfather about it?"

"I don't want to upset him. Besides, he said that, except for her
television appearances, he hadn't seen her in a couple of years. If you
call her office at the paper, you're invited to leave a message on her answering machine."

After they ordered a light supper, he said, "I'd like to help you
with this problem of Juliet if I can. Are you concerned about her because you want to be friends, or what?"

"I don't know if we can be friends, but I want to know why we look alike. Pop told me to leave it alone, but I can't. I'm wondering if Juliet can explain it. If not, she ought to be as concerned as I am."

He'd keep his views on that to himself. "I'd say the best chance of finding her is through her husband. If he's uncooperative, tell him why you're looking for her. That'll pique his interest."

They finished the meal and left the hotel. He parked behind her when they reached her house, thinking that he would walk with her to her door, tell her good night in some fashion or another, and go home. But when they got out of their cars, she suggested that they walk.

"I always loved the nights. From my bed, I heard the lapping of the ocean waves, and I would open the window shutters wide and let the moonlight pour in. Nights in Honolulu were magic. My imagination took me all over the world, and when I was older, I would fantasize about hosting parties for my hundreds of relatives, attending weddings and family reunions. At those times, my world was perfect."

Their steps took them to the banks of the Neuse River, where, in the bright moonlight, they found a boulder and huddled close in the night's chill. "Did you dream the world as you wanted it to be?" she asked him.

"I lost myself in books," he said, recalling the day he discovered both Langston Hughes and Countee Cullen. "They gave me a freedom from family and friends and from the turmoil that had inserted itself into my life. They made me want to be my own man, to become someone important."

"Then you must be satisfied, because you succeeded in that admirably."

He didn't know how long they sat there, holding hands but rarely speaking. He didn't mind the silence; she had shared something important with him: loneliness was her childhood companion, as it had been his, and deep down inside it still hounded her. If they were to have a meaningful relationship, he had his job cut out.

Whatever he'd expected, it wasn't the quick kiss on his lips just before she inserted her key into her front door. "I've got a lot of work to do on my feelings and . . . maybe on myself. This evening with you . . . well, I guess it broadened my knowledge of you and my understanding of myself." The back of her hand skimmed over the side of his face. "Good night."

*   *   *

As he prepared for their meeting with James Carlson the next morning, he heard her enter her office and wondered if her night had been anything like his. Hours of self-searching, of reliving the past and guessing the future. Resenting the intrusion, he let the phone ring several times before answering.

"Duval speaking. Yes, sir," he said to the general. "I'm a little rusty, but if you think you need a civilian for that lecture, I can do that." He listened to his mentor, the officer who pinned the first bar to the epaulets of his uniform. "Thank you, sir. I'll be there day after tomorrow."

He hung up and pondered the effect that two weeks away from his work at the Craven would have on Regina's mid-October deadline. He'd make it by the skin of his teeth, but he'd keep his promise.

"Sleep well?" he asked her as they walked together to James's office.

"Fair. Too many things on my mind and in my head."

"Tell me about it!" He waited to see where she'd sit, and as he expected, she sat at James's right, half facing him. Talk about self-confidence! On her, that show of self-possession didn't grate on his nerves; Regina did everything with class. If she told you what for, she handed it to you with elegance and style. He sat at James's left and dropped the bomb he knew would set her off.

"I'll be away for two weeks starting day after tomorrow. As a reservist, the army may call me whenever I'm needed."

She jumped to her feet. "What are you doing to me?"

The fire in her eyes, the bent of her shoulders, her whole demeanor shouted to them that she was spoiling for a fight. He ignored her signals. "I'm not doing anything to you."

"Don't tell *me* you're not. When will the manufacturer make the furniture?"

He prepared himself for a harangue of major proportions. "It's mostly upholstery. I'm finishing the wooden pieces by hand." Suddenly, he bristled at her effrontery in attacking him in James's presence. "Anyway, it's my worry, not yours. It'll be ready for occupancy the fifteenth of October, and you can get strident with me when I fall down on my job. Not before."

She fastened her knuckles to her hips and seemed to strengthen her stance. Her expression could only be described as furious. "You know how important this is to me, Justin. I told you Hayes reserved the right to break the contract if he can't move in according to the terms. You knew this last night, and you buttered me up to . . . to—"

"To what? What did I do to you? I don't recall a damned thing happening between you and me that would fall in the category of buttering. I bought you an eleven-dollar supper of shrimp and salad and walked down to the river with you. If you call that soft soap, I'd like to know where you've been for the last forty years. Believe me, I can be a lot more devious than that." He looked at James. "Would you mind postponing this meeting?"

James tapped his pen on his desk several times, sat back in his chair, and made a pyramid of his ten fingers. "I'm not postponing the meeting. I thought the two of you had worked out your problems and gotten rid of your animosity. Where will you be if we need to consult you, Justin?"

"Camp Lejeune. About an hour away."

A puzzled expression clouded James's face. "But that's the Marine Corps base, isn't it?"

"Yes. All branches of the service are participating in the workshop. The idea is to enlighten the average citizen about the service. Most of it will be televised."

James looked at Regina, and a smile settled around his mouth. "It won't be easy, but we'll get along without him, won't we Regina?"

"Absolutely," she said, with not a little vehemence. James responded with a gale of laughter, irritating her further.

"We get on well most of the time," Justin said with his gaze on James, "but this work is stressful. An unremitting diet of it would break a Goliath."

"Speak for yourself," she said. "I'm looking forward to two weeks free of aggravation and angst."

He couldn't resist pulling her chain. "You definitely need more than two weeks of it, and I'm sorry I can't accommodate you. But you know how it is. If you don't need me for anything else, James, I'd better get busy."

James stood and draped an arm across Justin's shoulder. "Do what you have to do. See you when you get back."

He glanced toward Regina, hoping for a measure of accord, a truce, but she didn't look his way. His left shoulder rose in a quick shrug, "See you in two weeks," he said, and walked out.

Regina knew without looking at him that James Carlson had locked his gaze on her. *It's his move,* she said to herself.

And move, he did. "Is Justin Duval anything to you other than a coworker?"

"What?"

"I said—"

"I know what you said, and I can't imagine where that question came from."

He narrowed his eyes. "Let's not play games, Regina. Justin's an able man, and you are equally competent, but the two of you stab at each other like swordsmen. I want the answer to my question."

"Why do you think you're entitled to know? That's a personal question."

"It isn't a matter of entitlement. I *need* to know."

Enlightenment must have shown in her eyes, for he smiled in a diffident way. "Right. You didn't think Justin's the only man with eyes, did you?"

The man wasn't joking. "Yes, I did, and I still think so, James."

His smile suggested the cool acceptance of a man of the world. "Then do something about it. I've known him for about a year, and I hope to have him for a friend for the rest of my life. Now that we've got the record straight, how many people are you expecting in that convention next week?"

"Six hundred civil engineers and their spouses or significant others. It's my first, and I can hardly wait."

"Take my word. You'll be glad when they leave. I'm planning a hotel in Winston-Salem. Interested in getting it started? You'd only be away from the Craven for a few months."

"Who'll design the interior?"

"I believe in staying with a winning team."

Her eyes blinked several times, and she knew they betrayed her surprise. "Well, can you beat that? I'll think about it."

"Good. While you're doing serious thinking, consider a better relationship with Justin."

"And when you next speak with Justin, tell him to work on improving his relationship with me. It flows two ways."

"Yeah, but this thing between the two of you isn't much further along than it was when you met."

She observed his cool facade—an elegant man flawlessly dressed in that little town of 30,000 people—and decided she had to get one thing straight.

"If I had said there was something between Justin and me, how would you have responded?"

He had the look of a surprised man. "But your response was tantamount to acknowledging it. You didn't make me want to dance, but as I said, I expect to be friends with Justin for the rest of my life, and I don't care for unnecessary complications in my personal affairs."

"It must be wonderful to have the ability to turn your emotions and feelings off and on, up and down, like a blasted thermostat," she said, rising to leave and not bothering to hide her irritation. "Justin isn't bad at that, either. You two ought to get along like bubble and squeak."

"Yeah? Well, get your act together, and you and Justin will glide along like Mozart and the piano. Let me know soon about Winston-Salem."

"I'll do that." As she rode the elevator down to the second floor, she thought of Mozart and the exquisite music he produced for the piano. And she thought of James Carlson's admission of interest, of his veiled warning that if she reciprocated that interest—and she didn't— his loyalty to Justin took precedence. The two men had much in common, she mused; one had a black face and the other a white one, but in both, the brain ruled. If she worked at the hotel in Winston-Salem with Justin as its interior designer, what could prevent their becoming lovers? Never again would she let herself fall into a long-term affair.

Eager for another try at bringing her family together, Regina approached Harold in his dressing room before his show with Maude that evening. "Could you please give me a list of my relatives on my father's side? Aunt Maude only listed you, Cephus, and your sister, Jewel. Any more?"

"You're barking up the wrong tree, Cuz. Besides, they're scattered everywhere. I have an uncle somewhere in Mississippi, but I don't know his address. A long time ago, I heard he was a holy-rolly preacher in a rural church. Skip him. I'll get to hell soon enough without having him send me there prematurely." He dipped a brush into what she assumed was liquid powder and spread it lightly over his face. "For an audience, the only thing worse that a tone-deaf, incompetent musician is having to look at shine on some dude's face."

Standing behind him as he worked with the aid of the mirror, she got the impulse to hug him and did so. "I wish you would stop putting yourself down. You're my friend as well as my cousin, and I don't like your doing that."

He put the brush on the table and blotted his face with a handful of tissues. "At the risk of sounding silly, I'm tempted to tell you I love you. But I won't. If everybody was as naive as you, we'd all be as happy as little pigs in hog heaven. Wake up, Cuz, before somebody hurts you."

She sat at stage-side that night, and for the first time, she heard a sadness in Harold's music. She expected that in his gut-searing blues, but when Maude sang George Harrison's "Something," a sexy love song, his saxophone wrung tears from her eyes.

"What was Harold's problem tonight?" she asked Maude at the evening's end. "He made me cry, and the song wasn't a sad one."

"Me, too. At first, I thought Johann might have put him up to it, but he didn't. Maybe he's nursing a broken heart."

"I haven't met his girlfriend. Have you? What's she like?"

Maude tightened the black lace stole around her shoulders, exposed by the strapless red silk sheath. "No, I haven't, but underneath Harold's sometimes sophisticated, sometimes bitchy behavior, I suspect there's a man who does a lot of hurting."

"He snapped at me the last time I phoned him, and he hasn't apologized. When we talked tonight, you'd have thought it never happened."

Maude sipped her beer. "Too bad I can't have my cigar in this hallowed temple." She patted Regina's hand. "Don't worry about Harold. If you need a friend, he'll be the first person to show up." She finished her drink and stood. "Johann's coming for me, and I promised I'd be at the front lobby at eleven-fifteen."

"Hmmm. Talking about surprises! How's it going?"

Maude looked at her niece. "Repeat after me, Regina. Say, 'Aunt Maude, how are you and Johann getting along?' "

"What?"

"You heard me. I want you to ask me how I'm getting along with my husband. Any niece would ask her aunt that. You're making progress, but you've still got a long way to go."

"All right. How are you getting along with him?"

"That's better. It's hard to say. He took me to bed, had my head and the rest of me spinning like a top, and ever since, he's acted as if he were my big brother. I probably won't murder him, but you can bet I'll come close to it. He intends to bend me, but wait'll he finds out who's gonna bend." Regina smothered a laugh. From where she sat, Johann hadn't done any bending, but somebody had.

"You were so casual about Johann when he first arrived. I hope you aren't letting him get you down."

Maude signaled for the waiter. He had become accustomed to her habits and arrived at the table with a glass of Heineken. She thanked him and turned to Regina. "Get me down? Girl, that man addles my brain. Ten years with Johann, and every time is like the first time. Just thinking about how he loves me, how he makes every nerve in my body scream for joy . . ." She closed her eyes and shook her head as though unable to describe the power of the experience.

"What I gave up when I left him! And being without him! I wasn't crazy, either; I knew what I was doing. But Lord, the way he's acting . . ." She slapped her right thigh. "I just feel so . . . so plain unnecessary."

"I hope you two get it together, and soon."

"I don't know how soon it'll be. He's got my number, but I've got the music that makes him dance, and Johann van der Kaa knows it."

Regina marveled at so much fuss about nothing. Maude's husband knew what he was doing. Her thoughts reverted to the topic that claimed her attention most hours of the day: Juliet. "Aunt Maude, do you think I'll cause Juliet any trouble if I go to see her husband and ask where she is? This is a small town, and I wouldn't think anybody could hide here, but she's been missing eight or nine days, and I want to know where she is. I want this monkey off my back."

"What monkey are you talking about?"

"Who is this impersonator?"

"She's your cousin, and for heaven's sake don't suggest otherwise unless you want to cause, uh . . . uh . . . a volcanic eruption. Take my word, and don't go *there*."

"Harold said Herbert Smith is only here for two weeks, and she's been off somewhere the entire time. I want to see him before he goes back on his run."

"Go ahead. But watch your mouth. Once you say something, you can't take it back."

Harold walked out of the elevator as she entered it to go up to her little apartment. She thought he'd left the hotel nearly an hour earlier, but didn't say so. Instead, she asked him, "How much more time can you give us? James Carlson, the owner, wants you to stay as long as possible, and I do too."

"Another two weeks, Cuz. Then I have to play with the Fayette-ville Symphony Orchestra Sunday afternoons and evenings. That's when I'm happy. I'll be sure you know where to reach me. Keep it to yourself, now."

She thanked him. "I've decided to find Juliet and have a talk with her. She ought to be just as concerned about our likeness as I am."

"I don't expect you to take my advice, Cuz. But if I were in your shoes, I'd say ignorance is bliss. Sometimes knowing hurts a lot worse than not knowing. Don't forget that. Leave it alone, Cuz. See you to-morrow." He whirled around and bumped into a man. "Sorry." His eyebrows shot up. "Keep the faith, brother."

She didn't know what to make of that as Harold strode through the lobby toward the hotel's entrance. Maybe she ought to find someone to give her a course in men; except for Pop, the ones she knew in New Bern needed more understanding that she could apply. Harold had two or three different personalities, or at least it seemed that way to her. Justin thought nothing of taking time to popularize the armed forces, when meeting his deadline at the Craven would challenge three men. James was willing to have an affair with her, provided of course that he didn't offend Justin. And Johann took his wife to bed once, after she'd had a sexual hiatus of nearly two years, shook her out of contented abstinence, and then began acting as if he were her brother.

If I woke up in the morning and discovered I didn't need them, life would be so much simpler. I'd probably dance an Irish jig. But with Justin sabotag-ing my thoughts during the day and interfering with my sleep at night, there isn't a chance of that.

She walked into her apartment, got the telephone book, and made a note of Juliet Smith's home address. Herbert Smith might get testy, but the shock of seeing her would dilute that in a minute.

Ten

Regina didn't intend to let anything or anybody prevent her from seeing Herbert Smith that morning, so she hesitated to answer the phone, knowing the call would delay her.

"Regina Pearson speaking."

"Regina, the guest in room four-ten says her card key doesn't open her door. I reprogrammed the lock and gave her another key, but she still can't open it and claims she's scared to go in the room. She swears somebody tampered with the lock."

Why did she need an assistant if he couldn't solve the simplest problem? "It's easy, Larry. Go with her to the room, open the door, and walk around the room with her until she's satisfied no one's been there."

"I should shake my bottom for that dame just because she's too ignorant to open a door?"

"You will shake your bottom because you like your job. The Craven gives service and ensures the comfort of its guests. If you can't handle that, you should be assistant manager in a motor lodge. And Larry, smile and make her feel cherished."

"You should have put *obsequious* in the job description."

"Sorry. I forgot it. I'll be away for a couple of hours this morning."

"But what about the fresh flowers? The truck turned over when the driver was making rounds this morning. He didn't get hurt, but the florist doesn't have any more flowers to send us, and we—"

"Yesterday's flowers haven't wilted. Anything else?"

"Room seven-forty-six missed the Trolley Tour and wanted me to send her in a Craven limousine to catch up with it. I told her she missed the first fifty minutes of a sixty-minute tour, and I'd exchange her ticket for tomorrow's tour. She got mad and said some mean things about my parentage. You should give me a raise for not wringing her neck."

"You have my sympathy. Any other problems?"

"Not yet. Give it another ten minutes. I'm not happy, Regina. I graduated from hotel training school, and you're asking me to be a patsy for these people."

"Relax, Larry. Instead of that Dior blue suit you insist on wearing, put on a black suit, white shirt, and red bow tie, and with your six-feet-three-inch height, you'll look sharp. And then you'll *really* be able to look down on practically everybody. The women will fall all over you."

She knew she'd pleased him when he asked, "What about the men?"

"What do you want from me, Larry? I'm just a hotel manager." His laughter assured her that she'd left him in a good mood. She'd never known a man with a more volatile personality, unless it was Harold.

Looking at the pile of notices, memoranda, and assorted other papers on her desk, she had the urge to shove it all into the wastebasket. Unfinished business. A lot of unattained goals. That was her life. Forty years old, and what had she accomplished? The big, loving family she yearned for—her reason for pulling up stakes in Hawaii and coming to New Bern—was still a dream. More elusive, it seemed, with each passing day. She hadn't seen one-third of the relatives on Maude's list, though the whole town knew she wanted to meet them, and those kinfolk knew where to find her.

She made a few notes as to what she would say to Herbert Smith and prepared to leave her office. When she passed Justin's door, she didn't see a light. If he left New Bern without at least telling her goodbye, she wouldn't forgive him.

Justin didn't plan to leave New Bern without seeing Regina. He tried not to have loose ends either in his business affairs or his personal relations. He added a few touches of brick red to his design for the chili can and liked it. He could take it to Abner and Johann, but it was Maude's product. He phoned her.

"Maude speaking. How y'all doing this morning?"

"I finished the sketch for your chili cans," he said after greeting her, and I'd like you to see it before I show it to Johann and your father. You busy now?"

"Looks like they're really going to market this stuff. Of course, when Johann sets his mind to something, it's as good as done."

He had the same impression of the man. "In that case, why don't you give in and make it easier for him?"

In his mind's eye, he saw her hands go to her hips, much as his Aunt Jo did when she needed to win an argument. "Shame on you, Justin. My husband was born poor and worked hard for everything he got. And let me tell you, he's got plenty. And he doesn't have much use for people who don't earn their way. Does that sound like a man who'd appreciate something for nothing?"

He had to admit she was right. "Well, no, but you're waging a war."

"I'm being me and he's being himself. If I'm smart, we'll both get what we want. Come on over and let me have a look at those angels."

When Maude answered the door, his first thought was, *how old is this woman?* She looked forty-five, but he guessed she was near the age of Regina's mother.

"Y'all come on in. My husband and my rejuvenated father haven't asked me whether I wanted a gang of strangers eating my chili." A wistful expression settled on her face. "Maybe it won't sell. What do you think?"

"You couldn't be serious. I'll fill my pantry with it. That chili is good stuff. Anybody who buys it once will buy it again."

She looked at his design. "It's wonderful. Just wonderful."

"You're sure it suits you?"

"Yes, indeed, and I'll bet Pop will like it, too."

On his previous visit to Maude's home, he'd recognized a deep love between father and daughter. He saw it in Maude then—her pride in her father—and told himself not to be jealous. A man's children completed him. He didn't have that, and he needed it.

"What about Johann?"

"Oh, I'm not worried about him. He and Pop are wearing the same shoes these days, and Pop wants my chili in cans. They're like the Bobsey Twins: what one wants, the other wants."

"What shall we call the product?"

She fingered her chin for a few seconds, and a smile blazed on her face. "Abner's Perfect Chili Con Carne."

"Great. He'll love that. I'll be away for a couple of weeks. Take care."

He dialed Abner's number on his cellular phone, aware for the first time that he liked the old man, that he was glad for a reason to visit him again. He told Abner he'd like his opinion of the design. "If you're not busy right now, I'd like to show it to you."

"Busy?" Abner snorted. "Humph. I'm too old to be busy. If anybody wants my company, I give 'em as much as they like, provided they don't get on my nerves. We'll save you a cup of coffee."

Drinking coffee with Abner and Johann at the table in Abner's little kitchen brought home forcibly to Justin that he hadn't spent much time enjoying the casual company of men he liked. A good soldier obeyed the rules, and he'd wanted to be the best. So he'd been circumspect as an enlisted man and even more so as an officer, a trait that guaranteed he would walk alone. As the years went by, he became the man he projected himself to be, and only recently had he begun to reach back toward that kid who loved pranks, wild music, the latest dance craze, and off-color jokes. He could be himself with Abner and Johann because both were without affectation: what you saw was what you got.

"You been here twenty-five minutes, and you haven't showed us a thing," Abner said. "My eyes are itching for the sight of that logo. Hope you put some red in it."

He was getting used to Abner's crusty manners, the license of one who has lived long years and weathered many storms. "That's why I'm here, sir. But I didn't want to seem pushy."

"Pushy? Humph." He looked at Johann. "You know anybody here named 'Sir'?" Johann shook his head. "You call me Pop, Justin. The whole family calls me that."

The whole family, huh? He opened his briefcase and showed them the design. "What do you think? The name of the product will be printed in white in a semicircle over the top."

"That's fantastic," Johann said. "I ought to get you to redo the logos for my companies."

"Well, this is really something fine," Abner said, a wistfulness in his voice. "Can't you just see rows of those cans on the shelves of every supermarket? I sure didn't think you were going to turn out anything this nice. What'll we call it?"

"Maude said it'll be 'Abner's Perfect Chili Con Carne,' and I like that. Whatta you say?"

"Perfect," Johann said. "That's the only name for it."

A fullness lodged in his chest when he saw the tears hanging at the tips of Abner's sparse lashes, refusing to drop, as stubborn as he imagined Abner could be.

"She didn't have to do that," he said, "but it's just like her. Always good to her father."

Justin stood to leave. "Then Abner's Perfect Chili Con Carne it is." He didn't want to leave them and was about to sit down again when Abner squinted at him and said, "Anything happening between you and my granddaughter?"

His shrug didn't reflect his feelings. "Hard to say, Pop. I suggest you ask Regina. Frankly, I don't know. I'd like us to be more than we are, but we're like sailboats flailing around in a storm and unable to reach dry land. Her priorities are getting her family together and making the Craven Hotel the pride of North Carolina. Both worthy goals."

"Yeah. But they won't get me any great-grandchildren. What about your family? They don't live around here, so where are they?"

"Baton Rouge. A million of 'em, and except for my mother and my sister, I stay far away from 'em as much as possible."

"That's not so good. Families are important. Trouble is, they're like fudge: mostly sweet, but they always contain a few nuts. And it's the nuts that get in the cracks of your teeth."

"Even so, you're lucky you have them," Johann said. "Here with Pop, I'm enjoying the first father-son relationship I ever knew. He may never get rid of me."

"Humph. I won't be sending you anywhere." He winked at Justin. "He changed my life, even my breakfast. I haven't had so much energy in years. The more I see of Johann, the more convinced I am that my daughter doesn't row with both oars."

Justin released a chuckle. "My impression of Maude is that both of her feet are planted squarely on God's good earth."

Abner brushed his thin fingers over the stubble on his right cheek. "You young people are smarter than I was. You don't trifle over the senseless things we did when I was young. And what for? I refused my elder daughter—my firstborn and my heart—my blessings when she wanted to marry. I had reasons I couldn't mention, but people said I didn't want her to marry a light-skinned, Catholic man. It wasn't true. Well, she went with him anyway, and she was dead for thirty-eight years before I knew about it. Forty years after she left here, her only child is the joy of my life. Sometimes it nearly kills me to think my stubbornness caused me to miss Regina's childhood and her youth. I compounded it by refusing to meet her when she came here, but she's got my genes in her and wouldn't tolerate that."

Johann had been quiet, but it appeared that his mind had been at work. "What was wrong with your daughter's fiancé being light-skinned, Pop? I don't get it."

"When I was growing up, a lot of African Americans used white as their standards. Still do. You'd see newspaper ads for a 'mulatto' waitress, a light-skinned maid; the closer to white you were, the easier time you had getting a job or being accepted in certain social circles. Dark-skinned women worked as maids in movies and sang the blues on stage. The light-colored considered themselves better than the dark ones.

"Dark-skinned people looked down on the light-skinned folk as descendants of black slave women who slept with their slave masters. Of course, we always knew most of those women were forced to do it, but we still regarded their offspring as a bastard race. A whole lot of stupidness."

"How is it that you accept me?" Johann asked him.

Abner winked at Justin. "I liked the man I met in those letters you wrote me. Strong, determined, and purposeful. You're that way in person, too. Only kind of man Maude would ever get along with. Half the time, I forget you're white."

Johann stretched out his legs and locked his hands behind his head. "I'm not sure that's a compliment, but I don't suppose you care. How'd you like to go to the Netherlands with me? It only takes about six hours."

"I thought the Grand Canyon was next."

"Soon as our chili starts flowing into cans, we'll do whatever you like, but right now, Amsterdam is where my money is."

After another hour of bantering, Justin left Abner and Johann, surprised but pleased that they made him a partner in the venture. "van der Kaa, Witherspoon, Witherspoon, and Duval" sounded good, but he'd have been happy to have as compensation a continuing supply of Abner's Perfect Chili Con Carne.

He passed his own office and knocked on Regina's door, and when she didn't answer he checked with Larry, learned that she wasn't in the Craven, and decided to go home, where he could work for a couple of hours undisturbed. *Too bad,* he thought. *I can't help it if she's not there. I just won't see her.*

When he got home, he phoned her, got no answer, and left a message on her answering machine. "I stopped by your office, but you weren't there or in the hotel. I'm leaving New Bern today at three. I'll call you. Good luck with the convention." Nothing personal in that message, but sweet-talking to a machine wasn't his style. At times, he thought they were getting closer, and then they drifted. She knew he was leaving and didn't tell him where she would be or how he could reach her. She cared about him, but she sure as hell didn't know how to show it.

About that time, Regina knocked on the door of Juliet Smith's house. The knocker produced chimes in the tune of the Gershwin song "Loved Walked In," and when the door swung open, a tall, thin man in a red plaid shirt stared down at her.

"Where the devil have you . . . Wha . . . What happened to you? What did you do to yourself?"

She had forgotten that seeing her might confuse him. "I'm Regina Pearson, Mr. Smith."

He squinted at her, as if to verify what he thought his eyes saw, and as he did so, his confusion changed to hostility. "You're who? What's the meaning of this?"

He had a right to be upset. His anger was almost palpable, and although he didn't appear threatening, he seemed on the verge of bursting out of himself in rage.

She hastened to explain. "Juliet and I are first cousins. Her father and my mother were brother and sister. I know how much we resemble, and that's what I want to speak with her about." She spoke softly, her tone that of an intercessor, for fear of upsetting him more.

It did little to placate him. "She's not here, and I don't know where she is."

What a wall! She could almost see him sliding it between them.

"Wait. Please. Can you and I talk? Nobody seems to care that she could be in some kind of difficulty."

His demeanor changed, and without the stridency and hostility, he seemed to shrink in size, a balloon leaking air. She had never seen a man lose his sense of self so rapidly and so completely that he appeared to fold up. Like a convicted man whose last appeal for clemency had been denied, his long arms dropped to his side and dangled there. After a bit, he stepped back, opened the door wider, and spoke in a different, weaker voice.

"Until you started talking, I thought she'd gone somewhere and got her skin lightened. She's so self-conscious about being dark. Hates it. That's one thing about this place I can't stand. People are so color-conscious. You got white people and then you got *shades* of black people. Sickening." He said the last with a sneer. "You can come in if you want to. She's been gone over a week, and not one word."

Regina walked inside and glanced around at a neat, well-furnished place, a home that bespoke its owners' middle-class status and upper-middle-class taste.

"Does Juliet play the piano?" she asked, with her gaze on the Steinway baby grand, wondering if they also had that skill in common.

He shrugged. "Expensive decoration. She wanted it, so I bought it. Have a seat."

An intelligent man apparently distressed that he didn't know his wife's whereabouts. She decided to take a chance and ask an obvious question. "Have you reported to the police that Juliet's missing? Maybe . . . Well, something might be wrong."

He shook his head. "I can't do that. She's a prominent person, and she's scared to death of bad publicity. Juliet spends most of her time protecting her image."

She asked him whether Juliet had disappeared before.

"Maybe for a day, but with me on the road all the time, she can't always let me know where she is." She didn't say the obvious, that since he was at their home, reaching him shouldn't be difficult. She kept the thought to herself and asked him something else that had bothered her for the past several days.

"The Witherspoons I've met don't seem concerned that Juliet might be in some kind of difficulty. Why's that?"

He took a handkerchief from his pocket and wiped his forehead with hands that trembled. "I guess because she doesn't associate with them. I tell her all the time that the most important things in life are your health, your family, and how you get along with God. Runs off her like water off a duck's back. She ignores all three. What did you want to ask her?"

"I want to ask her whether she knows why we look like identical twins. It's making me a wreck. After living in another part of the world for forty years, I meet a woman, a cousin, who could be me. I

want to know why. My aunt Maude shrugged it off as a genetic accident, but I can't accept that. Did Juliet ever tell you her feelings about
it?"

He studied her, and his friendliness was short-lived, evaporating
like steam before fire. "Didn't it occur to you that she might not *want*
to talk about it, that she might not give a hoot if you're all shook up because *you* look like *her?* Where do you get the right to storm in here
and start messing up people's lives?"

"Look, I don't want to hurt her, but I've got to try and fill some
gaps in my life."

"Yeah? Looks to me like you've lived a long time with those gaps.
Give it a rest, lady."

"But—"

He interrupted her, waving his hand as if her problems were of no
consequence. "Ask your grandfather. He always has an answer for
everything. And leave my wife out of it."

She made one last effort. "If you hear from her, would you please
let me know?"

He wrote a phone number on a slip of paper and handed it to her.
"All right. I hope you'll do the same for me. Call me at this number if
you hear anything."

She told him she would and left when he didn't accept her offer to
shake hands.

The more she thought of Pop's advice that she shouldn't open
Pandora's box, the more certain she was that her likeness to Juliet was
not a riddle as far as he was concerned. She made up her mind to dig
it out of him, and would have gone to his house that morning if she
hadn't encountered Harold in the Craven's lobby when she got back
to the hotel.

"Hey, Cuz, I'm on my way up to your office."

Headed in the wrong direction, too. "Well, come on. I'm going
there now."

"Cephus just called me," he said, settling on the arm of the leather
chair beside her desk. "I don't understand it and never did, but if you
want information about Juliet, see my dear half-brother."

In the process of sitting, she remained suspended above her desk
chair. "Harold, for heaven's sake, if you know something, out with it."

He stared at her, a flicker of unfriendliness in his grayish-brown
eyes. "Why do you think I'm here when I could be in bed asleep? As I

was about to say, I never thought Cephus and Juliet were getting it on, but . . . well, this is the age of stupidity." He examined his nails and buffed them on his gray silk suit. "And your guess is as good as mine. Seems your highfalutin cousin went to Raleigh to apply for the position of feature editor at the Raleigh *News & Observer*. She planned to be away just for the afternoon and to surprise hubby if she got the job. So what does she do but kiss a cement post head-on and total that Toyota she drives."

She couldn't stand another minute of his drama. "Harold, for goodness' sake, what happened to Juliet?"

He pulled air through his front teeth. "Oh, don't get so wound up; she's not dead. Her Highness wouldn't think of dying. She's not that considerate. No, indeed! Claims she changed pocketbooks and neglected to transfer her wallet. She didn't have her driver's license, car papers, or other identification with her, so she's been flat on her fanny in a charity ward in General Hospital."

When Regina jumped up and grabbed her purse, Harold yelled, "Where're you going? Take it easy. You could cause her a lot of trouble. She phoned Cephus as soon as they let her get up, and he got the charges against her dropped."

"Charges? What kind of charges?"

"She fell asleep at the wheel."

Hmmm. "Why wouldn't the police get her identity from the car's license plates? Sounds strange to me."

Harold rolled his eyes in the manner of one suffering the chatter of fools. "She may think she's royalty, but to those Raleigh police, she was just a black gal on the left side of the law. Wake up, Cuz."

She couldn't get used to thinking that way and wasn't sure she wanted to. "Why didn't she call her husband?"

"Look, Cuz, don't get into that, though I don't suppose my half-brother wants her, since she's too dark-skinned for him. Anyhow, Herbert doesn't have the clout to get her out of trouble with the law, but Cephus does. Cephus doesn't think she told him everything, and I don't, either."

He stretched his arms above his head and yawned. "Musicians need to sleep during the day, but I can't go back to bed. I'm due to volunteer at St. Catherine's Thrift Shop in less than three hours."

She had to keep her promise to Herbert Smith and told Harold as much. "I gave him my word."

He threw up his hands and rolled his eyes toward the ceiling. "All right. Tell him whatever you like so long as you don't mention Cephus. I told him I'd keep a lid on it."

She telephoned Herbert Smith, but after thanking her, his voice changed like a sudden shifting of the wind, and she could almost feel him cooling off.

"How'd you find out about this?"

She hadn't prepared herself for that question. "One of my cousins called to ask if I knew she'd had an accident."

"And he—it was a he, wasn't it?—didn't think I'd want to know?"

Her reaction to that was a stinging desire to box his ears. "I'm relatively new here, Herbert, and I don't know whether he knows you or if he knows you're not on your run but here in New Bern."

"Everybody here knows everybody. Well, thanks. I'll get on over there."

She wouldn't gain a thing if she tried to speak with Juliet in Herbert's presence, so she'd have to live with her angst for at least one more day.

At first, she told herself that if Odette and Maude didn't care what happened to Juliet, she wouldn't bother to tell them, but she considered that uncharitable and phoned Maude.

"We've located Juliet, Aunt Maude. She's in General Hospital over in Raleigh, recovering from an accident, or so Harold told me."

"Why didn't she let somebody know? It's not like nobody cared about her."

"I'm going to see her tomorrow. Maybe since she's hospitalized, she'll be more receptive. At least I hope so."

"Listen, child, you're gonna keep on till you open up a nasty can of worms. When you see something this far out of the ordinary, you know if you start digging you'll find more than a little dust on a bottle. You start unearthing secrets, and before you know it, you've ruined somebody's life."

"After what you just said, surely you don't think I'll leave it alone. You've got suspicions or you wouldn't tell me to back off. Well, if I didn't have a backbone, I'd be in Honolulu. I've never had an easy life. Money? Yes. But affection, understanding, and acceptance? That's all new to me. I'm tough, and I can take it."

"You been talking to Pop?"

She realized she'd wound the telephone cord so tightly around her wrist that it pained her. She loosened it. "Not since day before yesterday. Why?"

"He's coming over for chili tonight. Why don't you eat with us? And . . . uh, Regina, please don't mention Juliet. Okay?"

She jerked upright. "Well . . . all right, I guess." She wasn't sure she was glad she'd called Maude, but she was positive that their conversation would stay with her for a long time. Something was not right.

"My, but you look good! You ought to wear that lavender-pink every day. Come on in. I just took the chili off the stove."

She hugged her aunt, and as Maude embraced her she thought back to the days when her fantasies revolved around the loving embraces she would one day receive from the score of relatives who loved her. Her arms tightened around Maude's back, causing her aunt to step away and gaze at her.

"What is bothering you? Still distressed about Juliet? You said she isn't in danger, so don't fret over it. Fretting won't do a thing for you but make you look old."

"Is that why you're so laid-back?" She caught herself, then remembered that Maude wouldn't consider her rude for having asked a personal question. "You don't look much older than I do."

"One of the reasons. But the real one is, I long ago decided that if I can't solve a problem and if I have to live with the situation, I grin and bear it. Accept it and go on living. Sometimes I'm amazed at how foolish I used to be. If God had given me everything I asked him for, I'd be a dried-up old hag by now."

Maude sat down, and a look of hope brightened her smooth, brown face. "What's with you and Justin?"

Regina rubbed the fingers of her right hand across her forehead. "I wish you'd tell *me*. When I lived in Hawaii, I made two humongous mistakes, and I don't want to repeat them. I'm strongly attracted to Justin, and I know it's mutual, but we can't seem to get past that. I think it's because we've both made awful mistakes, need a lot more than chemistry, and don't intend to trash our lives again."

"I like Justin, and I wish the two of you would get together, but you're right to be careful. I had three bad marriages. You talk about living in hell."

"Did your husbands abuse you?"

"One of them did. *One time.* I kept walking and never looked back. One tried psychological abuse, but he wasn't smart enough to pull it off. The other one just plain got on my nerves. Him and his damned garlic, odoriferous cheese, and distaste for soap and water. When I got rid of him, I went to church and thanked the Lord."

He must have had something going for him. To Maude she said, "How'd you happen to marry him?"

Maude threw up her hands and appeared nonplussed. "I asked myself that question. True, he started that garlic-and-cheese business and got careless with his personal hygiene after we married, but . . ." She blew out a heavy breath. "I don't know what I was thinking about. He sure didn't make me holler in bed. Johann can make me scream, beg, plead, and do all kinds of wild things."

"Are you going to make up with Johann?"

"We . . . There's the doorbell." She snuffed out the cigar. "You open it, and give Pop a nice surprise."

As she rushed to the door, a sense of security and belonging radiated through her at the prospect of being with the old man again. "Hi, Pop," she said, and opened her arms to him.

His face beamed like moonlight. "She didn't tell me you'd be here." The unsteadiness of his voice and its gruffness betrayed his emotions as he folded her into his arms. "I don't know what I did to deserve this," he said while walking with her into the dining room, "but I'm glad to accept it as my due."

Maude greeted her father with a smile and hug, looked past him, and frowned. "Where's Johann?"

"He's *your* husband. Why you asking *me* about him?" Pop said, taking his usual seat at the head of the table. "I don't carry him around in my pocket."

"Pop, where is Johann? Isn't he coming?"

Abner looked at Regina and motioned to the chair on his right. "Have a seat, child. I look forward all week to this. Maude's chili is to food what a Rolls Royce is to automobiles."

"You're up to something, Pop. Now, tell me where Johann is."

With an expression of amazement pasted on his face, Abner looked at his daughter. "Danged if you ain't getting to be a jigsaw puzzle. If you ignore your husband, you got no right to know where he is or what he's doing. But since you ask, he's home. Probably packing."

"He's *what?*"

Regina stared at her aunt's rapidly retreating back, amazed that a sixty-year-old woman could move that fast.

Maude's trembling hands and shaking fingers made error after error as she tried to dial the number; in desperation, she asked the operator for assistance.

"How you doing, Maude? I hear tell Juliet Smith's in trouble over there in Raleigh. Somebody said Herbert finally got tired of her shenanigans and swiped her a few times. Soon be summer, warm as it was today."

She wanted to scream at the operator but controlled the impulse. "Ruth, could you please get this number for me. I'll call tomorrow and we'll talk about Juliet. All right?" She hoped she'd placated the woman. Perspiration beaded her forehead as she waited for the ring and then for Johann's voice.

"Hello. Abner Witherspoon's home. He's out. I'll take a message."

She didn't waste niceties. "Johann, why didn't you come with Pop?"

"Hello, babe." That didn't sound as if she'd be able to affect a reconciliation with him. Calling her "babe" meant that he'd been thinking about her and found her wanting. He wasn't pleased.

"Pop has a standing invitation to dinner with you every Wednesday. I don't. If you remembered during the last seven days that you have a husband, you didn't communicate that to me. You expect me to force myself on you?" He'd primed himself to be difficult, and she had never learned how to handle him when he was like that.

Increasingly agitated at the thought that he might leave the States, she showed her impatience. "I don't want none of your cat-and-mouse stuff, Johann. You come on over here."

When his voice deepened, she knew he'd hardened his stance. "Listen to me, babe. I let you know I needed you, laid myself open to you. I went to you, and it was good with us, but you haven't reciprocated. You haven't reached out to me. I love you, babe, but I am not your fool."

"You talking a lot of nonsense. Pop said you were probably packing. Packing to go where? You bring your behind on over here right this minute." She heard her voice rising in panic and couldn't control it. "I mean it, Johann. Nobody's eating till you get here."

"Are you inviting me or ordering me?"

She paced the floor of her bedroom, trying to shut out the fear that he might leave her, but she couldn't allow him to know she teetered toward capitulation. "Both. You're trying to punish me because I won't crawl, but I won't prostrate myself before you or any other man no matter how much I hurt. You hear me?"

"I never asked or wanted you to do that, and you know it. And another thing. When did you start ordering me to do anything? Why can't you admit you're wrong and that you want us to straighten out our lives?"

"Would you really get on that plane and leave here without seeing me?" She hated the tremors in her voice.

"That was my plan, Kitten. You aren't the only one who can hurt, feel rejected, and shed tears about it."

Her lower lip dropped. Never before had he admitted feeling that she rejected him. "Don't . . . I . . . Honey, I want you to come over right now." She refused to plead. His silence lasted so long that she nearly screamed in frustration and panic. "And . . . bring your toothbrush."

"See you in ten minutes."

She sank to the side of the bed and let tears stream down her cheeks.

Ten minutes later, with her face refreshed, a smile on her face, and her regal coolness wrapped around her, she opened the door and stared at her husband of ten years. She knew Johann well enough to know she had to make the first move, so she held out her hand.

"I'm glad you came."

He looked at her the way one reads a newspaper whose print is too fine, as if looking for little signals or markers that would steer him safely through a proverbial mine field.

"If you hadn't made that call, I was definitely going to be on that plane tomorrow evening. When I do go, I'd like to take Pop with me."

At last she could get a full breath. She needed intimacy with him, in any degree at all, so she squeezed his hand. "How long will you stay?"

He stared into her eyes so long that she wished she hadn't asked him. "A week, two weeks, forever. It depends on you and what you're offering. But we shouldn't get into that now."

"No. We shouldn't." She brightened her face with a smile, though bright was far from what she felt. "I didn't tell Regina and Pop that you were coming. You didn't give me time enough to adjust to it. In fact, I just flopped down on the bed and . . . and . . . Oh, well, it doesn't matter."

The feel of his arm around her waist reminded her of his physical and moral strength, of his will and determination. Pop was like that, too. Small wonder that her father and her husband got on so well together. Indeed, they were so much alike that the thought frightened her as much as it comforted her. All of New Bern knew how uncompromising Pop could be.

Abner treated Johann's arrival as if it were not out of the ordinary. "You could have come when I did," he said to Johann, "and I could have been eating my chili. You remember my granddaughter, don't you?"

"Indeed I do. How's it going, Regina?"

"Fine. Nice seeing you again," Regina said. "I think you ought to know that the average American doesn't greet people that way. It's—"

He interrupted her. "I know. It's mainly African-American slang but, yesterday I heard the president admonish somebody to 'tell it like it is,' and I *know* that emanated from the Black Power movement."

Maude couldn't help wondering how Johann spent his days, because he seemed to have absorbed a lot of local culture. "This is true," she said in response to Johann, "but it wouldn't hurt you to learn to say, 'How do you do'?"

Abner glared at her. "You want him to sound like a goat trying to communicate with sheep. Nobody talks like that anymore. In these parts, good manners are as dead as a five-cent cigar." Maude set a large bowl of chili con carne in the middle of the table, along with a dish of rice, a green salad, and a pan of cracklin' bread.

"Thank the Lord, I can finally eat," Abner said, and bowed his head. "Lord, you gave us sense, but we don't use it; good health that we take great pains to ruin; and strong bodies that we weaken in only you know how many ways. But Lord, you gave us food, and this daughter of mine only makes it better. For what we are about to eat, we do thank you. Amen."

"Pop, that was pretty long considering that you were practically dying of starvation," Johann said. "But I liked what you said so much I might translate it into Dutch."

"Don't try to butter me up," Abner said, and blew on a spoonful of chili to cool it. "I'm watching what's going on. This circumspect behavior between man and wife is about as phony as a tin rifle. Don't let me get in the way. I came here by myself, and I'm prepared to go back the same way."

"You know I wouldn't hear of that, Pop," Regina said. "I'll be happy to drive you home."

"He knows that," Maude said, "but we all know Pop likes to make his points."

"Humph. It wouldn't hurt you none to make a point once in a while. If a man's life is in order, you don't find him walking around in the house at three o'clock in the morning. *Getting a drink of water.* Nonsense. People don't want water when they're sound asleep. You'd better take care of business."

She made the mistake of glancing at Johann, who mouthed the word "Right."

Thank God for napkins. Twice she spilled chili in her lap, and once it landed on the edge of the table. She couldn't remember having had such a fit of nerves. As soon as Abner and Regina left, Johann would let her know what was on his mind, and she wasn't sure she was ready for that information.

"I want us to have a family party," Regina said. "Pop, I still haven't met your son Robert and his family, Odette's brother, Jake, and none of the Pearsons except Harold and Cephus. Where does Harold's sister, Jewel, live?"

Abner cleared his throat and drank several swallows of water. "Regina, sometimes I think you're the only one of my offspring who has any of my genes. I've been . . . What's so funny about that?" he asked Johann, whose laughter was teetering out of control.

"Ever since my children grew up and scattered, it's been my dream to get them and my grandchildren together, to get them to love each other. My granddaughter here is the only one of them who cares about family. The only one. Maude, you did make some apple turnovers or an apple crisp, didn't you? Johann, her apple things are almost as good as the chili. Maybe—"

Johann threw up his hands. "First things first, Pop. Let's get the chili in cans before we start freezing apple turnovers and . . . What was that other thing?'

Maude looked at the three of them bursting with laughter, and Johann ignoring her. And she thought of the noose dangling over her bedroom door.

* * *

"I didn't bring my toothbrush," Johann said when they were alone, the kitchen and dining room tidied, and they finally had to deal with each other.

"Why not? I asked you to bring it."

"So you could whet my appetite and send me on back to Pop?"

"Wait a minute. I wanted you to stay that morning, but you said you had to fix Pop's breakfast."

"I did. And it didn't occur to you to go with me, did it? You could have said, let's go to Palm Beach, Denver, Oakland, New York—anywhere—and I'd have taken you. Just to be with you. But you won't crawl—your words—and I won't beg."

The bile of fear shimmied through her body, and she swallowed with difficulty. "Johann, have you got a woman back there in Amsterdam?"

He grabbed both of her arms. "You mean to tell me you care?"

She shook herself loose and stepped back so he could see her face and everything about her. "Damn right, I care. And you know it."

He stepped closer. "Didn't you wonder who was giving me comfort those eighteen months when you were here enjoying your language and your sunny weather? Did you even think about that?"

She couldn't lie and wouldn't. "Yes, I wondered, and I hurt. I told myself that I couldn't have you as long as you lived in that dreary place. I taught myself not to want what I couldn't have. No man touched me, Johann. Not a single one."

"Oh, I believe that. You were almost as tight as a virgin, and considering your temperament, that was some feat. I won't say I did the same, because I didn't. I took care of my needs."

"What is she like?" She felt as if the bottom had fallen out of her belly, but he would never know it.

Both of his eyebrows shot up. " 'She' who? I said I took care of my needs, not that I formed a relationship with a woman. I didn't. But if things don't change, I will. I hate sex without passion or affection."

"But you were going away from here without telling me or seeing me."

"I'm not going back over that ground with you. If you didn't call me for a whole week, and at a cost of only about twenty-five cents per call, why should I call you to tell you *anything?* And especially since I made the last move."

"When are you going?"

His shrug didn't fool her. "I need to attend to some record company business, and I want to set up the company that will can the chili. And I'm taking Pop with me."

Now she'd heard it all. "He said he'd go?"

He nodded. "We sent for his passport today, along with the ticket. So he'll have it within a week."

"You're taking him because he's involved in the chili company?"

"He's a full partner. If I go alone, he'll worry that I'm not coming back, so I'm taking him with me."

"Are you going to spend the night with me?"

"I don't know. You got a beer?"

Eleven

An uneasy feeling pervaded Regina as she headed down the corridor toward room OB-12 in General Hospital. She wondered about the OB, which to her signified childbearing or a gynecological problem, but shrugged it off: hospital staff might place emergency cases wherever they had room. The odor of disinfectants and medicines attacked her nostrils, and she had to resist an urge to turn back. She held her breath, but when she finally had to breathe, she thought she would be sick.

"What's the matter, sis?" a woman who obviously worked there asked her. "You all right?"

"I'm all right," she said, although she wasn't. "Would you please tell me where room OB-12 is?"

"You look kinda out of it to me. It's two doors further down."

Regina thanked the woman and walked with deliberate steps toward her destination. She thought she recognized a man's voice, and stopped to listen. She took a step farther and realized it was Herbert Smith's voice.

"I don't believe you. Nobody makes an accordion out of a Toyota and walks away without a scratch."

"I was knocked unconscious."

"So you say. But if you were two and a half months pregnant, how come I didn't know it? Woman, you talking shit. You got rid of it. Had me taking every kind of poison under the sun thinking I couldn't get you pregnant. And you swearing you wanted a baby. Find yourself another fool."

"Herbert, please. Why don't you believe me? Ask the doctor."

"I did, and he said you came in here bleeding."

"But I'd just been in an automobile accident!"

"I told him that, and he just shrugged and kept on staring at the chart in his hand."

Regina looked around at the empty corridor. She ought to move, and she told herself to get away from there but remained rooted to the spot. Stunned.

"All this time you been pretending," Herbert went on, his voice low and with a dangerous overtone. "Woman, I would have given my life for you."

Juliet's voice took on the quality of defeat, the diffidence of one no longer self-assured. "If you don't believe me, Herbert, what can I do? As God is my witness, I've told you the truth."

His silence, long and deafening, caused Regina's breathing to accelerate. Surely he would believe his wife. *He had to.* But seconds later, without uttering another word, Herbert Smith bolted from the room and into the corridor, nearly knocking her off her feet.

"Excuse me," he said without sparing her a glance.

Her thoughts as she prepared to walk into Juliet's hospital room had nothing to do with confrontation and everything to do with sympathetic understanding. She didn't think she'd ever seen a man's face so disfigured with anger. Herbert Smith would not soon be placated.

Regina opened the door wider, walked into the room, and gasped. Juliet shared it with three other female patients, and they had witnessed Herbert Smith's explosive accusations. If any of them had connections in New Bern, Juliet's reputation was irreparably tarnished. She stood beside her cousin's bed, looking down at the tears gushing from the woman's tightly closed eyelids.

"Don't cry. After he thinks it over, he'll realize he's wrong," she whispered.

Juliet's eyelids shot up, and her eyes widened as she stared at Regina. "What? Where'd you come from? What're you doing here?"

Regina sat in the only chair available for Juliet's guests and told herself not to get angry no matter what Juliet said to her. "I came because I heard you'd had an accident, and I wanted to know whether I could help you."

Juliet turned her face away from Regina. "Why do you think you can help me, and why would you want to? You came here to gloat."

She decided to tell the truth. "I admit I wanted to confront you about your seeming indifference to the fact that we are mirror images of each other, but when I overheard your husband talking that foolishness, I knew you needed a friend. Men can be hotheaded. That's their knee-jerk reaction to whatever doesn't please them, and especially when it comes as a surprise. If there's anything I'm learning, it's that African-American men are like Hawaiian and German men in at least this respect: if they take a blow to the ego, they act out."

Slowly and as if pained, Juliet faced Regina. "Why are you being so nice? You want me to believe you're sweet Miss Goody Two-shoes?"

Ignore that, Regina admonished herself. To Juliet she said, "Trust me, I can defend myself with the best of them. That is one thing that living here in New Bern with my African-American sisters and brothers has drilled into me: stand up for yourself or you'll find yourself facedown eating dirt."

"Why should I believe you're here out of the goodness of your heart?"

Regina's shrug was intended to convey the message that she wouldn't waste time worrying about whether Juliet believed she had good intentions, but her words carried a different message. "Look. Meeting you was as much of a shock to me as it was to you. Several of my relatives had asked me if I'd met you, but didn't even hint as to why I would find you interesting, so I was hoping you'd be a friend, someone like a sister." She waved her right hand. "That aside, first things first."

"What do you mean?" Juliet asked and tried to prop herself up in the bed.

"I mean, how are you going to deal with your husband's suspicions? Can you get an affidavit from another doctor?"

"No. That one was the attending physician." Juliet stared at her. "You believe me, don't you?"

Regina leaned forward, so that the other patients in the room wouldn't overhear her. "Why shouldn't I? What you told him made sense to me. You ought to sue that doctor."

Juliet eased back down in bed. "What for? Do you think that white doctor cares if he deflated my husband's ego or if he busted up a marriage either through his ignorance or his incompetence? Well, let me tell you he does not."

The more she heard of that sentiment, the better Honolulu looked. "When do you expect to get out of here?"

"Tomorrow, but I don't have a car." She threw up her hands. "This is terrible. I never even called the paper to tell the editor why I didn't keep my appointment for that interview."

Regina handed Juliet her cellular phone. "If you remember the number, you may call now. I'll step out while you—"

"Thanks. Just sit right there."

Regina listened to what passed for an apology, a far cry from the arrogance that she associated with Juliet. Seeing an opportunity to plant the seed of friendship, she stood to leave. "I'll come for you tomorrow at noon and drive you home."

Juliet returned the phone. *"You would do that?* I've got half a hundred kinfolk in New Bern and Havelock, and they all know I'm in this hospital, because a nurse's aid told me it was in the papers. Did one of them show up here?" She sighed. "Only you. Well, I'll be ready to go at noon. And . . . thanks."

She told Juliet good-bye and left. But as she walked across the parking lot to her car, her father's words filled her thoughts. "The chickens coming home to roost," he would say when he observed a person suffering the consequences of unwise behavior. Or he would shake his head, point his right index finger, and say, "You always live long enough to reap what you sow."

Regina got in her car, turned on the ignition and headed for New Bern, her thoughts once more on Justin. She wished she could separate the Justin with whom she worked from the man to whom she was so fiercely attracted. Native Hawaiian men saw a woman they liked and went after her. No equivocating and certainly no concern for consequences, because the outcome would always be in their favor—or so they thought. On the other hand, Justin thought through everything he did. He considered himself responsible for his actions and behaved honorably and justly. She appreciated that in him, but at times, she wanted to go to bed with him and forget the hang-ups, his and hers.

When she reached her office, she found a note from her secretary. *Mr. Pearson is downstairs at the bar. He wants to see you.*

She put her briefcase in her desk drawer, locked the drawer, and retraced her steps. She found Harold in the Starlight Lounge drinking ginger ale.

"Hi. You wanted to see me?"

"Yeah. I just got some awful news at the hair salon a little while ago. Seems Juliet had an abortion and Herbert's walked out on her. He's been sucking up to that woman ever since she married him, but she finally did something to make him trip. Imagine Miss High and Mighty getting herself in a mess like that. Gawd. I almost feel sorry for her."

"You don't," she said. "You sound as if you're happy about it. She didn't do any such thing. She had a miscarriage as a result of that accident, but the doctor let Herbert believe she deliberately terminated the pregnancy. If a pregnant woman is driving a car that is wrecked so badly the front end is almost touching the back, wouldn't you think that would make her lose the baby?"

"Maybe she wasn't in that car. From what I heard, she didn't get a scratch."

"Come off it, Harold. She was taken to the hospital unconscious. Cephus told you that."

He shrugged. "Maybe. But she's been so nasty to me, Cuz. That woman has made me cry over the things she's said to me and about me. One of these days, I'll show her. I'll show them all."

So much has passed among my relatives that I don't know about and can't understand, she thought, *but I do know that Harold's hurt goes deep.* She eased her right arm across his shoulder, not wanting him to think she felt sorry for him. "There's no point in hating Juliet. Right now she deserves your sympathy. I'm going back to Raleigh tomorrow morning to bring her home."

He swung around and stared at her. "Listen, Cuz, with that gossip column of hers, Juliet has driven nails in the backs of half the folks in New Bern." When she raised an eyebrow, he went on. "That's all it is, a bloody gossip column disguised as editorial commentary. If you don't believe me, ask Abner Witherspoon."

She would, she decided. "You're always giving me snippets about my relatives. Why don't you help me get to know them and understand them? For starters, give me a list of the persons I haven't met, and that includes all of them except you and Cephus. I need to know my background, where I came from, and that means knowing the Pearsons and Witherspoons. Everybody needs a loving family, but people can't love you if they don't know you."

"All right. I'll make you a list, but don't expect them to run to you waving a welcome flag. Every one of them knows you're here, but you haven't seen them, have you? If you ask me, they're a bunch of jealous people wondering how you got this big job if you didn't sleep with somebody in order to get it.

She removed her arm from his shoulder. "Is that what you think, Harold?"

He laid his head to the side and squinted at her. "Cuz, you're as straight as the crow flies. I got my shortcomings, but I know people, and you're a straight shooter, right up front."

"Thanks."

"Forget it. While I'm into your business, let me tell you something: You're crazy for a family, but the best way to get one is to start your own, and the only man around here worth your time is Justin Duval."

"Harold, I don't want to dis—"

"You listen to me, Cuz. You're too powerful for most of the guys around here; they want a woman they can look down on. Somebody to gaze up at 'em and tell them how great they are. You aren't going to do that. I know what I'm talking about. And don't forget, you're forty already. What's wrong with Duval?"

"Nothing. He . . . He's doing his own thing."

"Yeah, and you're doing yours. But that man wants *you*. At least for now."

"What is that supposed to mean?"

"It means if you don't act right, his testosterone will send him to the closest refueling station. And he might stay there. Even if he wanted to be a martyr, too many smart women around here to let him do that. You'd better wake up."

She didn't doubt the veracity of his words, but she didn't need to hear them. She raised herself to her full five feet, seven inches—something she never did in the company of her Hawaiian friends, because she towered over them—and stared at Harold. "And what about you? I don't see you rushing into matrimonial bliss and parenthood."

He shrugged. "It's not for me. My music is my life."

Maybe, but his voice lacked its usual conviction, and she had a sense of remorse for having attacked him in what appeared to be a vulnerable spot.

She patted his shoulder. "Sorry. I was out of line. Get me that list as soon as you can. Will you?"

"If you insist, but I will not be responsible for what you run into."

"Fair enough. I'd better get to work. See you at the show tonight."

He nodded, but the sadness beclouding his face let her know that she'd knocked the props from under him. *I wish I knew why he's so vul-*

nerable. The telephone rang as she entered her office. "Lucien Hayes on two, Regina," her secretary said.

"How may I help you, Mr. Hayes?" she asked, adopting her most businesslike manner. If the man meant to harass her about that suite, she was having none of it.

"How's the suite coming?"

"Oh, I'm sorry sir, but I have no idea. I don't pester Colonel Duval about his work. If he had a problem with it, he would tell me. He hasn't mentioned a thing, so I suspect he's doing fine."

She had written a thirty-day grace period into the contract. If he didn't read it, too bad. With Justin busy showing his patriotism for his country, she was glad she'd done it. Only by some miracle would he have that suite ready on time. Hayes wasn't satisfied, but he was enough of a businessman to concede that he had no gripe unless the Craven failed to honor the deadline. She canvassed booking agents for a replacement for Maude and Harold but couldn't find anyone who suited her. In exasperation she phoned Maude.

"Aunt Maude, how do you feel about singing at the Craven for two weeks without Harold? I need someone for the cooking school convention the end of September, and Harold says he has other plans."

"I know. He said he needs a vacation, but I can't sing with just anybody. That saxophone of his sets me on fire, and when he lets go with those mournful swings, it looks like my whole soul opens up. That man can blow that sax."

"He's great, all right, but don't be so modest. You'd sound good singing a cappella. Got any ideas?"

"Let me think about it. Harold said you're planning to bring Juliet home from the hospital. I sure hope you know what you're doing."

She loved Maude, or thought she did, but she bristled at her aunt's uninvited advice. "Bringing her home is all I'm doing. You think she should walk from Raleigh to New Bern?"

"Get your behind off your shoulders." The words sounded as if Maude had screamed them. "You don't know what you're meddling in. I hear tell Herbert put new locks on the doors. So how's she going to get into the house?"

Regina sucked in her breath. This got worse by the minute. "If he did that, I'll call Cephus, and he'll get it straightened out."

"Better let her call him. If you do it, he'll have you in his pocket for the rest of your life. And believe me, Cephus puts a high price on his services. Kinship doesn't mean a thing to him. Ask Harold, if you think it does."

She'd had a surfeit of negative comments about her relatives. At times she wondered how they managed to stay in the same county with each other. "Thanks for telling me," she said to Maude. "Call me as soon as you think of someone who can accompany you."

"I will, but . . . Honey, you worry me. Whatever's wrong with this family was wrong before you were born. You can't plow into here like a bull in a china shop, digging up a lot of wretched stuff nobody's thought about for years. All the Witherspoons and Pearsons know one another, and if we don't sip from the loving cup, your coming here will never change that, and if I have to prove it to you, I will."

Regina hung up, dissatisfied. Irritated. And distressed at her aunt's frank assessment of her dream, of her need that was as much a part of her as breathing. She was learning that rumor was like Sunday morning gospel, that gossip seemed to be New Bern's main industry, and the truth didn't much matter. Even her aunt, a worldly woman who hated gossip, was so immersed in local ways and attitudes as to be unaware of her own transgressions. When her phone rang, excitement raced through her but quickly abated when she heard Pop's voice.

"I called in case you might need me for something," he said. "My son-in-law—you know, Johann—is taking me to Hol—I mean the Netherlands this weekend, and we may be gone two or three weeks."

In spite of her disappointment that Justin wasn't her caller, she got a warm feeling from the childlike joy she heard in her grandfather's voice. "That's wonderful, Pop. Johann will see that you have a good time."

"Oh, he will, though it's a business trip for both of us." She smiled at the self-assurance of a successful businessman that his voice projected. "I also don't mind finding out what it is about the place that my daughter, Maude, can't stand. Not many women are so crazy that they'd walk away from a man like Johann. You be careful you don't step right into her tracks."

"I know what you're saying, Pop, but it's not entirely up to me."

"Humph. He said it was, and you can quote me on that. He's a good man, child, and he's willing to see that I get me some great grandchildren during what's left of my lifetime."

She nearly dropped the phone. "He . . . Justin told you that?" she sputtered. "Why, I'll . . . I'll—"

"Now, now, give me a little credit. He didn't have to say those exact same words, but I've been a man myself for over ninety years, and I figured out what he didn't say from what he said. Pay attention, and you'll find out I'm right."

She'd better change the subject before her displeasure with Justin burned out of control, but in her attempt to do that, she spoke without thinking. "Pop, do you know Juliet's in the hospital?" Even as the words left her mouth, she wanted to take them back.

"Yes, I sure do." The words came out on what seemed like a long sigh. "I read the Raleigh *News & Observer,* you know. Pretty strong stuff, but she's made so many enemies with that column of hers that I don't know what to believe."

"I went to see her, and I'm bringing her home tomorrow."

"Hmmm." He let the silence between them hang for a while, and she waited for his next words. "Well, the Lord may bless you for that, but you may get punished for disobeying your old grandfather if you open that kettle of worms. Shouldn't be difficult to see why first cousins look alike."

She couldn't tell him she would take his advice, because she wouldn't. "What day are you leaving for Europe? If I can, I'll go see you off."

"I notice you didn't comment on what I said. I'm going Saturday morning, but don't bother. That's one of your busiest days, and your first convention starts Saturday. You all ready for it?"

"Yes, sir." She heard the pride in her voice but figured that after handling all the near-disasters, threatened labor problems, and Larry's temperament, she was entitled to a bit of vanity.

"Put some extra help on the registration desk," he advised. "Nothing makes people madder than hanging around your lobby after traveling for hours."

She told him she would. "We'll talk again before you leave."

With Regina's words and sentiments about family clouding her mind, Maude telephoned her brother. "Robert, when did you last talk to Pop?"

"Some time last week," he said to his older sister. "Why?"

"Did he tell you where he's going this coming Saturday?"

Departing from his usual taciturn manner, he said, "Didn't say nothing to me about going nowhere. I could barely touch base with him. Something about a company he's forming with your ex-husband. I don't think we ought to leave him there by himself, though Rose's got as much here as she can handle."

She sucked her teeth and looked toward the ceiling. "Rose? Don't worry, your wife isn't threatened. Pop is as sound as the United States dollar. And Johann is not my ex. I'm still married to him. He's taking Pop to Amsterdam, and he hasn't said one single solitary word to me about going with them."

"I 'spect he thinks if you wanted to go, you'd say something. What's this I hear about Juliet wrecking somebody's car, tearing up her own, and practically killing herself?"

She shook her head, exasperated. "Robert, damned if you're not getting to be just like those peanuts you grow."

"Snort at me all you like. I ain't dirt poor, and as long as people crave these nuts, I ain't likely to be."

Talking with Robert was increasingly difficult; his world began and ended with his peanut farm, his three children, and his second wife, Rose. She doubted he knew Reagan was no longer president. And that was just as well, because the knowledge would probably make him cry. She closed the conversation and called her father.

"I know you won't like to hear this, Pop," she said after they greeted each other, "but you've inserted yourself between man and wife, and you've been doing that ever since Johann got here."

"Humph. Your head's full of feathers. That's pure rot, and you know it. If it wasn't for me, you wouldn't know whether he was living or dead."

"You're making it easy for him to stay away from me."

"*Me?* What happened to your common sense, girl? You're the only person who can do that. He's miserable." His voice was suddenly that of an old man. A tired man. "He's pushed back the clock for me, Maude, given me a whole new life. You're a good daughter, always have been, but Johann is . . . Well, he's more than a son-in-law. I'd thank God on my knees if one of my sons needed me as much as he does."

Pop was up to his old tricks, turning everything he touched to an advantage. "Johann is fifty, and a man that old shouldn't need a daddy."

"Unless he never had one. Every man needs someone he can open up to and express himself without worrying about what the other person thinks of him. Men don't do that with women, 'cause we're supposed to know all and be all. The Rock of Gibraltar. He said where he comes from you can have that with your brother—maybe. If he's got a brother, he doesn't know it."

She didn't want to hear it. "You encourage him to stay away from me."

"Meddling is meddling. I don't encourage and I don't discourage. 'Least not since I figured out he's got your number."

She didn't remember ever winning an argument with Pop, and maybe that was because she adored him so much that she didn't want to push him into a corner. "Take some warm clothing, a sweater, and your raincoat. That North Sea air is cold even in summer. Where y'all going besides Amsterdam?"

The eagerness returned to his voice. "He asked me if I wanted to see Paris and London, but I don't know about that. I wanted to see Paris once, but that was sixty years ago. I wouldn't mind seeing the Roman Colosseum. I'll be over tomorrow for my chili as usual."

"I love you, Pop."

"I know, girl. I know. If you want your husband to come with me, you'd better ask him, 'cause I don't plan to mention it."

Only a foolish woman would make that mistake twice, and that wasn't her estimation of herself.

Regina prowled around her home that evening, out of sorts. She tried not to hope, not to care whether the caller was Justin, but her belly rolled in opposition to her efforts at calm.

"Hello," she said in as casual a manner as she could muster.

"Hello, Regina. Did you get my message?"

She sat down and stretched out her legs. Relieved. Excited. And cautious. "Yes," she said, as if hearing his voice were of no special import. "I got it. How are you?"

"Bushed. They're getting their money's worth out of me. Do you remember agreeing to go away with me so we can find out how we feel about each other?"

She stopped swinging her leg. "I remember saying it was a good idea that we spend some time together."

"I remember that you agreed. Keeping your word?"

"Let's talk about it after this first convention is out of the way and . . . Why don't we wait till you get back?"

"Have you changed your mind?"

He was pushing her, and she didn't like it, but she supposed he had a right to know where he stood. "No, I haven't."

"Interesting. I don't detect any enthusiasm. If I'm important to you apart from what I do to make the Craven Hotel a success, I want to know it right now."

She got up and paced to the window and back. He wanted some kind of declaration, and she wasn't going to give him one. Skirting the issue, she said, "I thought we settled that, Justin."

"All right. I'm holding you to it, and when I get back, we'll settle it again."

"When are you coming back?"

"One week from tomorrow, and I'd really like to see you that evening."

"Me, too, but I think we shouldn't get into this any more deeply so long as we're working together."

"We've been over that, Regina, and as far as I'm concerned, it's a dead issue." He gave her the telephone number at which she could reach him. "I like to get phone calls. Don't forget that. And have some ideas for me when I get back, will you? Some place you've always wanted to go. And don't forget to call me. I'm not going to fade away like a puff of smoke in the wind, Regina. I'm going to be in your life for a long, long time."

"But—"

He interrupted her. "If I ever said anything to the contrary, I didn't know what I was talking about."

"Is that so? You haven't been, shall we say, driven to get the two of us together. What made you change?"

"You must have realized that I've been moving in this direction for . . . well, a couple of months."

She couldn't resist a dig at him. "No, I didn't notice. Your pace was imperceptible."

"Have it your way. I'm no longer uncertain. Back in this military environment, I see that what used to seem manly is empty swaggering—a lot of boasting about nothing, chasing women to cover up loneliness, grabbing at happiness without an iota of sense as to what happiness is. The emptiness. In the midst of this, a sensible man can't help but take stock of his life."

Stunned that he would be so candid, she was sorry for her flippancy. "I'd hate to face that kind of reckoning, but I suppose at one time or another, we all have to do it." And better now than later.

She was tired of trudging uphill. For once, in her personal life, she would love to sail with the wind at her back. She got Maude's list, perused it, and telephoned a third cousin, the granddaughter of Abner's deceased sister, who lived twenty miles away in Havelock.

"Miss Walker, this is Regina Pearson. I'm calling—"

"Regina Pearson? I don't know you, do I?"

"According to my aunt Maude Witherspoon, you and I are cousins."

"What? Maude must be off her rocker. I don't have any Pearson relatives, and if I did, I wouldn't own up to it."

The next thing Regina heard was a dial tone. She crossed Olivia Walker off the list, returned it to her briefcase, and walked to the window overlooking her garden to gaze at the moonlit, cloudless night. "I'm forty years old," she told herself aloud, "and when you get right down to it, I don't have a thing that's mine to show for it. Forty years."

Beauty all around her, and no one with whom to share it. Not a man she cared for, a relative, or a girlfriend. She propped her elbows on the window sill and cupped her chin with her hands. What she wouldn't give if she could tell someone, even a neighbor's child, how she felt about the loveliness before her eyes. The longer she looked at the scene, the whiter the night became and the more eerie the shades and shadows. The hunger inside her had nothing to do with food. She could go back to the Craven and watch Maude and Harold bedazzle their audience, or she could grit her teeth and go to bed. She went to bed.

Justin could count the times in his thirty-eight years that his relations with a woman depressed him. The prospect of a divorce hadn't done it. But he traced directly to Regina the weight that hung over him. A couple of days back in the arms of the military were sufficient to shake him out of the complacency he'd developed about her. He hadn't realized the emptiness of his life until he saw it again in the men around him, officers and enlisted men alike. He'd all but told Regina he was ready for a commitment if they suited each other.

When he slid between the sheets, they failed to sooth his naked body. He released a strong expletive. The thought of sex with Regina was a tease, like trying to arrive at a bend in the Norwegian fjords only to realize that when you reached where you thought it was, the bend seemed another half mile away.

The next afternoon, Regina parked in front of Juliet's house, walked around to the front passenger door, opened it, and helped her cousin out of the car. Juliet put firm feet on the pavement and walked to her front door as steadily as if she hadn't had the accident and hadn't miscarried. Regina walked behind her, nursing the nasty thought that Juliet could have opened the car door and gotten out of it unassisted.

"Can I get something for you?" Regina asked her after they walked into the living room.

"No. I'll be all right. Thanks." She sat on the sofa and flipped on the television. "I wonder where Herbert is?" The question, obviously rhetorical, was barely audible.

Juliet wasn't showing her minimum hospitality, not to mention gratitude, but Regina sat down anyway. "You seem stronger than yesterday," she said, "so maybe I'll tell you what's been bothering me."

The rapid upward quirk of Juliet's eyebrows warned her to expect resistance, but after getting that far, it didn't make sense to back off.

"I intend to find out why skin color is all that keeps you and me from looking like identical twins right down to our shoe size, and I need your help." She remembered too late Herbert's having said that Juliet hated being dark, and figured she'd just jeopardized her cause.

"My help? We're first cousins, for heaven's sake."

"All right. Both Pop and Aunt Maude discouraged my digging into this, and they were emphatic. Do you and I resemble your father?"

Regina stared in amazement at the cloud of fury that suddenly blazed in Juliet's face as she sprang to her feet. "You've got one hell of a lot of nerve, barging in here messing up people's heads and meddling in things that don't concern you. Who are you, anyway? I'm an honored person in this town, and I am not going to let you screw things up for me. Go look after your hotel and leave me alone." Taken about by the open hostility, Regina couldn't move.

"You heard me. I want you to leave here this minute."

Who was this chameleon? She'd just driven nearly a hundred

miles to get the woman from the hospital and bring her home, and for thanks she was told to get out of Juliet Smith's house.

Rising to her feet, she stood head to head with Juliet and looked her in the eye. "I didn't want to believe the tales I heard about you, but girlfriend, you are one piece of work. I'll find out without you, and I won't keep what I discover a secret."

She let herself out, squared her shoulders, and quickened her steps. Besting Juliet wouldn't be much of a victory; that would come when she solved the riddle of their uncanny likeness. She didn't want to upset her grandfather, who was about to take his first trip abroad, so she'd begin with her aunt Maude. The next morning, she phoned her.

Maude was not in the mood for unnecessary drama, as she put it. "I'm trying my chili con carne receipt for Johann and Pop's canning business. I have to measure everything in grams, kilograms, liters, and milliliters. Pounds and ounces are so much more civilized. It took me years to get comfortable with the metric system used in Europe, and it's the first thing I happily forgot here in New Bern."

"They can't begin the actual canning now, so why do they need the recipe?"

"I don't know. Perhaps the authorities will want to know what's going into those cans. Come on over for supper, why don't you? That is, if you want chili."

"All right. Did you remember to invite Johann?"

She put the glass measuring cup on the counter, where its reflection bounced off the gleaming Formica, and snapped her fingers. "Y'all don't think I'm such a nincompoop that I'll repeat that mistake after little more than a week, do you? Child, I don't fool with Johann. That man's playing hardball, but I'll get him."

"You sure seem confident."

"Why shouldn't I? I know the music that makes him dance, and I intend to play it for him as long as I breathe. Come over right after work."

She typed up the recipe, added her name, and signed beneath it. Maybe Pop and Johann knew what they were doing. If not, she didn't care; the idea and the excitement it generated brought her father new life. She had to thank Johann, too, for giving Pop the love and care he hadn't received from Robert, the one son who lived nearby. In their youth, his sons fought his authority in order to achieve independence, but in later years, they failed to see that he no longer towered over them or tried to control them.

Her brother, Robert, the youngest of Abner's sons, might bring solace and comfort to the old man if his eyes weren't covered with peanut husks and dollar signs. As she saw it, even with that handicap Robert could spend more time with his father than the monthly visit of an hour or two that he managed. Travis, the second-oldest boy and Juliet's father, left his wife and child when Juliet was four, and hadn't been heard from since. However, Travis had been a solid family man, loving and supporting his wife and child right up to the day he'd suddenly left. Pop hadn't grieved so hard about it, and that made his leaving suspect.

Though he was wayward as a youth, Donald's faithfulness to his father wasn't fairly tested. The eldest son, he succumbed in an automobile accident when he was thirty and his children, Odette and Jake, had just begun school. Maude didn't think Pop had ever gotten over the pain of Donald's death.

As she ruminated about her brothers and the past, she understood her father's attachment to Johann. Her husband didn't make a secret of his feelings, and Pop had no reservations about accepting his son-in-law's love and adulation and wanted him to be a permanent part of his life. She imagined her father's spirit would crumble if Johann ever disappointed him, but knowing her husband, she didn't worry about the possibility.

The phone rang, and she wiped her hands on her apron and answered. "Maude speaking. How y'all doing this morning?"

"Why don't you record that and save yourself some breath? Of course, you'd have to do that for different times of the day."

"Now, that's a thought, Odette. 'Scuse me a second." She cut the end of the cigar that lay on the kitchen counter, relit it, and took a few puffs. "Did you know Pop's going to Europe Saturday?"

"Lord. Do tell. You talking about Abner Witherspoon, my grandfather?"

"One and the same. He and Johann are leaving Craven County Airport at ten o'clock Saturday morning, and Pop's acting as if he casually flies to Europe whenever the mood hits him."

"What's come over him? I never knew Pop to go anywhere that wasn't necessary except prayer meeting and Sunday service."

Her throat trapped some cigar smoke, and she had to cough a few times. "He's acting like he's fifty instead of ninety-one. Johann's the best thing that's happened to Pop in years."

"Sounds like it. Did you hear what happened to Juliet?"

After smothering the cigar, she said, "I've heard all kind of tales. What did you hear?"

"How can you be so casual? She nearly died from a botched abortion. You'd think she had better sense. Somebody needs to give that girl a lecture about contraceptives. Worst thing is, she did it because it wasn't Herbert's. Honey, what goes around comes around."

Bored with the gossip, Maude spoke sharply to her niece. "Odette, don't repeat those lies to anybody else. Not a word of it's true."

"How do you know?"

"Because Regina visited her in the hospital and talked with her. That's how I know."

"Well, you'd expect Juliet to whitewash herself. Miss Importance wouldn't tell the truth about a thing like that. If you ask me, she's got it coming to her. She doesn't control that pen of hers when she's writing her columns. Remember when she blasted poor Harold? And what about Jake? Insinuating that he had three OW's. All three of those women said they'd never been near Jake—wouldn't know him if they saw him."

Maude laughed in spite of her annoyance at the unfounded gossip. "Yeah, but Jake didn't mind the publicity. Your brother parades around with *stud* written all over him. Anyway, you should talk what you know. Loose words come back to haunt you."

"I think I'll go out to the airport Saturday morning to see Pop off. Y'all take care."

"You, too."

At least she wouldn't have to listen to that kind of talk at dinner; Regina didn't believe it, Johann didn't know about it, and Pop wouldn't tolerate it. She got her guitar and worked at learning the two new songs Harold wrote for her. She felt a strong kinship with Harold even though they were not blood relatives, because he had to overcome the kind of stigma the good people of New Bern heaped on her when she started singing in small clubs. However, once they discovered that the Europeans idolized her, you'd think she'd always been the toast of New Bern.

"I got a long memory," she told Pop when she called to let him know she'd finished testing the recipe. "These people want to rub up against me now, but I remember when they treated me as if I were the trash beneath their feet. These nights, they'll sit in the Craven as long as I'll sing."

"Humph. Maybe you sing better that you used to."

In her mind's eye, she could see the twinkle that always danced in his eyes when he allowed himself a moment of wickedness.

"Pop, I used to hurt something awful when these people snubbed me, but I figured out long ago that if you show them you don't give a hoot what they think, they treat you a lot better."

"'Course they do. Not even a child will keep punching holes in a balloon if no air comes out of it. Good or bad, people want to see results."

"Pop, I wish you'd come to hear me sing."

"I heard you sing. Sounded pretty good, too. Your mother would have been proud."

"What about you, Pop? I always wanted to make you proud."

"You can rest your mind. You're an honest woman, and you gave me a fine son-in-law."

"Consider yourself hugged. For you, that was high praise."

"Did you ask my son-in-law to have some chili tonight?"

"I sure did. You don't think I'd make that mistake twice."

"Humph. I thought you were too clever to make it the first time."

She opened the door at six-thirty, hugged her father, and looked up into Johann's flashing green eyes.

"Hi," he said, and reached into the inside pocket of his beige linen jacket, showed her his toothbrush, and winked. "How's that for dessert?"

So much for playing it cool. No one had to tell her that her face was one big grin. "Works for me." She took Johann's hand and followed her father to the dining room, where Regina and Odette waited.

Abner took his seat at the head of the table, said grace, and added, "Somebody's up to something, Lord. My family hasn't been this big in years."

Odette had the appearance of one anticipating exposure of past deeds that were best forgotten. She locked her gaze on her bowl of chili. "What do you mean by that, Pop?"

He rested his spoon and burned her with a stare that was not intended to soothe. "My daughter Maude here always has time for me, and my granddaughter there"—he pointed to Regina—"is all a grandfather could want. But when did I last see or hear from you?"

"I know, Pop, but you're always after me about—"

He cut her off. "Begging. No member of my family's got any business standing around with their hand out. You've got good property and plenty of money, and you ought to be ashamed of yourself. I wouldn't be a bit surprised if you stuck your hand out and tried to panhandle me."

"Oh, Pop," Maude said, hoping to change the topic of conversation. "Odette dropped by to say hello and stayed when I told her you'd be here. Y'all do justice to my chili, now."

He savored a spoonful, looked at Johann, nodded his approval, and turned his attention back to Odette. "I live and breathe three hundred and sixty-five days a year, Odette, not just occasionally when one of you gets a guilty conscience and calls or comes by. I've had more contact with my granddaughter Regina here these few months she's been here that I've had with you the last five years."

"I'm sorry, Pop, but . . . if you'd stay off my case, I'd—"

"I'll get off your case when you stop begging." Maude laughed as Abner's eyes twinkled with the devilment that she always loved in him, but which was so subtle that few people recognized the trait.

Odette showed talent for diverting her grandfather's attention from her when she said, "You know, this is the first time I met your husband, Maude. You never let nobody know he was white till the night the Craven opened, did you? Soon as folks found out, it was all over town. I'm sitting here trying to remember who it was that first told me about it."

How many times in the two years I've been back here have I wanted to stuff something down this woman's throat? thought Maude. "If I'd thought he jeopardized your safety, that his presence put you in danger, I'd have given you a rundown on him. But since they've pulled out his fangs and declawed him, I didn't bother to mention him. Also, it was none of your d . . . your business who I married."

"Well, don't get bent out of shape," Odette said, seemingly neither embarrassed nor remorseful. "You know how people talk."

"They're good at character assassination, too," Regina said, remembering Maude's account of Odette's tale about Juliet. "First time somebody tells me a whopping lie about you, Odette, I'll make certain you know it."

"In other words," Pop said, "somebody's been making up stories about Juliet. What we need in this town is a good year-round circus—with animals."

Maude wondered at Johann's silence and, on impulse, nudged his foot with her own. He rewarded her with a grin that seem to envelop his whole face. "Want to go to Amsterdam with Pop and me? I can get your ticket is less than an hour."

Pop's spoon clattered against the plate. "I am not chaperoning any honeymooners." He picked up the spoon and waved it at Maude. "And no battling half-lovers, either."

The round of laughter saved her a serious reply, so she said, "Johann is teasing me. He wouldn't think of spoiling Pop's trip."

Johann seemed unconcerned as he savored his chili. "This stuff can't miss, Pop." He grinned at his wife. "And neither can I."

Maude slouched against the dining room doorjamb and watched her husband play host, holding the front door as her father, Regina, and Odette left.

"My granddaughter Regina will drive me home," she heard Pop tell Johann, "so you just take it easy."

Johann's hand rested on the old man's shoulder. "Be sure to lock the front door, Pop. You're a little too careless about that sometimes."

He closed the door and locked it, and as she turned to go to the kitchen, she felt his hand on her shoulder. "Where are you going, Kitten?"

She swallowed so hard that she nearly choked. "I'll take a few minutes to clean the kitchen."

He turned her fully to face him. "Not tonight."

That said, he took possession of her mouth, her breasts, buttocks, and, at last, with his tongue deep in her mouth, his hand captured the V between her legs. She slumped against him in capitulation, and he picked her up and carried his trophy to her bed.

He awakened her the next morning with a hot cup of coffee. "The kitchen's clean. I have to go fix Pop's breakfast."

That was overdoing it. "You don't. He's been fixing his own for the last thirty-five years."

"He didn't have me. How do you feel about last night?"

She stretched like a satisfied feline and rimmed her lips with her tongue. "I could get used to it."

"Good. I'll be looking for some proof."

Twelve

Justin, too, was seeking proof, but he didn't expect Regina to abandon her single-minded pursuit of family ties long enough to contemplate their relationship with the seriousness it deserved. She'd said she would call him. What the hell! He'd deal with that later. Being a civilian in a military environment didn't suit him one bit; he missed his rank and the status that went with it, but on the other hand, he didn't have to tell anybody when and where he went.

He e-mailed the carpet design—his last one for the Craven assignment—to the manufacturer, closed the computer, and put on his jacket. He figured he deserved a drink of the best Scotch whisky known to man. He didn't have to drive, so he might as well enjoy himself. From the day he arrived at Camp Lejeune, he'd put in eight hours daily lecturing, seven hours on his designs for the Craven Hotel, and had nine hours in which to gulp down his food, take care of his person, and sleep. He'd finished the job, and he needed Regina. But she wasn't there, she hadn't called him, and he wasn't sure he cared any longer.

He switched off the radio and had started for the door when the telephone rang. He had a mind to ignore it, because the last thing he needed was a session with some men who'd tanked themselves up with alcohol. "Hello."

"May I please speak with Colonel Duval?"

He spoke with a cool voice and detached manner. "Regina, this is Justin. I thought you had decided not to call me."

"I've called twice, but you weren't there. Are you in a dormitory?"

"A cottage. Done any thinking about where we'll go when I get back there?"

"Wait a minute. We can't go any place till that suite's finished."

"Sure we can. I can't do anything else until the stuff's delivered to the hotel."

"What about the wallpaper?"

"What about it? I'm not a paper hanger. Quit stalling, woman."

"Want to go to Honolulu?"

He sat down. "That hadn't occurred to me, but if you'd like that, it's what we'll do. As I think of it, it's a great idea."

And it was, he mused after they terminated the conversation. Perhaps if she saw Honolulu and her old acquaintances with different, more experienced eyes, she'd be able to leave her demons out there in the Pacific, just as being among servicemen again had forced him to see his hang-ups and deal with them.

That Saturday morning in late September, Abner Witherspoon sat in the first-class lounge at Craven County Airport, looking at the faces of the three descendants who came to see him off on his first trip to Europe. He shifted in his chair, crossed and uncrossed his knees, and folded his hands across his belly. Then he unfolded them and put them in his pants pockets. At ninety-one, he had no right to be so excited, but thank God he'd experienced enough of life to be able to keep his fit of nerves to himself.

Maude looked at her father as a benevolent parent would upon a child leaving home for the first time. "You be sure and call me as soon as you get there, Pop."

"Yes, you be sure, now," Odette added in a voice less authoritative, as if she were uncertain of her right to say it.

Regina, who sat closest to him, patted his hand as if to reassure him, but none of it seemed to faze Abner.

"Anybody else want to tell me what to do?" he asked, looking at Regina. "If I don't get there all right, the whole world will know it. Won't it?" He winked at her. "I got a couple of weeks to have the time of my life, and I don't aim to spend them thinking about anybody here in New Bern."

Regina frowned. "Johann, would you please give me the addresses and phone numbers where I can reach you? If Pop wants to get high-nosed, I guess he's earned the right."

Johann wrote something on the back of an envelope and handed it to Regina. "I'll keep up with him if I can, but after we settle the business, he's got a long list of things he plans to do. I ask you, what could be interesting in a pewter factory?"

Abner crossed and uncrossed his knees, leaned back, and let a smile brighten his face. "You'd think a smart man like my son-in-law here would know that a pewter factory is where they make pewter, and if somebody wants to see how pewter is made, that's where they should go."

Johann spread his legs and leaned forward, bracing his forearms on his thighs. "Right on, Pop."

Abner's eyebrows shot up. "You're learning a lot of black expressions that you didn't get from me. Like I was saying, I want to see how they cut those diamonds. Never wanted to own any, but I've always been curious about how they cut 'em. Maybe we'll run over to Antwerp in Belgium and visit one of those diamond factories. And cheese. The Dutch make cheese. I want to go to a cheese factory, too. You see, I got a lot to do over there, so don't expect me to hang around a hotel making phone calls."

A glance at her watch, and Maude's heartbeat accelerated. Five minutes to boarding time. "Don't overdo it, Pop."

He looked at Johann. "I wish somebody'd tell me why it is that your children don't listen to what you tell *them,* but they think you ought to obey them." He shook his head. "Doesn't make a bit of sense."

Johann walked away from the group, leaned against the bar, picked a pretzel stick from its container, and twirled it. When his gaze locked on her, Maude got up and joined him.

"What is it, Johann?"

"While I'm gone, think about where you want us to go. You said you don't want a divorce, so I want us to live together, sharing the same house, the same table, and the same bed." His right index finger tipped up her chin. "Do you follow me, Kitten? It's that, or I'll head back to Amsterdam."

"I won't live in that cold, dreary climate. And no sun. I got three shades lighter while I lived there."

A smile played around his lips but didn't touch his eyes. "I know. And there're no collards or fatback."

"Fatback? Where'd you hear about that?"

"Pop and I were in the supermarket, and he told me that's what people here cook string beans with."

Her right hand went to her hip, but having been taught as a child that it was not ladylike, she quickly removed her hand. "You're letting him teach you bad habits. Pop wouldn't think of eating anything cooked with fatback. That stuff will definitely clog your arteries."

A white man stared at them, his lips twisted in a snarl. She hadn't thought that Johann noticed him, until he opened his arms and enfolded her—though he detested public displays of affection—sending the man what she knew was a challenge.

"Don't let it get to you, baby," he said. "If he persists, I'll give him something to think about."

As she gripped his arms, her fingers shook. "I'll still be here in this Southern town while you're in the Netherlands, so please ignore him."

Johann stared down at her, his eyes hard and his face cold and solemn. "I'd think you would prefer a cold, dreary place where color doesn't matter to what you've got here."

Her fingers crawled up his arms. "If someone laid claim to your land, would you walk away and let him have it, or would you fight for what was rightfully yours?"

"Point taken," he said, "but you factor this in your decision. There's no other choice for me, Kitten. You agree that we live together, or forget it."

She slapped her hands on her hips and rolled her eyes. "There you go giving me ultimatums, and you know all that does is fill me full of attitude and make me do the opposite of what you want." She softened her tone. "At least, say please . . . or something like that."

"Flight eight seventy-one to New York boarding in five minutes."

"Please," he said, and took the kiss she offered.

"Flight eight seventy-one to New York now receiving first-class passengers."

She looked into Johann's eyes, at what they promised, and wondered if she was crazy for not going with him.

"Are we getting on this plane?"

With lips apart, Maude swung around and looked at her father, whose presence she had momentarily forgotten.

"You should have taken care of that last night. They called first class, and that's us. If you're smart, you'll keep that frame of mind till we get back here."

She opened her arms to her father. "You have a good time, Pop, and be sure he comes back here with you."

His arms—weaker than in years past but still strong enough to communicate a father's love—curved around her. "That's all up to you, daughter. If you show him you want him back, he'll come." He hugged Regina and Odette. "You don't know what it's meant to me that you came here to be with me this morning."

Maude watched her father and her husband until they walked down the ramp and she could no longer see them. "Pop's a brand-new man," she said to her nieces. "I hadn't thought he needed attention. Since I've been back here, I've looked after him as well as he'd let me."

The three women made their way out of the airport and walked across the parking lot to their cars. "Johann treats him as if they were equals. He ignores their forty-year age gap, and Pop responds to that," Regina said.

Odette had a different explanation. "That's not how I see it," she said. "The real reason is that Pop finally got himself a son. Men always stick out their chests, flex their biceps, and feel powerful when they get a son. I never could figure it out; in my book, the human male ain't no big deal."

"Funny thing," Maude said. "Johann's father married his mother because she was pregnant, and didn't even have a drink with her after the ceremony. In effect, he never had a father. Pop is proud of Johann's accomplishments; he understands him and has grown to care deeply for him. Johann loves Pop and treats him the way a devoted son treats his father. I think they needed each other."

"That does not explain why men get so excited when they get a son. Big deal. I'm still waiting for a decent man," Odette said.

Maude sucked her teeth and looked toward the sky. "Odette, if you want to get the kind of man you think you deserve, you'll have to change your habits."

A Lincoln Town Car parked beside them, and when the driver got out, Odette stepped over to him and held out her hand. "Could you give me a little something, please?"

The man seemed taken aback but nonetheless put his hand in his pocket, peeled off a bill, handed it to her, and didn't wait to be thanked.

Maude opened Odette's hand and looked at the money in it. "You see what I mean? You'd like to have a man who drives a silver Town Car, but you traded that one for a ten-dollar bill. Everybody in New Bern knows about you, and no man worth his salary wants a woman who's a panhandler."

Odette's gaze dropped to her feet. "See y'all later." She drove away.

Maude shook her head from side to side. "When a decent-looking woman can't find a man to her liking, she ought to take a good look at herself. If you call Johann, let me know what's happening."

Regina's perplexed expression didn't surprise her, but if Johann didn't give her his telephone number, she wasn't going to ask him for it. "Sure. Don't you have his number?"

"He didn't give it to me," said Maude, "and I definitely wasn't asking him for it. See you later." Maybe she was shooting herself in the foot, but she had never chased a man, didn't know how, and didn't see the need to learn. She waved at Regina, got in her car, and headed for New Bern.

I guess there's a lot I don't know about getting along with a man, Regina said to herself as she headed her car toward New Bern. Somehow, taking independence to the extreme that Maude did seemed counterproductive. What she needed was a plan, a way to meet her kinfolk, establish a relationship with them, work things out with Justin, and put the Craven Hotel squarely on the United States map.

Horns honked behind her, and the driver of one car shook her fist at Regina as she drove past her. She looked at the speedometer and saw that she was driving at half the legal speed limit. Unwilling to accelerate, she pulled off Route 17 at Queen Street and drove through the historic district, where legacies of slavery and colonialism still gleamed unsullied after centuries.

On an impulse, she parked in front of the George H. White House and gazed at the old Georgian structure. It stood as a monument to White, a prominent African-American lawyer who served in the United States Congress from 1897 to 1901. *If White could attain such heights with the obstacles facing him, I'm not about to be defeated.* She lowered the window, took a deep breath of crisp, fresh air, closed the window, and headed for the hotel, where, invigorated, she strode with brisk steps through the lobby and up the stairs to her office.

"Ms. Pearson, Harold Pearson wants to see you. He's here in the lobby," the receptionist said, speaking through the intercom.

"Tell him to come up, please." She didn't mind seeing Harold, because his affection and friendship were important to her, but she'd appreciate it if he would at least call before barging in on her whenever it suited him. Laughter welled up in her; five months earlier, she couldn't have imagined requiring anything of a relative other than love. She was learning that family might not prove to be the singular vital ingredient in one's life.

She got up and opened the door when Harold knocked. She didn't know why she hadn't asked him to come in, but the vulnerableness she always sensed in him, even when he displayed a mean streak, made her protective of him.

He kissed her on both cheeks. "Hi. I was afraid you wouldn't be here, and I had to talk with somebody. You're the only person around here who tries to understand me." He took a folded sheet of paper from the inside pocket of his jacket and handed it to her. "I'd better give you this before I forget it. It's your sixteen other Pearson relatives. I hope you can stand 'em."

She thanked him and put the paper into her briefcase. "Now, what do you want us to talk about?"

He leaned forward, his fair skin mottled with the blood that rushed to it, and ran his fingers through his hair. "Cuz, this is the best thing that ever happened to me, and I can't accept it."

She took one of his hands in hers and tried to calm him. "What happened to you?"

"It's the Toronto Symphony. The conductor heard me playing Mozart's Concerto for Wind Instruments with some members of the Fayetteville Symphony, and offered me a job in the reed section."

She must have squeezed his fingers too hard, because he moved his hand. "Harold, that's wonderful. I'm so glad. But what's the matter? Why can't you take the job?"

"I'd have to buy three tuxedos with complete accessories, including a pair of patent leather shoes for formal occasions. Every player has to have them. And Cuz, I don't even own a warm coat, boots, gloves—none of that cold-weather stuff. I figured it's two or three thousand dollars if you add a place to stay. And I have to keep my apartment here in New Bern. Musicians playing a gig here and there don't save that kind of money, and I don't believe in debts."

Harold got up, walked to the window, and looked out. "For just one minute, Cuz, I had it licked. I could tell these creeps who're always looking down on me and making little of me where they can go. If I played with the Toronto Symphony Orchestra, every person in this two-bit town would know I'm somebody."

She leaned back in the chair, her mind on his words, and her gaze on his demeanor, for his limp was more pronounced than she'd seen it.

His shoulders slumped, and he seemed shorter than his five feet, nine inches.

"Please don't mention this to anybody, Cuz. It'll be just one more thing they'll have to laugh about."

She'd didn't remember having heard anybody denigrate Harold, but she didn't have a wide circle of acquaintances in New Bern. Patting the chair beside her desk, she said, "Harold, would you sit here so we can talk?"

"Nothing to talk about, Cuz. I can still do my twice-a-month Sunday-afternoon gigs with the Fayetteville orchestra October through April. It's better than nothing. I gotta be going. Thanks for your ear." He stopped and looked hard at her. "I told you I'd need you more than you would need me. Now you know what I meant."

"Would you please sit down?" He dropped into the chair. "You're going to Canada. I'll give you whatever you need."

He jumped up. "You can't do that, and it isn't why I came here. I needed to talk with somebody, and you're the only person I've got."

"Would you *please* sit down? I can do it, and I will. You may pay me back when you can. And before you leave for Toronto, put some order in the music you composed and give it to me. I'm going to get it published in a single volume. Is it scored for orchestra as well as for soloists? What you need is an agent. Promotion is what I'm best at; I did it for Royal Hotels in Hawaii."

He raised himself up, braced the palms of his hands on her desk, and leaned toward her. "If you're playing with me, I don't think I can stand it."

"I'm serious. Give me a curriculum vitae and a list of your compositions, and call that conductor in Canada." She handed him the phone. "Here. Do it now."

"I c-can't. J-just give me a minute, p-please," he said as tears streamed down his face.

She went into her bathroom to give him privacy, and when she returned, his face beamed through the water that poured from his eyes.

"He said . . . He said he'll be expecting me October the fifteenth, and I should receive my tickets and travel orders any day. Me, Harold Pearson, playing with a first-rate symphony. Cuz, if you ever need me, even if I'm in Australia, just call, and I'll drop everything and come. You changed my life. From the time I met you, I knew I had at least one friend." He reached toward her but didn't touch her. "Please don't mention this. If I make it, I'll tell, but if I don't and they know, I'll be disgraced."

She didn't understand Harold's preoccupation with the image that his relatives and others held of him, but she had a hunch his concern was well founded.

"I'm in your corner. Let me know what kind of opportunities you envisage, and I'll get you started."

He told her he had to be in Canada Sundays and Mondays during the symphony's season and to join its tours. "I'll give you the schedule." He shook his head as would one seeing an apparition. "I just can't believe it. I'd better start getting things together."

She went down to the lobby two hours later and stopped dead in her tracts. "Did Harold Pearson just walk out of here?" she asked a porter.

"Yes ma'am. Would you like me to call him?"

"Uh . . . no. Thanks."

She spoke to the receptionist about the evening's programs and observed the staff registering new arrivals, something she did periodically to ensure that they gave the hotel a friendly but elegant atmosphere. Satisfied, she headed back to her office, sat down, and mused over what Harold could possibly have been doing in the hotel for the past two hours. He could have been in one of the three sound-proof music rooms playing the piano or some other instrument, but she doubted that. He could have been photocopying sheets of music, but that didn't ring right, either.

I'm not going to second-guess him, she said to herself. *If it bothers me, I'll ask him.*

Maude didn't feel like singing the blues that night, but Harold had given her notice that he was in the mood for some down-to-earth soulful music. After half an hour of pleading with him, he let her choose. She'd always decided what songs she would sing, and she couldn't understand his asserting himself about something that was her domain. He didn't make a fuss about giving in to her, so she dismissed it as another of the oddities that Harold evinced from time to time.

She opened with Duke Ellington's "Mood Indigo" and ended the set with his "Creole Love Call," which was too high for her mezzo voice, but she could easily sing it since it didn't have words. Her flesh crawled as she listened to the haunting strains of Harold's cornet. Goose pimples dotted her arms, and she had to shake herself to force her concentration on the notes she had to sing. At the deafening applause, she stepped aside to give Harold the credit he deserved, but he walked over to her, took her hand, and then bowed.

After the show, as she sat with him, Regina, and James Carlson in the Starlight Lounge, she'd never seen Harold so self-assured. She wondered if he'd fallen in love, but that wasn't a question she could ask him in the presence of others.

"You sang your ass off tonight, Maude," Harold said. "I'm trying to play my horn, and that singing . . . I kept thinking of somebody lost in a wilderness. When you ended that eight-bar crescendo with a pianissimo, I nearly dropped my horn. It went all through me. Gawd! But you can sing!"

His eyes sparkled, and his facial features were more animated than she'd ever seen them as he smiled at the well-wishers who passed their table.

"Maude sings all the time as if she owns music," James said, "but you hit your stride tonight, Harold. I began listening to you at the Zanzibar when I first started this hotel, and I know you're a great jazz artist, but from the way you played that cornet, I think there's more. See that you develop it."

Regina nodded. The saxophone was Harold's plaything, but the cornet was his professional instrument. He'd said he would show them, and she didn't doubt it. "First time I heard you play the cornet," she said to Harold.

"No, it's not. I borrowed one that night at the Zanzibar. Remember?" He waved a hand as if the matter were of no consequence. "I always play my best when I got my own horn."

"I'd have given anything if Pop had been here tonight," Maude said. "I don't think I ever sang better, not even when I was young."

"Shame on him," Harold said. "That is one cussed man. He invented stubbornness. The whole of New Bern knows that if Abner Witherspoon says no, it's written in stone."

"Not exactly," Regina said. "He and I are on the best of terms."

Harold's eyes widened. "Get outta here. Since when?"

"Since before the Craven opened. He was a big help to me."

Harold leaned back in his chair and spread his hands palms out. "I take it back. The old man's a pussycat."

"That pussycat is having the time of his life in Amsterdam right now," Maude said.

A frown slid over Harold's face. "Amsterdam, New York? What on earth can he do in that one-horse town."

Maude laughed and took a hefty sip of her Heineken. "Pop's in the Netherlands with my husband."

"You're kidding."

Maude shook her head. "Ask Regina. My ninety-one-year-old father has found the fountain of youth."

James called the bartender. "Bring us a couple of bottles of vintage champagne. Let's drink to that." He looked at Regina. "Where's Justin?"

"You know he's at Camp Lejeune." Her shrug, though seemingly casual, carried a message, Maude thought. She had brushed off a few men in her day, and she knew the act when she saw it. *Hmmm.* So Carlson wanted Regina, and she wasn't interested.

"Y'all hurry and drink up this two hundred dollars James just spent. If I don't get my sleep, my voice won't be worth doodledy squat tomorrow night."

Regina looked hard at her. "Won't be worth *what?*"

"I forget," Maude said, "You're not fully black yet. But you get my message. Did you call to see about Pop?"

Regina laughed. "If you want me to call Johann, just say so, but please tell me what you want me to say."

Maude drank the last of her beer. "You may not be quite black, but you sure are a quick study. Five months ago, nobody would have called you a smartass."

When Regina could stop laughing, she said, "That's true, but I fit right in now, don't I?"

James closed his gaping mouth, then turned to Harold. "Are these insults?"

"Lord, no," Harold said. "They adore each other. Wish I was that sure of . . . of anybody."

Regina stood on the balcony looking down at the crowd of conventioneers in the lobby, registering, greeting each other, milling around as if acquainting themselves with their temporary home. She'd done it. Eight hundred sixteen chefs and their companions. What a sight!

Dressed in a navy blue suit with white shirt, red tie, and red, white, and blue handkerchief, Larry walked through the crowd, introducing himself and welcoming the guests. She hadn't suggested he do that, but it was a gracious touch. She thanked God he hadn't chosen to wear his Dior blue suit and canary yellow tie that gave him the appearance of a man on the make. Satisfied, she went back to her office, and as she sat down, her gaze fell on Harold's list of relatives she might contact.

She scanned the paper until she saw the name of Jewel Pearson, Harold's sister and Cephus's half-sister. "May I please speak with Jewel Pearson," she said when a low, sultry female voice answered the phone.

"I'm Jewel. Who's this?"

Not much warmth there. "Regina Pearson. I've wanted to meet you, Jewel, and I asked Harold for your number."

"I'm surprised he knows it. I heard a lot about you. What's up?"

It wasn't a blast of cold air, but it wasn't a jubilant hosanna either. "Jewel, I've been here about six months, and I've only met five of my relatives, though I'm told there're Pearsons and Witherspoons all over this region. I'd like us to get to know each other."

"If you've met five, you're doing good. Our folks don't hang out together; if they do, they don't include me. We could have a drink some time. What's this I hear about you being a dead ringer for Juliet Smith? I hope you're nicer than she is."

Whew! Talk about blunt! "Would you like to meet me here at the hotel for lunch or dinner? I don't drink much."

"Well, I like a little gin and tonic once in a while. What time you get off from work?"

"Uh . . . I can make myself free most anytime that suits you."

"Yeah? Well, 'scuse me. I'll come by 'bout five-thirty on my way home one day. Take care."

After hanging up, Regina mused over the encounter, wondering what, if anything, she had accomplished with that call. Maybe nothing. Not to be defeated, she dialed the next number.

A voice that was surely battered and ravaged with time said, "Thank y'all for calling. Please speak loudly."

She tried several times to make herself understood and finally gave up when she decided that her cousin Martha Pearson Stout couldn't hear. Harold should have warned her. She made a note to visit the woman as soon as she could. Fourteen more individuals on the list—blood relatives who didn't and probably never would give a damn about her. She expelled a long, labored breath and put the list in her briefcase.

After eating supper in the hotel, she hurried home to change her clothes, hoping to fish in the Neuse River before the sun set around eight-thirty. But as she was about to leave, the phone rang.

"This is Regina Pearson. Hello."

"Regina, can I come over there? I'm scared to death that Herbert's leaving me. P-please. He said . . ."

She sat down. "Juliet, what's going on?" She couldn't imagine receiving a call from her cousin after Juliet's ugly behavior, repaying her kindness with the demand that she leave Juliet's house.

"I don't know what to do. I called Cephus, but he's off someplace with the governor. Somebody, please talk to Herbert. I'm a good wife I am. I am. Regina, talk to Herbert. *Please!* I haven't done anything to deserve this, and he's accepted all the nasty things people are saying about me. At least you believed me." More words tumbled out of Juliet so fast that Regina could hardly understand what her cousin said, her voice rising like that of a tortured animal.

"Don't cry," Regina said, trying to calm her. "Stand up to him, and tell *him* you've been a good wife and you won't tolerate his accusations. Turn the screw in the opposite direction. Put him on the defensive. Ask him what kind of man takes sides against his wife and fails to defend her when she needs him."

"Oh. You . . . uh . . . You know, you're right. But suppose that doesn't work."

Sensing that her advice fitted well with Juliet's personality, she said, "It will, at least for a while. In the meantime, we'll figure out a strategy. You'd better not have company when you take him on, because the last thing you need is for him to have an ego trip."

"You're right. I . . . I don't know how to thank you."

"Don't bother. It's not solved yet."

She hung up, called Harold and told him as much as she knew. "Do you know how to get in touch with Cephus? If that doctor can be made to tell Herbert the truth, that'll put an end to this crisis."

"I hate to say it, Cuz, but . . ."

She didn't want to hear it again. "She's been just as nasty to me as she has to anybody, but she needs help. Be magnanimous. It won't hurt you, and it'll allow you to feel superior."

He chuckled, and she realized he still reveled in the excitement of his appointment to the Toronto Symphony. "Okay, I'll call Cephus and tell him to scare the hell out of that ofay doctor."

An hour and a half later, Cephus called Regina. "It's all taken care of. I told that charlatan doctor that if he didn't produce those records and give Herbert Smith unaltered copies, he'd be looking for work because the state would take his license."

"Did you tell Juliet?"

"Pul-leeze! I tried to, but she was so busy bawling her thanks I hung up."

She appreciated his help, but nonetheless he grated on her nerves. She looked at the dying daylight and threw up her hands. By the time she got to the river, it would be too dark to fish. Since coming to New Bern, she had allowed many of the hobbies she once enjoyed to go by the way. Most of all, she missed sculpting and long solitary walks on the sandy beach at sunset—pleasures exchanged for feeble attempts to mold some strangers into a family.

Impulsively she grabbed her purse, got in her car, and drove to Dillon's department store, where she bought blocks of dark chocolate. She was paying for it when she looked up and saw Odette.

"Heard from Pop?" Odette asked her. "I'm ashamed that I haven't stayed closer to him, but if I spend one minute with Pop, he lectures to me. Still, he's all right. He is that. I couldn't believe how young he seems." Something in the vicinity of her feet seemed to have caught her attention. "Maybe we could have a little party or something for him when he comes home," she said without looking up.

"That's a wonder. . . . I think it's a great idea, Odette, but Pop hates parties."

Odette wasn't convinced. "That's what he says. We don't have to believe him, do we?"

"I don't know. I had a hard enough time getting him to even admit I existed; I am definitely not doing anything to annoy him."

"Let's ask Maude. She's the closest person to him. . . . How do you stay so slim if you eat chocolates?"

"I don't eat it. I buy these bulk pieces because I carve figures out of them." An idea hit her, exciting her, but she didn't share it with Odette.

"Do tell! Won't it melt?"

Regina put the chocolate in the small shopping bag she carried. "No, because I work a few minutes and refrigerate it a few minutes. I've done busts of Mary McLeod Bethune, Martin Luther King Jr.,

Eleanor Roosevelt, and Jimmy Carter, as well as some other people."
And when she got home, she would begin work on a bust of Pop.

"I'd better be going," Odette said. "I'll mention the party to Maude
and ask her to call and let you know what she thinks."

Regina watched Odette make her way out of the store. She had
seemed mellow, gentle, and, yes, personable. And she hadn't mentioned Juliet. She also didn't stop any of the men she met on her way
out of the store and ask them for money. Absolutely out of character.
She hoped her cousin wasn't sick.

At home, she changed into pants and an old T-shirt, got her artist's
tools, and sat down at her kitchen table to begin the bust of her grandfather. On an impulse, she reached over and turned on the radio,
which she kept tuned to WNXT-FM for local news. Her hand remained suspended in the air, and her lower lip dropped as Dragmar,
the station's features reporter, intoned, "Columnist Juliet Smith is battling a divorce. Seems hubby is about to sue, and the lady is pleading mercy.
How the mighty have fallen!"

Regina put the chocolate in the refrigerator and debated whether
to call Juliet or Cephus. She suspected that she was already in debt to
Cephus, though for what she wasn't sure, and she didn't want to com-
promise herself further. The phone rang.

"Is your radio on, Cuz? Dragmar's ruining Juliet. They've been at
each other for years, just like two cats brawling over rights to a back
alley. I have to hand it to Juliet, though; she never got as far down in
the sewer as Dragmar. I'm feeling so magnanimous today that I already called Cephus. If he gets a retraction from her, this town won't
be big enough for his head."

"You think he can straighten this out, too?"

"Listen, Cuz. Cephus is not a nice person. He keeps records of people's infractions and improprieties. Never let him catch you with your
pants down—oops. Well, you know what I mean. Can I come by and
bring my music? I've organized it, made a table of contents, and filled
out the copyright forms. Cuz, my feet won't hardly touch the ground.
I wish I knew how to thank you."

"You can thank me by writing out a thorough, honest curriculum
vitae. I can't work on your bookings if I don't know anything about
you. Also, let me know where and with whom you'd like to play. We'll
try to get an orchestra to play one of your pieces." When he didn't respond, she called, "Harold? Harold, are you there?"

"I . . . I'm here. I'm just so full, I can't speak."

"I'll expect you in about an hour. All right?"

Much as she liked Harold, he disconcerted her with his personality changes. Inconsistency in a person could be baffling, but Harold's vacillations from strength to weakness, kindness to cruelty, and insecurity to self-assurance mystified her. She saw changes in herself daily, but she welcomed most of them as necessary adjustments to her new life. They were not the spontaneous reactions to circumstances that Harold displayed.

Fundamentally, she remained the same person she was when her father died; her values and goals hadn't changed, although she'd begun to shift her priorities. Her father had believed that the less you knew about a person the more you'd like them, and she supposed he used that bit of philosophy to keep people, including his daughter, at arm's length. But she was learning that *like* didn't mean much and that she preferred to care about people. The more deeply she knew and understood her relatives, the more she cared for them. She couldn't even dismiss Cephus as easily as when she first encountered him.

She couldn't sculpt, because Harold would interrupt her, and there seemed no point in calling Juliet, for the same reason, so she telephoned her aunt Maude.

"I tried to phone you," Maude said. "Did you hear Dragmar tonight? That sister sank to the gutter this time. I hope Juliet didn't hear that broadcast, because she was already miserable, and knowing that the whole town's talking about it will just sicken her."

"Aunt Maude, I'm not used to all this mudslinging, and I don't want to get used to it. If that's what I have to tolerate here, I'd as soon be back in Honolulu virtually alone."

"Let's not get carried away, here. Juliet attracts notoriety, so she has to pay for it. I was thinking about going to the Antique Auto Show. It's a little late this year, but it's always exciting. Want to go?"

Mmmm. That was a quick change of subject. "We could go Sunday afternoon," Regina said, "unless you'd rather rest for your evening performance."

"Let's see the show. Uh . . ." A pause ensued, and Regina sat erect, waiting. Diffidence, however slight, was not a trait she associated with her aunt.

"What is it, Aunt Maude? Is something wrong?"

"No, not a thing. Uh . . . you would tell me if you'd spoken with Johann, wouldn't you?"

So that was it. Maude thought she'd overplayed her hand. "I'm going to call him tomorrow. Any message?" she asked, careful to say it in as casual a tone as possible.

"No. Nothing special except he's taking his time getting back here."

They'd only been gone four days, but she didn't remind Maude of their plan to stay about three weeks. "I'll tell him. There's the doorbell. Can we finish this tomorrow?"

"Sure. Wasn't important anyway."

But it was. Maude hadn't called out of concern for Juliet, but for news of Johann. All her aunt had to do was telephone him, but she'd rather worry. Regina hastened to the front door. Only the Lord knew what she would face when Harold stepped into her house.

He greeted her and looked around. "I knew you'd surround yourself with elegance. Paintings, Persian carpets, and"—he ran his fingers over the arm of a chair—"this rich velvet on your furniture. This is my taste, and one of these days, I'll be able to cater to it. Just look at these paintings! Elizabeth Catlett and Beardon. Cuz, you're a mess." He handed her a manila folder. "My bio and copies of my compositions."

She set the table of contents he'd prepared aside and looked at his compositions. "I studied music, but with this I'm out of my league, so I'll get an expert to help you shape up this book."

Splotches of crimson appeared on his face, and he sat on the edge of the chair, wringing his hands. "Cuz, you're talking a lot of money, and except for a few hundred dollars, I'm strapped."

She didn't plan to tell him or anyone else of the wealth she inherited from her father, but she didn't want him to worry, so she joshed, "When I die, Harold, you'll be one of my beneficiaries, so all we're doing is using money that you'd have gotten anyway. Besides, you'll be wealthy within a few years because I'm going to package you properly."

He gazed at her, searching, as if trying to read her, to see inside her. "Nobody's ever been this good to me. People around here don't take me seriously, but from the time we met, you acted as if I was somebody special." He shook his head. "The good Lord must have sent you."

She winked at him. "He did. As soon as you join the Toronto Symphony, I'll begin booking solo appearances for you. The first year, we'll ask twenty-five hundred, and then—"

He jumped up and grabbed her shoulders. "Are you crazy? No-body's going to pay me . . ." His voice trailed off. "You're serious, aren't you?"

He was like a child on Christmas morning, and she couldn't help rejoicing with him. "Of course I'm serious. If you don't value yourself, neither will anyone else. In three years, we'll triple that." After getting as much information from him as she needed, she made tea for herself and coffee for him and brought it, along with a plate of chocolate chip cookies, into the living room.

"Before we go any further, Cuz, send me a contract making your-self my agent/publicist and listing your cut as fifteen percent. I want it legalized."

It made sense, she thought. "I won't take the cut till after you earn a hundred thousand. It's a deal. What am I going to do about Juliet, Harold? She needs someone."

"Well, if you want to go see her, do it, but don't be surprised if your good deed backfires."

The following day, Thursday, Regina spent the morning in her of-fice, dealing with staff problems, conflicts in bookings, and other things she considered trivial and which Larry could have handled. She called him on her intercom. "I'll be away much of the afternoon. If you need me, reach me on my cell phone."

She telephoned Juliet, arranged to go to her house around one-thirty, and then contemplated phoning Johann in Amsterdam. Why not? She wanted to know about Pop, and she would probably be able to put her aunt at ease. Johann answered on the first ring, and all she understood was "van der Kaa."

"Johann, this is Regina in New Bern. How are you and Pop doing?"

"I'm exhausted, but Pop wants to go back to the Bali Restaurant for dinner. It's pouring rain, but he doesn't want to stay inside, so today we did the museums. I thought he'd be bushed. How are you?"

"Just fine." She waited for him to ask about Maude, but he didn't.

"Aunt Maude wants to know when you're coming back. She seems to think you've been gone a long time, but I told her you left four days ago." Let him think about that.

"Thanks, Regina. Since you're our intermediary, ask her why she doesn't call me if she misses me. I miss her, but I'm too damned stub-born to do anything about it. Tell her I said that."

"I will. Is Pop anywhere around?"

"Yeah. He was teaching me how to play cribbage, but he got bored and tuned in CNN."

"Hi, Pop. This is Regina. Enjoying yourself?"

His voice reached her as clearly as if he were in the room with her. Oh, the wonder of Telstar! "I knew if I got a call, it would be from you. My daughter Maude won't call, 'cause she's scared Johann will think she wants him. I'll bet she's sitting by the phone."

"Not exactly, Pop, but she wants him to hurry and come back."

"He's got a fine place here. We already got the chili company set up, and I've been doing a lot of sightseeing. There must have been a million flowers in that square yesterday morning. My son-in law is taking me to Belgium, France, and London this trip, so don't be upset if you can't reach me." In his enthusiasm, words seemed to spill out of him.

Shudders raced through her at the thought he might collapse from exertion. "Try not to do too much in one day, Pop. I don't think you're used to this."

"I'm not, and it's too bad. Best thing ever happened to me. I've got a few things to tell my daughter Maude when I get back, and she won't like a word I say. These Dutch women know a man when they see one, but my daughter is not cursed with that virtue. And if I find out you're still jerking Duval around, I'll have some words for you, too."

"What do you want to see in Paris?" she asked him in an effort to change the subject.

"I'll work that out when I get there. I'm going to see Brussels, Antwerp, and London first. How is your convention crowd? I've been a little anxious about them."

"Great, Pop. Before they left, their attorney signed a contract to hold their next three conventions at the Craven. Pop, I feel so good about that, and I have to thank you for warning me about so many potential crises. I did just what you told me."

She heard him sigh and thought he might be tired until he said, "I'm glad you came to me. If I'd had you with me all those years when I struggled alone with the Witherspoon Hotel . . ." He didn't finish the sentence.

"Maude was in Europe most of the time, and Travis—when he was home there—and Robert had no use for the hotel. Well, no point in going back over that. Johann will e-mail you our travel schedule, so you can reach me if you need me. I'd better go. They dress for dinner here. My son-in-law is taking me back to that Bali Restaurant for some Indonesian food. It sure was good night before last. Mind yourself with Duval, now. You hear?" She was learning that her grandfather was not easily sidetracked.

She sat at her desk for a long while, marveling that a man her grandfather's age was so open to adventure, ideas, and new foods. He could teach her more than the skillful management of a hotel. She phoned her aunt, marveling as she did so at the joy such a simple act gave her. At the wonder of it. Whenever she felt like it, she could dial her mother's sister and get a warm reception.

"Maude speaking. How y'all doing this afternoon?"

"Aunt Maude, Pop is running Johann ragged, and Johann said if you miss him why don't you call him."

"Cheeky, isn't he." The relief in her aunt's voice was unmistakable. "If I read that right, he doesn't miss *me.*"

Regina stifled a laugh. "Oh, he does, but he said he's, quote, 'too damned stubborn to do anything about it,' unquote."

"You just wait till I get my hands on that man."

Regina let the laughter pour out of her, and when she got it under control, she said, "I can imagine what you'll do when you get your hands on him."

"Honey, you may be smart, but I don't think your mind can divine *that!* Thanks for calling him and delivering my message."

"You're welcome. See you this evening."

She locked her desk, got her briefcase and purse, left the hotel, and set out for Juliet's house. Her right hand shook so badly that she had to steady it with her left one in order to fit the key into the door of her car. She finally got the key into the ignition, started it, and had to cut it off and calm herself; her heart seemed as if it would fly out of her chest. She didn't think she had ever been as nervous or as scared. She parked in front of Juliet's house, walked up to the door, and knocked. Of all the trials she'd experienced, none had greater potential for disrupting her life than the one she now faced. She would befriend her cousin, but she would demand a reckoning about their identities.

Thirteen

Maude didn't want Johann to get cocky about his chances with her. She didn't want to live in Europe, but her conscience had begun to eat at her. She had never thought of herself as self-centered, and she didn't like people who showered their love on themselves alone. Regina's words rang in her head like funeral bells tolling for the dead. *"He said he misses you, but that he's too damned stubborn to do anything about it."* The worst of that was her certain knowledge that he'd spoken the truth. If he decided not to kneel, he wouldn't, no matter what it cost him, and back there on his home turf, where stoicism marked most anybody you met, he might decide he'd gone far enough with her.

She couldn't focus on learning the new song Harold wanted them to perform at the Craven that night, and began pacing from her living room to the kitchen, wiping specks of dust from furniture, smoothing the doilies on her tea tray, moving about listlessly, with no goal in view.

She made no apologies for having divorced her first three husbands. Lawrence Hicks had abused her and every living creature in his path, including their dog. Julius Nickerson realized she didn't suit him, and had the sense to cut his losses early and get out. She'd married Henri Duprés because he idolized her and because being alone in Paris was proving a chilling experience. But the romance ended when he said "I do," and from then on she was to be maid, cook, and provider of sex when he wasn't getting his needs met elsewhere. He also considered himself a fair substitute for her career, even though when he met her, she was the toast of Paris. His passion for garlic and distaste for soap and water hadn't helped his cause. She had refused to tolerate him.

Johann was sitting alone at a table in Neukirk's Jazz Club, situated in the heart of Rotterdam, when she first saw him. He was no more than six feet from the stage, and his face bore the expression of a man who liked what he saw and wanted it. She couldn't keep her gaze from him and finally capitulated and sang directly to him, her heart fluttering and the muscles squeezing and contracting in her belly. He smiled, and though she held out for months, she was his from that moment.

They had ten years of marriage, good years, the happiest of her life, but in all that time, she couldn't stop longing for her own people, for sunshine and her own culture. What was the point in using the vernacular if nobody understood it? And sometimes, saying she was dragging her ass or that she was plain crapped out was the only way to express exactly how she felt. But that was Greek to her Dutch acquaintances. In addition to that—and that was a lot—the Dutch didn't know collards from squash. She saw many Indonesians there, most of them darker than she, but they considered themselves white. Occasionally, she longed to see a plain African-like black face so that she wouldn't get a shock when she looked in the mirror.

She opened a bottle of Heineken, went back to the porch, relit her cigar, and rocked back and forth. She'd spent the last half hour thinking about her life, but if Johann gave her an ultimatum—and he might—she still didn't know what she'd do. She knew only that she didn't want to live in Europe and she didn't want to live without Johann. Oh, what the heck! According to her watch, it was seven o'clock in Amsterdam. She might catch him before he and Pop left for dinner. She dialed the number Regina gave her, thinking she'd been foolish not to ask him for it. After all, wasn't he taking her ninety-one-year-old father out of the country?

"Abner Witherspoon speaking. Mr. van der Kaa will be back after a while. Who's calling?"

She couldn't believe he had the courage to answer the phone, not knowing whether the caller spoke English. "Pop, this is Maude. How are you?"

"I'm fine. You finally decided to call your husband, did you?"

Johann could have called *her*, too, but she wasn't about to get into a trans-Atlantic discussion with her father on the subject of her behavior as a wife. "You must be having a good time. You haven't called us."

"My granddaughter called me, so you knew how I was. I don't see a thing wrong with Amsterdam. It rains a lot, but it rains just as much in New Bern. I think you need your head examined."

She didn't want to shock him by agreeing, so she said, "Pop, will you please tell Johann I called him?"

"A minute ago, you led me to think you were calling to see about me. Humph. I'll tell him, but you'd better straighten up. You hear?"

"Yes, Pop. When you coming home?"

"I haven't been to Paris and London yet. Should I tell your husband you're anxious for him to get back there?"

She couldn't help laughing. "Pop, I can see right through you. All right, if you want to. Love you."

Maybe it was talking with Pop, or perhaps it was because he would tell Johann she had called him and missed him; for whatever reason, she felt lighthearted, twirling around in the kitchen as she hummed "I'm just Foolin' Myself," a tune Billie Holiday made famous. He would call her, and then what? She knew he wouldn't accept anything less that her full commitment to their marriage.

About that time, Regina faced her moment of reconciliation with fate, the likelihood of her cousin's denial, and anger, as Juliet Smith's door opened.

"I thought you were the cleaning woman. Come on in," Juliet said, then walked back into the living room and left Regina to make her own way.

Regina stood at the door, debating with herself. She could go in or she could ignore Juliet and solve the mystery without her help.

"Come on in," Juliet called. "I'm not feeling too good. I don't know what that doctor did to me, but I'm still spotting a little."

Regina went in, closed the door, and followed Juliet's voice to the living room. "Do you want to go to the hospital here?"

"I thought about it, but I think I'll wait a while and see if I'm any better. Thanks for coming over. I don't know why you'd bother after the way I treated you."

She sat on the green velvet sofa across from Juliet, who sat on the edge of a matching oversized chair. "I am not a Pollyanna, Juliet, and I don't allow myself to be a doormat for anyone. I'm here because you called me when you needed someone and because I have to have the answer to our strange likeness." She watched her cousin's face for a reaction. "Maybe it isn't so strange, but I intend to find out. But first, was Cephus able to help you?"

"He had the doctor send my records to me by FedEx so I can show them to Herbert when he comes."

She already knew that much, but she was after the outcome, and she realized she hadn't completely shaken that ingrained Hawaiian habit of not probing. "Did you tell your husband you have the records?"

"I told him, and he said he'd come on his next pass. I'd be happier, though, if he didn't have to see the proof, but this is better than what I had facing me."

Might as well get down to business. "Do you have any idea where Uncle Travis is?"

Juliet shook her head. "I haven't heard anything from him or about him since he left here when I was four years old. Mama said she got home from school one day—she taught elementary school, you know—and my father was standing beside his car with one suitcase. All he said was, 'I'm leaving.' Mama went to the kitchen so he wouldn't see her cry. His bank book was on the table, and he'd withdrawn half of what was in his account and left the rest for us. She heard the front door close, and that was the end of their marriage. Nobody knows where he is. Not even Pop."

"Your mother and both of my parents are dead. He's the only one who knows about this, so if he's alive I'm going to find him. Did your mother have any clues as to where he might have gone?"

"He polished minerals as a hobby, and mama thought he might be in Colorado or New Mexico. Someplace like that."

"I'll get a detective. You might have to take a DNA test. Would you be willing to do that?"

Juliet's eyes widened and her lower lip dropped. "You mean . . . Well, yes, because it won't make me a bit unhappy to know I'm not related to him. My mother cried herself to death about that man."

"But it might show that you are. I'll have to take it, too. Have you ever mentioned this to Herbert? How much we look alike, I mean."

"No, but I suppose he saw it for himself when you came here."

Regina had a suspicion that Juliet didn't open up to her husband, and that a lot of dust lay beneath their marital rug. "Now's your chance to clear up any problem and any misunderstanding with him. He's wronged you and he'll need your forgiveness, so if there's anything unsettled between you, I'd get it straightened out now."

She noticed her cousin's restlessness and the way she shifted her gaze. "What's the matter?" she asked her.

"I really did have a miscarriage in that accident. We've been trying so long to have a child. We've both had every test and treatment for infertility known to mankind, including old wives' remedies. Then, when we decided to give up, I got pregnant.

"I hadn't told Herbert, because I didn't want to raise his hopes for fear something would happen. I was waiting till he noticed it."

"But why? I don't see how you could keep such good news to yourself."

She rubbed her upper lip, looked up, and seemed to measure her words. "Regina, when I was sixteen a midwife gave me a botched abortion, and the doctor who treated me said I couldn't have any children. I never told Herbert I was pregnant, because I didn't expect to carry that baby to term."

"If I were you, I'd find a good time to tell him everything. I'm no expert on husband-wife relations, but I'm not a stranger to men, either. Try to clear out all the debris. He loves you; I'm certain of that."

"I know. There's some iced tea in the refrigerator. Would you like some?"

The word *no* lay on the tip of her tongue, but she didn't release it. She wanted to build a friendship with her cousin, and that meant accepting her hospitality.

"I'd love it," she said. "No. No. No. I can get it. You sit there. I'll bring some for you, too."

In the elegant, spotless kitchen, she found oatmeal cookies in the pantry and took them along with two glasses of tea into the living room.

"I love your kitchen."

"Thanks. I only cook when Herbert is here, and I don't do much of it then. He's a lot better at it than I am."

"I grew up among Native Hawaiians, and the men expect their wives to do everything. Life here is so different, so much more progressive than among them. Getting used to the difference is a challenge."

"I've never been there. Some time you'll have to tell me what it's like and how different it is living among African Americans. Maybe I'll write a piece for my column." She hesitated and a look of alarm clouded her face. "Only if you wanted to. I wouldn't print a word if you didn't agree."

What a change! Perhaps they could be friends after all.

* * *

That night, after dressing in her tiny apartment in the Craven Hotel, Regina walked down the corridor to the staircase leading to the lobby. With the first step down, she nearly tripped. Standing beside the center table beneath the huge chandelier, in the company of James Carlson, was Justin Duval, speaking with a woman she didn't know.

As soon as he saw her, he went to meet her. "My Lord, but you're a sight for sore eyes," he said, his face blooming into a smile. "I would have told you I'd be here, but James drove by and said, 'How about riding with me to the Craven?' I didn't need an excuse." Suddenly, he gripped both of her shoulders and kissed her on the mouth so quickly, she barely felt it.

She steadied herself after the shock of it and looked around; nobody paid them any special attention. "Who's your friend?"

For an answer, he grasped her arm and walked back to James and the woman. "Regina Pearson, this is Claudia Sharp. She's doing a story on James and would like to interview you about the hotel, which James tells her is the crown in his enterprises." After greeting the woman and James, she watched to see which of the men Ms. Sharp paid the most attention to, and decided that James had his hands full.

After ten minutes or so, Justin nudged her left elbow. "Could we go over there"—he pointed toward the lounge—"and talk? I have to go back tonight.

"My designs are with the manufacturers, and I expect they'll have the reproductions ready in a couple of weeks. So I'll have time that I can use for a much needed vacation, say a week. What do you say we head for Honolulu? If Larry can't handle the hotel for a week, he's in the wrong job. If he gets into trouble, tell him to call Pop."

"Pop? You mean I didn't tell you Pop's in Europe with Johann having the time of his life?"

"Wait a minute. Don't make jokes."

"Poor Johann intimated that he could use some rest; Pop doesn't even stay in when it rains. I'm so happy for him."

"Maude didn't go with him, I see. She's singing tonight."

Regina smothered a laugh. "Pop said he wasn't chaperoning any honeymooners. I'm satisfied she and Johann will get together, because she loves that man."

"Enough to go back to Europe? He's a patient man. I'm not sure I want that much patience." He looked her in the eye. "If I had it, I wouldn't use it. When can we get some days to ourselves?"

"I can't be away on a holiday weekend."

He laughed. "No problem. Labor day has come and gone, and by Thanksgiving, we'll know whether we love or can't stand each other. So don't be chicken. When I get back, maybe you'll bring me up to date about Juliet." She told him she would.

"I sense a sadness—for want of a better word—about you, Regina, and I think it's done something to your spirit. Am I right? Never mind. You don't have to answer that. I'm here for you if you want to talk."

She couldn't lie about it, and she couldn't ignore his comment. "I'll just say it's not my health or my job. Let's go in; it's almost time for Aunt Maude to go onstage," she said, glad for the opportunity to change the subject.

She told him about the list of relatives Harold gave her, and added, "I've called three of them, with poor results. Harold warned me, but I have to do this."

He squeezed her hand, and his teeth sparkled against his dark face. "I told you the best way for you to get the family you want is to have your own."

"If I have any children," she blurted out, "they're going to have a father to raise them and love them. Period."

"Come on. Harold's tuning up the band."

"What about James and Claudia?"

"She wants him all to herself, poor fellow," he said, "but she's swimming after the wrong whale."

They sat down at a table near the stage. "If you think I can't raise children and love them, forget about Honolulu." He crossed his leg at the knee, put his hands in his front pants pockets, and leaned back in his chair. She might as well have been sitting alone. She watched Maude deliver her song and saw Harold just behind her aunt, seeming to engross himself in his music, but she had no idea what her aunt sang or Harold played. From the corner of her eye, she observed Justin—distant, turned inward, and obviously unhappy. His applause, sparse and perfunctory, confirmed her suspicion that he was as inattentive as she.

At the end of the set, he stood. "I want to speak with Maude; then I'm heading back to Camp Lejeune. If you decide to explain that comment, I'll listen."

She stared after him, vacillating between anger and chagrin, until he disappeared backstage. Hardly aware that she'd folded her arms across her bosom, crossed her legs at the knee, and sunk deeper into her chair, she said aloud, "Damned if I'm going to pussyfoot around a man's ego just to keep him interested. I had to do that in Honolulu, but this is another place and another time. I don't mind my own company. In fact, I like it."

"Sour grapes. I heard that."

"What?" she looked up to see Harold straddling the chair that Justin vacated.

"Talking about blood changing to water. One minute he was eating you up, and the next, he wasn't even here. Cuz, you're going to mess around till you don't even know what state that guy lives in. What did you say to him?"

"Nothing important."

"Maybe not to you, but it sure rang his bell. All kinds of people out here in the street, Cuz. That guy's special, and he doesn't have to put up with your shilly-shallying. The sistahs are waiting in line."

"Let 'em wait." He had a point, and she had to learn restraint in voicing her thoughts, but she felt bad enough without his lecture.

"If you want to know what it's like to be lonely," he said, "give me a couple of hours and I'll tell you how it is to hug yourself because nobody else will hug you; to go to movies and concerts because you can't stand being alone, and hurt like hell because none of the hundreds of people around you gives a damn whether you live or die; to see couples laughing, engrossed in each other, and want company—any company—so badly you want to scream. I can tell you about *lonely*, and if you don't watch it, that's where you're headed. Accept the guy or break it off."

Looking into Harold's eyes, she saw some of herself mirrored there. Fumbling to find his way, as she was doing—and not only with Justin but also with her family.

"I'm scared. I've been down this road twice, and each time I suffered, losing my sense of self, compromising my integrity and my self-respect. Native Hawaiian women live for their man, to satisfy his wants, whims, and desires. I grew to maturity in that culture. This place is spring rain after a long drought, and I'm not—"

He interrupted her. "Since you know it's different here, that women have status and most of the men you'll meet respect it, stop reliving the past. Cuz, I don't want to see you break your own heart.

Take a chance. I understand people, and I don't think he'll let you down."

"He wants us to go away together for a week, but Harold, we've just gotten to the kissing stage."

Harold's left eyebrow shot up. "Well, shut my mouth. You trying to tell me an army man's got that much self-control? Girl, shake your bottom and get this thing on track. Celibacy's bad for the blood, at least for mine."

The bass player got Harold's attention with a few riffs, and he stood and looked down at her, his countenance stern and his face immobile. "If you go away with him, at least you'll have privacy to work out your problems. Nothings worse than having to make out. Not to speak of a lot of colored people watching your every breath and reporting your pulse rate. Ready to take you apart." He gave her the thumbs-up sign and winked. "Gotta get back onstage. Get it together with the guy. You hear?"

As he walked away, his limp more noticeable than usual, she had a sense of rightness about Harold and her, that he was her friend—maybe her best friend—her confidant and, most important, her brother. And he was family.

"I've located an investigator," Regina told Juliet the next morning, "and I'll give him the information you just gave me." But as she looked through the window at that gray, misty morning, thinking of the forces she'd set in motion, goose pimples covered her arms, and her breath came in little pants.

"I'm nervous about this," Juliet said, "but I realize we have to find him if we can. We don't know who we are. And with all these other things I have to deal with, Herbert just called and said he'd be home in a few days."

"You'll handle that, and you'll have one less problem."

"Cephus offered to talk to him, but I don't think Herbert wants to hear anything out of any man's mouth."

"I second that. Let's stay in touch."

She wondered at Juliet's hesitation, at her long silence. And then what sounded like fear colored her cousin's voice. "I was going to suggest we meet at Drake's for lunch, but I'm still not feeling good. Regina, I'm . . . I have to go out some time, and I know everybody will be sneering at me. Maybe if you went with me to Drake's . . ."

Herbert would be a better buffer, but she didn't say that. "Of course I will. Let me know when you feel like it."

She opened her calendar and noted with pride that she'd booked as many conferences as the hotel could service through the middle of the next year. Larry hadn't thought she would get many African-American groups, because they had previously ignored New Bern as a conference city; but with Pop's guidance she had enticed African-American librarians, lawyers, cooks, sororities, and fraternities as well as large integrated groups.

The light flashed on her intercom, and she pressed the button. "Yes?"

"I'm downstairs at the desk, Cuz. I just wanted you to know that I got measured for my tuxedos, and I bought some real winter clothes. I'm beginning to think I'm really going to play in that orchestra."

"Of course you are. Did you get me that list of orchestra leaders and their addresses?"

"In my hand, Cuz. I'll leave 'em at the desk for you. I'm still in the clouds. See you tonight."

The next morning Regina decided she ought to have lunch with Juliet at Drake's before Herbert came home. She reasoned that facing the public might help restore her cousin's self-confidence, and she would need that before she faced her husband. She telephoned Juliet a few minutes before ten.

"How about lunch around one today?"

"Great. That would give me time to set my hair. I'll be there."

"Come looking fantastic. People don't look down on an elegant woman."

"Gotcha. Thanks."

Three hours later, she sat at a table in the center of Drake's Restaurant, facing the door, as Juliet walked toward her in a red linen suit, broad-brimmed red linen hat, and spike-heeled black patent shoes with matching handbag. If she was looking for attention, she got it, and from the expression on the faces on most of the women, she got their envy as well. How could a woman look one way and behave another? To her mind, Juliet would have been the epitome of elegance if she had glided to the table rather than bounced.

She rose and greeted Juliet with a hug, and realizing she meant it gave her unexpected pleasure.

"Everybody's staring at us," Juliet said, seating herself.

"That's what we expected. Let 'em look. When's Herbert coming home?"

Juliet picked up the menu and focused her gaze on it. "Day after tomorrow, but I've been thinking about what you told me, and I'm not so nervous about it. I . . . uh, I'm going to do better by everybody. I know hundreds of people around here, but you, Aunt Maude, and Cephus are the only ones who reached out to me. You don't have to tell me that means I need to reform."

"Aunt Maude?"

"Yes, but I know she's not crazy about me—and for good reason. She called me a number of times to see if I needed anything."

They gave the waitress their orders, and Juliet seemed unable to resist glancing at the other diners. "Don't let it get to you," Regina said. "I'm just sorry I didn't wear red. If I had, that would have bamboozled them a-plenty."

Juliet shifted in her chair, obviously uncomfortable. "How can you be so kind when you know I don't deserve it. It's as if you're deliberately punishing me. I'm not a nice person, and you know it."

It dismayed Regina that their lunch had turned into a confessional. "There's no need to berate yourself. Only one person who ever walked this earth was without fault," she said, quoting Justin.

Juliet leaned forward, determination blazing on her face. "I'm trying to tell you something. I knew there was a relationship—I mean, that something was going on between you and Justin Duval—but I made a play for him. And more than once, too. I wanted to prove to myself that I could take him away from you."

Regina could feel her lips curl in annoyance. "You'd risk your marriage for such stupid conceit?"

Juliet didn't look at her. "I wasn't going to take it to the dangerous stage. Anyhow, I needn't have worried about that; he brushed me off and all but told me I was out of line." Then she sighed with such relief that Regina knew Juliet had unburdened herself of a load of guilt.

"You're not attracted to him? Is that what you're telling me?"

Juliet shook her head. "You're right, it was stupid. I can't see any man but Herbert, and I've been unfair to him, too, because I never let him know how crazy I am about him. I always thought that would make him love me less." She lowered her face into her hands. "Oh, Lord. I'm so mixed up."

Regina reached across the table and grasped Juliet's hand. "Start making amends with Herbert, and don't forget to write something nice about Harold for a change. He says you've hurt him."

"I guess I have. People say things about him. I don't know if any of it's true, and I suppose I've made it worse."

Their food arrived, and Juliet picked at her salad. "Until recently, I hated just about everybody. I'd pass a school, see children playing, and curse because I couldn't have any. I used my column as a kind of equalizer; I was unhappy and I tore down anybody that I could. Nobody, not even Herbert, knew how miserable I was because I couldn't have a child."

Unclog the dam, and the river overflowed. She hadn't dreamed that Juliet lived with such misery, that she had allowed her unhappiness to warp her personality. "When you tell Herbert the truth," she said, "why not ask him if you can adopt children?"

"I think I will."

When they separated at around three o'clock, Regina had the feeling that she could like Juliet, and she meant to try.

Back in her office, she made a booking for Harold on her first try, as guest soloist with the Boston Pops Orchestra. When he didn't answer his phone, she left a message.

"You'll soon be famous. If you want to know more, give your Cuz a call."

She wanted to make amends with Justin, but how did you call a man and say, "Hi. I want to go away with you for a week"? When she could stop laughing, she lifted the receiver and dialed his number.

"Your call is being transferred to Colonel Duval's voice mail. Please speak clearly. Your call will be returned promptly." She didn't want him to call her; she preferred to be the one to terminate the call if it wasn't going her way. With no alternative, she left a message and hung up, aware that she had no idea as to his whereabouts.

At the time, Justin was at his mother's home in Baton Rouge, and Regina was paramount in his thoughts. The nine-year gap in age between him and his younger sister, his only sibling, prevented the companionship that sisters and brothers of similar age enjoyed, and even when very young, he promised himself that he would have a big family. Regina was already forty, and common sense said he should look elsewhere if he wanted children. But he wanted Regina, and he might have to give up fatherhood in order to have her.

He stood at the living room window of his mother's house and watched his cousin's seven-year-old boy jump through a hoop that he had suspended from a tree branch, and his thoughts went back to his loneliness as a child that age. "I'm damned if I do and damned if I don't."

He answered his cell phone, checked the time with a glance at his watch, and dialed her office number.

"Hello."

"Hello, Regina. This is Justin."

"Hi, Justin. I'm going to Honolulu with you, and I wish I'd had the foresight not to make that comment about children needing fathers."

No preliminaries. No explanation and not much of an apology. He let the wall beside the window take his weight, and his right shoulder the brunt of the contact. *I am not asleep, and I am not dreaming. At least, I hope I'm not.*

"You certainly know how to hike up a man's blood pressure. Give me time to adjust. Will you?"

"Of course," she said displaying that air of innocence with which he was becoming familiar. "Is it a deal?"

"You bet it is. I'll be back in New Bern Monday, and we'll firm it up."

Maude walked into the living room massaging hand cream into her smooth, brown fingers—fingers that said she was forty rather that sixty—and scrutinized Regina the way she did when her niece first arrived in New Bern. She had always been able to read people, especially when they weren't paying attention to her, but Regina was not an easy study. Usually, neither her face nor her body language revealed her mood or attitude; her posture varied little. But on this occasion, her demeanor betrayed her feelings.

"What you looking so forlorn about?" Maude asked her. "Seems to me you haven't been yourself since last Thursday, when Justin came to the show with you. I thought he was at Camp Lejeune. What's this all about?"

Not since Regina moved into her own house had she spoken with her niece on a daily basis, but sure as sunrise, Regina had called her every morning that week, precisely when she sat down to eat her breakfast. And this was the third consecutive evening on which Regina had "dropped by" after work. Something was amiss.

When children got hurt, they ran to Mama, and she suspected Regina had her filling that role. The thought brought a smile to her face because as far as she knew, nobody had ever applauded her maternal instincts. She softened her voice.

"What's the matter, child? You missing Justin?"

Regina picked a toasted pecan from the French Lalique bowl—a legacy of Maude's marriage to Henri Dupré—and nibbled on it in a way that said her thoughts were elsewhere.

"Do you realize that at the age of forty I've had to reinvent myself, change my values, goals, friends, acquaintances, interests, job . . . you name it—my whole outlook on life."

Maude sat down, selected a cigar from the humidor on the table beside her chair, cut it, and lit it. "I'd say you've adjusted pretty well. Maybe you will never have a bunch of Pearsons and Witherspoons hanging around you; you see how many Witherspoons and Cobbs— my mother's people—you've met over here."

She puffed on the cigar. "Honey, family is like stocks and bonds: riches on paper, but when you try to cash in, you're subject to find there ain't much there." She got up to answer the phone.

"It's for you."

Regina got up slowly. She hadn't told anyone she would be at Maude's house. "This is Regina."

"Hi, Cuz. I got some news that will blow your mind. What time will you be home?"

"In about an hour. You want to come over?"

"Of course. Why do you think I asked? See you in an hour."

She hung up and looked at Maude. "Harold didn't want to talk with you?"

Maude shook her head. "He knows he doesn't have to worry about my feelings. I give a man all the room he wants. These days, Harold's a bird that just got its wings back. Something's happening with him, and it must be good. If it is, I'm happy for him."

Regina saw Harold sitting on her steps before she reached her house. He raced to the car while she was still parking it. "Cuz, you won't believe this. My first gig with the symphony is going to be televised, and they're going to do one of my pieces. I'll get introduced. I'm dying. I just know it, Cuz. Nobody ever treated me like this; I must be on my way to heaven." He picked her up and swung her around. "Maybe now, Cephus will give me some respect."

The sight of his tears stung her deeply, and she hugged him. If only she could get the courage to ask him why he hurt so badly!

"You're going to make all of New Bern eat crow, Harold. You're on your way, so stop thinking about the past." She didn't have the heart to tell him nobody in New Bern would see a broadcast unless they could tune in CBC-Toronto.

"I try to do that, but I've been hurting so long, it's hard to let go of it. I wake up wet with sweat after dreaming this is another one of Cephus's nasty jokes." As if realizing only then that her arms enveloped him, he stepped away. "We're out here in the street. If anybody sees you hugging me, your reputation will be shot." Obviously amused, he permitted himself a shrug. "Mine, too."

"This is some office you got here," Maude said to Regina when she visited her the following noon. "And your folks certainly are protective of you; even after I told 'em who I was, that string bean wearing the yellow tie insisted on checking my driver's license."

"Larry knows who you are, Aunt Maude. He likes to feel his importance. Have a seat. Have you found a saxophonist to replace Harold?"

"I rehearsed with an old guy this morning, and it went well 'cause he's first-rate and has that New Orleans style, but Harold is so special. He feeds my soul. It's not easy to replace him."

"The two of you are magic together."

Maude looked hard at Regina. Something wasn't right. The longing in her niece's eyes tied a knot in her stomach. "What ails you, girl?"

Regina examined her nails before looking squarely at Maude. "Suppose some more of my folks, ones I haven't met, would be as wonderful to know as you, Pop, and Harold. Even Odette. Think of what I'm probably missing."

Maude strummed her fingers on the arm of the chair a few times. "Yeah. That's just what I *am* thinking, and the other part of my thoughts rest on how lucky you are to miss them."

A chuckle staggered out of her throat. "My brother Robert graduated from what used to be A&T College in Greensboro—now it's

University of North Carolina, Greensboro—but he can't say fifty words without mentioning peanuts. I'll bet he's the only person in the English-speaking world who thinks the World Trade Center is still standing. He gets on my nerves and I'm his sister. If you think he's a fountain of love and warmth that you just can't wait to cultivate, ask Pop how often he has the pleasure of one of Robert's ten-minute visits. Maybe twice a year."

"But he *does* visit him, and no matter what you say, I think I should meet my relatives. You know yours, and you know whether you want a relationship with them. Why can't I know the same? Things are working out between Juliet and me, aren't they?"

"You mean, Juliet is letting you help her straighten out the mess she's made of her life. Don't get too comfortable; your little investigation is likely to blow up in your face."

Regina shrugged. "The worst that can happen is that she and I end up where we started."

Maude leaned forward and braced her hands on the arms of the chair. "The connection between you and Juliet is my brother Travis and my sister Louise. That leads you to Pop. How do you know your ties to Juliet don't come from my mother, or her mother, or even from your great-grandfather? You don't have to look like your parents. Ever heard of recidivism? Genes can show up after generations. And you don't know what those old people did back then. Let sleeping dogs lie, and stop looking for problems."

"Every time you or Pop warns me about this, something in me drives me more forcibly than ever to get at the bottom of it. It's not in my nature to be satisfied living in darkness."

Maude threw up her hand. "All right. That's my last word on the subject. What do you plan to do about Justin Duval? You're not dragging your feet because he's dark-skinned, are you?" Regina's face clouded with a frown and reddened in what was obviously rising anger. Maude grinned, having known the answer before she asked the question.

"Since you know how little this skin-color prejudice means to me, I don't know why you wasted your breath with that question." She propped her elbows on her desk and cupped her jaw with both hands. "Justin is important to me, Aunt Maude. Sometimes when I'm with him, I want him so badly, I ache."

"And at other times?"

"I look at him, feel him, smell him, taste him, and get the sensation that I'm sinking, that he can sap my will. Aunt Maude, he scares me. I've had two unsatisfying affairs. I'd rather be alone."

She spread her hands. "I can deal with loneliness; I'm used to it. Until you embraced me at the airport and I walked into your house, loneliness was my most constant companion and had been since mother's death. And I know now that my loneliest moments were spent in the arms of my lovers, self-centered men who didn't worry about how I felt. I didn't know what I missed until—"

"Until Justin got hold of you. Tell me about it! I went through that with three husbands, the first two of 'em pretty good men, especially if you count their attributes from the waist up. Johann shook me up, twirled me around like a tornado, and had me begging for more. And he still does it."

Regina leaned back in the chair, locked her hands behind her head, crossed her knees, and swung her legs. She could see contentment stealing over her niece, a change that seemed to envelope her whole being.

"I'm going back to Hawaii for a week—with Justin. He wants us to . . . spend some time together, and I just decided that I'm eager for it. I can hardly wait."

"Yeah? Be sure he knows it. If he's put his cards on the table, let him know you need him."

Her sigh told a long story, and her words supported it. "I've got some work to do there, some demons to exorcise. By the way, when will Pop and Johann be back?"

Maude examined her nails with great care. "You asking me? When I talked with Johann last night, he said Pop wants to see the Roman Forum, so he's taking my ninety-one—or is it nineteen-year-old?—father to Rome. Girl, I won't recognize Pop when he gets back here." She walked to the door and stood there shaking her head. "I've just come to realize what an exceptional man my father is."

Regina's lips flattened in a grin. "He's also formidable. I want him to come back here before he passes out. And now that he's broadened his horizons, so to speak, I'll see that he comes to the Craven and eats at my house."

She watched her aunt breathe deeply of the autumn breeze that drifted through the open window and then grin at her niece. "Well, the Lord said faith would move mountains. I hope yours is intact, 'cause my father is a mountain."

The door closed behind Maude, and Regina lifted the receiver. "Regina Pearson speaking."

"I decided to come back this afternoon. Can I see you tonight?" No preliminaries. Just a couple of words that rocked her world.

"I'll be at home. What time may I expect you?"

She thought she heard him smother a laugh. "Around seven, and when I get there, I hope we don't act the way we sound—like two prime ministers discussing world peace. Woman, I'm anxious to see you."

"Same here. Did you get the tickets?"

"What? You didn't say when we could go."

"Any time. As you said, if Larry can't manage this place for one week, he's in the wrong job, and I should know it."

"Whew! See you at seven. Bank on leaving day after tomorrow."

On her way home from the Craven, Maude stopped at *The Enchanted Frog* on Middle Street to buy a gift for her brother Robert's birthday and encountered Rose, Robert's wife, who was apparently on the same mission.

"Would you mind telling me why Regina Pearson wants to come to my house? I got enough to do without being bothered with distant relatives. This is the peanut-gathering season, and I'm busy."

Maude had never had much tolerance for her sister-in-law, and it stretched her not to apprise her of that fact. "Rose, Regina is not a distant relative; she is Robert's niece, and she wants to meet her mother's brother and his family. What's wrong with that?"

"She lived a whole lot of years without knowing a thing about us. I'm not going to satisfy her curiosity. She's living in luxury in the Craven. Isn't that enough for her?" A strong statement coming from mousy little Rose.

She spread her hands, palms out. "Regina doesn't live at the hotel, and if she doesn't meet you, Rose, I doubt it will kill her. How are the children?"

"Just like they always are. More interested in school and books than in helping me. I hear Regina called Cousin Ida, too. And you can imagine what kind of hoopla that caused."

Maude stared at her. "What do you mean?"

"Well everybody knows Cousin Ida isn't really your cousin. You know how country folk are always calling each other cousin, aunt, and uncle till after a while people forget it's not real. Seems Cousin Ida's got something against Regina. I don't know what it is, but that woman was mad as a wildcat."

"Did she call you?"

"No. Cousin Ida doesn't speak to us. Odette told me about it."

"Cousin Ida will get over it," Maude said in a show of impatience. "Good to see you," she added in as much of a lie as she could manage. She'd have to ask Pop whether Cousin Ida was related to the Witherspoons; she'd always thought so and had put her name on Regina's list.

She purchased a western saddle for Robert, had it wrapped, and headed for the door. But not soon enough to escape more gossip surrounding Regina's efforts to round up her relatives.

"I hear tell Jake's going to be modeling at the Craven. Now that ought to turn New Bern on its head," the store guard said to her. "Man, I wish I'd thought of that. It beats standing at this door casing shoplifters."

"First I heard of it, Cliff," Maude said.

"He told me she invited him to the Craven, and you know Jake's not going to do anything except model—when he can find the work, that is."

She shook her head and smiled as best she could. "Good to see you, Cliff."

She imagined Jake, Odett's brother, would love to model at the Craven, though she doubted his ego could stand that much massaging, but she couldn't imagine Regina asking him to do it. She walked into her house and raced to answer the ringing phone.

"Maude speaking. How y'all doing this afternoon?"

"I heard the Craven is hiring. Is Regina Pearson giving preference to her kinfolk?"

"Why you asking me? Call Regina," she said to a maternal cousin she hadn't heard from in months. "Listen, Carrie, I just work there." She hung up. Before it was over, Regina would wish she'd never heard of the word *family.*

Fourteen

Although it seemed to her as if weeks had passed, several days after giving Justin her firm commitment, Regina walked along Waikiki Beach at sunrise, her bare feet once more imprinting the sand she loved. She raised her face to greet the breeze and to feast her gaze on the dazzling colors streaking the sky. It was her world, her time and place to escape real life, to dream and fantasize about the future and the family she would one day have—or it had been. She couldn't quite put her finger on the reason, but the joy she expected didn't fully materialize; the freedom she had once found in those early-morning walks on the beach eluded her. She stopped and put on her sandals, and her stroll became a brisk walk.

When she entered the hotel, Justin stood at the reception desk using the telephone. She hesitated to join him, thinking that his call might be private, but he looked up, saw her, and put the phone back in its cradle.

"Here I was calling you in the hope that we could walk along the beach together before the tourists took over, and you went off and left me. I thought we were here to spend some time together."

But she had reverted to her old ways, her habit of walking alone. "I guess ingrained habits die hard. Let's go back. Maybe this time I'll enjoy it."

Justin was not a stranger to Honolulu, for he'd spent a number of his army days there in special training activities. He liked the weather, the beach, and the ocean, but not much else. The sun completed its painter's wizardry and began to warm the earth, which was another reason why he'd never been enchanted with the place. Afternoons could sizzle with the heat. He squeezed Regina's fingers, and she looked up at him and smiled.

"Tell me who you were when you lived here."

"I was a docile daughter pleading for fatherly affection; a woman who didn't know what to expect of a man, and tolerated what I suppose you would call indignities from the two men who claimed to care for me; an excellent student because I discovered that what I learned was all I could call my own; and the best hotel publicist and event planner in Honolulu."

He looked into the distance, trying to put some meaning into that statement—meaning that could help him understand her and build the relationship with her that he needed.

"That's important, but who were you inside? Deep down, I mean?"

"Lonely. Just plain lonely. All the time."

She slapped her hand over her mouth and stared at him with large, rounded eyes. No one had to tell him she had just experienced a moment of self-revelation, had surprised herself. He eased his right arm around her, and they walked on in silence. He couldn't think of anything to say, and if words occurred to her, she kept them to herself.

After ten minutes or so of awkward silence, he remembered the luau the hotel planned for that evening, and seized upon it as a means of breaking the silence. "Did you bring one of those crazy-looking native dresses for the luau?"

"I gave away all of my Native Hawaiian things before I left here. I hadn't thought I would ever come back." She looked away from him. "I wouldn't have believed I've changed so much in six months. I'm seeing all this with new eyes, and the sense that I don't belong here is like something hammering at my brain. Maybe I shouldn't have come back." She spoke more to herself than to him.

"I don't agree. You're going through a catharsis, and you needed it in order to get on with your life. Something here has held you back, at least in our relationship."

She spoke as if she hadn't heard him. "I went to New Bern to find my large, caring family, but what I got was a hotel and four out of the dozens of my relatives who are within a fifty-mile radius of my house."

"Regina, you are not going to like people just because you have some of their genes. I can think of a lot of individuals I like better than most of my relatives. The truth is that except for my mother, sister, and two cousins, I don't care about that clan. I have an aunt who'd make the witches in Macbeth seem like fairy godmothers."

"I know. Cephus Pearson can turn me off, Odette comes close to it, and some of those I contacted recently let me know they weren't interested in meeting *me*, and some others expected jobs at the hotel."

"You have Pop, Maude, and Harold. That's more family than most people can count on. And remember. You were alone when you thought you needed a gang of relatives."

"Yes, but I've been to gatherings of over a hundred family members, people who came from all over the world for the occasion, who greeted each other warmly and affectionately, shared experiences that excluded outsiders, and filled the environment with love. I was so envious."

"And you still have that need?"

She seemed to contemplate the question. "Not as much as I did. Maybe . . ."

He placed his hands on her shoulders and guided her to face him. "Don't I take up any of that slack? Do I make up for it, even a little? You had a need to belong to people who loved you. I love you. Do you think you can find that with me?"

He knew he'd shocked her. He'd shocked himself, because he hadn't planned to tell her what he felt. She gaped at him.

"Why are you surprised? Did you think I've been . . . just killing time with you?"

"But we still work together, and—"

"Not after November first, we won't. So don't use that as an excuse to avoid deciding whether you want to . . . see if we can make a go of it. I need a resolution to this relationship."

Although her face was the image of someone appalled, she covered the hand that still rested on her right shoulder, and stroked it. "I've just realized I have a couple of ghosts to slay. Let's go back. I'll meet you in the lobby at seven for the luau."

A muscle twitched in his jaw, and he bit back an expletive. Their first day in Honolulu, and she was telling him he should spend it alone while she slew her past. "If you free yourself before then, page me. I'll probably be in the pool or somewhere near it." She nodded, but he could see that her thoughts had already drifted elsewhere. It was just as well. "Do what you have to do," he said. "It's time we came to terms with this."

Regina sensed Justin's growing exasperation. He wouldn't continue to pursue a relationship with her if she didn't give him more encouragement. She knew it was foolish to let her past experiences define her and circumscribe her life, and she also knew Justin was no more like Ken Pahoa and Helmut Neukirk than black was like red; both were colors, but the similarity ended there. She went to her room in the Royal Hotel, two floors below the one in which Justin stayed, and telephoned Kalani, who was overjoyed that she was in Hawaii.

"I thought I came back for a short vacation," she said, "but I realized a little while ago that I have to get a few things straight. Let's meet for lunch tomorrow, but I need to . . . Do you know where I can find Ken?"

"Oh, Regina. I don't know if it's a good idea to resume that . . . uh . . . relationship."

"Never! I need to clear up something with him. Where is he?"

"Same place." She gave Regina Ken's telephone number. "Seasons change, friend, but Ken's arrogance is as predictable as daybreak."

"Thanks. See you tomorrow." She held the receiver until the dial tone startled her. That conversation held no evidence of the camaraderie she once enjoyed with Kalani; it lacked intimacy as well as the warmth she had always felt for her dearest and only friend.

She didn't telephone Ken, figuring that surprising him with a visit was more likely to yield the results she needed. She dressed in a mauve-colored linen suit, put her hair up because Ken liked it down, and took a taxi to *Oahu News*, the paper that catered to Native Hawaiians. She considered it her good fortune that his secretary was not at her desk, knocked on his door, and stepped inside when he gave permission.

"Have a seat. I'll be right with you," he said without taking his gaze from the computer screen.

"How are you, Ken?"

His head snapped up. *"What's this?* Where'd you come from?"

"I arrived last night from the mainland."

His bewilderment was short-lived. A smile of self-satisfaction awakened his facial features, and within seconds he was pulling her into his arms and searching for her mouth.

"I knew you'd come back to me."

She braced both hands against his chest. "I haven't come back to you. I'm here to find my self-respect. I want you to tell me why you treated me the way you did. I don't care how raw you make it. Tell me the truth."

He backed off as quickly as if she had scalded him. "What's come over you? I don't know what you're talking about."

Her left index finger poked his chest. "Yes, you do. The years when you played around with other women and didn't care if I knew it, certain that it was your right and my lot to tolerate it. Explain that to me. And all of your boasting and posturing about your prowess as a lover, when you took and took but gave me nothing because you knew I didn't know the difference. One conversation with my aunt was enough to open my eyes to your phoniness. And you acted as if you had the right to dictate my life."

She pounded her right fist into her left palm. "Talk to me. You laid an attitude on me, and I want to know why you treated me as you did. *I said, talk to me.*"

When his upper lip curled into a snarl, she knew he hadn't changed, that he probably never would. "You asked for it. You wanted to be loved, at least what you and your people call love. What you really wanted was a father, and you substituted me for one. You didn't have to do what I told you to do. You were working, weren't you? But you stayed. You're not Hawaiian, and you never will be. Our women accept our ways. You didn't understand our ways, but you told yourself you did. I'm a Hawaiian man, and I act like one."

"With no concessions to anyone else's way of life. Right?"

"You didn't have a culture; you just aped us. And some of you rubbed off on Kalani. No Hawaiian man will marry her. She argues, and she's got some notion about going to the mainland and working for the government. Our women don't work outside the home, and they're obedient."

She looked at him and wondered what she ever saw in him, a perfect case of the horror a woman reaps when she *makes do* with a man because she can't find the kind of man she wants.

"You're full of it, Ken. Hundreds of Native Hawaiian women work outside the home, many in professional jobs; I suspect some of your other observations are no more accurate than that one." She narrowed her eyes. "The woman you've got now—how do you treat her?"

He shoved his hands into the pockets of his trousers and kicked at the carpet. "Why would I treat her any differently? She's Asian, and she's a woman. She understands men."

"Is your father like you?"

"He's . . . uh . . . older, and from a different school."

A weight fell away from her like dead bark from a tree. "I got what I came for. Thanks."

As she turned to go, he grabbed her hand. "What's that supposed to mean?"

"It wasn't me, Ken. It was you, and I thank you for making it so clear. I thought all Hawaiian men were like you, that you were the standard, and I'm glad to know I was wrong. Have a good life."

Light steps propelled her along Puu Panini Avenue, and she looked neither toward her old home on Huauni Place nor her beloved Diamond Head. Thomas Wolfe said you couldn't go home again, and she had the evidence that proved his point. She had thought she needed a confrontation with Helmut, too, but she didn't require a diagram to see that the two men she chose while her father lived were of the same ilk. Thank God, she no longer needed or wanted whatever it was she had sought in them.

Yawning overcame her as she walked into her hotel room, and she succumbed to the effects of the seven-hour time change and was soon fast asleep.

"Hello."

"Are you asleep? You were supposed to meet me down here at seven o'clock. What happened? Are you all right?"

She enjoyed a languorous stretch of her body. "I'm fine. I only . . . Justin? For goodness' sake, what time is it?"

"Seven-fifteen."

"Gee whiz! I didn't even eat lunch. Give me twenty minutes. What're you wearing?"

"The loudest shirt anybody ever saw. I bought it in the hotel this afternoon, and it'll be in the waste basket when I check out. Hurry up."

Justin had partaken of enough Hawaiian luaus to last him forever. Attending the luau earlier that evening was merely a reason to be with Regina. What he wanted from their trip was a genuine bonding with her. He didn't want her to bare her soul, because he wasn't going to bare his, and he didn't believe he had the price of another person's privacy and dignity. He wanted to know who Regina was.

He strolled along Waikiki Beach, kicked at a withering lei—the native symbol meaning "natural circle of achievements"—walked on past one night couple after another: some in awkward positions and embarrassed, some holding hands with the innocence of new love, and at least one angry and disillusioned pair. The wind whipped up, increasing its velocity and making the night less friendly as the ocean waves lapped and lashed—an eerie sound in the darkness.

Hours earlier, he had at last cooled his loins in the heat of Regina's body, and the violence of his release, his absolute capitulation to her body's demands, worried him. She gave him her person, shared her emotions, but withheld her innermost self. Damned if he'd settle for that again.

"I've closed the book on my past here," she told him minutes before taking his hand and leading him to her room. And it was good that she had; he would willingly pay for his own sins, but from the day he met her, she'd been giving him the bills for the transgressions of her father and her lovers. He shook his head as he walked in the dark. Two affairs that lasted for years, and she had never been fulfilled. Amending that had proved so easy, he had to conclude that her lovers didn't care and took advantage of her lack of knowledge and meaningful experience.

Looking up, he realized he'd walked all the way down to Diamond Head, several miles from the hotel. With his hands in his pockets, and his shoulders hunched forward, he bent into the wind and retraced his steps.

In her hotel room, Regina, too, was having moments of reflection, reflection colored with a sense of guilt. *He knows I haven't leveled with him, and he's going to challenge me about it. But it . . . it's like laying my insides on a table. I can't. I just can't.* But until she did, he would withhold a part of him that she needed.

Several days later, having returned from her vacation and still euphoric from her tryst with Justin in Honolulu, Regina stood with Harold in Craven County Airport, waiting for his flight to Toronto.

"Supposed I fall on my face in front of all those people," Harold said, his insecurity as pronounced as she had ever witnessed.

"Why would you do that? The orchestra will be playing your music, and if you don't know *that—*"

He grabbed her arm. "Of course I know it, but I'm already nervous. Cuz, this is my life we're talking here, my one chance. I gotta make good. And not just for me. You're taking a big chance with me, and if you want to manage another musician, people will point to me, and—"

She understood his fears and hastened to allay them. "Listen to me, Harold. Six weeks from now, you'll laugh about this. Once you get that horn in your hands, you'll soar."

He hugged her. "I don't know why you're so good to me, but I sure thank the Lord for you."

"I've ordered tapes of the performance, and I'm going to get TV station WKTN to run the program."

His face lit up. "You will? I'll show 'em, Cuz. They'll finally know I'm a real musician and a real person, someone they have to respect. Yeah." He knocked his fist into his palm and picked up the carry-on luggage in which he'd packed his precious cornet. "I'm gonna suck gold out of this horn. You just wait. I'm gonna blow this baby till the whole concert hall looks like a desert sunset." He kissed her cheek. "I love you, Cuz."

As she drove back to New Bern, she mused over Harold's volatile personality. In ten minutes, he switched from dejection to elation, from self-doubt to cockiness. She wouldn't say he was unstable, or that his self-doubt was a serious deficiency. Harold knew he was a good musician. She shook her head in wonder. What an enigma he was!

She hurried back to her office. After a week away, she'd have enough to keep her busy far into the night. She phoned Larry. "Let's have lunch and you can bring me up to date."

"Welcome back, Regina. No major problems, except the sorority due here in March has two hundred and twenty more registrants than the number of rooms booked, and the Sheraton's the only one able to handle the overflow. We also have a group of writers coming that weekend."

"Did you arrange it with the Sheraton?"

"It's ninety dollars more per room. We're giving a big discount, but they haven't offered that."

"I'll see if I can bargain with them. How about one o'clock?"

"Cool."

Sitting across the small table from Larry, she couldn't help observing his perfectly manicured nails and flawless attire, his beige-and-blue-striped tie matching the blue of his shirt and his beige-colored suit. She imagined that if she looked at his socks and shoes, she'd find the color scheme extended to them.

The thoughts that occurred to her shook her somewhat, but she went with her gut instinct and, at the end of the meal and of their business discussion, she put a question to Larry that, months earlier, she'd have thought improper.

"Are you and Harold friends?"

His expression hardened, and he pulled air through his teeth. "That unreliable little bastard? Of course not." He ignored the gasp that flew out of her. "Don't mention him to me."

Larry knew Harold was her cousin, and if he risked such a venomous comment about him, it was due to strong personal feelings. If she was to learn anything, she'd better control her reaction.

"Why do you say that?"

"You don't need to know. Take my word for it: he's a little worm."

She bristled at that last shot. "I thought you knew Harold is my first cousin."

He lifted his left shoulder in a shrug, then flattened his lips and narrowed his right eye. "Yeah. Good riddance."

It wasn't the first time she'd detected in him what she surmised was the capacity for cruelty. She folded her napkin, pushed back her chair, and stood.

"I guess that's it for now. I'll be in my office."

He looked up at her and took his time standing. This from Larry, who could exude charm and flawless manners. "Sorry if I rang your bell."

"If you *had* done that, you would definitely know it," she flung over her shoulder as she walked away.

She didn't care what Larry did in his private life, but if she caught him fooling around when he was supposed to be working, she'd have it out with him. Now she knew how Harold could spend a couple of hours in the hotel at midday when he wasn't swimming, eating, or practicing his music.

She phoned the station manager at WKTN-TV and got his agreement to air the tape of Harold's solo debut. "I thought I would send out invitations to watch the show from the Craven's auditorium when Harold comes back here."

"Fabulous. It's a deal."

The telephone was getting to be her worst enemy. "Regina Pearson. What can I do for you?"

"This is Leonard Watson," the caller said, sending shivers from one end of her body to the other. "I haven't contacted Travis Witherspoon yet, but I know where he is. You want to meet him, or you want him to contact you?"

She braced one hand against her desk and closed her eyes. Calming herself. Maybe she shouldn't have pursued it but should have let the matter lie, as Pop and Maude had advised.

"You still there?"

"Yes. Yes. I'm here. I . . . uh . . . have to think about the answer to your question."

"If he doesn't want to be found, you would do well to surprise him, though getting to the Klondike would be one onerous trip. My sources say he's leading a normal life, as if he has nothing to hide."

"He hasn't," she hastened to say. "Give me his home address and phone number, and I want to know where he works and what he does. Get word to him that his daughter and his niece are looking for him, and tell him how to get in touch with me at once." She knew her uncle would think she had bad news of his father, but if that would cause him to telephone her, she didn't mind. After ignoring his father for twenty-six years, he deserved a shock. She wrote down the information that the detective gave her.

In fairness, she ought to share the news with Juliet, but she stayed in her office trying to deal with the tangled state of her nerves. Around four-thirty, she forced herself to do what she knew was right: left her office and drove to Juliet's house. She half hoped her cousin wouldn't be home, and turned away after ringing the doorbell the third time.

"Coming. Coming," she heard a male voice, which she determined to be Herbert's, say. "Just hold your horses."

"This takes some getting used to," he said, after his eyes widened and his shoulders slumped. "Come on in, Regina. She's in the den."

She followed him to the dimly lighted room. Her first thought upon seeing the cozy nook was that Juliet furnished her home with sex and romance in mind. About fifty candles arranged in pyramid fashion burned on the mantel piece, and a low flame, which she realized was artificial, danced in the fireplace below it. Juliet reclined on the sofa in a burnt-orange velveteen jumpsuit.

When she saw Regina, she sprang to her feet. "Hi. I'm so glad to see you. When did you get back?"

"Last night. I've got some news."

Juliet grabbed Regina's hand and pulled her to the sofa. "I'm scared to know what it is. I've been uneasy ever since I agreed we would do this."

"I'm not exactly dancing for joy, but I have to know who I am. Does Herbert know what we're doing?"

"Does Herbert know what?" He walked into the room, sat on the arm of his wife's chair, and slung his arm around her shoulder as if he'd never condemned her.

She could see that they had solved their disagreement when Juliet smiled up at him and rubbed his thigh. "Darling, we're trying to find out why we look so much alike. Both of us think it's unnatural for cousins to look like twins, but maybe we're just being paranoid."

He got up, walked over to the fireplace, and stood with his back to them. "I hope you know what you're doing. It's a shock looking at the two of you; I grant you that. But suppose you discover something you'd rather not know. Then what?"

"It can't be worse than not knowing," Regina said. "When I get the answer to this riddle, I'll begin to understand other things in my life that have burdened me for the last thirty-six years."

It occurred to her then that Juliet hadn't asked what the news was, and that she didn't plan to ask, so she took her cousin's hand and told her. "Juliet, my news is that your father is in the Klondike region of Canada, alive and well. I've sent word for him to call me."

Herbert swung around. "All these years, he's been alive and never once called or wrote to his father? Or his daughter? He doesn't want to see me, 'cause I've got some choice words for a man who'd do a thing like that. I might even let him feel the sting of my fist." As if the thought angered him, he rushed from the room.

"Looks as if you and Herbert made up. Is he satisfied that you didn't have an abortion?"

Juliet's face darkened. "Yes, he is, but it's a tainted victory because he had to see the proof. It can't be the same for me, knowing that he would think those terrible things about me. Part of it's my fault, I suppose. If he had known how much I love him, maybe he would have believed in me and trusted me. But I still have him, and that's what's important to me."

"Did you mention adopting a child?"

"Yes, and he said he wanted to do that but was afraid that if he mentioned it, I'd be hurt. We'll start working on that as soon as you and I get at the bottom of this strange likeness. I can't handle but one kind of drama at a time."

"Let's hope this won't take long. And . . . Juliet, I don't think we should mention your father's whereabouts to anyone until we have the proof. It could be a terrible blow to Pop if the detective is wrong."

"You're right. Herbert won't mention it." When Regina stood to leave, Juliet hugged her and said, "Please, let's see each other often."

Regina returned the warmth. "I'd like that." If only she could look at Juliet without having the eerie feeling that she was seeing herself in some other life or era.

Driving back to work, Regina prayed she wouldn't have to go to the Klondike, at the northern tip of Canada, in order to confront Travis Witherspoon. Yet she knew that if he didn't get in touch with her, she would do precisely that. She marveled that Juliet could be married to a man, love him, and not discuss with him so amazing an enigma as her likeness to her cousin, and that she hadn't confided to him their intention to locate Travis Witherspoon. *You haven't mentioned it to Justin, either,* her conscience nagged. Indeed, she hadn't let him know how deeply she felt about it and how much she feared the truth.

The first thing she saw when she walked into her office was the red light flashing on her answering machine. To her disappointment, the voice she heard wasn't Justin's but that of Judy, her secretary. "I think I've got some kind of virus, so I'm going on home. I hope you don't get it; I feel as if I don't have a limb in my body."

She phoned Judy and reassured her, then checked her calendar. Pop and Johann were due back in a couple of days, and she made a mental note to join them for chili Wednesday night, the day after their return. She lifted the receiver, punched in Justin's extension number, remembered that he wasn't in his office, and hung up. The weight of her disappointment was in the thud of her right arm on her desk.

Regina sat in front of her lighted fireplace that evening, trying to force down a turkey breast sandwich and musing about her vacation in Honolulu. She no longer felt at home there, and knew it even before Ken gave his ruthless assessment of her as a make-believe Hawaiian. New Bern was home, but neither it nor most of her kinfolk embraced her.

The doorbell rang, and she stuck her feet into her rabbit mules and went to answer it before she remembered that Harold, the only person who would visit her at home without notice, was in Toronto, Canada. She hooked the chain in place and opened the door.

"If y'all would stay in your office," Maude said, "you'd know I wanted to drive by this evening. How was Honolulu?"

"Come on in. In some ways, Honolulu was great, and in others it was a bust."

"I sure hope the part that was a bust didn't have anything to do with Justin. Is this a smoke-free room?"

Regina got a saucer and gave it to her aunt. "The whole house is smoke-free, unless you're here."

"I hear you were over at Juliet's again today. What's going on with you two?"

"Same old same-old."

Maude cut the end of a fresh cigar and lit it. "Must be all right. That article she wrote on you—it's the best thing she's written, and not a single bitchy word in it. Very flattering. You two getting to be thick as thieves."

"I didn't see the article. I was away when the *Chronicle* published it. I'll read it in the library." She regarded her aunt, her mother's sister, her blood kin, and a strange and comforting peace settled over her, filling her with hope. Yes, and alleviating her dread of the truth about Juliet. "Wouldn't you want an explanation if you were the spitting image of somebody who wasn't your twin or your sibling?"

"I expect so, but you be careful you're not walking into something you can't find your way out of."

Maude left minutes before Regina received the call for which she had been waiting all day.

"I phoned you twice at your office," Justin said, "but I didn't leave a message. Sometimes I rebel against machines, and giving a personal message to one is idiotic. How are you, and how did it go at work today?"

That was her cue to tell him how excited, scared, and just plain stressed she was, and why, but she let the opportunity pass. "Getting back into harness was easier than I had expected. Would you believe Larry didn't dump a slew of problems on me?"

He didn't answer that. Instead, he let her know that he hadn't called to make small talk. "How about going to Baton Rouge with me this weekend? My mother has been pestering me to bring you down there. What do you say?"

What *could* she say? She had focused her energies on Travis Witherspoon, and she dare not leave New Bern and miss his call. But because she hadn't taken Justin into her confidence, she couldn't give him an abbreviated explanation and expect him to accept and understand it. Yet, she didn't want him to think he wasn't important to her.

Finally, she hedged. "This isn't a good weekend for me, Justin. Do you mind if we go another time."

"Is that all you have to say? You're always preaching to me about the importance of family and urging me to get closer to my folks. Don't you realize what my taking you down there will mean to them?" He obviously didn't care if she detected his testiness, for he spoke in a tone harsher than his words.

"Yes, I do, but please understand. I just can't go this weekend."

"Do you think I'm capable of understanding your reason? And don't tell me you can't leave the hotel. If Larry managed for ten days, he can handle it for two."

"Please don't be so hasty in judging me. I'm involved with . . . with my folks right now, and leaving here this weekend isn't a good idea."

His voice lowered and lost its warmth. "When we last discussed your folks, the only ones you cared about were Pop, Maude, and Harold. Have you gotten attached to some more in the last twenty-four hours?" Suddenly, his demeanor changed. "Somewhere, I must have made a wrong move. Sorry. Call when you have time. Be seeing you."

She stared at the receiver, unwilling to believe or to accept that Justin had hung up in a fit of annoyance at her. "I'll cry tomorrow," she said aloud as anger surged within her.

A glance at the hall mirror as she passed on her way to the kitchen was sufficient to settle her mind on what concerned her most—communicating with Travis Witherspoon. She wrote a letter telling him why she needed to see him, sealed and stamped it, and put it in a drawer. If she didn't hear from him within three days, she would mail that letter. And if he didn't answer it within ten days, she would book a flight to the Klondike.

Fifteen

For the sixth time that afternoon, Maude dialed her husband at their home in Amsterdam, the Netherlands, and didn't get an answer. He and her father were due back in Amsterdam from Rome that morning. They should be home, exhausted from sightseeing in Paris and Rome. She didn't like it. Her mind conjured up numerous scenarios that would logically explain their failure to answer the phone.

She found herself dialing the number again, dropped the phone in its cradle, and threw up her hands, exasperated. *Why am I doing this? I never chased Johann. And what will I do with him? I am definitely not going to live in Amsterdam or any other European city.* But after coming to New Bern, he had reminded her of the joy she knew every time he took her into his arms.

Here I am, sixty years old, letting my vagina make a fool of me. But she had to admit that Justin gave her far more that sexual gratification. She existed as a complete woman only when she was in his company.

She lit a used cigar, realized she had forgotten to cut it, and grimaced. "My mind must be out to lunch; I haven't done that in years," she said aloud.

By evening, she had dialed the number fifteen times, and was about to call her brother Robert in alarm when her doorbell rang. Since she wasn't expecting anyone, she hesitated to answer it. The bell pealed persistently until, angered, she rushed to the door and yanked it open.

"*Johann!* Johann, what are you doing here? My Lord! Are you . . . ?" She grabbed his arm and squeezed it. "You're . . . you're real; you're not . . . Is Pop all right?"

As was his wont, he settled the matter by locking her to him. She doubted she'd live long enough to count the times her husband had kissed her, but she didn't remember a kiss such as that one. He went about it as if he had a score to settle, and maybe he did. But for that punishment, she would commit the offense again and again if she knew what it was. When he finally released her, he slammed the door shut behind him, took her hand, and walked down the hall to the living room.

"Where's Pop?"

"Home. Watching the Giants and the Eagles."

"And he didn't call me? How's he doing?"

"He's in great shape. Slept from Rome to New York. We didn't go back to Amsterdam. My admiration for Pop is bottomless; he's an amazing human being."

"You've given him new life."

He sat down and settled her on his knee. "I'll be here for the next three weeks and four days, Kitten. If I don't move into this house and into your bedroom within three weeks and three days, I'm headed home—for keeps."

"You would leave me?"

"I don't have you now, so what's the difference? Getting my libido blown out of socket while I walk five blocks anticipating a loss in the sack with my wife is not what I call a state of bliss. I want it all or nothing."

His position didn't surprise her, but she hadn't expected his ultimatum. *"Fight fire with fire,"* Pop always said. "Where's your suitcase? You can get your things and move in now."

"All right. I will. But if I decide I want to live in Amsterdam, then what?"

She frowned. "You know my position on that."

He kicked out his right leg and adjusted his trouser leg at the knee. "You're too honest to play hardball for sport, Kitten, but you're playing it nonetheless. You're giving me an either-or, and I don't like it."

She slipped an arm around his neck, careful not to make her game plan obvious. "Isn't that what you're doing to me?" Sliding further up on his lap, she let her hand caress his shoulder and adjusted her position, undulating a little as she did so. In a flash, she had the result she wanted.

"I have a supply of toothbrushes. I bought them last week."

He stared into her eyes until she feared he thought she had abused her advantage. "I hope you're as hungry as I am, Kitten, because if you're not, you're in for it."

"Have I ever hollered 'Uncle'?"

The perplexity of his gaze reminded her that he didn't understand most American slang. "Have I ever said I'd had enough?"

His grin electrified her. "Since you know the answer, it shouldn't surprise you that I don't intend to let you break up our marriage."

Music to her ears. If he was going to make a night of it, she'd better start it right. "I was just about to take a shower. Care to join me?"

His eyes lit up like flashes of lightning. "You bet."

She'd never made love in the shower. Her first three husbands didn't have that much imagination, and although Johann had made love to her in numerous places—including a balcony during the rain, a walk-in closet, various chairs, the top of their dining room table, and on the bathroom floor—somehow, he'd overlooked the shower.

She thought about her hair but only for a second; considering the pleasure awaiting her, a trip to the hairdresser was nothing. She leaned against the tile and watched him. He turned on the shower and adjusted the water's temperature, and she marveled at the finesse with which he slipped out of his clothes, socks, and shoes. After ten years of marriage, seeing him naked was still a shot to her womb.

He told her with a wink that he knew his body tantalized her, and that the knowledge pleased him. "Like what you see?"

She let out a pent-up sigh. "Lord, yes!"

As if he had waited for those words, he peeled away her garments with such speed that she barely saw his hands. And in a bold move, he hooked his hand into her red bikini panties and tore them from her, exciting her and sending her libido into a uncontrollable gallop.

He stepped into the shower and held out his hand to her, and when she joined him, he closed the glass door and picked up the bar of Miss Dior soap. The warm spray drenched her nakedness and danced on her nerve ends. Or was it his hands moving over her breasts, pinching her nipples and squeezing them into submission, that addled and besotted her?

His hands, slick with soap, slid over her buttocks and thighs until she tingled with exhilaration. She wanted to hold him, to caress and fondle him, but he let her know it was her feast. She threw back her head and let the water splash on her face and neck, open to him, giving him carte blanche for whatever he wanted to do to her.

She thought she would die when he pulled her nipple into his mouth, intensifying his assault on her body, sucking vigorously, stroking her thighs and buttocks while the fire of unquenched desire roared through her. Frantically she spread her legs, nearly toppling them both.

"It's been so long," she moaned. "If you don't get in me, I'll die."

He paid no heed, as she'd known he wouldn't, but knelt before her, the water beating his head and back, hooked her left leg over his shoulder, and drove his tongue into her, twirling, teasing, and sucking until she gripped his shoulders and let out a keening cry.

"Oh, Lord!" she yelled as he increased his motions. His tongue danced a lover's dance within her, firing the bottoms of her feet and igniting a powerful surge in her vagina.

She tried to move away, wanting to delay that first release until he lay above her, buried deep in her body. But he gripped her hips and held her, and she let him have his way and exploded into orgasm. He stood and held her in a loving embrace, but he'd made his statement, and she intended to make hers. She lathered her hands with soap and stroked his body until she could feel the heat that threatened to consume him, until she nearly burned from his fire. After rinsing off the soap, she kissed him from his shoulders to his loins.

A kind of wildness overtook her as she knelt before him, free to do to him as she pleased. She stroked him until he groaned, until he begged her to take him. Then she slipped him between her lips and loved him until tremors shook him and he pushed her away.

Obviously shaken, he knelt beside her, pulled her to her feet, and wrapped a towel around her.

"You're still hard."

"You'll take care of that in a minute." He stepped out of the shower, picked her up, and carried her to bed.

When she awakened the next morning, he was lying on top of her, still locked within her. She caressed his back, and he began the strokes that, moments later, flung them once more to mindless oblivion.

"I'd get up," he said an hour later, "if I was sure I could stand."

"You're the one who tried to set a record."

"Damned straight. And I set one, too. How many fifty-year-old men do you know who can live up to that standard?"

She slapped his buttocks in a playful gesture. "None that I know, but if I have your permission, I'll check it out."

"The hell you say!" He swung his feet off the bed.

"Are you leaving? Each time you've spent the night with me here, you left early the next morning. Why?"

He rested his elbows on his thighs and cupped his chin with both hands. "Pop enjoys having me fix his breakfast. I know he can do it, but he walks into the kitchen and sits at the little table, sometimes with the morning paper, and it's all ready for him. He said it's his favorite time of day. It's important to me, Kitten. I'm aware that I may not always be here to do that for him, but when I'm here, I want to do it."

She slid across the bed, enclosed his hips within her thighs, and wrapped her arms around his chest. "It's not for nothing that I love you."

He stood and looked down at her, his expression wistful. "I knock myself out trying to please this female, but does she melt? I say something nice about her father, and she tells me she loves me. Well, I guess I'll take what I can get." He stroked her jaw. "I love you, too, Kitten. So prepare yourself for a long, happy marriage—to me."

"Then you're not planning to live in Europe?"

He didn't give quarter. "Kitten, from what I know of history—and that's most of what I read—only one person lived on this earth and never compromised. You're not expected to be perfect like the Lord; make up your mind to give a little."

After the night they'd spent making love for hours, she didn't feel like arguing with him. "Want me to go with you over to Pop's house?"

He bent over and kissed her. "Hurry and get dressed. I'll shower in the guest room, because I don't dare risk one with you."

Abner dressed, tightened the scarf around his neck, went to the front door and picked up his copy of *The New Bern Chronicle*, tucked it under his arm, and went out on the back porch to read. He loved the nip in the air, because it energized him and enlivened his senses. The scent and smoke of leaves burning in his neighbor's backyard wafted over to him as he glanced over the morning headlines. He sniffed a few times, looked for Juliet's column in the features section, and didn't see that or the photograph of her that had punctuated the section's first page for the past six years. He understood that if she was sick she couldn't write, but she was still features editor, wasn't she? He checked the paper's roster and determined that she still had her job.

Usually, he'd be drinking his coffee about that time, and Johann would be there cooking his breakfast. He missed the pampering, but he would rather Johann spent his time fussing over his recalcitrant wife. He heard the door open and pretended he didn't; what his son-in-law did was his business.

Seconds later, he heard Johann's footsteps, and the scent of Maude's perfume sent his heart into a trot. She'd come with her husband, but he steeled himself against showing his pleasure and cast a thankful glance toward heaven.

"Pop, you stayed in this town overnight and didn't call me," she grumbled, sliding her arms around his neck from where she stood at his back. She walked around to face him. "Let me look at you. Johann said you ran him ragged." She leaned over and kissed him. "You look so good."

"Humph. I didn't go over there to recline on my fanny twenty-four hours a day. You got a real nice house over there." He picked up the paper as if he intended to read. "And it's empty. You also got a fine husband, who's not living in it with you. I should have had four children exactly like him."

"I guess we disappointed you."

"You're a good daughter, and I'd be satisfied with you if you had the sense to know a man when you see one."

"I know I have a lot of faults, Pop, but that kind of blindness is not one of 'em. He didn't stay over here with you last night, did he?"

"No, but considering how smart you are, he may spend every one of the next twenty-four nights over here. I don't like to think of what I might consider doing to a wife like you." He folded the paper and dropped it in the rack. "Course, I wouldn't have a wife like you."

Johann called to him from the kitchen window just above his head. "Breakfast will be ready in about five minutes, Pop."

He washed his hands, went into the kitchen, and sat at the table. *Lord, I hope these old eyes aren't fooling me.* Maude and Johann stood in a corner holding hands and gazing at each other. He shook himself a little and told himself not to expect too much. They had appeared ready to act sensibly before, and nothing had come of it. Still, it meant he could hope. He cleared his throat.

"I made it special this morning, Pop. You get a couple of those Belgian Waffles you fell in love with when we were in Brussels, with strawberries, whipped cream, and two slices of double-smoked bacon."

They joined him at the table, and he reached out to hold their hands. "Lord, I do thank you for taking us to Europe and bringing us back safely. And for this food and these, my children, I thank you especially, Lord. Amen."

He tasted the waffles, nodded approval, and eyed Maude. "You ought to let Johann teach you how to make these. In case you continue your present foolishness past December the sixth, when Johann leaves here, I'll still be able to enjoy these waffles."

She placed her fork beside her plate and let out a groan. "Pop, will you please get off my case? Getting along with a man is hard enough, but if you keep making Johann out to be a saint and me a witch, I won't stand a chance. He's tough enough without all the help you're giving him."

Abner looked at Johann. "These waffles are first-class. People know fire will burn their feet, but some of them will walk barefooted right through it. Never could figure that out. Too bad we can't can this." He stopped eating as a thought occurred to him. "But couldn't you work out a recipe, dry it out like Bisquick, and package it?"

Johann's laughter filled the room. "Ease up on her, Pop. We're not going to break up; I won't permit it."

"So now you're a miracle worker. Good."

"You'll see."

"You haven't told me about your trip, Pop."

"I didn't think you wanted me to repeat what I said on the phone."

"Start with the flight over."

"Don't remember much. Soon as they fed us, I went to sleep. I liked Amsterdam. 'Course, I wasn't trying to make a life there. Still, I found plenty to hold my attention, none of which had anything to do with the color of my skin. That's a recommendation for just about anyplace."

"How'd you like Paris?" Maude asked him.

Paris, indeed! He could have done without it, but he wouldn't tell Johann that. "It was all right, especially the Louvre. Never saw so much cheese in my life. I preferred Amsterdam. I liked the people. Now, Rome—I could have stayed there indefinitely. It was like I was born there—all those things I'd read about, seen on television. And the food. Those people know how to eat! Only thing they lack is some of your chili, and we're going to see that they get that."

"Yeah," Johann said, refilling Abner's coffee cup, "I didn't tell you the first cans of your chili will come off the belt in Amsterdam the end of January or thereabouts, and we're going to start production in Havelock in June."

"You're kidding," Maude said. "Don't you have to build a factory?"

Johann shook his head. "No, we're going to convert what used to be a tomato-canning factory. That's why we chose Havelock."

"Yes indeed," Abner said as he stretched out his legs and clasped his hands across his middle. "I expect to go to Amsterdam to lift the first can of Abner's Perfect Chili Con Carne off the belt. God willing, of course." He looked at Maude and allowed himself a wink. "I'll let you take the first can off the belt at the Havelock factory."

"I'll bet. I could pedal there on my bicycle. You're so generous, Pop."

It's taken nearly a hundred years, he thought, looking at the two of them, but he was going to live to see a lasting monument to himself. The hotel he had struggled so hard first to build and then to keep was finally lost to him, and he had the love and loyalty of only one of his five children. But in spite of his curmudgeonly behavior in years past, God had nevertheless smiled on him and sent his granddaughter—his Regina—and his beloved son-in-law, Johann, to brighten his last days. He said a word of silent prayer and gave himself over to the joy he felt.

The next morning, Maude rolled out of Johann's arms, showered quickly, and went to the kitchen. She had forgotten how much she hated cooking breakfast; indeed, she hadn't done it since she left Amsterdam. For her, a bowl of any kind of cereal sufficed. However, Johann referred to that as pig food and wouldn't touch it. "How the devil do you scramble an egg without getting it too hard?" she said aloud in a voice laden with scorn and annoyance.

"You crack the eggs in a bowl, put some butter and olive oil in a hot Teflon pan, pour in the eggs, and start stirring."

She whirled around to face Johann. "Thanks. I leave it in your capable hands."

"If we set up housekeeping together, I'll get a cook for you. Anything you want. But Kitten, I will never give you a divorce no matter what you do. What would you like for breakfast?"

"Some of those waffles you made for Pop."

As they sat in her kitchen enjoying their first meal alone in almost two years, she reflected on the solace that his presence always gave her: how she enjoyed talking with him, teasing, and swapping tall tales. She mused over their relationship and the equanimity she drew from it, and it occurred to her that, in trying to gather a family around her, Regina was reaching for that contentment, that sense of belonging, in relatives. But recently, she had allowed concern for her likeness to Juliet to derail her efforts to draw a family around her.

"I think I'm going to give a big party," Maude said to Johann. "My relatives and near-relatives are curious about you, and Regina has been browbeating me to help her gather her family around her. It's time I let them see you and that I straightened Regina out."

"Any of 'em like Odette? That woman's a real trip, as you say here."

The forkful of waffle didn't get to her mouth but landed on her plate as she gaped at him. *"What?* Did she beg you for money?"

When he frowned, she let herself breathe. "No. Does she do that?"

"Sure does. And she doesn't need it; she's wealthy."

He got up and took their dishes to the dishwasher. "Well, I'll be damned."

She didn't tell him she planned to invite both the Pearsons and the Witherspoons and that the party was primarily for Regina's sake, though she alluded to that. "Regina's got her head in the clouds, Johann. It's time she faced reality and got on with her life. If she wants a family, she'd better start with Justin, and she'd better hurry. Forty is pretty late for a woman to start having children."

At the time, Regina's concerns didn't center on prospects of a family. She sat at her desk, moving the papers that lay there from one place to another, opening and closing drawers, doodling mindlessly on scraps of paper. She had allowed Travis Witherspoon three days in which to call her, but in that time she had not received one word from him. She took a letter from the drawer and buzzed her secretary.

"Judy would you send this certified mail? I want it to go off this morning."

"Sure thing, Regina. I'll take it to the post office right now."

She thanked Judy and watch her stride out of the room, but knowing the letter was on its way to her uncle didn't still her restlessness. "I've got to get some work done," she told herself, but nonetheless welcomed the noisy ring of the telephone.

"Regina Pearson speaking."

"I did it, Cuz. I busted my ass out there, Cuz. The people stood up for me. I had nine curtain calls, and I could have had more, but I just wasn't able to make it back out on the stage. I cried like a baby."

"Oh, Harold, I'm so happy for you. I told you you'd be great. You're on your way now. When you come back, WKTN-TV will air the tape, and I'll have some invited guests view it from the Craven's auditorium. We'll have a big reception. Let me know wh—"

"You mean . . . you mean all of New Bern will get to see me and see that ovation? This is too much. I'm hyperventilating. Gawd. I'm not sure I can handle this."

"You can and you will."

"I can be there Tuesday afternoon, but I have to be back here for rehearsal Friday noon."

"I'm proud of you, Harold. I'll call the station and get back to you."

After hanging up, she called the station manager, and the man gushed with reverence. "Miss Pearson, I am so honored that you chose WKTN for Mr. Pearson's New Bern debut. We taped it from CBC-TV, Toronto. It was a stunning performance. I was awed. You may have any time spot you choose."

She thanked him and chose the coming Thursday. Then she wrote out an invitation, got the guest list for the Craven's opening, added the Pearsons she hadn't known about, and gave it to her assistant manager for special affairs. She meant to have a word with Larry. If he valued his job, he would have to treat Harold with respect that evening.

"This will definitely set New Bern on its nose," the assistant manager said, mostly under her breath, as she left Regina's office.

And so it did. Guests poured into the auditorium from seven o'clock onward, and she stood near the center of the lobby until she could no longer bear the suspense, craning her neck in search of Justin and watching for evidence of hostility in Larry. At seven-thirty, she headed for her office, hoping to regain control of her nerves.

"I wondered where you were." She looked up to see Justin walking down the stairs toward her. "How are you, Regina?"

"A wreck. A sane person wouldn't have tried to organize this in one week. How are you?"

He stared down at her. "My question is, *How are we?*"

She expelled a long breath. He wasn't a man she could treat lightly and count on for shared affection. He had made that clear, for in the week that passed, she'd had no evidence that he remembered she existed. She wanted him, so she had to bring him into her life.

"I'm dealing with something important that I haven't told you about. Now isn't the time to discuss it, but that explains why I couldn't go to Baton Rouge with you. I should have told you then, but I . . . I didn't. If we can have a few minutes together after the concert, I'd like us to talk."

"All right. Do we sit together?" She nodded. "By the way, where is Harold?"

"In the dressing room trying to calm himself. He said he wants to play a solo after the concert is aired."

For long minutes after the concert ended, Regina sat forward, on edge, as her guests remained silent. Then, near-pandemonium broke out as they cheered, screamed, stomped, and yelled. She knew very few of them and wondered which ones were her relatives.

As if in a daze, Harold stood and half-bowed, barely acknowledging the ovation. Regina searched the crowd for Larry and eventually realized, to her relief, that he was not in the room. The ovation lasted so long that Harold didn't get to play the solo he wrote for the occasion, but she could see that, in his joy and triumph, it didn't matter.

Regina nearly swallowed her tongue when Cephus jumped up on the stage and, towering over Harold, beamed at the audience, held up his hand to signal quiet, and said, "My baby brother here has put New Bern, North Carolina, on the world map. Let's all salute him. Hip, hip, hurray!" The audience echoed the praise.

"You'll read a full account of this preeminent occasion in tomorrow's paper," Juliet told Regina after hugging her and congratulating her. She started off, turned, and said, "Girl, Cephus is a trip. Would you believe what he just did?"

"I'm trying to handle the shock," Regina said.

"What's that all about?" Justin asked.

"It's a part of what I need to discuss with you later."

He raised on eyebrow. "This should be interesting."

After toasting Harold, she and Justin left the party to try and iron out some of their problems.

"Would you really go to the Klondike to confront him?" Justin asked her after hearing her story.

"Wherever. I'd go anywhere."

"But you haven't told me why you think it's so important to get at this so-called mystery."

"I'm afraid to articulate it, to let myself think something I find so, well . . . farfetched. Do you understand?"

"I think so. Let me know if I can help. Did you know the carpet for that suite arrived yesterday? The workers have already laid most of it. We'll bring it in on time."

Her eyes widened. "I admit I've been so involved with finding Juliet's father and giving Harold his moment of glory here in New Bern, that I may have missed a few things where the Craven is concerned. And Larry is annoyed with me for giving Harold this party, so he didn't tell me about the carpet. I won't lie and say I never doubted you'd get it done on time, but it doesn't surprise me."

"After you contact Travis Witherspoon, will you go with me to Baton Rouge? This is the last time I'll ask you."

She didn't hesitate. "Yes, I'll go. But while we're clearing our slates, I have a question for you. Asking it isn't easy, but I need the truth."

"What is it?"

She locked her gaze on his face. "You made love with me five or six times when we were in Honolulu, and though you gave me what I'd never had, you didn't give me yourself. Even with my warped experience, I knew that, although you gave me the physical fulfillment I craved, you withheld a part of yourself that I also needed. Was it deliberate?"

He looked her in the eye and showed no reticence in answering. "You're right. I'm aware of that, and it wasn't deliberate. I knew you withheld from me things of importance to both of us, that although you agreed that we would open up to each other and share our dreams, goals, problems, and needs, I sensed that you either wouldn't or couldn't do it. You gave yourself when we made love, but you didn't trust me to love you warts and all, so I couldn't show my faults to you—in bed or out of it."

"What about now? Can you do that now?"

"I don't know. Let's see how it goes. After four years of marriage, I still didn't know my wife. I don't want that false intimacy again. I feel, deep in my gut, that you're right for me, but . . ." He shrugged. "This is the level of understanding we should have sought in Honolulu."

Her fingers touched his wrist, and, as if they did it of their own volition, she quickly withdrew them. "I didn't know how to reveal myself, and I'm not sure I do now. Revealing what's inside of me wasn't a part of my conditioning. Will you help me?"

"I suppose that's something a girl learns from her mother. I'll try. Come on, I'll tail you home."

So she could still hope. She smiled, though she knew it was a weak reflection of her feelings. "Pop and Johann are back. Want to go with me to Aunt Maude's Wednesday night for chili?"

His face brightened. "Say, I'd love it. I want to hear how the plans for Maude's chili went, and I want to know about Pop's adventures."

"From what I know already, it will be a tall tale, sure as my name is Regina. I'll tell Aunt Maude you're coming."

"Child, you didn't have to call me about Justin," Maude said when Regina phoned her. "He's welcome anytime you want to bring him, but mind you Pop doesn't get on your case right in front of Justin."

"Aunt Maude, that's the least of my worries. Pop will be so full of his travels and so focused on getting you and Johann together permanently that he won't give Justin and me much thought."

"Yeah? Shows how well you know Pop. I was going to invite Harold but decided against it; Harold needs recognition, and we'd all be focusing on Pop and his trip to Europe. Guess what? Harold telephoned to tell me Odette was in Drake's Restaurant right then with a humdinger of a man."

"You're kidding."

"It's the truth, so help me. I tell you, I got as far as the front steps on my way to see for myself, but Johann called me back 'cause I was wearing my bedroom slippers."

"Well, I'll be doggoned. The man could have been a client."

"We'll see. Lately, she's been acting strangely. Say, I hope you read today's *Chronicle*. Juliet made up for all the mean things she's said about Harold with a great story on his concert and the party you gave for him. Harold must be a happy man right now—the town's most famous citizen, and he didn't have to commit the crime of the century to earn the honor. See you day after tomorrow."

Maude couldn't get used to working along with Johann, and she wished he would go over to Pop's house or somewhere and let her finish the dinner and set the table. If she left a crumb of seasoning out of that chili, Pop would notice it.

"Hon," she called to Johann, "go over and get Pop while I shower and dress."

He stopped chopping scallions and took his time rinsing his hands and drying them. "You'd better get used to having me around. I know you've accustomed yourself to living like a single woman these two years, but that's history, babe. I'll go get Pop, because I'd planned to do that, but from now on, you and I do things together."

He was right; she'd give him that much, but she preferred doing things her way, and Johann didn't dance to anyone else's tune. "Not to worry. It will all come together," she said. And she meant it. A woman passing sixty wouldn't likely find another man like her husband—fifty years old, successful, intelligent, a great physique, and the testosterone level a thirty-year-old man would envy—and she'd better remember that whenever her trademark waywardness raised its ugly head.

To Maude's surprise, Johann didn't assert himself in the presence of others as she had thought he might. When Pop arrived that Wednesday for his weekly feast of chili con carne, her husband remained in the dining room with Justin and Regina, who had arrived earlier, and let her open the door.

"I can smell it from here," Pop said when he entered the house. His gaze landed on Justin, who went to meet him. "Glad you're here, Justin; now I won't have to write out a report. I'll just tell you what we did."

"Sorry, Pop," Johann said, "but this group goes by the rules, and as secretary—"

"All right, all right. I'll dictate my report to you, and you can type it up." He sat down at the head of the table and looked around, a satisfied, proud man. "Now that we're back home and my son-in-law here has put Abner's Perfect Chili Con Carne into business, we need to say a word of thanks."

Abner looked at Maude. "I don't suppose you remember your prayers, so I'll say 'em for you." He made a pyramid of his hands and bowed his head. "Lord, you've given us a lot, not everything we asked for, but more than we needed. And looks like you're giving me some sons. I do thank you, and I ask your blessings on this chili and every person who buys a can of it. Amen."

They ate in silence for a few minutes, savoring the food and enjoying the company. Maude observed her father, an old man in his last years, shinning with contentment and basking in the affection of loved ones. And for the first time, she had a tinge of regret that she didn't have any children. Her gaze fell on Johann, whose smile caressed her, but she couldn't return it, wondering as she did whether he felt cheated because he had married a woman too old to give him a family. She didn't dare ask him.

"You look as if you lost twenty years," Justin said to Abner. "That trip was good for you."

"Wish I could say it was good for me," Johann said. "We got the business done, but that only took two days. From then on, I was following Pop around, and I swear I haven't been so tired in my life. I can't seem to get enough rest, and he's acting like a teenager."

"Humph. Wasn't me dragging you around that did it; it was all that Heineken you drank. You and my daughter Maude here are keeping that company in business."

Regina followed Maude to the kitchen. "Let me help you with the apple turnovers."

Maude looked at her niece. A woman adored by a such a man as Justin Duval should be glowing with happiness. "You've hardly said a word since you've been here, and I never saw you with such a gloomy expression. What's the matter?"

"I don't know. I ought to be happy, but it's like I'm being shredded. So many things: my work, Harold, my relatives who're behaving as if they don't know I exist, and . . . and Juliet. I—"

"So you've gone ahead and done what I told you not to do, and you're scared of what you'll find. Sometimes, child, you're better off being ignorant, 'cause what you don't know won't hurt you. Get your priorities straight, Regina. Justin Duval doesn't have to beg for female attention. I'm telling you for the last time: leave that business about Juliet alone. You can't rewrite history."

"I can't drop it. Every word you've said drives me in the direction you don't want me to go."

"You should be taking Justin seriously."

"I could say the same to you about Johann. I can't turn back now, Aunt Maude. The closer I get to it, the more certain I am that the truth won't please me, but I can't stop."

They took the dessert and coffee into the dining room, and Maude watched Justin as his gaze followed Regina. He might have patience, she mused, but it wasn't inexhaustible. She'd better do something to get Regina's mind off Juliet and her passion for a family or Justin would be history.

Her gaze settled on her father. He had resisted knowing Regina, but as his old eyes adored his granddaughter, Maude wiped a tear with the back of her index finger and gave silent thanks. First Regina and then Johann had blessed her father's life. She had to find a way to keep her husband in New Bern, or at least somewhere nearby, for as long as Pop lived.

Melancholia in no way described Abner's mood, she saw, as his eyes twinkled with their special glints of devilment. "I see you walked in here holding my granddaughter's hand," he said to Justin. "Pretty cozy. You're a fine man. All the same, I want to know your intentions toward my granddaughter." Regina's gasp nearly eclipsed Maude's screech as she threw up her hands.

"Now, Pop," Maude said in a voice of one horrified, "people don't . . . I mean, fathers don't ask men that anymore."

"Humph. Then they're stupid. From what I can see—and I can see plenty—men haven't changed one iota since I was courting." He looked at Justin, obviously awaiting an answer.

If the question disarmed Justin, he didn't make it apparent. Rather, the half smile around his mouth suggested that he might be amused. He let them all stew for a few minutes. "Pop, if my father was living, I'd ask him to call Regina on the carpet about her intentions toward me. In fact, I'm taking her to Baton Rouge so my mother can get after her about stringing me along."

"You what?" Regina's words came out in a sputter.

Justin patted her hand. "Not to worry. I'll tell her to go easy on you."

It didn't surprise Maude that the patter failed to placate Pop. "I want to see at least one of my great-grandchildren before I leave here, and even a nincompoop would know that can't be too long."

"What about Juliet, Odette, and Jake?" Regina asked him, her face barely masking her discomfort at the turn of the conversation.

"They're not serious, neither one of 'em. Jake doesn't know the difference between his libido and that Harley-Davidson he roars around town in. And if Odette doesn't quit her begging, any man she finds will be too stupid to father children. Herbert's never home. All of 'em have a problem. I'm looking at my best bet."

"Why don't we all have Thanksgiving dinner at my house?" Regina said.

Maude couldn't help gaping at her. No one had to tell her that Regina's invitation was a spur-of-the-moment decision articulated as a means of diverting Pop's attention from her relationship with Justin.

"Good idea," Pop said, giving Maude another shock. She would have expected most anything but that. A premonition settled over her. What would be would be.

Sixteen

"Where are you going to put all of these people?" Johann asked Maude. He perused the list of Whitherspoons and Pearsons, their spouses and significant others—sixty-four in all. "Wouldn't it be better to hold this at the Craven?"

Maude shook her head. "They won't come. Half of them will think the Craven outclasses them, and the rest will stay away because they think that if they go they'll be honoring Regina. And Lord forbid they should do *that*. But every one of 'em is dying to see how I live and whether you'll be here."

"You're not cooking for that crowd."

"The hotel can cater it, but I'll make my chili. When we tell them you, Pop, Justin, and I have a company that cans it, that'll knock their socks off."

He'd been skeptical from the moment she mentioned it to him, and as the time approached, he seemed less and less sure that the idea of getting Regina's relatives together, merely to have them all in the same place, made sense.

"Seems to me," he said, "if they wanted to see each other, they'd manage it without all this hoopla."

She didn't care to continue debating it."You may be right, but I've mailed the invitations. Are you with me or not?"

He stopped polishing a silver candlestick. "Don't get unglued there, babe. From now on, you and I write with the same pen, as my uncle used to say. I know it's important to you."

"I'd rather have it on the weekend, but I'm singing Friday and

Saturday nights, and Harold's in Canada on weekends. So it's Wednesday night."

"What about Pop's chili?"

"If he doesn't come, I'll send him some."

On that cold Wednesday evening in mid-November, Regina stood near Maude's front door with Justin beside her. She had fought the idea of his standing there with her, until he made it clear that he'd stand there or go home.

"I've finished my work at the Craven, and James approved it this morning. We're no longer working together. If you'd rather not be seen with me, say so."

"It would just be simpler if they didn't have to think about who you are and why you're with me."

He lifted his left shoulder in a slight shrug. "Let them think what they like. Do I stay here with you or head for home?"

"All right, all right," she said as Maude opened the door to an old woman who carried a wooden cane and an earphone shaped like a small foghorn. She surmised at once that she faced her cousin Martha Pearson Stout. Maude confirmed it, but Regina couldn't communicate with the woman. Justin smiled at her and patted her shoulders, and the woman beamed contentment.

"See? I'm good for something," he said.

Regina shook Jake Witherspoon's hand. She had heard of his leather pants, motorcycle, and way with women, but none of that prepared her for her cousin's good looks, towering physique, and liquid charm. His gaze swept over her and focused on the crowd as if judging its worthiness of his august presence.

"He wouldn't recognize me if I walked over to him this minute," she said to Justin.

"Lucky you."

Finally Harold arrived, creating a titter among the sixty-some people milling around and eating, inspecting Maude's house, and paying little attention to each other. Cephus arrived a few minutes later, shook her hand, and greeted Justin as if he were Colin Powell.

"I'm glad Maude organized this," he said. "I've never seen some of these folks, and it's good to know one's kinfolk, though it's hard to figure out who's a Pearson and who's not." He saw Harold, excused himself, went to the center of the room, and clapped his hands for attention.

"I suppose you all saw my brother's debut performance with the Toronto Symphony. If you didn't, I brought along CDs that you can have for three bucks, the cost of making them. It was a great day for the Pearson family and for New Bern. Let's all give it up for Harold."

The hand-clapping began as a smattering, a token acknowledgment, but soon escalated to a strong applause. Regina looked from Harold to Cephus and realized that Cephus really did take pride in Harold's accomplishment, and that Harold knew it.

"Excuse me a minute," she said to Justin, and moved over to Cephus. "I have something to add to that. As Harold's business manager and agent," she announced, "I'm pleased to tell you that on the twenty-first, he will be guest soloist with the Seattle Symphony. And he has some similar dates after Christmas. We all should be proud of Harold." She expected a ringing applause and shouts of "Hear, hear!" but the scattered response let her know that the assembled folk either had not fully accepted Harold or were jealous of his new status. She hugged Harold and decided she would like Cephus in spite of his self-serving antics.

"They're nothing, the bunch of them," Cephus said in what approximated a growl, his graying hair and dapper attire giving him the appearance of a diplomat. "They'll come to me like they always do when they need something, and I'll help them remember how nice they were to Harold. A bunch of jerks jealous of a brother who made it big. You're a good person, Regina; I'll see that the governor knows it."

With every opportunity, Cephus pulled her a little deeper into his debt, though she had neither asked nor received anything of him. "Harold doesn't need this group," she said. "Before long, he'll be dining at the White House."

But Harold hadn't uttered one word throughout the episode, and a glance at him was proof that he saw the lack of response to her announcement as another case of rejection.

"Thanks, Cephus. And you, Cuz. You both did your best for me. I'll be leaving as soon as I can find Maude."

Jewel Pearson, Harold's sister, arrived, and Regina prayed she wouldn't stop to talk after asking her, "How come Maude's spending all this money on this shebang? She always was a show-off." And she couldn't muster any sympathy for her Uncle Robert, who, dressed in a silk suit, explained that he and his Rose came in his pick-up truck because it used less gas and because he was delivering peanuts to save an extra trip to New Bern.

"Thank God they found each other," she said of Robert and his wife.

Justin's shrug expressed his boredom, and Regina, too, began to weary of the party, a group of strangers who treated each other as such. When Odette arrived with a man who, from all appearances, had accomplished much, a hush fell over the room, followed by whispers that, Regina surmised, were condemnations of Odette.

"Regina, Colonel Duval, this is Claude," Odette said. "Lord, I'm starting to wish we hadn't come."

Claude greeted them casually. "Glad to meet you both. I've been looking for a golfing partner ever since I came to town, but no luck so far. You good for a couple of rounds?" he asked Justin.

"You bet. Give me a call." He handed Claude his card.

Johann, who had been standing by the living room fireplace, rushed toward the door. "Pop! Pop!" he exclaimed.

With her arms spread wide, Maude ran to her father. "Pop! We're so glad you came. I didn't even pray hard for this."

A hush fell over the crowd as he stood among them, taller than most remembered. "I was hoping to hear Harold play that cornet. I saw the broadcast of him with the symphony. And naturally, I want some chili."

The crowd stood back as if awed, but Odette walked up to her grandfather. "Pop, this is Claude. We're . . . we're serious."

He peered down at her. "You done any changing since we last spoke?"

"Yes, sir, she has," Claude said. "I put her in her place when she approached me, and she convinced me she was a better person than that."

"Humph. I wouldn't have stayed around to listen."

"I wanted you to know that's past, Pop."

His long, thin fingers brushed her shoulders. "You come see me. You hear?"

One by one, his descendants greeted him, but having them around him evidently didn't give him satisfaction.

Cephus stood beside him and, once more, raised his hand and voice to silence the crowd. "We're all surprised and pleased to see Abner Witherspoon among us," Cephus began. "He's the reason why most of you are here. Give him a big hand."

The explosion of applause brought a grimace to the old man's face. "Every Witherspoon raise your hand," he said, then looked at Cephus. "About forty, wouldn't you say?" Cephus nodded. "Will those of you who know five of your relatives here—not by name and sight, but as close acquaintance—raise your hand." He counted seven hands.

"Never thought I'd see this many Pearsons around me. How many of you know five of your kinfolk here?" Only Harold and Cephus raised their hands.

"Well, I'll have my chili, and then I'll be going. I hope you all met my granddaughter, Regina, who runs the Craven Hotel, and my son-in-law, Johann, here. We're putting the chili you're eating in cans and selling it all over the world. So you look for Abner's Perfect Chili Con Carne next year. Colonel Duval over there designed the cans."

He ignored the gasps, walked over to Harold, and patted his shoulder. "I'll bet they gave you a hard time, but don't you worry; that big tree out there was once a little acorn that held its ground. I hope to see you perform some time."

"Thank you, sir. You don't know what it means to me to hear you say that, sir," Harold said, his voice reflecting the hollow sound of tears.

Abner went into the kitchen, sat down in front of the chili Maude placed on the table for him, and looked at Johann."You see any signs of family among these people?"

Johann shook his head. "Not much. I always thought I'd been deprived, not having any real family, but from what I've witnessed this evening, I'm not so sure."

Abner left him, went back into the living room, and raised his voice. "All of my adult life," he told the group, "I wanted my family around me—wanted to enjoy the love and warmth of my children and grandchildren—but I don't mind telling you what I feel in here isn't family but a bunch of strangers checking each other out. Still, I guess I ought to be glad I got to see all of you.

He went back to the kitchen. "When you get to be my age, Johann, you can say anything you please; nobody has the nerve to challenge you."

Regina stood a little closer to Justin, glad that he had ignored her declaration of independence and hadn't left her to greet the Witherspoons and Pearsons by herself. Maude and Johann walked with Abner to the door, and the old man stopped at Regina's side.

"You've brought a fresh breeze to this town." His frail fingers clasped her left arm. "Enjoy yourself down there in Baton Rouge. This is a good man you got here." He returned her hug and focused on Justin. "Remember to come see me when you get back."

Justin smiled as he looked at Abner. "Bet on it."

"It wouldn't have felt right if you hadn't come, Pop," Maude said. "Shouldn't you tell everybody good-bye?"

"What for? They won't even know I left. Still, you did a good thing, daughter." His gaze shifted to Regina. "I hope you can cook; I haven't been part of a family Thanksgiving dinner since Lois left me, God rest her soul. Wasn't anybody's fault but my own; I just never felt like it."

She supposed her face was a wreath of smiles, reflecting the pleasure she felt in knowing that her grandfather would join her for Thanksgiving dinner. "I can cook, Pop, and you don't have to wait till Thanksgiving to sample it."

"I think I'll walk home with Pop," Johann said. "I've had enough of family for now."

Maude closed the door behind her father and her husband and faced Regina. "Wonder what happened to Juliet?"

Regina's eyebrows lifted. "Gee, I don't know. I've been so concerned about Harold that I didn't think about her."

"Pop's got a second sense," Maude said. "He knew this gang would roast Harold. That's why he was so nice to him. But Juliet . . ." All at once, she seemed preoccupied. "He didn't mention her. I was so sure she'd come."

"Me, too," Regina said. "I'm disappointed."

An hour later, the party over, Justin stood just inside Regina's door, looking down at her. He, too, wondered about Juliet and whether her absence from the family gathering had an ominous relevance for Regina's quest to clarify her identity. He decided not to mention his qualms to Regina but to focus instead on his own agenda.

"I've finished the suite. When will you show it to the buyer, Lucien Hayes?"

"Tomorrow."

He jammed his hands into his pants pockets, pushing back the lapels of his jacket. "When can we leave for Baton Rouge?" It was important to him, and he refused to drop it. "I've met your folks, and it's time you met mine. Especially since you've been urging me to get closer to them. What do you say?"

"I'll call Lucien Hayes tomorrow morning and tell him he can inspect the suite. I . . . uh . . . If he's satisfied, we can go this weekend."

"Even if he's finicky as a poodle, he'll like that suite. So will you. Let's plan to leave early Friday morning."

She agreed, and he relaxed, though only for a second, when it occurred to him that he might have to put a lock on his aunt Jo's mouth. She was his least favorite close relative, and to his mind, she could benefit from a course in finesse.

He let the wall of her foyer support his back and hips and opened his arms to her. Nothing felt as good to him as her breast, soft against his chest, and her hands, gentle on his neck and shoulders. A man felt like a man when he had a loving woman in his arms. Holding her reminded him of his lonely days as an unsophisticated youth, and in a voice that sounded soft and strange to him, he heard himself articulate it.

"I think I told you I joined the army as soon as I finished high school, more to escape my kinfolk than out of patriotism. In the days and nights that followed, I dreamed of finding a woman who suited me, who could fill that void I couldn't shake. I was so eager that I settled for less than I needed. Many times since, I've wondered why I ignored my good judgment. I knew it wasn't right."

Regina wasn't ready to hear the rest of it, but she didn't want to look back in grief for not having listened. "What are you saying?" Her question could be construed as encouragement, but maybe that was her intention.

"You're right for me. You suit me in every way, and you and I can grow with each other. While we're in Baton Rouge, think about the future and whether you see us together or apart."

"Justin, this isn't . . . Look. Don't go so fast. I'm not even sure I know who I am. My first priority is finding my Uncle Travis and—"

He pulled her closer, more forcefully, she knew, than he had intended. "And if you never find him? Then what? Will you be like Don Quixote chasing his windmills?"

She stepped away from him. "My life has been a question mark for as long as I've known myself. My instincts tell me that if I can solve this one puzzle, if I can get at the bottom of . . . of this unbelievable likeness to a woman who's not my mother or twin, I'll understand feelings I've had and things I've done. I'll have a better grip on my life. Can you understand that?"

"I can, and I do."

"You help me, because I know you're here for me. Want to . . . stay for a while?"

He lessened his hold on her; he gazed into her face and tried to smile but couldn't manage it. "Yeah. I want to stay all night. But if I do that, I'll feel like hell when I wake up tomorrow morning and have to sneak out before daybreak to avoid compromising you. This is still New Bern. God forbid I shouldn't be able to start my car tonight, and it sat in front of your door till morning. You'd replace your cousin as the current topic of discussion."

He let one of the marble tiles on the floor of her foyer feel the brunt of his shoe. "If that weren't enough, look at it this way. Feed a starving animal, and he'll come back to you every time he's hungry. He'll fol-low you around begging for crumbs. Handouts. He won't love you for it, but he'll take what you give—that is, until he can find a more con venient way of feeding himself."

The back of his hand drifted over her cheek. "I love you, sweet-heart, but I don't plan to choke on crumbs. Have a look at the suite. I'll be here for you Friday morning at seven o'clock." His lips covered her mouth, and seconds later she heard his Buick roar to life.

"You mean you invited my father over here to hear you play?" Maude asked Harold the morning after the party.

"I called to thank him for being so nice to me, and when he asked when he was going to hear me play, I told him I could come over at your house today. He said he'd rather I should come over Wednesday night for chili and bring my horn. Think you can accompany me on a little Mozart?"

"Not hardly. I haven't played Mozart in thirty years, so you bring somebody who can. What do you want to play?" He told her."Pop will love that," she said.

Abner Witherspoon listened as Harold played a movement of Mozart's horn concerto. At the end of the piece, Harold balanced him-self on tiptoe and stood with eyes wide and lips parted. Waiting. When Abner stood and applauded, Harold groped for a chair and sat down.

"You played one of my favorite pieces of music, and you didn't miss a single note of it," Abner said. "It was . . . Well, let me tell you, son, you're going a long way." He looked at Maude. "While we're at it, why don't you sing something?"

"Well . . . I—"

"I was hoping you would asked her, Pop," Johann said. "It's what she wants most: to sing for you. Come on, Kitten,"

She ran to the piano and looked through a folder of music. "I want to. I want to . . . but I'm . . . I'm flabbergasted." She handed the music to Harold and the pianist, who called himself Africa, leaned against the piano, and let Duke Ellington's "Mood Indigo" float in melodious mezzo tones from her throat. When she ended the song, she wiped the dampness from her cheeks and looked to her father for approval.

"You're blessed by God," he said. "The radio doesn't do you justice. I never dreamed you sang so beautifully."

She hugged him. "It's been years since I sang that well, or that I tried to. I'm so glad you asked me, Pop." She looked at him expectantly when the twinkle began to dance in his eyes.

"So am I. Who said you can't teach an old dog new tricks? I may go to one of your concerts one night. Now, if you don't mind, I'll have my chili, and I hope these good folks are joining us."

Abner bowed his head. "Dear Lord, we thank you for the good things of our lives, including the food we're about to eat. We've all sinned, Lord, but we know better and we're sorry. So please don't judge us too harshly. Amen." He told Harold and Africa about the chili factories. "My son-in-law here and Colonel Duval got the thing going. Soon as it's in the stores, keep your pantry crammed full of it."

"That won't cost me no sweat," Harold said. "This stuff is great." Chewing with great relish, Africa nodded his approval.

"I'll be back as soon as I drive Pop to prayer meeting," Johann said when they had finished supper.

"We'd better be going, too," Harold said. "I have to give a talk at the Havelock high school tomorrow, and I haven't prepared a thing." He slipped his oxford gray chesterfield over his gray silk suit and patted his pockets as if to flatten them.

"You turned my life around, Regina. I'd give you my right arm if I could blow my horn without it. You're something special, Cuz." He kissed her cheek, raised his head, and looked at Justin. "Not to worry. She's safe with me."

Justin's white teeth gleamed against his copper-colored face. "Trust me, I didn't fret over it for a split second."

Indeed, Justin seldom worried about anything. He repaired what needed fixing—if that was possible—and cleared his mind of problems he couldn't solve, so he didn't journey to Baton Rouge mired in concern about all the things that could go wrong while Regina visited his family. However, the visit was not stress-free. His first shock came at the airport, when he saw his mother, Aunt Jo, and twenty or so other relatives waiting to greet them. He figured his weekend would slide down from there, but as if someone had coached them all, including his five-year-old cousin Billy-from-hell, they gave him one pleasant surprise after another.

"We're having lunch over at your aunt Jo's," his mother said. "My daughter, Oleana, is on tour, and we're sorry you won't meet her, Regina. She practically worships Justin." The expression on her face as she regarded her son was one of adoration. "We're all proud of him. I intend to stay at the Craven for a few nights, soon as it gets warm. I want to see my son's work."

"I hope she likes Cajun food," his Aunt Jo whispered to him. "I made all my best dishes. You landed a beauty."

"I haven't 'landed her,' as you say."

She reached up and patted his shoulder. "But you will. I'm praying for that every second."

Stunned, he stared at her. "Why?"

"Because you deserve a fine woman, and that's what she is."

At lunch, his uncle Louis handed him a pair of tickets to the city's famous puppet theater, and the children gave Regina flowers and a book of poems the older ones wrote.

"I'm overwhelmed," Regina told them. "You've made me feel as if I'm home among old friends."

"That's the point," a young boy said. "We're supposed to make a good impression."

"I don't know these people," Justin said to Regina. "I can't imagine what's come over them."

"Maybe you don't know them," Regina said. "It's possible you still see them as they were twenty years ago. Nothing and no one remains unchanged that long. Pop's the best example of that." Her comment echoed his private thoughts, but he didn't respond.

"Wanna go fishing?" one of his cousins, a girl of about six, asked Regina. "My daddy will come along and put the worms on the hook."

"We go early mornings," the child's mother said, "and Cameron and I would be just tickled pink if you'd come along. You ever seen the Mississippi River? We'll be right near it, so we can take you over there."

"I've never seen the Mississippi, and I love to fish," Regina said. "Just let me know what time I should be ready."

"You're welcome to join us, Justin," she said.

"Thanks, Nadine. I think I will."

On Saturday night, long after his mother's house was dark and all but he had gone to bed, he sat in the garden musing over events of the past two days. He had hardly been alone with Regina. His family embraced her, seemingly without reservation, and she returned their welcome with affection and obvious delight. And for the first time in his memory, his aunt Jo treated him as the adult he was.

"Why are you sitting out here? Couldn't you sleep?"

At the sound of his mother's voice, he stood and walked toward the back porch. "Just thinking things over. Mama, what happened to Aunt Jo? She hasn't once complained that everybody gets more than she does from Daddy's estate, and I haven't heard her accuse Oleana of ignoring the family—not once—and she's actually treating me as a man. I never could stand being around her, because all she did was foment dissent. Nobody's mad at her. I can't understand it."

"I know. Jo never was half as bad as you thought. Anyhow, the more you ignored her, the worse she got. She thinks a lot of you."

"But Mama, she's not trying to dominate everybody."

"True. While you were in Hawaii, Jo won fifty-six thousand dollars in the lottery, and nobody asked her for a penny of it. In fact, your uncle Oscar gave a party to celebrate it, and everybody came. Oscar roasted a big pig on a spit, the Rolling River Boys played, and we danced all afternoon and half the night. Jo's been peaches and cream ever since."

"If I'd known fifty-six thousand dollars would do that to her, I'd have given it to her. It's a different family."

Simone sat in the swing and patted the place beside her. "Come sit here. I'm glad you brought Regina to meet me. Get busy before she's too old to have children. She'll make a wonderful mother."

He draped his left ankle over his right knee, locked his hands behind his head, and leaned back in the swing. "What about *wife?* You think that's less important than the kind of mother she would be?"

"I think you've satisfied yourself as to the kind of wife she'll be. Come on in and go to sleep. You don't have a single thing to worry about."

Little did she know, Regina's mind had only temporarily been diverted from her compulsion to find out why she and Juliet looked alike, and until she succeeded, her thoughts wouldn't rest with him.

"I like your folks," Regina told him on their flight back to the Craven County Airport. "I like them a lot."

"It appears to be mutual. At times, I felt like an outsider, but I'm glad they like you. It's important to me."

"Me, too."

Ten days passed. Juliet didn't give Maude an explanation for not attending the family gathering, and she didn't return Regina's telephone call.

"I don't want to go to the Klondike," Regina told the detective she hired to search for Travis Witherspoon, "but if I don't hear from him this week, I'm booking a flight."

"I'll alert him to that possibility," the man told her, "and it's my hunch he doesn't want that."

That night, after her aunt's performance at the Craven, Regina mentioned Juliet's silence to her. "It's as if she's in hiding."

"You're closing Justin out with your fixation on this Juliet business," Maude told her. "Where is he, anyhow?"

"In Winston-Salem with James Carlson, working on their next project."

"Hmmm. Is he coming here for Thanksgiving?"

Regina nodded.

"At least you're still in touch."

Regina stared at her aunt. "Of course we're still in touch. He hasn't forced me to show my hand, so I haven't done it. I still have some slack."

"And if he does?"

"I'd have to plead 'no contest.' I know what floats my boat."

However, Regina soon wished for the comfort of Justin's presence, because what she read sapped the strength out of her.

"When did you get this?" she asked Juliet, who surprised her with a visit to her house shortly after sunset three days before Thanksgiving.

"I've had it for weeks, since a couple of days before that family gathering. It's the reason why I didn't go."

"But why didn't you tell me?"

"I just collapsed. Herbert told me last night that I had to bring this to you."

Regina looked at the few words scrawled on a postcard. *"Tell her to back off,"* she read. *"You don't want to know."*

Regina stiffened her back. "Like hell, I don't." She dialed the detective's number and read to him the cryptic phrases.

"He'll change his mind if he hasn't already done so. According to my sources, he doesn't want a visitor. Hang in there."

She didn't wait long. The next morning, she received the telegram that would change her life. She tipped the delivery man, sat down, and mumbled a few words of prayer. Then she forced herself to open the message.

> *Dear Ms. Pearson, she read. You'd probably be happier if you had left yourself in the dark. When my wife confessed to me that I was not the father of our child, who we named Juliet Arnice Witherspoon, I gave her half of what I owned, plus the house, and left her. As of this writing, I have no children. I hope this finds you well. Travis Witherspoon.*

She didn't know how long she sat there or how many times she read the telegram. Nor was she aware of the tears that fell in her lap. Realizing that the phone was ringing, she groped for it.

"Hello?"

"Regina? It's ten o'clock. Did you forget we're meeting this morning with the owners of those four suites to talk about that swimming pool?"

She slapped her forehead with the palm of her right hand. "My Lord, Larry! Something came up, and it slipped my mind. See if you can reschedule it."

"I'd better tell 'em you're home with a fever and didn't wake up till I called you." He sounded as if he was near panic, and she didn't blame him.

"Whatever. I'll be in this afternoon."

She took off her skirt and hung it over the shower curtain to dry, washed her face, and made fresh coffee. It would be a blow to Juliet, but she had to tell her. *I'd better go see Pop first. Maybe Juliet doesn't need to know this.*

Her fingers shook so badly as she tried to dial her grandfather's phone number that she didn't succeed until the third attempt.

After greeting him, she managed to say, "Do you mind if I come over, Pop? I need to discuss something with you."

"Of course. You don't have to ask, child."

"Where's Johann?" she asked when he opened the door.

"Over in Havelock dealing with the chili canning factory. You look as if you've been indicted for murder. Come on in here and I'll get us some coffee."

She followed him into the kitchen and sat at the table, too nervous to speak, while he heated the coffee and served it along with brioche and jam.

He sipped his coffee, replaced the cup in the saucer, and focused on her. "Something's wrong. What is it?"

"I disobeyed you, Pop. I made some inquiries, and this morning I received a telegram from Uncle Travis. He's in Canada, the Klondike."

Abner sprang forward, his eyes shining and the muscles of his jaw twitching. Then he slumped back down in the chair. "Well, well. The dead yet live. I supposed you asked him about you and Juliet."

"I did." She handed him the telegram.

His expression pensive, he looked beyond her. "You can't keep it from her, and you shouldn't. I still think you should have left it alone. Now you're going to have to deal with it.

"People around here thought I refused Miles Pearson permission to marry my Louise, your mother, because his folks were Catholic and light-skinned. That was pure hog rot. I knew she was seeing another man, and I knew what she was doing with him. I also heard her losing her breakfast mornings. But Miles wanted her and she went with him."

Cold sweat covered her body, and she couldn't stop the trembling of her lips. "Wh . . . wh . . . what else?"

"A little over three years later, that same fellah took up with Hedley, Juliet's mother, and I had him run out of town, because I didn't want Travis to hang for killing him. And he would have if he found out. When Travis took off from here suddenly, telling me nothing but he was leaving town and didn't know when or if he'd be back, I suspected something happened between him and Hedley. It had taken four years for it to come to a head. I wasn't sure what it was, though, till I saw you. Juliet's your sister, and I think you'd just about guessed that."

Her stomach cramped, and she wrapped her arms tight around her middle, rocking herself and fighting back the tears. "Then . . . I'm not a Pearson, and my father knew it, because I never felt his love, and he didn't show me any affection. Oh, he took care of me, educated me, and willed me what he had, which was a lot. I don't see how he did it, how he lived with that all those years. And to think that I resented him."

"He was good to you because he loved your mother."

"Who is my biological father, Pop, and where is he?"

"You don't need to go digging that up. He's been dead for years."

She twisted her hands in obvious frustration, or maybe despair, but he couldn't help her. If you didn't want onions, you shouldn't plant the bulbs.

"What will I tell Juliet? I can't just act like I don't know this."

"Bring her over here. I want to talk to the two of you together. She has to tell her husband, and I 'spect you'll tell Justin. Maude already knows. Let it rest right where it is. Telling the world won't change a thing."

Abner stood at his living room window and watched Regina as she walked with slow and uncertain steps to her car. He had hoped she wouldn't dig up that old stuff, but she had, and only God knew what would come of it. One thing was certain: Louise hadn't drowned accidentally; she was women's swimming champion at North Carolina Central University in Durham and had four trophies as proof. He could only surmise that she'd done it deliberately when Miles confronted her with the evidence of her treachery.

He answered the phone, hoping for news from Johann as to the progress of the chili factory in Havelock, but he heard instead the voice of his son, Robert.

"Pop, I just made a killing with my peanuts," Robert said. "I got a deal with a peanut butter company that wants all of my peanuts every year, and they're paying me good money. Good money, Pop."

"Now, I'm glad to hear that, son."

"It means I can hire somebody to help me, and Rose won't have to work so hard. I'll be able to give you a few hundred dollars a month, too. It's been hard, Pop. All these years, I've been clearing just a little more than enough for us to get along, but things'll be different now. You'll see."

Humph. Just getting along, and wearing silk suits. "I don't need the money, Robert, because I took care of what I made. If you were having it tough, you should have told me instead of letting me think you didn't remember you had a father. I'll be happy if I can see you and my grandchildren a lot more often."

"We'll try to see you at least once a week, Pop. And we want you to come see us, too."

The suddenness of it was about as much as he could take. "You sure that deal you made is the reason why you're acting like a son all of a sudden?"

In his mind's eye, he could see Robert's chin jut out as it always did when someone challenged him. "Pop, you don't need this white fellow Maude married to do things for you, at least not as long as I'm living."

So that was it. He laughed aloud. "You always did treat the truth as if it were some kind of virus. I see you're improving. Don't worry about Johann and me. He's a gift to me from God. Beside, I expect he'll be going back to Hol—the Netherlands in a few weeks."

"You mean . . . I thought they were still married."

"They are, and they probably always will be. You coming over Sunday?"

"Yes, sir. If it's not too cold, we can all go fishing down at the Neuse and cook the catch there on the banks."

He hadn't done that in years. "Sounds good. We'll think about that when you get here."

Later that afternoon, he looked at Juliet and Regina, who sat on his living room sofa facing him and not looking at each other. Juliet seemed fascinated with the floor, but Regina sat erect, relaxed, and self-possessed, as if the day's events were merely an anticlimax. She had wasted no time getting the three of them together. Resolute and purposeful. He liked that about her, though he could do without some of her stubbornness. *That much like you,* an inner voice reminded him.

"I suspected something like this when I got that card from . . . from the Klondike," Juliet said, apparently unwilling to call Travis Witherspoon "Father" after what she had learned. "I never felt any real connection to my kinfolks, and I couldn't understand why." She trained brooding, troubled eyes on him. "What do I do now, Pop?"

He didn't want it to go any further. Their small town was populated with small-minded people, and they would rip apart a woman of Juliet's prominence, and especially in view of her past arrogance and, some would say, overbearing behavior.

"Tell your husband, and that's plenty. You can't change a thing by blabbing it all over New Bern. Besides, you haven't lost anything, and you got yourself a sister."

She had the appearance of one thoroughly confused, and he didn't blame her; two good shocks such as that one would shake up a strong man.

"What about you and me?" Juliet asked him.

He had already settled that within himself, and hearing her ask it didn't surprise him. "I'm still your pop, and I'll always be."

She jumped up and hugged him in what was the first affection she'd shown him since she was a child. "You come see me, now. You hear?"

She nodded. They told him good-bye, both solemn and deep in their thoughts, and he watched them leave his house walking hand in hand. Maybe something good had come of it.

Thanksgiving Day arrived with strong winds, an overcast sky, and a nip in the air. Justin built a fire in the stone fireplace that dominated Regina's living room, cut some chestnuts, and took a seat before the flames.

"Was Regina satisfied with the family gathering?" Johann asked him as he, too, settled himself on the floor facing the fire.

"I think she loved the party, because it was . . . well, the fulfillment of a dream. But I have a feeling she learned that genes don't make a family. To my knowledge, not one of them has gotten in touch with her." He picked up the iron poker and teased the flames with it. "Strange. Since I was eighteen, I've stayed away from my family as much as possible. But a few weeks ago, my mother organized a family gathering to introduce the gang to Regina, and they were . . . I still can't get over it. I hated to leave them."

Johann's arm eased around his shoulder. "I suspect you've remembered a boy's reaction to them, but this time, you saw them through the eyes of an experienced man. I'm happy for you. How did it go with Regina?"

"She was enchanted with them—even my supercilious Aunt Jo—

and they with her, down to the smallest child." He shook his head. "I never saw anything like it."

Maude let her gaze travel to the collection of people around Regina's Thanksgiving table: Pop, Odette and her Claude, Juliet and Herbert, Justin and Regina, Johann and herself, and Harold. She thought, *There's a reason for this, and it's got something to do with Juliet.* She had to give up her cigar for Pop's sake, since he hated for her to smoke, but she was not going to exchange her Heineken for white wine. She went to the refrigerator, got a bottle of Heineken from the six-pack she brought with her, and returned to the table.

"We've all plenty to be thankful for," Pop said as he began the grace. "Lord, my family is around me on this day for the first time in over thirty-five years. And my children and my six grandchildren have blessed me with their presence this day," he went on, referring to Robert's visit that morning along with his three children, and to Maude, Odette, Juliet, and Regina. "For your love, for this blessing, and for this food, we do thank you. Amen."

She didn't pray often, and maybe she'd soon have to make a habit of that, but she said a few words of silent prayer as Harold's face bloomed like flowers in spring, and Pop wore a glow of happiness as he reached for his fork.

"What's this?" he asked. He picked up the little two-inch-high bust of himself and turned it around, staring at it. "My, my. It's a chocolate . . . Would you look at this? Somebody carved a bust of me."

"Regina carves those," Odette said. "I saw her when she was buying the chocolate."

"Well, this is just about the nicest thing I . . . It's just . . . just nice," he said in a voice that wobbled with emotion.

"I'm glad you like it, Pop. Tastes good, too," Regina said.

"I hope you don't think I'd eat my own head. I'm gonna get me a glass box and keep it in the refrigerator. This is sculpture."

Abner took a few bites of turkey and dressing and looked at Johann. "My granddaughter Regina here is clever. Maybe you'd better give her the recipe for those Belgian waffles." The twinkle danced in his old eyes. "Wouldn't hurt to give it to my granddaughters, Odette and Juliet, too. I've got lots of places I can eat breakfast when you go back home."

Maude cocked an ear, knowing she had the clue she'd been seeking. Pop knew who Juliet's father was, and he wouldn't have made that statement if it hadn't come into question. In her book, Abner Witherspoon stood tall among men, and he'd just proved it for the nth time. Well, she could keep a secret as well as anybody.

"You can take turns eating waffles with your granddaughters, Pop," Juliet said. "I'll make them Monday and Wednesday."

"I'll take Sunday and Thursday," Odette said, "and Regina can make 'em on the other days."

"He'll soon get tired of 'em," Justin said. "I would."

"I don't get tired of my chili, do I? I'm glad it'll be in cans in case my daughter Maude comes to her senses."

"Pop, don't get on my case now," Maude said, and pleased herself with a hefty slug of Heineken.

"This is what family ought to be," Herbert said, speaking for the first time. He raised his glass of wine. "I'm proud to be included in your family, Pop."

Maude looked at her husband, unusually quiet and too pensive for her comfort. He hadn't said one word. She reached under the table and stroked his knee, but his smile didn't light his eyes. Cold shivers streaked through her, and she rested her fork on the side of her plate, her taste for the food gone. Johann had decided what he'd do, but she wasn't going to lose her mind worrying about *that*. When he got ready, he'd tell her. She let a smile brighten her face, picked up her fork, and ate the rest of her collards.

"You're a fine cook and I like your house," Abner told Regina, and nodded his head toward Maude. "See that you don't self-destruct. Justin is a good man."

"I know that, Pop. He has a wonderful family, too."

"Good, good. You had your family here today, and we're all you can count on, except maybe Robert. You understand? Leave it alone now. If they reach out, accept them, but *your happiness does not depend on them.*"

"I know." She hugged him and enjoyed his frail embrace. "Thanks for coming."

"I wouldn't have missed it."

It was December fifth, and Maude stood on her back porch dressed in her nightgown, robe, and bedroom slippers, unable to watch Johann pack. Over and over, she relived the night before, her face awash with tears. Her husband had stripped her of her will, had bared her soul to him and to her. And he had not withheld from her his own raw feelings and emotions but had let her see the depth and power of his need. She saw herself then as she had writhed beneath him in one explosive orgasm after another until, weakened physically and emotionally, she tried without success to hold back.

And still he showed her what she would miss, pounding into her brain and her body how much she needed and loved him. When at last she cried out in a voice filled with agony, "I love you. I love you," he gave himself to her.

"You can walk away, turn your back on what we are to each other because of the weather?" he asked her that morning.

"If I go back with you, I know I won't stay, because I can't. I was out of place, and I felt it every single day. The language, the weather, my superficial relations with people, and most of all, my culture."

"You mean collards and sweet potatoes? I'll—"

"Having no soul food was merely symbolic of what I missed. It was basic. A woman there told me something exciting and I said, 'Get outta here.' She thought I ordered her out of our home, and was insulted. I tried to explain, but she didn't understand and never spoke to me again."

"Well, why did you say it?"

"You see? It was an automatic response, an expression meaning *'that's unbelievable,' or 'you don't say.'* That isn't the only time it happened. I loved the people, and I was in my element onstage, on the street, in stores, restaurants, and public places. But I was out of place with one or two people, who didn't understand where I was coming from. Say to one of them, 'Tell it like it is, sister,' and they think you're telling them not to lie. At my age, I need contentment, to feel at home among people, as much as I need love."

The back door opened, and she spun around, her mind once more in the present. "I want to stay here with you, babe, but I won't count myself a man if I don't stand up for what I know is right. You won't budge an inch, although you know I'm not going to let you spin me around like a top. You'd walk over me if I did. I'm sending for Pop in mid-January so he can take the first can of chili off the belt. Meanwhile, take good care of him and of yourself."

"You . . . you're really going to leave me, aren't you?"

He picked up his suitcase and slung his garment bag over his left shoulder. "I'm only accepting your verdict. I'm going by Pop's and he'll see me to the airport." He stared at her, his eyes blinking rapidly, and swallowed hard. "So long, babe."

She cut a cigar and lit it, got a bottle of Heineken, and sat down in the apple-green swing. After half an hour, she dried her eyes and began to rock the swing to and fro, to and fro. She rocked it until night-fall.

Across town, the drama of life played for two people who dealt with a different kind of reconciliation. Regina marveled at the patience with which Justin listened to what she learned from Abner and Travis Witherspoon about her life—a long rambling tale, to which he listened without comment until at last she finished it. They sat in his car in front of her house, unwilling to separate and uncertain of the wisdom of sharing themselves through the night.

"How do you feel about it and about not telling Harold?"

"I don't feel one thing as a result of learning I'm not a Pearson, but I think it would hurt Harold. He accepted my role in his career because I'm his cousin and he knows I care about him. He needs my unqualified support. It's strange; the relative I loved first and who is closest to me in spirit isn't a blood relative at all. I suppose there's a message in that." She shook her head, reflecting upon her life's upheavals, shocks, and cruelties. She would never be certain of her identity, but at last she had a niche, her own place in the lives of people who loved her, and she would put the past behind her.

"Harold needs me," she said, "so I'm not going to tell him."

"Why did you tell me?"

She didn't like the question. It was another way he had of drawing her out without committing himself.

"Because you have a right to know."

Laughter poured out of him. Not a nervous reaction, but a joyous sound that she loved. "Come home with me for Christmas. Pop will be with Maude, and my folks will be expecting you. Can you get away from the hotel?"

She told him she could, and from that minute, getting back to his family in Baton Rouge pushed almost everything else out of her mind.

* * *

"We open gifts Christmas Eve after dinner," Simone Duval said to Regina, "so get a good rest. You must be tired after that trip. I'll knock in a couple of hours, and we can have some iced tea and cookies."

Regina thanked her and unpacked her things in Simone's guest room. She liked Justin's mother and his other relatives as well and couldn't understand his attitude toward them. She had waited with impatience to see them all again, to laugh and dance among them while they all talked and shouted at once, throwing their arms around each other, hugging and kissing. And to her amazement, when the dancing began, Justin proved he could wind with the best of them. She wondered if he knew how like them he was.

After a dinner of sautéed crayfish, turkey that was deep-fried whole, stuffed avocados, wild rice with mushrooms, turnip greens, and praline cheese cake for dessert, the teenagers cleaned the dining room and kitchen and then joined other family members around the tree. Twenty people for a sit-down Christmas dinner.

"The thought of all that work makes me tired," Regina told Simone.

"It wasn't much. Several of us cooked the different dishes, and a couple of others set the table. We always do it that way." She held up the navy blue cut-velvet shawl embroidered in sunset colors that was her gift from Justin, leaned over and kissed his cheek.

"My son told me he wants to marry you," Simone said to Regina, "but that you're kind of stingy with the encouragement. Seems to me any woman would want to marry a man like Justin—if she loved him, that is. If you don't mind, I'd like to know your intentions toward him."

The red, bell-figured green package fell from Regina's hands, her eyes widened, and she was certain her mouth hung open. She glanced in Justin's direction and saw that she was on her own, so she decided to give as good as she got.

She squared her shoulders. "Mrs. Duval, your son has not asked me to marry him. He hasn't even hinted it. Well, not strongly, anyway. And as for my intentions toward him, right now, I'd like to give him a good whack." Laughter spilled out of Justin as she got a taste of his brand of devilment.

"They do things like this all the time, Regina," Verna, Justin's twelve-year-old cousin, said. "They're always playing stupid jokes. Cousin Justin will do anything to get the better of somebody. Ignore them."

"If Pop could ask me that, I figured my mother could ask you," Justin said.

She joined the laughter but found it difficult to reconcile the Justin she knew in Baton Rouge with the more solemn man she had worked with at the Craven.

Later that evening, as they sat alone on the porch swing listening to the night sounds, he confirmed his wish to marry her. "I want to move on from here, start my family, and settle into my life's work."

"I want to stay in New Bern, at least as long as Pop's alive, and I'd like my sister to stand up with me at our wedding."

"It's the right thing to do."

They announced their engagement at breakfast on Christmas morning. Justin's male cousins and his uncles tossed Regina among them, the women hugged her, and Simone Duval made her special celebration cake. More relatives arrived after hearing the news, and the house soon overflowed with music, laughter, and dancing. Tall tales and stories that had obviously passed among them for generations punctuated the joyous day. In it all, they saluted Regina and lovingly embraced her.

She slipped upstairs to her room and sat on the edge of the bed to deal with her thoughts. A big, happy, loving family that she had dreamed of for years, and of which she envied her Native Hawaiian friends. And now, it would be hers. They didn't call themselves Witherspoon, but she belonged to them and they to her.

"What are you doing up here by yourself? Is it wearing you down?"

She smiled as Justin walked toward her. "It's what I always wanted. I think your folks are wonderful, and I don't see why you don't love being with them."

He sat beside her. "I find that I do. Growing up, I hated the arguments after my father died, but with a child's vision I didn't see their love for each other and for me. After Maude's party, I began to compare them with members of your family that I met there—people who could barely tolerate each other. That helped me to put things into perspective."

"It's humbling. I finally have the family I longed for. You, Pop, Maude, Odette, Juliet, Harold, and these wonderful people. It's . . . it's a miracle."

"Yes," he said, "and we have each other. That's the real miracle."

Epilogue

Abner Witherspoon walked into the waiting room at Schipold Airport, in Amsterdam, and looked around. *Martin Luther King Jr.'s birthday, and here I am all the way over here in Europe.* Very soon, his gaze caught Johann rushing toward him.

"You don't look so good," Abner told him in his blunt fashion, after their embrace. "I was hoping you'd gotten over her."

Johann stepped back and studied his father-in-law. "Are you saying that because you know she's over me?"

"Naah. I'm just telling you what I told her. You stayed together for ten years, and now you're both hell-bent on showing how stupid you can be. How's the chili?"

Johann picked up Abner's flight bag, threw his other arm across Abner's shoulder, and headed for the baggage claim section. They left Abner's luggage at the house Johann had shared with Maude—a two-story concrete structure facing a canal—and headed for the factory.

"Everything is standing still waiting for you," Johann said, his voice lacking its usual strength. "I'd give anything if Maude were here too."

The motors began to hum, and with Abner standing at the front end of the belt, the first can of Abner's Perfect Chili Con Carne rolled out and into his hands.

"It's a beautiful thing," Abner said, shaking his head, "and if it wasn't for you, it would never have happened. Let's see, it's seven o'clock this morning in New Bern; I want to call my daughter Maude. This is a great moment for me, Johann. I can't tell you what this means."

"Maude speaking. How y'all doing so early this morning?"

"I got a can of my chili in my hand, daughter, and I want to thank you for this. You don't know how good it is to succeed in something that means this much. Not many men my age have been blessed as I have so late in life. Here's your husband."

"Hello, Kitten. I'd give anything if you were here."

"Humph. I hope she's as honest as you are," Abner said, standing behind Johann.

"It's not working, Kitten. Would you agree to rotating? You know, three months here, three months in New Bern? You can stand it here for three months, and we can bring enough collards to last that long, and keep them in the freezer. Look, Kitten, don't you want to put an end to this?"

"Of course she does, and she's lying if she says otherwise."

"Oh, that? That was Pop answering for you. Yeah, but if I stay there three months, you have to stay here the succeeding three months. *You mean that?* You w . . . will? You'll really do it? Thank God. I'm . . . er . . . I'm going back along with Pop. I—I miss you like hell. All right, baby. See you at the airport."

Johann turned to him. "She said she's miserable and she wants to be with me. Maybe you were right when you said we'd probably be together forever."

" 'Course I was. The two of you belong together. Anybody can see that."

BLUES FROM DOWN DEEP

GWYNNE FORSTER

ABOUT THIS GUIDE

The suggested questions are intended to enhance your
group's reading of Gwynne Forster's
BLUES FROM DOWN DEEP.

You can contact the author at:

Gywnne Forster
P.O. Box 45
New York, NY 10044
e-mail: *GwynneF@aol.com*
website: *www.gwynneforster.com*

DISCUSSION QUESTIONS

1. What assumption does Regina make about family and blood ties? Do you think it is tenable?

2. Do her subsequent experiences support her assumption?

3. How do the culture and the environment in which Regina grows up influence her ideas about, and attitude toward, family and family life?

4. What, if anything, is wrong about these ideas? What justifies them?

5. In Regina's relationship with her father, what were the positive and negative elements?

6. What was his legacy vis-à-vis her judgment and values?

7. Which characters most affect Regina's transformation from a woman ignorant of her heritage and culture to one capable of understanding and accepting it?

8. What does Maude represent in this story? In Regina's evolution to a personal truth?

9. What does Harold symbolize in the story? In Regina's life? How does he influence her views on kinship and on the role and importance of family in one's life?

10. Why does Abner resist meeting and accepting Regina, though he is gracious to her at the first opportunity?

11. What does the chili con carne symbolize?

12. Why did Maude leave Johann? Why did she do it surreptitiously? What, excluding color and wealth, sets him apart from her other husbands?

13. Explain the basis of the strong affection that develops between Abner and Johann?

14. Do you agree with Maude in accusing Abner of meddling in her relationship with Johann? Does he help or hinder their relationship? What is his motive?

15. Can you identify with her dilemma about Johann? Why?

16. What, other than romantic interest, does Justin Duval bring to Regina's life? In the conflict between them, how is she strengthened? In what ways does he change from the time he meets her to the end of the story?

17. What does Regina give Justin that is lacking in his life when he meets her?

18. Regina's attitude toward family is the antithesis of Justin's. Why and in what respects?

19. Why does meeting Juliet Smith shock Regina, and what is Regina's reaction? Juliet's reaction?

20. Should Regina have obeyed Maude and her grandfather and resisted digging into the reason for her likeness to Juliet? In her efforts to unearth the mystery, what does she risk? What brings Regina and Juliet together—the truth, or the pain it causes?

21. The story includes many references to racial disharmony, but it also alludes to communion among the races. What is the paramount example of this?

22. Abner Witherspoon is the voice of morality. In what specific instances does he show his considerable measure as a man?

23. When at last Regina is surrounded by more than sixty of her kinfolk, what is her reaction to this realization of her dream? Of them, who will constitute her family and why?

24. What is Abner's advice to her about her happiness in relation to her kinfolk?

25. Paradoxically, the person who is most like a sibling to Regina has no blood ties to her. What is the lesson here, and how does Regina demonstrate it?

26. What is it about Justin's family that enthralls Regina and binds her to them?

27. *Blues From Down Deep* refers to three people. Who are they?